W9-ALL-006

OVERTAKEN

Also by Mark H. Kruger

Overpowered

OVERTAKEN

MARK H. KRUGER

SIMON & SCHUSTER BFYR

New York   London   Toronto   Sydney   New Delhi

An imprint of Simon & Schuster Children's Publishing Division
1230 Avenue of the Americas, New York, New York 10020
This book is a work of fiction. Any references to historical events, real people,
or real places are used fictitiously. Other names, characters, places,
and events are products of the author's imagination, and any resemblance to actual events
or places or persons, living or dead, is entirely coincidental.
Text copyright © 2015 by Mark H. Kruger
Jacket illustration copyright © 2015 by We Monsters
All rights reserved, including the right of reproduction in whole or in part in any form.
SIMON & SCHUSTER BFYR is a trademark of Simon & Schuster, Inc.
For information about special discounts for bulk purchases, please contact Simon & Schuster
Special Sales at 1-866-506-1949 or business@simonandschuster.com.
The Simon & Schuster Speakers Bureau can bring authors to your live event.
For more information or to book an event, contact the Simon & Schuster Speakers Bureau
at 1-866-248-3049 or visit our website at www.simonspeakers.com.
Jacket design by Chloë Foglia
Interior design by Hilary Zarycky
The text for this book is set in Janson.
Manufactured in the United States of America
2 4 6 8 10 9 7 5 3 1
Library of Congress Cataloging-in-Publication Data
Kruger, Mark H.
Overtaken / Mark H. Kruger.—First edition.
pages cm
Sequel to: Overpowered.
Summary: "After the mysterious pulses changed Nica Ashley's life forever, she was sure
things could only get worse when Dana Fox returned. Her reappearance after having gone
missing for months surely meant losing her friendship with Jackson but also that something
more ominous is simmering under the surface of quiet Barrington"—Provided by publisher.
ISBN 978-1-4424-3131-7 (hardcover)
ISBN 978-1-4424-3133-1 (eBook)
[1. Science fiction. 2. Conspiracies—Fiction.] I. Title.
PZ7.K9414Ovt 2015
[Fic]—dc23
2014030095

FIRST
EDITION

For Mel and Evan

1. NEW WORLD ORDER

I wasn't in the mood for partying.

Every fiber of my being wanted to disappear into a black hole of nothingness. Unfortunately, blissful escape wasn't possible. Not while my life was ensnared in so much drama and turmoil. OD'ing on existential despair into oblivion wasn't exactly on the evening's menu.

Instead, I found myself wedged in a corner of Dana Fox's sprawling rec room like a naughty child getting a time-out, as a crush of gleeful kids danced and partied all around me. All for Dana's homecoming.

News of her sudden return to Barrington that morning had spread through the town rumor mill like a raging California brush fire, incinerating everything else in its wake. Even memories of that pulse, which had nearly leveled the high school and almost exposed Jackson, Oliver, and me to Richard Cochran and Bar Tech only a day before, vaporized in the wake of Dana's reappearance.

Without missing a beat, Dana's overjoyed parents had

transformed their faux-French-château pool house into a raucous party central. It seemed as though the entire school had turned out en masse to pay tribute to the beloved and much-missed Dana Fox. Being a glutton for punishment as well as a budding masochist, I'd had to attend Dana's party and experience it firsthand. I'd had to get to know the girl who had so damaged Jackson's heart and cast a pall over his life.

Lime Jell-O shots spiked with silver mescal, which Chase's football pals had smuggled in underneath oversized parkas, were downed with reckless abandon by everyone. The thought of consuming Jell-O anything made me sick to my stomach. And as much as I desperately wanted to get lost in an alcoholic haze of misery where I didn't give a shit, I just couldn't bring myself to toast Dana's return.

Bitchy and small-minded of me, perhaps. Petty, even. I guiltily admit having those ugly feelings. But there was also something else churning away in my brain. Nagging suspicions about why that girl had disappeared in the first place and where she'd been hiding for more than seven months without so much as a peep. If I wanted to find out the truth about Dana's whereabouts, I had to keep my wits about me. I needed to keep up my guard and stay alert . . . frosty.

Ever since Dana had strolled up Jackson's driveway that morning and hugged him tightly, Jackson and I hadn't had a private moment to talk. Our communication that evening had been reduced to tense, ambiguous glances at each other from across the crowded room. As the electro-funk mix was cranked up to a full-on, mind-numbing blast, I watched Jackson dance uncomfortably with a beaming, radiant Dana. Dressed simply in a beautiful slim-fit ghost white cashmere pullover and black leggings, she owned the night and looked thrilled to be back with her long-pining boyfriend. A fairy-tale ending come to life.

As deeply and intensely as my feelings were for Jackson, I had no claim on him or his affections. Still, reality was a bitch—an icy slap across my raw face. It was painful for me to see Jackson and Dana together. Not just imagining them in my mind anymore as some vague past couple, but actually seeing them as a couple in the flesh. That hit me squarely in the gut.

Up until early that morning, Dana Fox had been an elusive phantom. A pretty face on a poster. MIA for more than seven months, she was presumably gone forever. Suddenly and incredibly, she reappeared, throwing my life (and Jackson's) into even more havoc and chaos than it was already. Only moments before Dana's miraculous return, Jackson and I had been arguing about the dangers of staying in Barrington. I knew we might have to leave town and follow in Maya's hasty footsteps to parts unknown or risk our secrets being found out by Richard Cochran and his minions at Bar Tech.

But I hadn't exactly been thinking with a straight head. I was still reeling from the aftershock of discovering that my father was an undercover government agent. Precisely how and why a medical doctor was spying for the Department of Defense still remained a mystery to me, one my dad had yet to fully explain. All I really knew for sure was that Dad had been covertly protecting me, as well as my friends, from being exposed to Richard Cochran and Bar Tech. And I had to protect my dad's deep, dark secret in return. No matter what the cost. Which meant concealing my father's true identity from everyone—even Oliver and Jackson.

I could see that Jackson was really shaken up by Dana's return. He had endured months of humiliation and being treated like a delusional mental patient. All because he'd dared to question the official story about why his girlfriend had suddenly disappeared from town one night without a word. Even lifelong friends like Chase and the other jocks had bailed on Jackson. The boy most likely to succeed had suddenly turned into radioactive waste, which they wanted to bury deep in the ground and forget about. That all changed because Jackson's girlfriend had come home. In a split second that morning on Jackson's driveway, the world around me and my friends had changed once again. Timing, as they say, was everything.

I'd felt both incredibly protective over Jackson and inexplicably angry. It was all I could do not to grab Dana by her lustrous, thick black hair and demand some answers. *Where the hell have you been all this time, bitch? Why didn't you ever call your boyfriend and let him know that you weren't dead? Why did you let him suffer like that? What do you know about Bar Tech?* But even as my blood was simmering and reaching its boiling point, I had just enough self-control and presence of mind to get the hell out of there. I was afraid I might do something stupid, which I would definitely regret and which might seriously jeopardize Jackson, Oliver, and me.

"Great meeting you, Dana," I had said halfheartedly, as I backed down Jackson's driveway toward the sidewalk, eager to make a hasty exit. "See you around." I'd had to get out of there.

"Wait up, Nica. I'll walk with you," Oliver piped up, anxious to leave as well. "Glad you're back, Dana."

"Thanks, Oliver," Dana replied, hooking her arm through Jackson's. It was a small but telling gesture that spoke volumes about her expectations with him and her status in the world. "Happy to be home."

Jackson looked at me with sad gray eyes. They looked as if their vibrant blue-green coloring had been bled out from his irises. He seemed utterly lost as to what to do or say at that very uncomfortable moment. So he just muttered: "Catch you guys later."

Oliver waited until we had turned the corner off Jackson's block and were safely out of earshot before speaking. "Holy shit, Nica. How weird was that?"

"Beyond," I muttered wanly as I just kept walking. I was concentrating on putting one foot in front of the other without breaking stride. It was the only thing I could do to keep from totally flipping out.

"That's all you have to say?" Oliver prodded, mystified by my seemingly indifferent reaction. "Mystery girl Dana frickin' Fox, Jackson's old girlfriend, returns from the dead," he added, "or wherever the hell else she's been holed up all this time. And all you have to say is 'beyond'?"

He hurried to keep up with me, since the effects of the previous days' pulse had finally worn off. But I didn't want to talk. Not to him or to anyone else at that moment. I didn't want to share my heartbreak or discuss Dana's return. I wanted to be left alone in my quiet misery. Just as I was about to break into a full-on sprint home, Oliver grabbed my arm. Tightly.

"Nica, stop," Oliver ordered, clutching my arm, not letting me go. "Talk to me." He seemed genuinely concerned.

Shaken back to Planet Earth, I stopped and turned to face him, trying not to lose my shit.

"What do you want me to say, Oliver? That I'm crushed that Dana's back? That's the least of my worries. Things are totally messed up. And I don't know what the hell this means for any of us."

Oliver saw how upset I was and finally released my arm.

"Sorry. Didn't mean to push you like that," he responded sympathetically. "For the record, we're in this mess together."

His kind words were just what I needed to hear. I felt awful for turning on him like a raving Fury.

"Thanks," I said, shaking my head as if I were trying to knock out all the crazy. "These last few weeks have really taken their toll. And now this."

"Understandable, given certain recent events," he said, with a warm, caring smile.

I started walking again. Slowly. Feeling adrift and confused and in no particular rush to race home to face my father. That was a whole other can of worms I wished I hadn't opened. But I had. And I wasn't sure how much Dana's return would complicate matters. All I knew was that my whole world had gone completely bonkers.

Oliver tagged along to keep me company and made sure I didn't get into any trouble. "Doesn't it seem like more than just an eerie coincidence," he declared, "that the day after the pulse hits and causes a nearly epic meltdown at school, that little girl lost shows up on Jackson's doorstep? I'm just saying. . . ."

"You're preaching to the choir," I chimed back, feeling those same nagging suspicions myself.

"What should we do?"

I shook my head, shrugged, and just laughed even as a tear streamed down my cheek.

"I don't have a fucking clue."

Oliver and I had aimlessly wandered the streets of Barrington for well over an hour, racking our brains for answers. I felt as though I were trapped inside one of those mind-twisting logic puzzles. Nothing but dead ends everywhere I turned. My head was ready to explode. Unfortunately, neither Oliver nor I got any closer to figuring out a solution.

"I'm starving," I suddenly announced to Oliver. "I need to eat something pronto, before I pass out." I felt a bit shaky, as though my blood-sugar level was nose-diving. "Preferably sugary and fattening."

"Now, that's a problem I can fix," Oliver announced with assurance.

He led me to Ebinger's Bakery, and a few minutes and several doughnuts later, Oliver and I, in the midst of our delirious sugar highs, stumbled out with huge grins across our faces. I marveled to myself how sometimes the silliest thing can make you forget your troubles and be happy, even for one brief moment. Maybe it was all the sugar in my body that suddenly made me hyper-aware, or the fact that I had stopped obsessing about my own angst long enough to observe the world around me, but suddenly something troubled me.

"Notice anything strange, Oliver?" I asked, pointing at Main Street.

Oliver gave me a quizzical look and then followed my gaze up and down the block. It took him a second to register exactly what I was talking about.

"Where's Bar Tech Security?" Oliver remarked. "I don't see one of their cars on the street." He seemed as surprised by this fact as I was. "Anywhere."

"And yesterday," I hastened to remind him, "they were literally everywhere." I reflected back on the day from the time I had left my house. "In fact, now that I think about it, I don't recall seeing a single security car around town at all today."

"Does this mean they're not looking for me—or us—anymore?" Oliver asked hopefully, but I could tell he was still very concerned they might snatch him at any moment like they'd done to Maya. "Especially considering that none-too-subtle spectacle I made at school yesterday. I wasn't exactly hiding anything. More like flaunting it."

"I'm not really sure what's going on. Maybe it's one of those collective amnesia experiences," I hypothesized.

"Like the way everyone seems to reset to normal the day after a pulse happens."

"Whatever it is, I intend to find out," I declared, determined to go on the offensive and get some answers.

"And how are you going to do that, supersleuth," Oliver pressed, "without exposing our secrets?"

"Leave that to me," I responded cryptically, formulating a plan in my head while we continued on.

After all, I did have my own personal Deep Throat . . . AKA my father.

Before Oliver and I parted ways and headed back to our homes, I asked what his mother said to him after we dropped him off the night before.

"She already knew about the trouble at school," he

replied, "and asked how I was doing. Of course, I was incredibly vague and acted like it was no big deal."

"She ask anything about the break-in at Bar Tech? Or you being chased by security?"

"Nope. Not a thing. And now that you mention it . . ." Oliver contemplated thoughtfully. "I remember thinking it seemed pretty odd, especially since she usually quizzes me about every stupid detail of my day. But truthfully, I was so relieved not to get the third degree by her that I went right up to my room. In retrospect, it's like she didn't *want* to know what had gone down."

Just like everyone in town, it seemed. Don't ask . . . don't tell . . .

As soon as I walked through the front door of my house, I heard my dad calling my name. There was an edge of concern in his voice. I found him in the kitchen, sitting at the table nursing a nearly empty mug of coffee. There was barely half a cup left in the coffeemaker. He'd obviously been waiting for me for quite a while. And he looked extremely relieved to see that I was all in one piece.

He rose to his feet and hugged me tightly. "Where did you disappear to so early this morning? I had no idea if something happened to you."

His long, muscular arms enveloped me in a cocoon of welcome paternal warmth.

"I'm fine," I replied, finally breaking free from his embrace. "I just had to get out of the house and clear my head." I didn't offer up any other specifics.

"And is it cleared? Your head?" He leaned forward, his expression tentative and worried.

"To be honest . . . no," I answered bluntly. "If fact, nothing seems clearer to me today than yesterday. Not about you. Or about anything else that's happened."

"The most important thing right now for both of us," he reinforced, looking directly at me, "is that we keep our secrets secret. And stick close to home."

"Does that mean I shouldn't leave the house at all?" Did he know something important that he wasn't telling me?

"Just let me know where you're going. Until this Maya thing blows over and Chase gets released from the hospital."

"So Chase is going to be okay?" I had to admit I was relieved about that bit of bright news.

"Looks as though he'll make a full recovery. Though he's still pretty out of it," Dad replied, slipping naturally into his doctor mode. "Which is no surprise, given that he's been in a coma for two days."

"Does he remember anything about what happened?" I pressed, still worried about what it meant for Maya and her future.

"No. But that doesn't mean Chase won't recover his memory. Eventually."

The implication was clear. There was a ticking clock. I knew the longer it took for Chase to remember, the safer Maya would be. Until then, it was up to Oliver, Jackson, and me to keep Maya's secret—even from my father. It seemed to be the wisest course of action, where my father's safety was concerned.

In the meantime, my father thought the best course of action for me was not to do anything rash or call undue attention to myself.

"Just be observant and try to act normal."

"Normal," I muttered with a bemused chuckle. I'd almost forgotten what that was.

"An alien concept, I know," my dad replied. "But do your best."

I promised to do as he asked. And he promised to continue working Cochran and Bar Tech from the inside. His main focus was to ferret out whether I or anyone else was in imminent danger of being identified by the security-goon squad. My father kept reiterating how important it was that we worked together—as a team.

In the spirit of domestic cooperation, the one new fact I did offer up to my dad was about Dana Fox's sudden return to Barrington.

"She's back?" he asked, genuinely surprised by my revelation and looking a bit disconcerted.

"I met her this morning." I didn't elaborate on any of the

specifics, but I couldn't help expressing my nagging doubt. "Though her sudden reappearance does seem suspicious to me." Of course, I deliberately failed to mention anything about my complicated relationship with Jackson to my dad.

"Agreed," my father admitted, nodding his head as he processed this latest wrinkle. "I doubt it's just a coincidence."

I doubted it, too. Timing was everything. And I intended to find out exactly what brought Dana back to Barrington.

Which was why, just a few hours later, I was standing in the middle of Dana's impromptu homecoming bash. What better place to start digging for answers than in her own backyard?

"I don't know what the hell is happening," Jackson whispered in my ear somewhat forbiddingly as he walked up behind me. He had on his old navy and burgundy school jacket, which I'd never seen him wear at all.

"Makes two of us," I remarked truthfully, trying my best to keep a stoic expression.

"I was so sure I'd never see Dana again," Jackson confessed.

"And yet here she is." I was desperate to get everything out in the open between the two of us. "Don't you have questions?" The floodgates opened, and so did my mouth. "Where she's been? Why has she never contacted you? Did her disappearance have anything to do with Bar Tech?"

"Of course I have questions, Nica," he countered, obviously angered by my insinuating tone but keeping his voice low so others couldn't hear what we were talking about. "I just need to give her time to open up."

"Time? Last night we were running for our lives," I snapped back, reminding him of the imminent danger that surrounded us. "And tonight we're partying?"

Before Jackson had a chance to respond, Dana abruptly interrupted us, flashing her big, warm grin. "You guys having fun?"

Jackson and I exchanged tense looks.

"Can't believe how quickly you pulled this all together in just a few hours," Jackson interjected, hoping to diffuse the awkwardness that hung in the air.

"You know me. Where there's a will, there's a way," Dana flipped back playfully. "Can't believe how much I've missed everyone."

"And everyone seems to have missed you," I replied in my sincerest voice. "Judging by the turnout."

Dana scanned the big crowd. Everyone seemed to be having fun. "I'm touched to know that people didn't forget about me," she said, humbly patting her heart with her right hand. "I'm just sorry that Maya's not here."

I stole a glance at Jackson, desperate for guidance.

What do we say about Maya's disappearance?

"Yeah, too bad," Jackson said, all cool and calm. "Haven't

seen her since school the other day. I don't know where she is."

"Well, I'm happy everyone else came. And I know we only just met, Nica," Dana added with a warm smile, "but I'm so glad you came too."

"Thanks for including me." I smiled back, relieved to be off Maya but also determined not to reveal even the slightest hint that I might not trust Dana.

"Now, if you don't mind," Dana said, slipping her arm through Jackson's, "I need to steal this guy for a few."

"Steal away," I retorted dryly, my eyes lingering on Jackson, wondering what he was thinking.

Jackson looked back at me, giving me a subtle nod, knowing we had much more to discuss. "Catch you later, Nica."

I nodded and watched Dana lead Jackson over to her suddenly effusive parents, who embraced him like a long-lost relative or future son-in-law—instead of the persona non grata he'd been since Dana's disappearance. I could read from Jackson's stiff body language that he was being polite but skeptical. He didn't seem to be buying their abrupt conversion any more than I was.

While everyone gorged on barbecue chicken wings and pasta salad, I felt claustrophobic and forced my way outside. The cold, crisp Colorado air hit my lungs. I needed to clear my head and try to think, which I seemed to be having a lot of trouble doing lately. I breathed deeply and looked up at the sky. Because of the altitude and our relative isolation, the sky was dotted with thousands of tiny stars. It was so beautiful.

"Everything okay out here, Nica?" A sweet voice expressed concern.

Busted, I spun around to see that none other than the hostess of the party, Dana Fox, had come outside to check up on me with a steaming mug of hot cocoa.

"Yes, fine," I sheepishly replied to Dana, taking the mug from her with a grateful smile. I was completely mortified at being found out. "Just needed some fresh air."

Dana furrowed her brow, definitely unconvinced. "You're going to freeze your ass off." Her arms were crossed and she was rubbing them briskly to keep warm. The sweater she wore over black leggings seemed to help.

"That wouldn't necessarily be such a bad thing," I joked, turning my head as I pretended to check out the size of my butt in my favorite black jeans.

Dana laughed and shook her head in casual dismay. "Anyone ever tell you you're—no offense—the tiniest bit crazy? And I mean that in a good way."

"I seem to recall the expression nut job being bandied about by various shrinks."

"Ugh, I hate shrinks," replied Dana. "All they want you to do is yak, yak, yak about bullshit. Just leave me alone."

"You went to one?" I was surprised by her admission. I

hadn't seen that one coming at all. But I used the unexpected opening to do a bit of snooping.

"Please," she remarked with a dismissive wave of her hand. "Who hasn't?"

"The curse of our generation," I quipped, trying to engage her and create a sympathetic bond.

"Tell me about it. My overprotective parents had me see this very nice woman in Denver last year. Specialized in teenagers. She meant well. Such a huge time suck."

"My mom sent me to one when I was ten," I confessed. "To make sure I was coping with my parents' divorce. What was your problem," I gently pressed, "if you don't mind me asking?"

"No big deal really." Dana shrugged and shook her head. "Jackson and I were going through . . . a rocky patch. Things just got too intense between us."

Her version of events certainly matched the official story I'd heard when I'd first arrived in Barrington.

"And that's why you left town," I probed, hoping to get some additional insight or clue about those missing months when she was away.

"I stayed with cousins in Connecticut. Anyway, old news," she declared with a sigh and an exasperated roll of the eyes, "because I'm back to stay." Signaling she didn't want to discuss the matter any further.

I was about to probe a little deeper into Dana's time away

when a gang of her BFFs from cheerleading, Annie, Emily, Maddie, and Jaden, suddenly came outside and surrounded her.

"Here you are," squealed Jaden. "The party's inside! C'mon!"

And the girls dragged a laughing, protesting Dana by the arms back into the jam-packed pool house.

I wasn't exactly sure if Dana had told me the truth and nothing but the truth about her time away, but it was a beginning I intended to build upon.

Dana's party finally started to wind down around eight forty-five p.m. My father was on call at the hospital and insisted on picking me up, even though Oliver's mother had offered to drive me home. With everything so uncertain, I had wanted to skip Dana's party so that we could continue strategizing, but my father had practically ordered me to attend. I hoped it was because he saw us as a clandestine father-daughter *Alias* spy duo. Except without the exotic and glamorous locations.

Exactly where that left my mother in this complex equation, I had no clue. To be honest, I was so wrapped up in my own personal angst and turmoil over my life that I couldn't worry about her. Paranoia and caution had gotten the better of me. It was hard for them not to. Instead, I chose to send a brief, bland e-mail filling Lydia in on my classes (I used "fine" a lot), extracurricular school activities (busy supporting our football team in the playoffs), and my hectic social life. I told myself it was better this way, that I was protecting my mother. What could she possibly do all the way from Antarctica anyway? When in fact the truth was a bit more complicated and something I wasn't quite ready to face just yet. And that was my (not so) repressed anger at her role in all this.

How could she have sent me to Barrington? Did she have any idea what was really going on? *She'd* worked here years before, when the incident occurred—while she was pregnant with me. Did she have any clue that sending me back to the "safest town in America" would actually be the most dangerous thing for me?

I just wasn't prepared to take on that drama—a problem wrapped in a riddle wrapped in a bunker-buster of a bummer: If she knew, it would break my heart, and if she didn't, I had no earthly way of explaining it to her. I didn't have a shred of proof except for my currently nonexistent powers and a few hastily scribbled journal entries detailing a scattered selection of the whiplash-inducing revelations of the past few months. It'd be enough to convince my mom that I'd somehow developed an overreliance on cough syrup but not exactly groundbreaking revelations.

My powers? Bar Tech?

Hi, Mom, long time. Listen, I— No, no, things are good. They're great, actually. I discovered my DNA is—yes, I know. Good stock. Not so much Dad's side, sure, but— Are you sitting down? Yeah, you're gonna want to do that. No, I'm not pregnant. That would be easier to say than . . . Um. Well. I can turn invisible.

Click

And that would be that. For as much as she loved to explore different philosophies, religions, and schools of thought, she was scientist and a journalist at heart. Rational to the core. Tales of superpowers and conspiracies were not even gonna make it in one ear and out the other; they'd be torn to shreds halfway by her twin Gatling guns of "Reason" and "Logic."

I felt my pocket buzz, and my eyes shot to a clock on the wall. Almost nine p.m. Curfew. The screen of my phone lit up with DAD. He didn't sound thrilled.

"I hate to do this to you, but do you think you can get a ride home?" Oh, Marcus. Always full of the best intentions, always coming up just a little short. I didn't need a super-power to see this coming.

"Sure, yeah. Everything all right?"

"Couple of scuff ups. Nothing serious, but we're slammed. Oh, and Chase seems to be recovering his memory."

It was obvious that Dad didn't want to say anything more explicit to me on the phone. And I knew not to ask. Who knew if Bar Tech was listening to our calls?

"I'm sure a ride won't be a problem."

"But with a parent, okay? No friends. I don't want to see you end up in here."

"Got it, Dad." *Click.*

Oliver was waving down a car as my dad wrapped up the call. I started to jog over to the old station wagon as he got inside.

"Oliver!" I shouted. "Can I get a ride?"

"You up to date on your shots? Car's a little messy."

"I can handle it."

I opened the door and was greeted by a sluice of files and folders that spilled out and piled at my feet. Oliver's mom turned around, and I realized in that moment that we'd never actually met. She was older than I expected—wiry haired and a little spastic—like if Doc Brown were a cat lady. And clearly not the most organized secretary Bar Tech had ever had, although now she managed Cattle Baron, the local steak restaurant.

"Sorry. Just put that stuff to the side. Wherever. Floor's fine. Sorry. Work, you know, and just, well, you eat in the car when you can between meetings and they tell you to drive here and drive there and it gets messy and you want to clean, but there's so little time. So. Little. Time."

I smiled as I stooped to pick up the papers before they got too messy. The neurosis that bubbled underneath her words hadn't wormed its way fully into Oliver's personality, but he displayed hints of it, and it was charming to see where it came from.

"It's okay! Plenty of space," I said, pushing some of the papers and books to the side, creating a clear patch to squeeze myself into. Somehow, everything I moved made its way back into my lap as Mrs. Monsalves finished rearranging the mess into a slightly different mess. Oliver turned around and offered a silent, mouthed apology. I shook my head and laughed. It was fine. Compared to my own family drama, other people's families were a comfort, even when they were strange.

"I'm Nica, by the way. It's so nice to finally meet you, Mrs. Monsalves." I couldn't really extend a hand to shake, so I tried to lean forward with as much glowing good-girl earnestness as I could.

"Oh, Nica! You're the mystery best friend I've heard so much about!"

"Mom . . . ," said Oliver, trying to shut down the quirk machine, probably before something really embarrassing leaked out.

"Guess so."

"I've always told Oliver he can have friends over whenever he wants, but he prefers to be in his room with those video games."

"Oh, we see plenty of each other," I assured her, hoping as I spoke that I wouldn't be squeezed for details of how our adventures had drawn us closer than most high school friends.

Oliver turned around in his seat. "So your dad's having a busy night at the hospital after all."

"Seems as though Chase's memory is returning." The urgency in my tone registered with Oliver. Chase's recovered memory would undoubtedly implicate Maya.

"Some guys have all the luck," snarked Oliver. "I can't believe that douche is my half brother."

It wasn't immediately clear to me that I'd set Oliver up to drop an offhand comment that was actually a grenade primed to explode. It wasn't until I saw Mrs. Monsalves's fingers clench the wheel that I realized a mistake had been made.

"Oliver."

"I don't think I'll ever be okay knowing Chase and I share DNA."

Mrs. Monsalves tried to play dumb. "What are you talking about?" A nervous laugh slipped through her teeth. "I thought I told you—no drinking." Oliver rolled his eyes at his mother's attempts to suppress the secret of his lineage.

"It's fine. Nica already knows." Oliver announced it like it was no big deal.

"Knows what?" Oliver's mother shot him a withering look.

"The whole thing, Mom. It's fine. Trust me."

"I don't even know this girl." Mrs. Monsalves's eyes darted up and fired at me from the rearview mirror. No putting that secret back in the bag.

"You don't have to. I do. She's my friend, and I'm telling you: It's fine."

The only thing worse than fighting with your parents was being trapped in a car with someone else fighting with their parents about you. I pushed back in my seat, wishing, praying, that my powers would come back so I could vanish—and then maybe fling open the door and dive out for good measure. Their voices started to rise:

"No, it's not fine. I told you that in confidence, Oliver!"

"And I had to talk to someone about it! Sorry I don't deal with my problems by pushing everyone out of my life the way you do."

I cringed and looked out the window, trying to get my mind far, far away from the morass I was in. That's when I saw it from the backseat, pulsing in the sky. By now my brain interpreted any light in the sky as an appearance of the pulse that changed us all, but this light was different. I honestly had no idea what it was at first. It was barely visible, no brighter than a far-off star, but it got exponentially bigger each time it pulsed, like a balloon slowly being inflated. I opened my mouth to say something, and in that instant, the light took over the sky with an immense, silent flash. It was so incredibly bright and violent that I would've thought it was a megaton nuclear bomb detonating if the flash weren't so . . . intensely green.

The same glowing, sickly, skin-crawling green pulse that

unlocked our powers in the past had suddenly infiltrated the entire sky. It was a clear night, and for a split second the rest of the evening's stars sparked from diamonds to emeralds.

And then we were upside down.

2. FIRE AND ICE

I don't know if Oliver's mom hit something or if the flash was so violent that she wrenched the wheel in shock, but my hair dropped toward the ceiling, and for a second I felt weightless. My seat belt slammed into my sternum like a body pillow made of concrete and all the air in my lungs escaped to join the rest of the debris crisscrossing my vision. The car was rotating upside down in midair.

My life wasn't flashing before my eyes. Instead, just a surge of overwhelming panic. There I hung, suspended between the sky and the ground and life and death, and I couldn't even conjure a comforting moment. I tried desperately to make eye contact with Oliver or his mom in the rearview mirror. Just eyes. A glance. Something before this all came to an end. But there was nothing. All I felt was the burning in my neck, something that felt like gravel in my chest, and my heart pounding in my ears.

An ancient oak tree trunk stopped our journey cold.

With the deafening crack of a thunderclap—*WHAM*—the windshield exploded into a thousand raindrop-sized shards, and the deadly torrent of glass washed over Oliver, his mother, myself and—

I came to upside down. What felt like miles and miles away.

"Nica?" Oliver sounded like he was shouting down a train tunnel.

I tried opening my mouth. It worked. Vocal cords? Intact. I scratched out a hoarse "Oliver." My body continued to reboot: hearing, check; vision, check; pain, check. Like a thousand checks on that last one. My body was screaming that I was wounded, but—cut? Broken? Bruised? I couldn't tell. I glanced around to get a look at myself but could barely make anything out in the dark.

"Nica?" Oliver called my name again. My mind raced and pinpointed that it was coming from outside the car, to my left.

"Here," I replied. "Here."

His face suddenly appeared in front of me, sideways and upside down. Confusion registered in his eyes even though he was staring right at me. "Nica?"

I started to get angry. Our game of Marco Polo was getting old. I needed to get out of the car and probably go straight to the hospital.

"I'm right here!" My voice was as ripped as my clothes felt like they were, and I could tell I was frightening him. I took a breath and calmed myself down. "Sorry. I'm here." His shaky, wide eyes told me the truth before he even dared vocalize it.

"No, you aren't."

Holy shit. There was no way. I held my arms out directly between Oliver's face and myself, trying to block him out with my hand, my forearm, anything. But I could still see him, staring right where I should be, where physics and common sense promised I would be, but wasn't there. There was no escaping it: The pulse had struck again scarcely more than twenty-four hours after the last one. And I had vanished.

I reached for the seat belt and—*ka-click*—let myself free. Gravity left me sprawled on the ground. I tested my legs. They weren't broken, but I wasn't getting to my feet anytime soon. Desperate to leave the cramped, broken confines of the wreck, I crawled forward, past a wide-eyed Oliver, and propped myself up against the side of the car. I watched his eyes follow the sound of my body scraping against the ground. When I settled, so did they, though about two feet to the side of my head. I tried to regain my composure, but my thoughts were scattered, panicked. I focused on the gentle shower of papers falling from the sky. Mrs. Monsalves's papers. Wait.

"Where's your mom?" I asked, searching Oliver's eyes for an answer. If the papers were falling, that meant they were propelled from the car, which means—

"In her seat," Oliver confirmed with a hint of fear in his voice. "She hit her head. She's breathing, but we need to get her to the hospital. There's a lot of blood."

Despite the grotesque image, I let out a small sigh of relief. At least she hadn't been tossed into the woods with her work.

"Is there a phone? Where's my phone?" I rifled around my pockets in a panic. I couldn't find it anywhere.

Oliver held out a shattered piece of plastic and circuitry.

"Shit." I recognized my case, reached for it, and turned it invisible as soon as my fingers touched it. As soon as it vanished, Oliver let go, surprised. The case reappeared moments later as it clattered onto the pavement—useless. "What about yours?" I desperately hoped that his phone was in better condition than mine.

"No idea."

"You check the woods?" I asked, trying to rein in my escalating worry.

Oliver shook his head, blinked away for a second, and reappeared moments later not six inches from where he had been.

"Oliver?" It was my turn to be shocked.

"Can't find it," he confessed. Then, suddenly having

another thought, Oliver gestured and held up his hand. "Hold on. Maybe on the other side of the roa—" Before he even finished his sentence, he pinballed around the edges of the road and then right back to me, this time reappearing almost on top of me. Unnerving to say the least.

"I don't think I'll ever get used to that," I said, still shaky and unsure of my balance, as I tried to stand on my feet.

"Oliver . . . ? Where are you?" Mrs. Monsalves muttered, dazed and confused as she regained consciousness.

"Right here," he replied, clasping his mother's hand to reassure her. "You're okay. I'm going to get help."

"NO," she exclaimed, frightened and disoriented as the full extent of the crash gradually became apparent to her. "Don't leave me." She clung to Oliver's arm tightly and whimpered.

As Oliver did his best to soothe his mother's fear, I looked down to where my body should've been but most definitely wasn't and realized I had to fight back my distress and focus, pain be damned. I couldn't very well barge into Dana's house in my invisible state. I took slow, deliberate steps away from the car and closed my eyes to try to calm my electric nerves. I put a hand to my chest and—ow, ow, ow—applied pressure, just to try to center myself. I am here. I exist. I gulped air instead of sipping it. The accident had left me so shaken I could barely count breaths, never mind individual seconds. Each desperate infusion of oxygen that didn't result in my reappearance prompted the next to come shallower, faster. Panic wasn't sinking in—I was beginning to sink in it.

Focus, dammit.

I pictured my dad standing in front of me, a gentle hand on my arm. I tried to read his thoughts and imagine what he would say as I took one breath after the other, catching myself and beginning to emerge from my spiral. There ya go. You got it. Then I allowed my mom into the picture as well. Lydia and Marcus, together again, rooting for me to find steady footing in each breath. I closed my eyes and drilled down even deeper, letting my parents guide me to check in with my lungs, my core, my heart, and my soul. Panic gave way to peace, and when I opened my eyes, I was back. Whole. Standing in the middle of a cold, dark stretch of road.

"Stay here. I'll go," I told Oliver. It was more of a command than a suggestion. No way would his mom calm down if he split and left me in charge. "I'll go back to Dana's and call an ambulance."

"Stay safe," he replied with an urgent tone, knowing it was the best plan despite his post-pulse speed and agility.

"Caution's my middle name," I quipped, doing everything in my power to keep focused.

As I took off down the road to get help, I heard Oliver gently assure his mother: "Everything will be okay, Mom. Nica's going to get help."

I ran all the way back to Dana's, almost forgetting my cuts and bruises and aching body. It took me about eight minutes—maybe less—to get there. I'd never run so fast in my life. When I arrived, breathless, legs aching and freezing cold, the front door was hanging open. Dana's house was as eerily silent as the road that I had just crashed on. No one was on the front lawn, no one was on the steps, and no one was on the porch. Kids had been streaming to their cars as we left just minutes earlier, but when I returned, it was as if everyone had mysteriously vanished.

I crept toward the quiet house and sensed something was very wrong. First there was that smell—a familiar post-pulse ozoney burnt aroma, which hung in the air. The closer I got to the open front door, the sharper and more unpleasant the smell became.

I hesitated at the door and called out, "Hello?"

No response. Only stillness and an unnerving silence.

Nevertheless, I needed to get to a phone. I took a step inside. As soon as my feet hit the hall floor—*ZZZZAP*—a surge of energy shot up through my legs with such force that it ricocheted around my head like tiny explosions. My hair came alive and stood on end. Every strand pulsated with electricity. Holy shit. I was afraid to move. Or touch anything. I didn't know what the hell was happening. It felt as if I'd suddenly grabbed on to one of those Van de Graaff generators that shoot electricity through your body at a children's science museum.

"Dana?" I could barely get her name out

No one answered. Just silence and . . . sparks. Everywhere. Some spat from the alarm system near the front door; others sizzled orange and white from a lamp in the corner of the dining room. As I focused and listened, I could hear the electricity echoing the whole way into the far end of the house.

What the hell happened here?

Even if some weird electric pulse had short-circuited most of the house, what was causing those sounds? But first things first: I had to find a phone and call an ambulance. I knew landlines weren't supposed to be connected to a house's main power. They supposedly worked no matter what was thrown their way. I clung to that hope as I booked it straight for the kitchen and pulled Dana's family's landline off the hook. A dial tone. Thank God. I quickly called 911, giving them the most precise location for the accident. Before I had even finished the call, I noticed something moving that stopped me dead in my tracks.

My eye caught a curious blue light pulsing on the wall. The size of a fingernail, maybe smaller, it looked like a strange firefly trapped between the paint and the wall itself. When I stooped to inspect it, I noticed it wasn't pulsing on the wall—it was pulsing in the wall. What's more, it wasn't alone. In my panic, I hadn't spotted the dozens of small pulses crawling through the wall—like ants at a picnic—all drawn toward something I couldn't see.

I tiptoed behind them as they pulsed, jittered, and flickered to their ultimate destination: Dana's living room.

There I discovered Jackson lying on his back, inert and unconscious. I was terrified. Had the pulse knocked him off his feet? Surrounding him were the only people who might have the answers—Dana's spellbound parents along with a few straggling partygoers, including the queen bee herself—all stunned into a frightened silence. Some clutched half-empty beer cans. Others just stared vacant and senseless, watching slack-jawed as the parade of bolts and sparks shot out from the floor and walls and rippled straight through Jackson's skin.

Horrified by what was happening before my eyes, I realized that Jackson's body seemed to be sucking electricity directly from the house itself. Streams of power flowed to him from every angle, filling him with a horrifyingly beautiful blue glow until his heart beat bright white in his chest . . .

. . . and then he began to float. Levitating up in the air like a weightless feather.

My heart pounded in my chest from dread that soon

everyone would discover the truth about the pulse and Jackson and Oliver and me. My body immediately swung into self-preservation mode. Before I could even think about what to do next, I had vanished. Completely. It was instinctive—defensive.

Barely a second after I disappeared, I heard a gasp followed by a stifled sob. Someone in the room was crying. I was surprised to see that tears flowed from the wide eyes of none other than Kyle Meldrum, one of Jackson's more macho football teammates.

"Jesus Christ," was all Kyle muttered as he rose to his feet. He was mesmerized by the unbelievable sight of Jackson pulsating like a human generator.

I should've known better than to let Kyle take more than a step closer to Jackson, but my own alarm and awe had momentarily turned me into a rigid statue. A tortoise could've run interference quicker between Kyle and his target. By the time I snapped back and realized what was about to happen, Kyle was already reaching for Jackson.

"Somebody do something," he begged. And then he made contact, his fingers touching Jackson.

The air crackled and split as electricity blasted from Jackson's body into Kyle. I hung back, terrified that Kyle's body and brain were about to be fried. And there was nothing I could do to stop what was happening. Invisibility could hide me but not protect me from Jackson's power. I had to stay out of the way or risk getting zapped, too.

Just when I feared that Kyle might ignite into flames—*WHAM!* A final discharge of power fired from Jackson's body. The explosion dropped Jackson to the floor and shot Kyle off his feet, slamming him spine-first into a wall a good twenty feet away with a loud *WHOOMP*. Kyle collapsed into a crumpled heap. The unearthly silence was suddenly pierced by Kyle's scream.

I stood there transfixed, not knowing what to do. That's when I noticed Dana was standing there too. She wasn't moving. There were tears in her eyes and she had a hand clutched over her mouth. What she'd witnessed was the cherry and whipped-cream topper on a wild homecoming party to end all parties.

I must've gasped because Dana heard it and spun around. I freaked. I could feel my body starting to return to its physical state. I had to get the hell out of that house before my secret was exposed.

I bolted out of there, leaving the front door open as I fled the house.

A solemn-looking female EMT was wheeling Oliver's mother over to the ambulance by the time I made it back to the accident site.

I beelined over to where Oliver was being grilled by the other EMT, a suspicious, bearded medic, who had just examined him. How had the accident happened? Had we moved Mrs. Monsalves? Had we been drinking? I immediately recognized the familiar irritability of Barrington citizens in the aftermath of a pulse. In this case, extra powerful meant extra aggressive.

"How is she?" I asked Oliver after the medic moved back to the ambulance to assist his partner with Mrs. Monsalves's gurney.

"Woozy and upset, but hanging in there," Oliver reported optimistically. His eyes narrowed a bit as he sized me up and realized something was very wrong. "Are you okay? You're shaking."

"We're in trouble," I whispered, making sure the EMTs couldn't hear what I was saying. My fingernails dug into my palms as I gave Oliver a concise Cliffs Notes version of what happened to Jackson back at Dana's house.

"They all saw?" he asked queasily, clutching my arm and staring at me in disbelief. He was looking pale and pretty shaky himself.

"Everyone." I nodded grimly.

But our conversation was cut short when the surly EMT waved us over to the ambulance. We were whisked into the back of the ambulance with Oliver's mother for the brief ride over to the hospital.

Oliver and I rode in silence. Words weren't necessary. We knew we were screwed. What a handful of our classmates just witnessed in Dana Fox's living room was totally inexplicable, and word would undoubtedly spread—fast—about Jackson, Barrington's newest power generator. I was afraid that we were going to wake up the next morning and find out that every last person in Barrington had heard the truth.

There were freaks living among them.

3. CODE BLUE

Once Oliver's mom had been stabilized and moved to an examination room, I tried to slip away to find my dad, who was on call. Immediately, the suspicious EMT stepped out in front of me, hands raised, and stopped me from leaving the ER.

"I'm fine," I insisted, anxious to get away from him and the unforgiving glare of the hospital's fluorescent lighting.

"You may feel fine," he snarked with a harsh gaze, cornering me, "but until a doctor signs off, you're not going anywhere."

The more I insisted I was okay and didn't need a doctor, the more the EMT acted like he didn't hear me. Was he deliberately trying to unnerve me? Did he suspect something? My nails sliced into my palms, trying to fight off my jangled nerves, but I could feel my control starting to slip.

Shit. I was trapped. I couldn't outrun the guy or even try to disappear. He knew my name and who I was. To make matters worse, up until that moment I'd been able to keep my invisibility under wraps while they focused on Mrs. Monsalves. Now his eyes were riveted solely on me. It was unnerving the way he kept staring at me.

The roller coaster events of the day had already left me feeling extremely vulnerable. And now the added pressure of having my body scrutinized by some random doctor was making me feel even more exposed. The clock was ticking. It would be just a matter of time before my secret was exposed and my cover blown.

I tried some old breathing exercises to steady my nerves. It was too late. That all-too-familiar hot, tingling sensation was already rising from the soles of my feet up through my legs, along with a fresh wave of panic and terror. I looked up and down the corridor, trying to come up with an emergency-escape plan. I had moments before I literally vanished before the EMT's eyes. I had to get out of there. But when I looked down again, the black-and-white-checkered tile floor had started to become visible through my disappearing feet. . . .

"Nica!" A familiar voice called out my name.

In a flash, I was enveloped in my father's strong, tall frame. He was my life raft. A tall white knight in hospital scrubs, rescuing me from impending doom. In those few seconds, I managed to catch my breath and steady my already frazzled nerves. Slowly in, slowly out. I quickly glanced back at my feet as my father and I separated from our embrace. A wave of incredible relief washed over me. My feet had success-fully rematerialized before the nosy EMT even noticed they were almost gone.

"Everything all right?" Dad instinctively knew to get me out of there. He pulled me away from the EMT and a couple of passing nurses before saying another word.

"Yes," I lied. "At least I think I am."

My father's commanding gaze was enough to send the still-lingering EMT packing. I was the chief of cardiology's daughter. My father was in charge, and the EMT knew bet-ter than to mess with him.

Just to be sure that I was still in one piece, Dad gave me a quick once-over there in the hospital corridor. All my limbs and extremities were still in place. Momentarily satisfied, he led me farther down the hallway to an empty examination room. When we were inside and alone, a second hug told me it was safe to start talking.

"There was a pulse right after we left the party," I blurted out as he shut the door. "That's what caused the accident. We spun out of control and hit a tree. Oliver's mom was knocked unconscious. I don't think she saw anything."

My dad was listening and nodding, but it was like he was on a five-second time delay. He was still examining me, checking my vision and pressure points and whatever else a worried physician did to triple-check the well-being of his only child.

"But the kids at the party . . . ," I continued. "They did see."

My father stopped what he was doing and stared at me, alarmed. "Tell me exactly what happened."

I took a breath before I launched into a blow-by-blow replay of Jackson's code blue and the ensuing serious sparkage, witnessed by a rapt audience including Dana Fox.

My father listened attentively before speaking. "Did you tell anyone?"

"Just Oliver," I meekly confessed. "I wanted to call Jackson afterward to make sure he was okay, but my cell phone was trashed in the accident."

Dad instantly dug his cell out of his scrubs and handed it over without me even having to ask. "Give Jackson a try," he suggested. Something in my dad's poker-faced expression looked less than optimistic that I might get an answer.

I dialed anyway. Jackson's was one of the only numbers I'd gone out of my way to learn by heart. It didn't even ring. I shook my head sullenly and promptly handed the phone back to my dad.

"Sweetie . . ." His voice, though sympathetic and paternal, was spiked with a hint of pity. He could read me like no one else, and JACKSON was printed in big, sad neon letters across my face. "I hadn't realized you two were so . . . tight."

I looked back up at my dad as a swell of emotion rose inside me. Dad's attempt at subtlety was heavy-handed at best. If he hadn't known before, my moon-eyed worry had all but given it away. I wasn't aware of the tears pooling in the corners of my eyes, but suddenly they were threatening to go fully torrential. If only going invisible were a cure for embarrassment.

"We need a plan," I declared, shifting into action mode, hoping to postpone my emotional meltdown until I was alone. "To figure out what we're going to do."

"There's no 'we' here, Nica," proclaimed Dad, who seemed to be wrestling with a crisis of conscience. "I can't keep letting you get in the middle of this. It's too dangerous."

"I am in the middle of it," I replied firmly. "No matter what you do or how much you try to protect me."

Dad exhaled and shook his head in resignation that I was right. Nevertheless, his overprotective tendencies were charging full-speed ahead. "My shift's almost over. I'm taking you home."

Dad set me aside in his office and quickly tended to his remaining responsibilities, then clocked out a little early. Being a respected doctor, not to mention one of Richard Cochran's favorite researchers, was a perk he didn't take advantage of often, but it was more than enough to grease the wheels when needed.

Tonight was one of those times.

I waited until we were in the car and pulling out of the parking lot to pitch him my plan.

"Dana's house is on the way home," I announced as if it were a fun fact my dad didn't know.

He shook his head, eyes on the road, guessing exactly what was on my mind. "You've had more than enough adventure for one night."

It was a no, but it wasn't firm enough to not risk a second pass.

"Please, Dad," I pleaded, staring right at him. He looked at me as I continued. "Just a quick drive-by. We don't have to go inside."

My dad didn't answer, but I could see the wheels spinning in his head. He just turned his eyes back toward the road and continued driving. It was past curfew, and the roads were completely empty. Just when I thought he was taking me home, he suddenly made a sharp turn that pointed us toward Dana's ritzy neighborhood.

"Just a drive-by," he insisted quite firmly. He was tightening the reins, making sure I felt the boundary.

I nodded and looked out the window. The other houses in Dana's neighborhood were just as impressive as the extravagant Fox compound. Not surprisingly, the Cochran home was also only a few blocks away. Tudor mansions and modern ski chalets blended together in an overwhelming theme: wealth. Each plot was expansive, dotted with trees wrapped in tiny white Christmas lights. I'd almost forgotten that the holiday was less than a month away.

My dad slowed down as Dana's house came into view. The Martha Stewart photo spread was ruined by the collection of Bar Tech Security cars parked outside, their red and yellow lights flashing.

As we rolled closer, we could see a half-dozen uniformed Bar Tech security guards mulling around on the front lawn. They weren't alone. Dana was with them.

"What's she doing?" I rolled down my window, but we weren't close enough to make out any words. I had to go see what was happening. My dad was already turning the corner, a necessary move to avoid their suspicions.

"Just drive out of sight," I advised. "I can sneak back on foot."

He glared at me like I had two heads. "No way am I letting you out of this car." There it was. The stern not-if-hell-freezes-over version of his "no" face.

"Dad. Please." I refused to take no for an answer. Danger or not, I had to know what happened to Jackson.

Dad didn't slow, but he didn't press into the gas yet either. I could feel my window of opportunity shrinking fast—probably another few blocks if that. I turned to look behind us. We'd crested a small hill. I couldn't see Dana's house anymore, which meant they couldn't see us.

"Please. Pull over." My voice had more urgency, bordering on desperation.

My father stopped the car short on the side of the road

and looked at me. He could tell by the worried look in my eyes how important this was to me—how important Jackson was to me. Dangerous or not, he knew I wouldn't let up. And couldn't let up.

"I don't like you putting yourself in danger."

Present tense! Relief ran through me. Dad was going to let me go.

"I'll be careful," I promised. My dad shook his head and exhaled audibly. "Five minutes. And don't get too close. Never know who's watching."

I nodded, then opened the car door and hopped out. I closed it as quietly as I could. Through the window, I held up five fingers as confirmation. I heard him and would obey. If only I could go invisible on command.

I hoofed it back over the small hill, careful to stay at just the edge of the road. I wasn't expecting any other drivers, but my dad would've murdered me if I ended up roadkill.

I crested the hill and had the Fox house back in my sights. My heart was pounding so loud I was sure everyone could hear it.

Three guards stood out front. There was no sign of Dana. Where was she? Where was everyone else? Nerves hit me as I skulked closer. Had they noticed my dad and me drive by? Still safely out of earshot, I jogged to the corner and around to the mouth of the driveway. As I double-checked the street, I counted six Bar Tech cars. It was unlikely any of the guards had parked there and walked home in this posh neighborhood.

Then through the large picture window I spotted a figure pacing by the Foxe's large Frasier fir Christmas tree and their equally enormous fireplace. Even though Christmas was almost a month away, the Fox family was already prepping for a very happy holiday now that beloved Dana was back home. As I squinted, I could make out a few more people in the living room. Not leftover kids from the party, however. These were the missing Bar Tech guards, warming their hands by the fire. I could barely make Dana's face out, though. Was she merely a nervous teenage girl, unsure of how to deal with a group of authoritative men demanding answers she couldn't give? Or was she a collaborating narc, selling out Jackson's secrets and celebrating over the unconsumed party food spread?

And where was Jackson? Was he okay? Or had he been carted off and locked away, never to be seen again?

I pushed closer to Dana's house. Each step was careful now. More measured. I was near enough to the guards that they'd hear a clumsy clod or two.

Focus, Nica.

Just past the guards, I pivoted to head toward the window, but a glittering expanse of fresh snow powder that had started to fall stopped me in my tracks. One more step, and I'd be two feet into a ghostly footprint the nearby guards would certainly take an interest in. Was it worth a try? Or was I just trying to talk myself into risky behavior because I was so anxious to find out what words Dana was exchanging with the guards inside.

As soon as my dad's voice chimed in, "Be careful, Nica; be safe, Nica," I deflated and knew the plan was toast. Of course the snow was going to keep me from getting to the bottom of this post-curfew Bar Tech house call.

What options did I have left?

I turned on my heels, slinking away as quickly as I'd come. Disappointment sucked the adrenaline from my veins, and the bitter-cold Colorado air wrapped around me as I hustled back to my dad's idling Prius. What good was my power if I couldn't even use it to help the guy who made my heart go crazy?

My dad was inside his car, neck anxiously craned around to the backseat, probably counting down the seconds as he awaited my return. I gave a dispirited shrug, but he continued to stare straight through me. It wasn't his fault, though. As physics would have it, he could stare straight through me. A few deep breaths, a cold front to shock my lungs, and I popped back into visible reality. Dad heaved an enormous sigh of relief as all the tension drained from his body. He turned around and quickly started the car as his free hand massaged his cramping neck.

I collapsed into the seat next to him and leaned into the

heat pouring from the Prius's vents. Being invisible didn't do shit with the cold. We pulled away from the side of the road before Dad pushed for a full report.

"They were inside. I couldn't hear anything," I lamented, visibly upset at my inability to find out anything of substance.

"I'll see what I can find out tomorrow," Dad promised sympathetically. He knew Jackson weighed heavily on my mind.

I stared out the window, worrying about Jackson, as we sped back home before Bar Tech ever became aware of us.

4. BLACKOUT

The ordinary chatter in the quad was exactly the small talk one would expect after a weekend: whispers of hookups, the flaunting of new outfits and electronics, and kids bitching about homework and their weird families like badges of honor. But this was the kind of catching up to be expected at a normal school in a normal town with normal kids, not surreal Barrington, where Jackson Winters had just publicly given his best Dr. Manhattan impression. Maybe it was worse in my mind, but an electric-blue-tinged snowboarding star conducting serious voltage through his body? Granted, I was biased, but how could the student body be talking about anything else? And where was Bar Tech Security?

The last day and a half of intensifying cabin fever had stoked my paranoia beyond reason. Dad had insisted I stay home behind locked doors after Dana's party had run so completely and thoroughly amok. He was aided by Bar Tech Security's own request (which really amounted to an order) for Barrington's citizens to stay indoors while the town's electrical grid was repaired. They blamed the downed cell and online services on a freak weather microburst. The company's latest tall tale would usually have resulted in an instantaneous explanation via Google, but the downed Internet gave me an excuse to crack open a book. Marcus Ashley's *Encyclopaedia Britannica* did not disappoint. The *M* volume was happy to be of service, its satiny pages delivering me a succinct summary of the localized weather oddity—an upside-down tornado of sorts. I had to give it to them. A microburst was a creative cover for Barrington's latest pulse, albeit still leaving the flash of green light, mass irritability, and resulting superpowers thoroughly unexplained.

My only contact with the outside world was a surprise package from my mother. The small box included a bunch of photos of Lydia outside and around the base, a social butterfly even among cloistered researchers. She'd also included a small jar of snow—long since melted, but impressively clear—and a few strange crafts she'd traded other residents for. Most of it was ostensibly junk, but it just made me miss her more.

I tried phoning her several times, but each attempt was met with the same infuriating "all circuits busy" recording and to try again later. I threw the phone across the room. Screw later. I was going crazy and needed to talk to my mother pronto. I needed a lifeline to some kind of normalcy outside the craziness that was my life. And at that moment my mother filled the bill. This so-called idyllic all-American, small-town existence my mother desperately wanted for me was proving to be way more treacherous and hazardous to my health (and that of my friends) than the stealth anacondas in the darkest Amazonian jungle.

Despite a brief text exchange Oliver was mostly unreachable, keeping vigil at his mother's hospital bedside. Considering she'd been bruised, battered, and tossed around during the accident itself, Mrs. Monsalves was in remarkably good condition (no broken bones, no internal injuries). So much so that she was discharged from the hospital by late Sunday afternoon.

Risky as I knew it was, I wished I could reach out to Maya. My anxiety level was reaching a feverish pitch, and I had to know she was safe. But I knew I couldn't. That was how people got caught.

Whatever Bar Tech was really doing with free rein of the deserted streets, I had no idea. The interminable isolation was maddening. My dad tried to find out more about what happened at Dana's without much success. Instead, he did his best to keep me from pulling my hair out: *X-Files* marathon! Father-daughter cook-off! All just momentary distractions from my biggest concern: Jackson.

What exactly happened to him after the party? I tried calling and texting him but couldn't reach him. Had his massive explosion of power altered and changed him? What if it were Jackson and not the pulse that had shorted out the entire town? As I stared out of my bedroom window at all the well-kept houses in our well-ordered town, each paranoid scenario I concocted in my head grew darker and more ominous. I had visions of Jackson being waterboarded in some abandoned warehouse or locked up behind Bar Tech bars or alone in the woods, burning up, unable to harness the electricity coursing through him. Or my worst nightmare of all: Jackson recovering from the pulse in Dana's loving arms. Did Dana now know everything about Jackson's power? And maybe Oliver's and mine as well? Our deepest secret had cemented our friendship. Had Dana's sudden reappearance weakened or destroyed it? Developing our powers together had taken our friendship to a whole new level. Or so I had thought.

At least now that I was finally at school, the horrid anticipation could come to an end. Was Bar Tech waiting to pounce on me as soon as I set foot on school grounds? Would they spirit me away to some deep, dark, secret location? I trod carefully as I scanned the quad for Jackson and Oliver. I just needed my friends to be alive and safe.

As if on cue, a hand on my shoulder sent a shudder up my spine. I turned, ready to wrap Jackson in the most platonic hug I could muster. But instead of looking up into his blue eyes, I looked straight ahead into Dana's emerald-green ones. She followed through on the hug before my body language could rescind the offer.

"It's so good to be back." Dana beamed at me, her smile wrongfully suggesting we were the closest of friends reuniting after a long separation.

"Yeah, I'm sure." I wriggled out of her embrace, my discomfort as obvious as Dana's ease.

"I'm ready to start over. Take on whatever's thrown my way. Tabula rasa. The possibilities seem endless." Dana oozed sincerity even though the sentiments were Hallmark at best.

"Uh-huh. So much . . . potential."

"Speaking of clean slates . . ." Dana's glossed lips curled as her voice took on a throaty, conspiratorial tone. "I saw Chase over the weekend."

"At the hospital?" I leaned back on my heel, immediately suspicious of how she'd dodged the town's house arrest.

"Yesterday afternoon," Dana volunteered.

"How is he?" While I'd heard that Chase was recovering, I hadn't heard he was well enough for visitors. My father hadn't said anything about that.

"Much better. He's been through a lot," Dana lamented with a sympathetic sigh. "I feel so bad. I had no idea . . ."

"He's not the only one who's been through a lot," I replied pointedly but cryptically, wondering what she was driving at.

"I heard how messed up things had gotten between Maya and him. Can't say I'm surprised. I always knew she was erratic. High-strung. He's lucky he wasn't more seriously injured."

"Sounds like he remembers what happened." I stepped closer to Dana, worried about what details Chase had shared with her.

"Bits and pieces," Dana recounted cryptically.

"Must be hard, not remembering everything," I said, laying on the compassion, hoping Dana would feel the need to divulge more.

"It is," Dana confided with a look of hesitation and uncertainty, which seemed unusual for her.

"What do you mean?" I was curious at what could possibly unbalance the indomitable Dana Fox.

"It's a little embarrassing." Her eyes bounced from me down to her rustic-chic Frye boots. "It's about my party."

"What about it?" Was the Chase discussion merely a pretext to knock me off guard? What did Dana know? I took a deep breath, trying to temper my pounding heart.

"I don't remember what happened," Dana continued. "I remember everyone being there. I was having so much fun . . . and then nothing but a blank. A memory gap."

I studied Dana's perfect face, searching for the truth. Had she actually forgotten what happened to Jackson? Or was she just playing me, hoping to trip me up? Did she somehow know that I'd returned to her house? I had to step carefully. One tiny slip of the tongue and my cover could be blown.

I mulled the possibilities. Perhaps Dana was just another unwitting victim of Bar Tech's machinations. Maybe they were behind her memory blackout and her brainwashing conveniently dovetailed with a night of teenage self-indulgence. The alternative, however, was much more troublesome. What if Dana's memory loss was all an act? A convenient solution, which painted her innocence in a seemingly foolproof lie? As sweet and as friendly as Dana presented on the surface, I didn't quite believe her sincerity. She seemed just a tiny bit eager to get me to like her. For all Dana's natural confidence and popularity, there was just something about her that felt forced and phony. Inauthentic. I couldn't quite put my finger on what was off about Dana Fox, but I knew I wasn't ready to trust her. She really was tabula rasa—a clean slate. And I was determined not to let her read me either.

"Wish I could help," I said with an empathetic smile and my best poker face. "But I wasn't the last to leave. You should ask Jackson."

"I will," replied Dana with a warm, friendly smile, not betraying any hint of anything being amiss with my suggestion. "But first I need to work out my stupid schedule. See you later."

I stood in the middle of the quad and watched Dana strut

off, smiling and greeting her old friends, eager to reclaim her rightful place in the Barrington universe. In the meantime, I was left with no real answers, only more questions.

"Lucky for Dana your eyes don't shoot lasers," Oliver quipped as he strolled up and parked beside me seconds later, "or she'd be one crispy critter."

Oliver and I stood side by side and surveyed everyone's faces as they strode by. I was struck by how disturbingly normal everyone appeared. No anxiety, no fear, just smiles and laughter. It was as if it were all for show.

"By the way," I said, looking at Oliver, "what are you doing here?"

"Mom's much better, so I decided to risk being rounded up by the Bar Tech storm troopers," he said, eyes on alert as he scanned the campus quad for impending danger.

"All quiet on the western front," I confirmed, letting him know that our favorite goon squad was nowhere in sight.

"For now," Oliver said as he gave me a wary sidelong glance. "Three days ago it seems like the world was coming to an end. Today it's sunshine and lollipops. A guy could get whiplash. What the hell's going on?"

"Beats me." I shook my head and shrugged, truly mystified. "But there's one person who might have a clue."

5. OCCAM'S RAZOR

Jackson was already seated in the back, right corner of biology class, fully locked into a beat-up Vonnegut paperback.

Amazingly, he was still alive and functioning. I contained my relief as I calmly strode down the aisle. Jackson looked up just as I arrived at his desk.

"Good weekend?" I rhetorically asked in an urgent, we-need-to-talk tone.

"Later," he responded firmly, shutting me down. His watchful eyes darted around the room as everyone else streamed in and grabbed their respective seats.

I nodded, disappointed but knowing Jackson was right. Talking there was not an option. It was downright stupid. Still, I lingered at his side a moment longer, wanting more than anything to take the empty chair next to him, but our alphabetical seating chart unfortunately relegated me directly opposite him in the front, left corner. As seemed to be the theme of late, I couldn't be pushed any farther away from him.

My gaze kept drifting toward Jackson as Mr. Bluni droned on about Watson and Crick's discovery of DNA and a research paper he was writing for one of those geeky science journals. My mind wandered back to Dana's party. All I could think about was whether Jackson knew what happened. As the lights were turned off in exchange for an overhead projector and a welcome audio-visual distraction, I found myself struggling to focus. I clicked the point of my pen in and out and honed in on the outrageously loud tock of the classroom clock's second hand. Then I stared into the humming fan on the back of the projector. What was going on? It was like someone had slipped me a triple espresso. Maybe the weekend stuck indoors was finally catching up with me.

I could hear my toe tapping against the floor with a fervor all its own. I stared down at it as if a threatening look would silence my own extremity and was startled to see the carpeting right through my foot.

Oh, no.

I forced a few hard blinks to sharpen my vision, but the top half of my foot was still horribly as clear as day. Shit-shitshitsh—

I held it up a little, along the side of my backpack, which I'd propped in front of my seat. The bag's logo stared right back at me from where I was pretty sure my toes were. I wiggled them inside my shoe. They were awake and intact, but it had no effect on their transparency.

Instinctively, I tucked my legs back under my chair, curling one around the other as if the compression would make them less detectable. Scrunching inward in my seat, I tried to wish it away, but my fear and panic were rising. When I lifted my leg back up for a second glance, I could see my invisibility was rising as well. To my shin.

I knew it wasn't safe to stay a sitting duck in the classroom. Thanks to the projector, it was still dark enough that no one besides me would notice, but in just the flip of a switch, the classroom lights could be back on and my transparent foot—and now lower leg, I upgraded as I stole another glance—would be exposed.

I had one real avenue of escape: the bathroom.

However, the last thing I needed at that moment was to draw attention to myself. Plus the embarrassment of a seemingly dire bathroom emergency in front of the whole class might upgrade me to fully invisible in one torturous anvil drop. Did I have a choice, though?

I raised my hand to half-mast, committing to embarrassment-door number one. Mr. Bluni was caught up in some discussion about the human genome project I had long since stopped tracking and seemed oblivious to my request. I looked down again. I was up to my knees in trouble. My hand reached higher. Have mercy.

Fortunately, Mr. Bluni finally caught sight of my hand. Instead of humiliating me, he discreetly gestured that I was free to go. I bolted for the door, almost stumbling face-first onto the floor as my feet got trapped on the projector's bundle of wires.

Jackson could tell by my panicked expression that something was very wrong, and it wasn't that I had to pee. I heard a few boys chuckle behind me, but no exclamations about my missing feet, so that was good enough for me to exit unscathed.

Hustling to the bathroom, I desperately hoped no one would be lurking in the hallway. My anxious gaze flew back over each shoulder, checking for spectators in any direction. All clear. Until I nearly collided with an angular, beanpole boy who had a shock of reddish-brown hair that stood up like a rooster's comb. He was just standing there, as if oddly frozen in space, looking as startled as I was by the sudden head-on.

"Sorry," he muttered, with a befuddled, deer-in-the-headlights expression.

I thought I recognized him from one of my classes, but I had no time for pleasantries. I grunted and zoomed by him before he had a chance to notice I was vanishing from the ground up.

I finally made it inside the bathroom, darting for the handicapped stall, the only one that wouldn't give my transparent legs away. Collapsing against the wall, it held me up, but not upright. I slowly slid down the wall, my butt hitting the floor and my head falling between my knees. I could finally breathe. And with more oxygen to my brain came a flood of questions.

Why was this happening? How was this happening? There hadn't been a pulse since Dana's party, which was two days ago. Under normal circumstances, there was no way my power should've lasted this long.

My powers had never lasted this long.

So what was different? The pulse had been huge, enough to startle Oliver's mom straight off the road. That was different. Was that pulse extra powerful? Did that, in turn, make me extra powerful? I had to talk to Oliver and Jackson. Were their powers still active too? My breathing transitioned from ragged to deep, and slowly my calves started to reappear. The process gave me more trouble than it had in the past (with the exception of my near freak-out after the accident), but once the process began to reverse, I breathed a sigh of relief.

I looked one hundred percent but felt about fifty when the class bell rang. I rushed back to the classroom to collect my stuff. Jackson had already split, which upset me. Wasn't he the least bit concerned about my abrupt exit? My hurt feelings would have to wait because Mr. Bluni looked ready to check in on me, so I darted off toward the cafeteria before he could follow through.

• • •

My mission was simple: Track down Oliver or Jackson. I pushed my way through the pizza line, much to the chagrin of those already waiting, and found Oliver near the front of the line.

"Dr. Ashley not feeding you?" Oliver joked at my determination to join him.

"We need to talk." The line wasn't nearly private enough, so I tried to pull Oliver along with me.

"And I need to eat." He dug his heels in until the server behind the counter handed him a fresh pepperoni pizza. It was the same kid I'd nearly mowed down in the hallway only minutes earlier.

"Hey, Topher," said Oliver, überfriendly. "You know Nica."

"Hey," he responded with an affirmative nod. "Think we have Spanish together."

"Yeah, hi."

Topher Hansen was the quiet, unassuming type. Super polite, a low flier on the radar, never got in anyone's way. He kept to himself so much that he seemed like the kid who wasn't there. And yet there he appeared in my life twice in the span of fifteen minutes.

"Can I get you anything, Nica?" Topher asked, staring at me with the same odd expression he'd had when I'd run into him in the hallway. He gave me an uneasy, paranoid feeling. Was he watching me?

"I'll just have some of his," I replied, pushing Oliver along, wanting to get away.

"No one remembers anything from Dana's party," I announced to Oliver moments after I dragged him over to an empty table at the back of the cafeteria. "Even the host."

Oliver almost gagged on a slice of piping-hot pepperoni pizza as he tried to speak. His first attempt was barely distinguishable as English. He swallowed a bit and tried again.

"Wait, what?"

"After the pulse, I mean," I whispered. "Jackson changing color and blasting a kid across the room. Shit, did you forget about it, too?"

"No," Oliver replied, "of course not. What exactly did Dana say?"

"That she blacked out."

"You think she's lying?"

"I don't have a clue what she's doing," I retorted. "For all I know, maybe she's telling the truth."

A tsunami of guilt hit me. Had I been so eager to suspect Dana that I had discounted Occam's razor's much-preferred explanation? The simplest explanation is usually the best one.

"Even so," Oliver added. "It's super creepy." Though not creepy enough to curb his voracious appetite. He snatched up his final quarter of pizza.

All I could do was nod in agreement. It was even impressive, in a supervillain sort of way. How had Bar Tech done it? How had they gotten into the minds of so many students and just wiped them out?

"It's a good thing, right?" Oliver's observation sent a chill up my spine. "At least our secret's safe."

"Maybe. Not to whoever covered it up," I pointed out.

Just then my phone buzzed. So did Oliver's.

"Jackson wants us to meet him," I announced, reading the brief message.

Oliver nodded. He'd gotten an identical text from Jackson. "What's in the library?"

Oliver and I hoofed it upstairs to the library. Trying to arrange secret meetings aside, I hated how awkward I was feeling around Jackson. Then again, I was barely used to having to compete for his attention. I'd been one of a whopping two people who would even speak to him at school. With Dana's return, I had no idea where that left me—or us. As I learned, though, the denizens of Barrington High could have quite short memories.

Oliver and I entered the library and headed toward the back. It was deathly quiet. Everyone was having lunch, even the faculty. Finally, something was actually going as planned.

Jackson looked upset. "What's going on, Nica?"

I took a deep breath. There was a lot to explain. A few deep breaths from my core—and my hand slowly started to disappear from the end of my fingertips up through my palm.

"Our powers have never lasted this long. Can you . . . ?" I looked to Oliver, but he had already loped the entire length of the library and back in barely the blink of eye.

"Actually . . . yeah," Oliver replied, stunned that he still had the ability and hadn't even known it.

We both looked to Jackson. He appeared to still be a few pages behind.

"When was there a pulse?" Jackson challenged with a puzzled expression.

Then it was mine and Oliver's turn to stare. Did Jackson not remember the party either? Was this Bar Tech's doing as well? Or did his supercharged display have something to do with his absent memory?

"Almost two days ago," I confirmed.

"The night of Dana's party." Jackson was truly stunned.

I nodded and detailed the events of the night just as I had done with Oliver outside his mother's crashed car. The story was just as crazy this time around, except that Jackson had lived it—and didn't remember a thing. He looked worried, weak even. It was a sliver of the vulnerable Jackson Winters that had caught my gaze the first time I'd seen him.

If there was a silver lining to be found, it was that Jackson wasn't the only one who didn't remember the events at the now-infamous after-party. I rattled off the kids, including Dana, who had clearly witnessed his display of power—and who now had zero recollection of the event.

Jackson stood there, silent, thoughtful, looking back and forth between Oliver and me. Trying to absorb the troubling information that he'd been so exposed—so vulnerable.

"What about you?" I asked Jackson. "Are you still . . . ?"

His eyes narrowed, a bit dazed by my question. The notion that his power hadn't dissipated after twenty-four hours was news to him. He held his hand out hesitantly. It took him a second before anything happened.

I knew the feeling; it was like getting back on a bike after a few years or picking up a neglected instrument. The muscle memory was there. It just needed a little wake-up call. The lights above our heads began to flicker. And *pop!* One of the low-energy lightbulbs exploded into a shower of glass shards.

Despite his absent memory, Jackson's powers were very much intact.

"What do you think is happening to us?" I asked.

Jackson combed the mane of hair off his face with his right hand, thinking carefully before conjecturing.

"Any number of things. Those last pulses were intense and happened so close together. Maybe they tripped an internal switch and triggered a reaction in our bodies?"

"Or maybe it was something in the atmosphere," Oliver chimed in, offering an alternate theory.

"Or it could be because—" Jackson abruptly stopped himself from finishing his thought. His blue eyes shifted down to the floor. Whatever it was seemed to have spooked him.

"Could be what?" I stared intensely, demanding Jackson come clean.

"That we've changed," Jackson calmly replied, looking up, "permanently."

"Shit," Oliver muttered, his eyes widening with comprehension that Jackson had hit upon a scary truth.

My mouth dropped open. Could it be the three of us would never be normal again? It wasn't that the thought of being permanently altered had never crossed my mind. It had many times. It was facing down the stark reality that threw me for a loop. This was the new me.

"What do we do now?" Feeling confused and scared seemed like an extravagant luxury that we couldn't afford when what we needed was a plan of action.

"Jackson?" a sweet voice called out, breaking our circle of secrecy. "You back there?"

I recognized the voice immediately and grabbed three books off the closest shelf and shoved them into Jackson's hands before Dana rounded the corner.

"This a secret club, or can anyone join?" Her smile sparkled. Not a trace of adolescent angst permeated her beautiful facade. Any club would be thrilled to have Dana as a member.

"No big secret," I blurted out nervously. "We just get

together to discuss books." Lame, I know. I realized how crazy I sounded only after the words flew out of my mouth. But it was too late to come up with a more plausible explanation.

"The Rise and Fall of the Third Reich?" Dana asked with a raised eyebrow as she snatched one of the books out of Jackson's hand. "Pretty heady stuff for a book group."

"You know what they say," interjected Oliver brightly. "Past is prologue."

"Actually, I think it was Shakespeare," Dana replied knowingly. *"The Tempest."* She studied our faces, still not buying it. "Are you guys really worried about Nazism infiltrating Barrington?"

"It's more a cautionary tale," I said, hoping to put an end to her persistent questioning. "Never know when and how evil will rear its ugly head."

Thankfully, just then the class bell rang. Lunch had ended, as did my brief encounter with Jackson and Oliver. No doubt we had more to discuss when Dana was not around.

"Walk me to Spanish?" Dana asked Jackson. There was an inflection in her tone of voice that made it sound less like a request and more like an order.

"Lead the way," Jackson answered, looking at me, uneasy at being put on the spot.

We exchanged a few polite nods and waves as Dana and Jackson left the library. I shoved the books about Nazi

Germany back onto the shelves where they belonged.

"This all feels different," I admitted to Oliver. "Deeper than before."

Oliver looked at me and nodded solemnly. "For me too."

Even though I had no definitive proof that what was happening to my body was a permanent change, I could feel it in my bones. My ability wasn't receding the way it had before. In some ways it felt stronger, more powerful. I had to prepare myself for it being part of me forever. Which only meant that Oliver, Jackson, and I were in even more danger than before.

It was undeniable. We might not be running for lives at that moment, but our Bar Tech nightmares weren't going away either. They were certain to get worse. I knew it; I could feel it in my gut. It was just a matter of time before Cochran showed his hand.

Something was building, but I didn't even know where to start. How do you fight the intangible?

6. TEARS OF A CLOWN

I counted off the minutes until I got out of school. After enduring an excruciatingly long day of feeling as though I'd been strapped inside a straitjacket, I fidgeted in my seat, unable to find a comfortable position and sit still. I hated feeling so paranoid and worried about disappearing in front of people. Obsessively checking my limbs every other minute to make sure I still had two of each, along with the rest of my body, was exhausting.

During my last class, I received a terse text from Jackson to meet him in the parking lot. He'd been so standoffish all day that I was relieved to hear from him, brief as it was. I was eager to continue our conversation from the library without the risk of Dana Fox or anyone else interrupting us.

As soon as the final bell rang, I grabbed my bag and dashed out of the classroom. I tore down the staircase from the second floor and was racing through the main lobby toward the exit sign when I heard someone shouting my name.

I almost ignored it. But my ingrained good-girl impulse forced me to slam on the brakes. My biology teacher, Mr. Bluni, strode right toward me. I was confused. He and I had barely ever exchanged more than a few words outside class before. What could he possibly want with me?

"Hey, Mr. Bluni. Everything okay?" My eyes were on the doors, looking for Jackson. I didn't want to miss him in case he was looking for me inside.

"You tell me, Nica." Bluni's laser-eyed gaze was unsettling. "You seemed distracted in class today."

"I did?" Caught off guard, I felt every joint in my body stiffen. What else might Mr. Bluni have noticed about me? Denying the charge was too risky. And I didn't want to seem defensive. "Sorry. I promise I'll be more focused tomorrow." I smiled sheepishly, copping to it so I could quickly get on my way.

"I hope so," he cautioned with an air of vague disapproval. Mr. Bluni had an agenda, and it didn't include letting me run off just yet. "I expect my research assistant to be attentive and prepared at all times."

"Research assistant?" I had no idea what he was talking about. Had I been so zoned out in class that I missed something important?

"For that journal article I'm writing on the human genome," he declared.

I racked my brain and vaguely recalled Mr. Bluni mentioning the article but not the research assistant part. And we certainly had never discussed me being his assistant.

"Nica," he continued, "you're smart, insightful, and could use the challenge."

"Oh—" Shit . . . is what I almost blurted out, but I wisely held my tongue. His offer totally flustered me. Truth was, I had enough challenges in my life without taking on another one.

"It's a terrific opportunity," he added, hoping to entice me and seal the deal. "Plus, it'll look great on college applications."

"I'm sure it will," I muttered. "And I'm honored by your offer and confidence in me, Mr. Bluni. Truly I am." I kept blabbering, hoping to land on a good excuse. "But I'm already overwhelmed and stressed by all the work as it is. I just don't think I'm the right person for the job. I'm really sorry."

"So am I," he responded icily, body going rigid with extreme displeasure. Then he turned and walked away quite brusquely. It was unnerving.

"Shit." It was obvious that Bluni was really pissed at me. But I had more pressing matters to deal with than worrying about hurting my biology teacher's feelings.

Jackson was impatiently waiting for me inside the cab of a truck, idling in the middle of the student parking lot. It was a loaner from his parents ever since he'd given Maya the keys to his beloved Mustang.

"What took you so long?" Jackson snapped at me, uncharacteristically testy.

"Pleasure to see you, too," I snapped right back as I threw open the passenger door and hopped into the seat next to him. "I got cornered by Bluni, if you must know."

"Anything serious?" Jackson asked with concern, as he threw the pickup into gear and sailed out of the lot.

Dared I tell him? It seemed so trivial. I shook my head and shrugged it off. We had more important things to talk about.

He drove through town, not saying a word for several minutes. Neither did I. It was an awkward, uncomfortable silence and reminded me of those early days after we first met. There was so much I wanted to say to Jackson, but I clenched my jaw tight, refusing to turn all weepy and sad about the state of our relationship or non-relationship. I was determined to sound rational and grown-up. But first I had to collect my thoughts about Dana, Bar Tech, him, and us. Except there were so many conflicting thoughts bouncing through my head that it was like a traffic jam up there. Finally, I couldn't hold my tongue any longer.

"I don't trust her," I declared, getting right to the point, which surprised me. Then again, skillful diplomacy was never my strong suit.

"You don't know Dana," countered Jackson. "Give her a chance."

"Is that what you're doing?" I avoided weepy and somehow went straight to accusatory and angry. I didn't mean to act crazy, but the words were just flying out of my mouth like unpinned grenades.

"Nica, I'm sorry," Jackson replied with a pained, anguished look. "Dana and I . . ."

"Have history. You and I . . . don't." I honestly didn't say it so coldly to be snarky or elicit pity or sympathy from Jackson, only to state the hard facts, which seemed to be in short supply.

"It's complicated. You know how I feel about you."

"I thought I knew," I responded, my heart pounding and emotion welling up from the pit of my stomach as I recalled being in Jackson's arms a few nights earlier. "I'm not so sure anymore." My anger was subsiding, with sadness taking its place. It was an awful, empty feeling. It was all I had.

"Give me time to figure stuff out," he asked.

"Time's in short supply," I reminded him, "in case you've forgotten. I'm not waiting around for Bar Tech to kidnap me or you or Oliver like they did Maya. I've got to do something before they find out that my—*our*—powers are here to stay."

"I'm not asking you to sit on your hands and do nothing, Nica. Just tread lightly. We don't know who our friends are. Who to trust."

"That's why, until I know which side Dana's on," I said, "I'm keeping my distance. And so should you."

"Please trust me," he pressed, his normally bright blue-green eyes projecting confusion and regret. "Let me handle things my own way."

I had to turn away. It was too painful to see him struggling with his complicated feelings about Dana and me.

Two minutes of silence later, he arrived at my house and pulled into the driveway. I quickly exited the pickup and slammed the door. Without saying another word, I hurried up the walkway and disappeared into my house, fighting off a wave of hurt and tears that I didn't want Jackson to see.

Once Jackson had pulled out of the driveway and I was safely behind the closed front door, I threw my bag across the foyer and screamed at the top of my lungs.

"Fuck!"

Jackson was right about not knowing whom to trust. Truth was, my emotions were all over the place. I didn't even know if I could trust myself anymore.

That's when the tears came.

I woke up several hours later buried underneath a mountain of bedcovers, completely disoriented as to whether it was day or night. Then I heard my dad calling me downstairs for dinner and the roller-coaster ride of a day came rushing back to me in living color, along with my looming problems.

One of which was the massive headache that was suddenly pounding in my head. I staggered to my feet in no condition to face anyone—least of all my father.

I shuffled down the stairs into the kitchen, not caring that my hair looked like a Medusa fright wig.

"What happened to you?" The expression on Dad's face said I looked far worse than I imagined. He was dishing up delicious chicken curry and lamb tikka masala from Dhaba, the one and only Indian restaurant in Barrington.

"Can we not talk about my day?" I grumbled.

My dad respectfully nodded and didn't press me to open up. Unlike Lydia, Dad respected boundaries and never tried to push me into sharing the source of my anguish. Although I sounded calm and in control, my desperation clearly shone through, because he pulled out a chair for me. I gratefully plopped into it. I didn't stop inhaling my meal until every ounce of food was gone. At least my appetite was unaffected by all the turmoil.

Later that evening my dad knocked on my bedroom door.

"Come in," I muttered from my cozy window seat while staring out at the neighborhood. I had sequestered myself into my room after dinner, pretending to do homework when I had in fact been texting back and forth with Oliver.

"Feeling better?" My dad opened the door and lingered in the doorway, not violating my space.

I nodded that I was feeling better even though it wasn't entirely true. It was obvious he had something on his mind he wanted to discuss.

"You found out something," I said, sitting up, hoping he'd have the answer to all my problems and make my life go back to normal. A pipe dream, I knew, but a dream I had nonetheless.

"Cochran is planning something major. Top secret. At the highest levels."

"Levels above him at Bar Tech? I thought he was the one in charge."

"He is," my dad acknowledged. "But Bar Tech's tentacles reach out from the company to all sorts of places."

"You mean like the military?"

"I wouldn't be surprised," he admitted. "What about you? Were there any run-ins with Bar Tech Security? Anything strange happen at school or with Dana?"

"No. Nothing. Which was weird. I didn't see security anywhere."

"That doesn't mean they're not watching," he said ominously, mulling over the significance of it all. He then turned to leave.

"Dad . . ." My throat constricted, suddenly parched.

"Yeah?" He paused and looked at me, half listening, his mind still preoccupied.

"There's one other thing that I probably should mention," I confessed. "Remember how I said my power only lasts twenty-four hours after the pulse?"

"Yes. What about it?" His attention riveted back on me.

"This time it didn't happen. My power didn't go away. And I'm scared it's permanent."

My father leaned back against the doorjamb. My revelation stunned him like a jab to the solar plexus.

"The frequency of pulses must've caused a kind of genetic critical mass," he said, "which permanently activated your ability. Like flicking on a light switch."

"Lucky me," I scoffed. "Some girls get nose jobs when they turn sixteen. I disappear."

Dad stayed up until the wee hours of the morning reassuring me that other than Bar Tech already knowing about Maya, they had no way of knowing who else was affected. And Maya was safely in hiding and out of reach. All the other blood samples drawn from students at school had also been tainted by my father, effectively creating a protective firewall around my friends.

"How long will it hold?" Dad heard the trepidation in my voice. He took me by the shoulders and looked me right in the eyes. Cool, calm, reassuring.

"I'll make sure Richard Cochran never harms you."

Dad planted a kiss on my forehead. It felt like his kiss

could protect me from all the evil that was out in the world. For that moment I felt safe. Protected.

Nothing could've been farther from the truth. But I was too self-involved and wrapped up in my own emotional turmoil to see anything else clearly. I should've been worrying about my father. Who was protecting him?

7. THE RETURN

Chase Cochran grabbed me in a bear hug and planted a kiss on my cheek. He was aiming for my mouth, but I had the sense to turn my head at the last moment. We were in the school quad at seven forty-five a.m., in full view of everyone, including teachers.

"Aw, come on," he groaned, acting like a sad Labrador puppy dog. "Don't be like that."

"I'm not like anything," I replied, gently pulling away, taken aback by his sudden appearance and quite public display of affection.

"I'm single now," Chase offered. "Still recovering from my coma. Take pity."

"You seem perfectly healthy to me," I bantered back, my guard up. "Glad you're okay."

"Awww," he said brightly, with the kind of hopeful, excited expression one has on Christmas morning. "Nica Ashley missed me."

"Don't get carried away, cowboy," I scoffed, rolling my

eyes, hoping to knock his ego down a few pegs.

"I'll take that as a yes." He grinned, nearly blinding me with his confident, megawatt smile. Some things never changed.

Fortunately, a steady stream of friends and wannabes swarmed around to welcome the prince back to his kingdom, so I took off while he was distracted.

It was nothing short of amazing how quickly Chase had recuperated from his close call with the hereafter. My dad and the team of doctors at the hospital gave him a clean bill of health and discharged him only two days after he had emerged from his coma. And here he was back at school as if nothing awful had happened.

Last time when Chase had attempted to kiss me, he was still dating Maya. For me, that cemented his status as a "never going to happen" once and for all. Besides, he was also Richard Cochran's son and Oliver's half brother, which made him extra toxic. Even worse, I had overheard him betraying Maya to his father. Even if I was interested in Chase Cochran, which I was definitely not, I knew for sure that I could never trust him.

I barely made it a few steps inside the school lobby when Dana spotted me and insisted we grab a preclass latte from the cafeteria. Despite my deep mistrust of Dana, I knew it was a golden opportunity for me to get closer and bond with her. You can catch more bees with honey, my grandmother used to say. Not to mention, I was also feeling awfully draggy from sleep deprivation after my previous night's heart-to-heart with Dad, so I took Dana up on her offer.

"Please tell me you were just playing hard to get," Dana remarked as she and I grabbed our large to-go cups frothy with steamy foam.

My furrowed brow and puzzled expression made one side of Dana's mouth turn up into a half smile.

"I saw Chase making eyes at yours truly," she explained with an encouraging wink.

"More like keeping the lion at bay with my bullwhip." My diaphragm forced up a fake laugh as cover. "I don't think so. Not really interested in joining the horde of hormonal girls vying for his divine attention."

"Just don't write him off, okay?" Dana pleaded. "I've known Chase since second grade. He might've been the jerk chugging milk for the attention of the whole cafeteria, but he's the same one who stopped 'Dana Pox' from catching on in middle school."

"No way." It slipped out before I could shut the gates. It was hard enough to imagine Dana on a bad hair day, let alone being made fun of by pimply adolescents.

"I was a disaster," she confided. "Probably could've sold my before and after to Proactiv. No lie. Chase is a much cooler guy than he lets on."

Dana's honesty was unexpectedly refreshing, giving me

a new perspective. Sure, Chase had his moments. Rarely. Occasionally. And he was sort of, maybe, a little bit—fine, absolutely—drop-dead good-looking. But Chase Cochran and me together? Not when Jackson was still deep in my heart. It would be bizarre on all fronts. Hypothetically speaking, of course. As if I'd let anything really happen.

Strolling down the hallway sipping my latte, I listened politely while Dana rattled off Chase's many stellar qualities (loyalty, generosity, hunky body, to mention a few) when I spotted Mr. Bluni in one of the Biology labs behind closed doors. Through the door's narrow vertical window I could see that he was locked in a heated discussion—argument, actually—with none other than Richard Cochran. I was so flustered to see them alone together that I stumbled and nearly tripped over my own feet, recovering my balance at the last second before making a fool of myself.

"Nice save," Dana said approvingly. Flashing a suggestive look, she added: "What was that about?"

Though Dana was insinuating that my head-in-the-clouds wobble had something to do with Chase, I was mulling the same question about an entirely different matter.

What secret business was Bluni and Cochran arguing about behind closed doors?

My curiosity and suspicion were definitely stoked by my all-too-wild imagination, weaving evil plots worthy of a James Bond villain. It must be more than random coincidence that they were together. Knowing Cochran even in the limited way that I did, I wasn't surprised that he might have hooks into a biology teacher like Mr. Bluni, whose interests ran to genetics.

Which then left me to wonder: Was my paranoia making connections and inventing conspiracies that weren't really there? Or had I truly discovered something beyond what I—or even my father—already knew? There was only one way to find out. And it required me eating a major slice of humble pie.

"So you've had a change of heart, Nica," Mr. Bluni said brusquely as he strode down the hallway without stopping, barely giving me more than a passing glance.

I'd been hovering by the cafeteria entrance during lunch, waiting for Bluni to make his routine walk by on his way to brown-bagging it in the teachers' lounge. As soon as he appeared, I scurried after him like a needy, slobbering puppy.

"You were totally right," I admitted with unbridled enthusiasm. "I just had a lot on my mind and wasn't think-ing clearly when I turned you down." I flashed a sweet smile so broad and unnaturally taut that my cheeks began to ache from overstretching my facial muscles. "Assisting you would be an amazing opportunity." I was willing to kiss a lot of ass to convince him.

"I know," Bluni snapped back, continuing on ahead,

never breaking stride. "Which is why I've offered it to someone else."

"Who?" Spirit unbowed, I trotted after him, not prepared to concede defeat so easily. I had to convince him to give me another shot.

"Lacey Dane," he announced.

"Seriously?" Though the girl was in my biology class, I barely knew her and had to think fast about what to do. "She said yes?" The insinuating inflection in my voice suggested that something was amiss with her.

Lacey Dane always reeked of a sinister bouquet of Listerine strips mixed with some pop music monstrosity's signature fragrance. Apparently all in a vain attempt to cover up her oh-so-rebellious but really gross habit of smoking in the bathroom between classes. The heavy-handed aroma that wafted around her designer-clad body was toxically sweet. I could always smell when Lacey Dane was approaching or had just left the area. Odorous excessiveness aside, I had nothing against her.

"Why wouldn't she?" Bluni stopped and stared at me with a sharp, suspicious eye. Head tilting, arms crossed expectantly, foot tapping impatiently. He demanded an answer.

"No reason . . ." I shrugged noncommittally, hesitating a half second before continuing. "I guess she's fine." Vague but pointed. "Forget I ever mentioned it."

And then I hustled off, leaving behind a concerned and

somewhat bewildered Mr. Bluni scratching his head in the middle of the corridor.

As I disappeared around the corner, I winced and gritted my teeth, fighting off a nasty bout of self-loathing. Had I actually resorted to playing a twisted game of mind-fuck the teacher? Even worse, trashing a nice-enough girl who had never done anything unkind to me? Deep in my heart I prayed for forgiveness and hoped that I wouldn't be struck down by lightning for being such an awful, hateful person, but I had to snag that assistant job if I wanted to find out more about Cochran's plans. Whether Mr. Bluni swallowed the bait remained to be seen.

Strangely enough, as the afternoon wore on, I kept running into Chase in a series of awkward encounters. I bumped into him several times in the stairwell between classes and once nearly collided with him as we came out of our respective bathrooms. It seemed weird. What were the odds of so many coincidences in a single day? Each time Chase made sure to say something flattering about my hair or clothes. Of course, I didn't fall for his phony fawning bullshit, though it was nice to be complimented. And since Jackson seemed to be sticking to Dana like glue every time I saw him, what was the harm in enjoying some meaningless flattery?

The more I saw Chase, the more I sensed that something had changed—something was different about him. Not that he and I had ever been good friends before, but

Chase Cochran was a pretty transparent guy. His wardrobe was predictable—J. Crew from head to toe. He liked football, being in charge, and throwing his money around. He also liked bossing Maya around and having her at his constant beck and call. He was certainly not one to betray emotion or vulnerability. And yet that's precisely what I caught him doing.

I spotted Chase sitting alone at one of the picnic tables in the quad after school. At first I thought he was asleep. His head was slumped down toward his chest. Locks of blond hair covered his eyes.

"We gotta stop meeting like this," I teased as I approached. But as I got closer, I realized that he'd actually been crying. I'd never seen him look so dejected and incredibly sad.

"Yeah." Chase quickly wiped his moist eyes and flashed a phony smile.

"Everything okay?"

He nodded. "Just waiting for my ride."

Even though Chase had been given the okay to return to school, he still wasn't allowed behind the wheel of his car just yet. Which meant that he needed to rely on his friends, or worse yet, his father, for a lift to and from school. A lift from Dad was humiliating enough when you're twelve—mortifying when you're seventeen.

"You sure you're all right?"

"Of course. *I'm me*," he said with a sarcastic laugh.

Though I definitely saw a crack in his normally invincible, devil-may-care facade.

"That you are," I retorted, keeping the mood light, not pressing him further. I needed to hustle off and find Oliver.

"Nica?"

"Yeah." I stopped and turned back.

"You heard from Maya at all?"

Maya? Really? Not what I was expecting. I covered up my surprise and just shook my head. "Sorry. Not a word."

Maybe Chase was playing me. Gossip around school that day branded Maya's disappearance a "private family matter." Which was Barrington-speak for don't ask too many questions about what happened. Eerily similar to what was said when Dana vanished. It was no secret that Maya had been publicly losing it those last few weeks, culminating with Chase's near-fatal brush with the great hereafter. The fact that Maya was gone meant that she'd either been sent to stay with relatives out of state, or sent to a mental hospital because of stress.

"It sucks not remembering what happened," Chase confessed with wounded pride. Stripped of all his usual bravado and coolness, he actually displayed a touching vulnerability.

For a brief moment, I felt sorry for him, the way I might feel compassion for a lost puppy that I found wandering the streets. Then I remembered what a conniving bastard Chase had been before his unfortunate coma. And what he'd done to Maya. Best to keep my distance and proceed with caution.

Just then a car horn honked twice. I looked up to see a sleek black Mercedes-Benz sedan pulling up to the drop-off area. All the muscles in my body instinctively tensed with apprehension. I recognized Richard Cochran's car even before the darkly tinted driver's-side window slid down to reveal him sitting there, flashing that charming but vaguely menacing cobra-like smile.

"How's our boy doing, Nica?" Impeccably attired in a crisp midnight-blue designer suit, Cochran tilted his green-mirrored aviator sunglasses down along the bridge of his aquiline nose.

Our? When had the man who I regarded as my mortal enemy suddenly gotten on such intimate terms with me?

"Great," I replied, turning back to Chase, hoping my face didn't betray any uneasiness or animosity at being in his father's immediate presence.

"You're late," snapped Chase as he hopped off the table and tramped over to the car. I'd never seen him act so testily before—least of all around his father.

"Busy afternoon," Cochran explained, never taking his sharp gaze off me. "Unavoidable."

"Always is." Chase shrugged dismissively, popping open the passenger door, having zero interest in his father's excuses.

"Can we drop you somewhere, Nica?" Cochran eyed me.

Through the window I could see Chase's body stiffen, stewing with rage.

"No, thanks," I responded with a polite but hesitant smile. "I'm meeting a friend."

Cochran didn't react or smile back. "Don't let me keep you." He just continued to stare in my direction, eyes hidden behind reflective lenses. Studying me, scrutinizing me.

A shudder of fear ran down my spine. I could've sworn Cochran was trying to read my thoughts, bore inside my brain. I held my stare and half smiled, determined not to be cowed or look away, all the while trying to erect an impenetrable Berlin Wall to protect me—from what, I didn't know.

Our brief contest of wills concluded when the driver's window abruptly rolled up, concealing Cochran behind the tinted glass. And the car drove off, leaving the school grounds.

"That was intense," quipped Oliver as he walked over to where I stood, watching the Mercedes as it disappeared down the street. "Trying to do a Vulcan mind meld?"

"If only I could," I replied with a fatalistic sigh. "Then I'd know what the hell's going on around here."

"What if there was another option?" Oliver teased with a sly smile.

"I'm all ears, Spock."

• • •

"Wait," I urged Oliver as we hoofed it through town on foot, sticking mostly to the quieter residential streets where there was little traffic. "Telling Cochran you're his son is extremely risky. There's still too much we don't know." I was diligently watching every vehicle that drove by to make sure Bar Tech Security or any other suspicious cars weren't tailing us on our way home.

"Whatever Bar Tech wants from us, I don't want to be a part of it," Oliver announced as he shrugged off my concerns. "They can't force us to do anything. Bar Tech doesn't own us."

"Not yet," I warned. "Did you forget what they did to Maya? Things may be weirdly quiet for the moment, but don't be fooled. Cochran is planning something."

"Problem is that Cochran doesn't see us as people," Oliver countered, "but as his genetic experiments. Investments. If I can get close to him, maybe I can persuade him that he's got it all wrong."

"How?" I looked at Oliver, hoping he had something clever up his sleeve. "What's your brilliant plan? That he'll welcome you with open arms?" While I really wanted to believe my friend was right, I wasn't convinced that he or any of us were in a position to change minds. Our destinies? Perhaps. But Cochran's plans? Highly doubtful anyone was going to be able to move that powerful billion-dollar mountain.

"That's the thing, Nica," Oliver replied with a hesitant laugh. "My brilliant plan requires help. Your help."

"If you're going to approach Cochran, it might be best to do it on your own. One-on-one."

"First I need proof."

"I doubt Cochran will consent to a cheek swab for some DNA." I was becoming warier by the second.

"Who says the DNA has to be from him?" Oliver shot me a long look, signaling that he had an alternate strategy.

I stopped in my tracks and stared at him, suddenly catching his drift. "You're talking about getting Chase's DNA."

Oliver nodded. "Just need a few strands of hair to prove he and I are brothers. No big deal."

"You can't seriously expect me to volunteer for that," I proclaimed, "especially when I've been doing everything in my power to avoid being alone with him."

Great. Oliver's plan started with me getting up close and personal with Chase. This was one situation where I wasn't sure how I felt about having Oliver's back.

"It'll be easy," countered Oliver. "It's not like Chase will miss a few strands of his precious golden locks."

"Okay," I said, trying to wrap my brain around this scheme. "Let's suppose for the sake of argument that I can actually get you some of his hair, then what?"

"I send it to one of those fancy labs with my own DNA and get back scientific proof that we share the same genes. Same father. It'll make it impossible for Cochran to turn me away."

And there lay my quandary: I could do what Oliver was asking and help him reunite with a man that I not only didn't trust but was convinced was actively evil, or I could risk one of my only friendships in Barrington by saying no. This was an impossible situation with way too many variables.

"How can you be sure Cochran doesn't know the truth already?"

"Because my mother never told him," answered Oliver, eyes moistening, emotions bubbling to the surface. "That night after the accident, when I saw my mom lying in the hospital . . . Everything suddenly became crystal clear. If she'd really been hurt . . . if something had happened to her . . . I'd be all alone."

Oliver's deep longing to connect with the father he never knew and fill that hole in his heart was palpable and real. And I didn't want to stand in Oliver's way to connect with his own father. But if he had to follow his heart, I had to follow my head.

"Oliver, I . . . just wish you'd wait."

It took a second for my reluctance and resistance to register with him, but after it did, his face went ash white.

"You're turning me down?" Oliver's shoulders slumped. He looked so crushed and disheartened, as if someone close to him had died.

"I can't imagine how difficult this all must be . . . what

you're going through. But there are so many things that can go wrong. Things that can expose you in ways you don't even know about. I just can't be a part of you putting yourself in a vulnerable position to be taken advantage of. Or worse."

"I better get going," muttered Oliver, barely making eye contact with me.

"Oliver . . ." At a loss for the right words, I stood there feeling helpless and torn apart about turning my best friend down.

Before I could apologize and say I was sorry, Oliver turned and ran off, practically leaving me in a cloud of dust. This was not how I'd planned for the afternoon to go.

8. THE CLUE

I had turned onto my street, relieved to see my house looming in the distance, when my pocket buzzed. I reached for
my phone, hoping it was Oliver. Our conversation had been
cut way too short. And I'd been swimming in an ocean of
regret about how badly I had (mis) handled the situation.
Maybe there was another way to deal with the whole father
issue that I hadn't considered. If Oliver and I just sat down
and really worked it out, maybe we could—

The text was from an unknown number. I tapped it open
with my thumb.

Won't find answers if you ask the wrong questions.

I stopped dead and looked around, suddenly feeling eyes
on my back that were not there. My breathing sped up and
my heart rate spiked. I clenched my jaw and focused, determined to keep my invisibility at bay. Paranoia be damned. I
was going to keep myself under control. Who had my number? Why didn't they say who they were? I summarized
them all as one:

What?

The answer didn't come right away. I had enough time to scoot off the street and into my house, where I felt like I could breathe again. Without thinking about it, I retreated to a bathroom with no windows as if to say, *Try it—invade my privacy now.*

My phone buzzed. I held it up. *1 New Message.* My finger hovered. Whatever the message contained, I had the sneaking suspicion it was going to make matters more complicated, not less. Maybe I should just ignore it; pretend I'd never received it. Or better yet, pretend it had never been sent. The little "message" symbol taunted me. It teased a mystery, and like always, I couldn't resist. I swept my thumb to the side and opened it.

9918 North Elm.

The address sounded familiar, though I couldn't place it. Somewhere off Main Street in the heart of town. I could only assume the mystery texter wanted to meet. I headed to my room to shake off my school clothes and put on something more appropriate for espionage. All black seemed a safe bet.

9918 North Elm. My eyes pinged off my phone and then to the gold numbers fastened to the storefront. I'd expected a dark parking garage or a back alley. Maybe a wooded area or an abandoned sewer tunnel. But I was way off. This was where the texter wanted to meet: Ebinger's Bakery. Great. Way to make sneaking around nice and easy, Mystery Texter. Send me to a place where a classmate or neighbor might be stopping in to get snacks or coffee. Next time maybe we could meet in the cafeteria during lunch. It would be about as private.

For a minute I considered slipping away. I thought about turning invisible and waiting for someone to open the door so I could sneak in without raising any suspicions. Of course, this presented the problem of how I could reappear in the small, tight space to greet the mystery texter without anyone noticing. It would be almost impossible. Not to mention my ability was still highly unpredictable. I also had to consider the fact that whoever had texted me wasn't necessarily a friend. Sure, it seemed like I was onto something good here, but what if it was a trap? What if I was being followed or watched? What if someone was trying to trick me into going invisible so they could prove I had a power? I couldn't take that chance. Besides, I had to assume that the mystery texter was indeed on my side and that they had thought this plan through enough to execute it without putting either of us in an awkward (or potentially dangerous) situation. With that, I wrapped my fingers around the chilly metal doorknob and pushed my way inside.

As I stepped inside the bakery, my senses dialed to eleven as I took in my surroundings. All it would take was a wave or a greeting from a friendly classmate to call attention to me and possibly ruin the whole meeting. I mentally cataloged everyone inside: a few grandparents, soccer moms, and a man in a dark-blue suit. My brain swam in a flood of endorphins as I realized any of these people could be the mystery texter. Who could it be? One of the soccer moms laughing and chatting over croissants? I imagined that one of them had a baby like me, whose very DNA was warped by Bar Tech's experiments. Maybe she didn't want her children to end up like us. Or could it be one of the grandparents? They all sat alone, reading newspapers—exactly the way I imagined a secret source would wait for someone. What motivation could they have, though? Was it possible that one was a disgruntled Bar Tech exec? A whistleblower whose conscience was finally getting the better of her?

Truth was, my mysterious texter could be anybody.

The only person who looked up when I sounded the door chime was the buttoned-up man in the dark-blue suit. I stared for a moment too long and his gaze caught mine. I quickly looked away, hoping he would just ignore me. He didn't make a sound or even a gesture as I moved past him.

So who was left? Maya? I didn't think so, but then again I hadn't heard from her in days. Maybe she'd gone incommunicado because she'd worked her way into a position where she could play both sides. Not something as big as working for Bar Tech, but maybe she'd made a friend on the road who knew something the rest of us didn't. Maybe she couldn't risk getting caught by continuing to text us, but once she got close enough to learn something important, she'd decided to reach out again. The bigger question was if she would really risk being seen in Barrington again. In any case, I had no choice but to settle in and wait.

With my head down, I headed straight for the counter to order a coffee. A guy I recognized from school—sporting a name tag that dubbed him NOAH—took my order. He had a surfer's cool but with a scientist's intense eyes—the kind that noticed everything.

I was on edge, so it could've been my imagination, but I could swear he was staring at me suspiciously. I ordered a coffee and scooted away to find a place to wait for my not-so-secret rendezvous.

I cozied into a chair by the door and gulped down coffee in an attempt to calm my jangling nerves. I felt Noah's eyes on my back and tried to focus on something mundane until before I knew it, I'd finished a second and a third cup of coffee and was quite buzzed and ready to leave. By now the bakery had started to empty out, the sun was long gone, and my dad was probably beginning to wonder where I was. He hadn't texted, so I was most likely in the clear, but not for much longer. I couldn't wait here all night, but I couldn't resist my curiosity.

What if the texter knew that? What if this was all some

sick joke being orchestrated by someone who wanted to see how long I'd play along? As that possibility loomed large in my mind, I grew agitated. The coffee I'd been sipping for the past seventy minutes didn't exactly curb my emotions. My inner switch had flipped from "intrigued" to "exasperated." *Screw this,* I thought. *If someone really has answers or questions or any kind of tips for me, there are better ways to get in touch. We don't have to play secret agent.*

As I stood up and headed for the door, I was struck by a thought: They didn't set a meeting. I assumed the address had been sent with the intention of meeting face-to-face, but the only person that ever indicated that was me. It wasn't mentioned in the texts at all. Maybe I had it all wrong. Maybe I wasn't sent here to meet someone. Maybe I was here to do something else. I snapped my head around to see if Noah was still standing behind the counter, but he'd vanished into the back. With no one else in sight, I started to circle the edges of the bakery, pretending to examine the local art that hung on the walls. Truth be told, I wasn't interested in the impressionistic mountain landscapes or the half-dozen attempts at splotchy "modern art," I just wanted to get a different angle on the place.

My eyes darted over tabletops as I moved, letting my fingers dance beneath them, searching for anything that might've been hidden there. Every spy movie I'd ever seen played back in my mind and every literary detective I've ever loved tried to help me guess what particular game was afoot. I finished checking the tables and came up empty-handed. I went into the bathroom next and checked the graffiti carved into the stall wall. Yes, Barrington keeps its streets clean, but not that clean. I took note of the phone numbers (though, I was honestly too skeeved out to dial any of them) and tried to decide if any of the filthy words Sharpied onto the smooth, tan plastic could have a double meaning. I almost went full Godfather and checked the toilet tanks, but that felt like a step too far. I headed back out to the main room.

Starting to get desperate, I eyed the blinking Christmas lights that draped around the edges of the windows. Were they programmed to convey some sort of Morse code? I hoped not, since I didn't know Morse code. For all I knew, they could be screaming the truth about UFOs and Area 51 and I would be none the wiser. I clenched my jaw, frustrated and ready to give up when I spotted the bulletin board by the door. I cocked my head and drifted toward it. It would be too easy to just leave a note. . . .

I scanned the ads and missing pet posters to see if anything seemed like a secret message, and caught my own face staring back at me. What in the . . . ? I pushed some other flyers to the side and revealed not just my face, but Oliver's, Jackson's, and Maya's as well—all smiling out from an ad for "Ellen Bowes Photography—School Portraits, Weddings, Events." Except the photos of my friends and I weren't portraits at all. They were selfies pulled from Instagram and Facebook. Either Barrington had a terrible photographer wannabe at large, or something was up.

My fingertips sizzled with anticipation as I snatched the ad off the board. What could it mean? I didn't see anything else out of place on the front, but as I turned away from the board, light hit the back of the paper and made it ever so slightly translucent. I flipped the ad over to read them. There I found a question staring back at me.

WHAT IS BLACKTHORNE?

Could it be a futuristic video game? Or was it an obscure Bolivian movie about Butch Cassidy? Or perhaps a dive rib joint in Boise, Idaho? These were among the many dubious possibilities I discovered during an exhaustive Internet search, which yielded little of actual substance. Certainly nothing that led me to connect Blackthorne to Bar Tech or Cochran or shadowy conspiracies.

I even risked reaching out to Maya and texted her, hoping that maybe she was behind the cryptic message, but no such luck. She assured me that she was still safely a thousand miles away, lying low somewhere in the Chicago area. And despite my attempts to connect with Oliver, he blew me off, not responding to any of my increasingly apologetic texts.

After hours of futile and exhausting bleary-eyed research, I shut my laptop and called it quits. I had to face the prospect that maybe Blackthorne and my secret texter were bogus—meant to distract and send me off on a wild-goose chase. For all I knew, this could've been one big setup by Richard Cochran to entrap me.

I stared at my phone like it was radioactive. Damn, I was definitely losing it. A good night's rest would hopefully clean the cobwebs out of my brain and help me think clearly in the morning. Blissful sleep was what I desperately needed.

BZZZZZZ. BZZZZZZ.

I sat upright in bed and looked around my room in a foggy haze. It was dark outside. 11:04 p.m. according to my clock. I had drifted off to sleep no more than ten minutes earlier and now my cell was buzzing. I looked around. Where was my phone? Not on my nightstand or anywhere on the bed. My hands felt around the coffee-colored shag carpeting, fingers combing through the long, dense fibers until I found the phone underneath the bed. The number was blocked on the incoming call, but I answered anyway. I hoped it was my mysterious texter wanting to establish verbal contact.

"Hello?" I waited for the caller to identify himself.

Nothing.

"Who's there?" I heard breathing. Someone was definitely on the other end.

CLICK.

I dropped the phone, unnerved by the disturbing call. I had no clue if it was my mystery texter or not, but it definitely made my skin crawl. I didn't think it was a wrong number. Spooked, I slid back under my comforter, longing for a safe place to hide. Not tonight. I was no longer tired. My eyes were wide open, fixed on my bedroom door. Staring. It wasn't that I expected an intruder to break in during the night and kill me, but a good night's sleep wasn't in the cards either. That would have to wait for another day.

9. BIG FREEZE

Paranoia had firmly taken root in my brain. My mother might have been the one living in Antarctica for nine months, but I was the one who would soon experience absolute zero—true coldness.

From the moment I arrived at school and wandered through the quad, I was eyeing everyone who glanced in my direction or passed by. They all seemed like potential suspects. Was the energetic redheaded soccer goalie with tree-trunk thighs my mysterious texter? Or the meek wallflower with bad skin whose face was always buried in Jane Austen or Harry Potter novels? Or the artsy drama geek with dreadlocks who insisted on wearing clothes only in lavender and black? Or perhaps it was one of the teachers? Or the bald, goateed Bar Tech Security guard with bulging biceps who seemed to be taking an unusual interest in what I was doing.

Better yet, maybe it wasn't anyone at school, in which case I was truly screwed. As if I didn't have enough to worry about with Bar Tech and Cochran's scheming, and Oliver hating me, not to mention Jackson's aloofness and what was going on with us.

It was at that moment that I became acutely aware of being watched. I casually looked around at the throngs of students crisscrossing my path as they hurried to their lockers. My eyes drew a bead on Lacey Dane, bundled up in a puffy red parka and white cashmere scarf, glaring daggers at me. She was hovering by the entrance, surrounded by a posse of friends, who were all giving me the evil eye as well. Other kids started turning around, whispering and nodding directly at me.

Shit. I knew I'd been busted. Mr. Bluni must've ratted me out to Lacey. Should I grovel and plead insanity? Lacey didn't exactly look like the forgiving type—at least not right now. It was probably best if I kept my distance. I had no clue what sort of retribution she had in mind. No matter what, I was screwed.

"Rough night?" The voice was friendly but jarred me nonetheless.

I spun around. Dana Fox, fresh faced and pretty as always, was looking at me with sympathetic green eyes.

"I look that awful?" A rhetorical question; I already knew the answer.

"Nothing a little lip gloss and blush can't cure," she gently replied with a reassuring nod.

Dana then took my arm and led me to the nearest girls' bathroom, where she magically transformed me, with a little help from Sephora, from looking like one of the pasty-faced Walking Dead into a slightly prettier version of me, with rosier cheeks and plumper pink lips. Not bad for a two-minute makeover.

"Voilà," she said, incredibly proud of her impressive artistry and her mastery of French.

I stared at myself in the mirror and had an out-of-body experience. I cracked a little smile and almost didn't recognize myself. "Where did you learn to do this?"

"From the master," she confided with a dismissive shrug, as if it were nothing. "Mom never leaves home without her full face on."

"Only beauty tip mine ever taught me was to exfoliate," I replied jokingly, but it was totally true.

Dana politely laughed as she tossed her trusty cosmetics case into her gorgeous caramel-colored leather saddlebag. "You should smile more often. Your whole face lights up."

"Okay." I felt myself blush, suddenly self-conscious. "I'll keep that in mind." I also felt a rush of warmth in my hands, which I quickly hid behind my back, in case I started disappearing before Dana's eyes.

"If you ever feel like talking about anything . . ."

I stiffened and chewed my lip, indecisive about whether

to say anything to her. Did Dana know more than she was letting on? Could she possibly be my mystery texter? The jury was still out on whether I could trust her or not. Nevertheless, I had to say something about why I was a bit of a train wreck that morning.

"Argument with my dad last night," I lied, waving it off, which seemed to make it sound more believable. "Just the usual shit."

"Sometimes it helps to vent anyway." Dana exuded this seductive warmth and had an openness about her that made one want to spill her guts. "My parents drive me crazy with their endless hovering. I just want to scream, fly your helicopter somewhere else," she admitted as an invitation for me to do the same.

I felt this overwhelming urge to unburden myself—to confess everything about the mystery texter, Bar Tech, my unrequited love for Jackson, and even how much I hated my hair that day. It was taking all my willpower to resist opening my mouth and divulging my innermost secrets. And I might've said something incriminating if it weren't for the ringing of the first-period bell.

"I've got bio," I announced, grabbing my bag and pushing the door open to leave. We exited the bathroom and were about to go our separate ways when Jackson appeared, walking toward us.

"Hey, babe," Dana cooed sweetly in her singsongy voice, giving him a peck on the cheek as he arrived.

"Hey," Jackson replied, awkwardly hugging her back and nodding to me as if I were just some random girl he knew.

That small gesture set me on edge. What exactly did it mean about the two of them? Or me? And why was Jackson suddenly wearing his varsity football jacket, which I had never seen him in?

"I better get to class." I hated feeling like I couldn't talk to him.

"Remember to smile," Dana reminded me, flashing her own bright grin, which really did seem to light up the hallway.

I nodded and hurried off to the nearest staircase just as I heard Jackson say: "See ya around."

"Hope you're ready to dive in," muttered Mr. Bluni as he dropped a six-inch-thick folder of articles and indecipherable scientific charts into my hands as I walked into biology seconds before the bell rang.

"Sure," I responded, uncomfortably aware that Lacey and almost everyone else in the class was scowling or staring me down with disapproving looks. I could've sworn a few were even mouthing the word "bitch." A frigid arctic blast, fueled by their collective hatred, had suddenly blown into the classroom and engulfed me. And although I desperately wished that I were anywhere else, it was all I could do to keep myself from literally vanishing in front of the entire class.

I held it together long enough to make it over to my seat, where I spent the entire period sitting in humiliated silence as Bluni lectured the class on DNA and RNA. I pretended to pay attention and take copious notes, all the while feeling Lacey's righteous antipathy and indignation about my heinous actions.

I had made my bed. Now I was going to have to lie in it.

The rest of the day went from bad to worse. After I survived biology, Bluni pulled me aside to break down our research schedule. I nearly had a coronary when I saw how much work he was expecting of me. Three afternoons a week after school, not to mention do a shitload of independent research on my own time. As I staggered out of his classroom, I was reminded of that cautionary adage: Be careful what you wish for . . . Well, I certainly was about to find that out firsthand.

By the time I finally lassoed Oliver in the quad at the end of the day and delivered my profuse apology, he pretended that he wasn't even angry anymore.

"You were right," he insisted. "Lame idea, the whole DNA thing."

"No, it's not dumb. Maybe there's another way to figure

this out." I knew how important it was to have Cochran know that Oliver was his son.

"Forget it. Not your problem." Oliver's eyes shifted around, never really looking directly at me.

"Is something else wrong?" I had a nagging suspicion that something else was going on with Oliver. But I couldn't put my finger on it.

"No. I just promised Dana that I'd help her with math. She's a little behind."

"Oh." I was a bit put off. I never knew Oliver and Dana traveled in the same social circle. "Don't let me keep you."

Off he fled without another word.

That night I finally got around to looking through the mountain of articles Bluni had given me. Most of them pertained to the human genome project and identifying genes. Standard stuff. Nothing unusual. I had hoped to dig up a connection to Bar Tech, but there was no smoking gun—at least none that I could find. Or any mention of Blackthorne either. I even searched online and tried cross-referencing the studies with whatever genetic research Bar Tech was publicly engaged in but came up empty-handed.

At dinner I casually pressed my father for any details he knew about Bar Tech's current studies.

"Tell me what you're looking for." He eagerly thumbed

through the clippings, which were from *Scientific American*, *Journal of Human Genetics*, *Journal of Biotechnology*, among others, and found nothing that made him suspicious.

"That's the problem. I'm not sure," I admitted. "Bluni was vague. Insisted I read this stuff first before we discussed the details of his research. Something to do with genetic testing."

"Every biotech company is hot on that trail these days," my father informed me. "If we knew exactly what they were looking for, then maybe we could put the pieces of the puzzle together."

"I know there's a connection between Bluni and Cochran."

"Their argument could've been about a million different things."

"What about the fact that Bluni has a PhD from MIT?" I'd found out this detail when I'd run across Bluni's doctoral thesis about nature versus nurture, which was published back in the 1990s in some obscure science journal. It had to do with inherited traits versus environmental factors. Not only that, but Bluni won several college science awards in biology. "What's he doing teaching high school biology?"

"Maybe he enjoys molding young minds," Dad hypothesized. "Lots of high school teachers have graduate degrees. All you have is supposition and inference. No hard facts."

Unfortunately, my dad was right. I didn't have any hard evidence yet to support my belief, or even to give me an idea of where to look. All I had was a feeling. Not much to go on. My gut told me there had to be a link.

"Just do your work, Nica. Don't nose around too much," my dad advised. "Let me work my end. If there's something there, it'll shake out."

That just meant I'd have to get closer to Bluni and prove that he could trust me if I wanted to find out about his connection to Cochran. That would take some time. Time I might not have. And with Oliver distracted by personal issues and Jackson distancing himself from me, I was very much alone.

The days that followed were an excruciating lonely time for me. As word spread around school about what I'd done to Lacey, I gradually became persona non grata, the girl everyone loved to hate. Most days I kept to myself, eating lunch alone. Sometimes Dana would invite me to join her and the other cheerleaders. The girls were polite, but conversation was filled with a lot of awkward silences, inside jokes, and oblique references to after-school clothes-shopping excursions that I was excluded from. Not that I was a shopping fanatic, but the gravitational pull of my world had definitely shifted.

I wondered why Dana never once asked about her former best friend. Wasn't she the least bit curious why Maya had vanished? Or was Dana just happy not to have the competition anymore? She could reign supreme. Socially and academically unchallenged. And reign she did.

I was amazed by how easily Dana settled back into the swing of social life full throttle without missing a beat. It was as if no time had passed. The cheerleading squad had happily welcomed her back with open arms, electing her captain again. She also became editor in chief of the school blog, which she immediately overhauled with a fresh new design esthetic. And Dana even volunteered several hours a week at my father's hospital, reading uplifting books to sick patients.

Stranger still, Jackson rejoined the football team. Not a huge deal in the scheme of things, but very telling about where Jackson's head was at emotionally. His previously subpar grades suddenly shot back up to straight As. He'd even dusted off his old snowboard and was planning an excursion with the Ski Club. Within just a few short weeks, rebel boy amazingly reverted back to the overachieving jock he was before Dana's disappearance. Involved, committed, and popular. The Jackson I had never known. Which only isolated me even further.

Sure, he was still nice to me, treating me with an offhanded benevolence when we'd pass each other in the hallways. Never once did we directly talk about what had happened between us the night before Dana returned. Or what it meant. It seemed like a vague, distant memory, forgotten in Dana's sudden reappearance. And Jackson seemed even more reluctant to mention the pulse or even talk about how we had changed and transformed. The only transformation on his mind these days was rewinding the clock to a world before the pulse.

Disheartened and nearly exiled, I threw myself into Bluni's research project as a way to keep my mind sharp. Unfortunately, he never let me get anywhere near his lab research, which was done at a private facility off site. I was relegated to writing endless briefs on bioethics topics ranging from genetic testing for sickle-cell anemia or Tay-Sachs disease, among others, to an evolutionary process called genetic drift.

Along with natural selection, mutation, and migration, genetic drift was one of the basic mechanisms of evolution. In each generation, some individuals might, just by chance, leave behind a few more genes than other individuals. The genes of the next generation would be the genes of the "lucky" individuals, not necessarily the healthier or "better" individuals. When I probed Bluni for specifics about how this impacted his secret lab work, he'd curtly shut me down and ordered me to focus on my own research.

On a few occasions when Bluni was stuck in an after-school meeting, I'd practice making myself invisible for longer and longer sessions so that I could snoop through his meticulously ordered research files. The man was beyond anal. He was a super control freak who kept everything password protected on his laptop. As if that weren't secure enough, all his notes were written in an alphanumeric scientific code, which I couldn't decipher. I needed Oliver's expertise and help for that. Help I wasn't going to get until I had something concrete that proved a connection with Bar Tech.

Ever since Dana's return to Barrington, I'd gone from being part of a team of warriors to a solo army of one. Except for my one-time mystery texter, who'd vanished as inexplicably as he'd first appeared, I had no one to rely on but myself.

Which meant I had to prepare for eventual battle. I arrived at school bright and early one morning. I always liked to get a head start on my day, but that day was different. No one would know I was even here. I planned to spend the entire day invisible. It was going to take a massive amount of control and energy to make it through the entire day without reappearing, but I wanted to try it for a couple reasons. First, the stranger things got in Barrington, the more I needed to know I could count on my power. While I'd proven to myself that I had the ability to control my invisibility under many different circumstances, I'd tested only it in relatively short bursts. If I was successfully able to use it for minutes at a time, why not test it in a more challenging situation? Not only did I need to know if such a thing was possible, but I also needed to know how my body would respond. Were there unseen dangers involved with being invisible for hours at a time? I couldn't afford to find out in the middle of an emergency at some point in the future. I had to troubleshoot now so I could be prepared for when everything turned to shit.

10. CHUTES AND LADDERS

Here I was the next day, on one of Barrington High's sleek, eco-friendly school buses, humming its way to the local ski resort on nearby Whiteface Mountain. I could see how that might not be regarded as any great defeat, but I was not an organized-activities kind of girl. Or a "choosing to be out-doors in single-degree windchill" kind of girl. I liked winter sports just fine: with snacks, an oversized hoodie, and Bob Costas bringing the Winter Olympics straight to my cozy living room.

The bus was full of kids, most of whom had been put on a pair of skis or a baby board before their training wheels had come off. Ski Club was just a way of life for them. I'd made the mistake of YouTubeing videos of Jackson's old snow-boarding competitions on my phone at lunch. Athletics suited him. He was strong, precise, agile, and fearless. And it was his fault I was in this mess in the first place.

The wheels on this bus had really started turning at school yesterday, while I was perusing the student body's bulletin board. I couldn't get Blackthorne out of my mind. There hadn't been any more communications between my mystery texter and me. Or, as I reminded myself, at least not any that I'd found yet. I'd scoured the school high and low for anything new hiding in plain sight and coded to catch only my attention. This had landed me at the school's social activities board—my very first visit. I read over each and every flyer, hoping to spot another piece of the Blackthorne puzzle.

What is Blackthorne?

I had no idea, and I was beginning to doubt the cast list for the Drama Club's rendition of *Beauty and the Beast* was going to tell me. I rustled past a few more notices—the brackets for the Chess Club tournament, a couple glittery signs advertising tickets to the upcoming Winter Formal, and flyers reminding students about the first basketball game of the season.

Then I'd spotted it: my name.

Not in the cast of the musical—thank God—but on a separate list right next to it. It was a sign-up sheet for Ski Club's first trip of the season to Whiteface, and I had definitely not signed up.

I ripped the sheet off the board and flipped it over in anticipation . . . but there was nothing waiting for me on the other side. Deflated, I turned it over once more and reexamined the list. Also included were Jackson, Oliver, and Dana. All in the same handwriting. I realized that in my excitement

I had missed another detail. The *i* in "Nica" had been dotted with a heart. Deflated, I decided the mystery texter would have to wait. I had a more immediate problem to solve.

I tracked down Jackson outside of his locker to ask him about it. We hadn't talked in several days.

"Hey." I leaned up against the locker next to his, trying to play it cool. Mostly it just hurt my bony shoulder. "I was hoping you could solve a mystery for me."

"If I can," he answered with the slightest hint of hesitation.

"Saw my name on the Ski Club sign-up sheet. But the mystery part is . . . I didn't put it there."

"Oh, right. Ski Club. I guess she didn't talk to you about it yet." She. It dropped a few decibels below the other words, like he was afraid to speak it. The silver lining was that it was finally Jackson's turn to feel awkward. "Dana signed us up."

"Well, I appreciate the enthusiasm, but I think she'll understand that I don't want to spend junior year with a full leg cast as my major accessory."

"It's not about the skiing, Nica."

"Then maybe someone should rename it."

"No, I mean it's more than just skiing. It's mostly about hanging out with friends."

"I hadn't pegged you as a sitting-around-the-fire-and-singing-Coldplay kind of guy," I joked, trying to keep things light.

"Didn't say that I was," Jackson snapped back. "But I

like to keep myself open to new experiences."

This made me laugh. The mental image of Jackson Winters 1.0, the former lone wolf of Barrington High, trying just about anything besides his James Dean routine was pure comedy.

He continued. "Don't be mad at Dana, okay? She's just trying to reach out. She really likes you."

Dammit, Jackson. I could feel it coming, an itch I wouldn't be able to resist scratching. I just wished I could turn and walk away from him.

"Just come." Jackson's blue-green eyes bored into me. In that moment, I was willing to jump off a bridge, wire money to his Nigerian prince friend, and give him a choice of my kidneys.

"I'll be there," I muttered as if all my willpower had evaporated into the thin mountain air.

A roar of laughter from the back of the bus rudely interrupted my memory of Jackson's appreciative smile. I turned to look over my shoulder, to see what was going on and then dismissed it with equal speed. It was jock one-upmanship of the lamest variety—exposed butts pressed against freezing bus windows to moon unsuspecting drivers in the oncoming lane. How they thought this would result in timeless glory was foggy at best. But, apparently, Jackson disagreed. I could pick his laugh out among the others, and I risked a second glance to verify.

Dana was laughing, too, but curled in against Jackson's chest, shielding her eyes from anything sun starved and untoward. I wanted to shout down the length of the bus how much fun I was having with her, how bonded I already felt. Instead, I pushed my sarcasm back down, internalizing another dose of acid to my probably growing ulcer.

Borrowing Dana's move, I leaned in to my own seat partner, Oliver, for support. Luckily, things between us had cooled off since our flare-up over Cochran. For the time being, it looked like we had reached a truce: We were both firmly invested in pretending like nothing had ever happened.

I gave him my most pathetic pout, the same one I used when my dad tried to order our takeout pizza with vegan cheese. "What are we doing here?"

He shrugged. "I don't know about you, but I'm going to shred some gnar and tear it up."

"Don't be gross."

"You have no idea what that means." Oliver was amused by my ignorance.

"And I'm pretty sure I don't want to."

"Take a chill pill," he said flippantly. "Everything's crunchy, dude."

"Now you're just messing with me." I felt irritable and inexplicably anxious about the trip.

Oliver's poker face cracked under the pressure. "Ha-ha,

fine. I might not be the best boarder, but it's pretty fun. And the lingo is straight out of the Keanu Reeves School of Bodacious Phrases."

Something behind me caught Oliver's gaze, and I turned to follow it. Topher was seated across the aisle, a large Ebinger's Bakery box situated in his lap. Opened just a moment ago, the box's still-fresh scent of caramelized sugar and spiced vanilla wafted over in sinful invitation.

Topher angled the box so we could see inside. It was a medley of doughnuts and sweets, at least a couple I'd be happy to put out of their misery. "This morning's castoffs," he offered. "Noah can't eat all of them, so I might as well grease some palms."

"In the most honest sense of the words," Oliver agreed, not needing any further encouragement to snatch up an oversized Boston cream. As he devoured the treat, I took a second glance at Noah, the boy seated with Topher. He had served me coffee at Ebinger's the day I'd found the Blackthorne clue. I hadn't been able to place him at the time, but now, in context, I was almost certain he was Topher's boyfriend. Played on a sports team, too—lacrosse, maybe? Or hockey? Something with muscly guys and scoring goals, anyway. As for whether or not he was my mystery texter, Noah didn't strike me as the shadowy whistleblower type, but maybe that just meant he was a great shadowy whistleblower.

"Please, take them away. I'm pretty sure I could eat the whole box, and that would be disastrous," Noah said, as he tried to pawn the pastries off on me.

I looked into the abyss of desserts, a plump apple fritter catching my eye. I was already on my way to an afternoon of torture, which meant I was not about to deny myself a momentary refuge of sugary pleasure.

"I'll eat the whole box if it means they'll take me home early," I kidded, savoring the flaky cinnamon glaze and sticky apples below.

"You too, huh?" Topher asked as he playfully ribbed Noah. "I'm glad to know I'm not the only person being dragged into this against their will."

"That's not what you said this morning!" Noah said, teasing right back. "Besides, you owe me after that entire night of subtitles last month."

"It was a J Horror retrospective at the coolest theater in Denver. And I paid."

They exchanged grins. Normally, bickering sent me into immediate wallflower mode, but it was obvious that Topher and Noah were just playing.

I considered a second doughnut, but remembered how susceptible I was to the sugar crash and didn't want to be on the slopes for that. I tried to pass the box back over the seat behind us, but Oliver stopped me. He snagged a third pastry and then, with a pained reluctance, relinquished the box.

"What you said this morning," Noah started, "was that you're keeping your mind open to new experiences."

"And I owed you one," Topher rejoined.

The chatter quieted when I noticed that Noah's phrasing—keeping your mind open to new experiences—was the exact same thing Jackson had said to me at school yesterday. It was just a coincidence, but still, not the stuff that was usually bandied around by teenagers. I wondered if it might be on an airbrushed inspirational poster in the school somewhere, subconsciously penetrating our group vocabulary.

Thirty minutes and forty dollars later, it was official: There was no turning back. I was shackled into a pair of downhill skis, being pushed up Whiteface against my will.

As I ascended higher into colder temperatures and noticeably stronger winds, Oliver pointed out the bunny hill, our destination. By our truly torturous speed, I guessed we were still a minute or two away from the exit point. The bunny hill, a deceitful name that made it sound much more fun than it looked, was packed with beginner skiers and snowboarders—almost all of them elementary-school-aged.

"As long as you don't knock down any of the kiddies, you should be fine," advised Oliver.

I noticed Oliver's phrasing had a distinctive lack of "we."

"You're not coming with me?" I was trying not to panic.

Oliver pointed farther up the lift, to where it deposited more advanced riders on a higher, steeper slope. "I was just going to head up to the blue trail. I guess I could stick around down here for a few runs, if you'd like." It sounded like he wanted to snowboard the bunny hill just as much as I did. I considered forcing him to stay, but I knew that would just result in two miserable people instead of one. I decided to let him off the hook.

"Oh, don't worry about it. I'm just being a baby. I just lean forward and point myself toward the bottom, right?"

Oliver laughed. "That'll probably get you there, one way or another.

"This is your stop," Oliver reminded me, as we reached the top of the bunny hill. I tried to mimic the eight-year-old gliding off the T-bar in front of me, but my sideways stumbling was decidedly less graceful.

Oliver shouted a "Good luck!" over his shoulder . . . and then I was on my own. As I navigated toward a pushing-off point, nothing seemed to work the way it should. Instead of gliding, it was a full upper-body workout just to move ahead a few feet at a time. My ski pulls felt like just more weight I had to carry around rather than providing me with any help. The bunny hill hadn't looked impressive from the entrance, but peeking over the edge, I wasn't so sure.

Scooting my skis up the beginning of the incline, inch after inch, I waited for the moment when gravity would take over and I would tip, descending like the heavier side of a see saw. Teeter, teeter, teeter . . . and I was off, finally getting that glide I'd been looking for. Getting it, in fact, a little too fast and continuing to accelerate. Nervous, I coiled myself in tighter, but as my center of gravity lowered, I only slid down the hill faster. Still completely unaware of the purpose of my ski poles, I dug them into the snow like an emergency brake. It worked, but instead of spraying a puff of snow in a dazzling stop like I had envisioned in my head, I tumbled headfirst, my upper body's momentum too far ahead of the impromptu anchor I'd made out of the ski pole.

I tried to catch my breath as I stayed still in the fresh powder. It looked light and fluffy, but it sure didn't feel that way against my face. I could hear a few nearby giggles as I sat upright, trying to brush the snow off myself. A mom nearby, arresting in head-to-toe hot pink, looked over to see if I was all right, but I waved her off. The concerned mom lost interest when I successfully hobbled to my feet. Just standing still would have to do for a minute. As I looked back over my shoulder, it was daunting to see all of that adventure had gotten me only about a third of the way down the hill. Surveying the remainder of my journey, I spotted two other people actually my age. It was Topher and Noah. Topher seemed to have about as much raw talent as I did, but he also had a patient boyfriend helping him along the way. It was adorable, and I was a little jealous.

I scoped out the bottom of the hill, where all the trails led back to one shining point: the lodge. It was so close, yet so far. I just had to summon what was left of my quickly dwindling energy and make it there. Then I could finally be released from these medieval torture contraptions on my feet. I started to shuffle away when I realized my less-than-fortuitous timing. I could make out two tiny figures in the distance, careening down the final stretch of Whiteface's most challenging run: Jackson and Dana. They were weaving in and out of each other's paths in a striking display of athleticism. It had just taken everything I had to survive (most of) the bunny hill, and there they were, the perfect couple. Effortless. The knife of jealousy slid into my side like butter.

As difficult as it was to watch the king and queen of Barrington High, I couldn't tear my eyes away. I had never seen Jackson in this light before. When I'd met him, he'd been broken, a shell of himself in the wake of his missing girlfriend and Barrington's increasingly strange events. What I had never considered was that Dana's return would restore him to someone entirely different—a complete stranger. He was someone I didn't know, and he seemed so blissfully happy. I wasn't sure I was ready to admit it, but I couldn't help wondering if Jackson and Dana were truly meant for each other.

Drained of any remaining enthusiasm, I ended up completely reversing my previous gung-ho strategy and tried to continue down the hill as slowly as possible. Maybe if I went slowly enough I could retreat to the lodge without having to go back up the hill again. I was ready to face a few condescending smirks at the equipment rental if it meant I could trade my gear for indoor heating and a warm beverage. Pushing off with the ski poles (at this point, I had picked up at least one thing from the surrounding tykes), I sent myself hurtling toward the bottom. It felt faster than it probably was and a little bit terrifying, but for a few moments I was actually enjoying myself. I wasn't about to close my eyes and reach a personal nirvana, but I suddenly got it. The wind didn't feel as cold, the sun seemed to shine a little brighter, and the world raced by around me. Everything slowed. The obnoxious kids, the doting parents, the chaos on all sides turned into a half-speed ballet that played out for my enjoyment.

Maybe, I thought, maaaaybe I could get used to this.

But then I realized I was dangerously close to the bottom of the hill. The lodge was looming, and I had no way of slowing down. I tried my e-brake trick again, a bit gentler this time, but the stutter stops just tossed me around like prey in the jaws of disaster. The ballet sped back up to real time and blended into swirls of color around me as I lost all sense of control. Up was down; down was up—

Crack. And in an instant, light was dark.

11. SKI CLUB PART 2

"Nica? You all right?"

I couldn't feel my ears. Holy shit. I'd hit my head—did I tear them off? I grabbed at the sides of my face, fingers quickly confirming that was crazy. Ears: check. Arms intact. Where was I?

"Hey, you're okay," the deep voice said reassuringly.

I blinked away the bright white light to see Chase Cochran standing over me.

"Wiped out," Chase affirmed. "Looked like you slammed your head pretty bad."

Oh, right. Ski Club. Whiteface. Colorado. America. The ringing in my ears began to subside as I gathered my senses and offered Chase my hand. He pulled me up. He was strong—unsurprising, I guess, but I wasn't expecting to be literally whisked off my feet. I could feel myself warming up already.

"Yeah. Guess I did. Everything look all right?"

His fingers gently touched my neck as I tilted my head

back and forth and he checked for injuries. "Flawless." He grinned as he pronounced his official medical judgment.

I smiled back. Don't judge. I was still dazed from the fall. Flirty as the moment was, I had no desire to stay out in the freezing cold. I wanted to be inside, wrapped in a blanket, thinking about what had just happened while I waited for the bus to take us all home.

"Okay, well, see you in there. . . ." I was still so dazed, I wasn't really sure what else to say. Without another word, I turned away from my would-be white knight.

I'd momentarily forgotten that there wasn't much traction to be found on the snowy ground, but my skis gave me a friendly reminder. As I moved, my feet shot in two different directions, and I fell over into a clumsy split. Chase caught the back of my jacket and kept me from spilling face-first into the snow.

"C'mon," he said. "Let me give you a lesson."

"No, I'm fine."

"Think you can make it the whole way to the clubhouse on your own?" His voice betrayed an unusual level of concern.

I looked up and saw the peaked roof in the distance, probably a hundred yards, but it seemed like miles. Dammit, Chase.

"Okay, one run and that's it," I relented.

Chase smiled and gave me his arm as we trudged back toward the lift.

Through the bright green pines trawling by, I spotted a fleck of dark concrete. It perched on the side of the mountain like a large, exposed boulder, but as the lift pulled us higher into the air and closer to the object, I realized it was man-made. I nudged Chase.

"What's that?" He followed my finger as I continued. "A cabin or something? Do people stay that far up the mountain?"

Chase squinted too, and then he cocked his head. "Probably one of Bar Tech's."

They're everywhere, I thought. But I couldn't say that to Chase. It was still up for debate as to whether or not his sudden kindness toward me was motivated by a misguided desire to hook up, or if there was something else going on. It remained to be seen if I could totally trust him. After all, I knew less about him than he did about me. I didn't really like it that way, so I decided to keep digging.

"Up here?" I gently pressed, as if I were just making random conversation. "I thought all their offices were in town."

"Now they are. Back when my dad first took over as president, there were buildings the whole way up Whiteface. The company was doing tons of research up here. Atmosphere something or other. Science stuff. They weren't making any money with it, so he shut the whole wing down. Saved them a lot of trouble, he said."

I nodded, keeping my eyes locked on the building. It's not that Chase's explanation was unreasonable, but the idea that Bar Tech had left a footprint here, in the otherwise pristine wilderness, chilled me more than the air whipping at my cheeks.

I stared at the building. Abandoned, huh? I dared a door to open or a guard to foolishly step out onto the roof so I could prove to myself that Chase was lying or that he was blind to the truth. I watched it until the chair evened out and the building disappeared behind the evergreens. I saw nothing.

I suspected everything.

Moments later I stood at the top of the bunny hill, staring down and fighting off vertigo.

"It's simple, Nica. Honestly. Side to side. Side to side." Chase demonstrated on the flat surface, bending his knees left and right. Here I was, a girl who could turn invisible at will but was unable to master the simple physics of gravity, inertia, and downhill motion.

"Simple for you," I shot back. "You grew up doing this."

"Did I?"

"Uh, I mean—" I suddenly felt foolish. "You did, didn't you?"

Chase shook his head. "You're not the only one who's had to learn how to fit in, Nica."

His admission caught me by surprise. In my mind, Chase Cochran had always been the king of the school, as bestowed upon him through birthright, but he seemed to be indicating otherwise.

"Freshman year," he continued, "I had, like, zero friends. My dad had to let some people go at Bar Tech and everyone knew he was to blame. A lot of angry kids took it out on me. I was the son of the big, bad boss. No one could separate him and me. Their parents were too upset."

Oh, Chase. You have no idea.

"Couldn't hang anywhere and no one wanted to come to my house. I joined Ski Club, but the only problem was that I was useless on these things. Maybe worse than you. I crashed every time I went down and sat up covered in snow."

"So who taught you how to get better?"

"No one. I had to teach myself."

In that moment, some of the ice I'd let build up around my heart started to thaw. Chase Cochran, self-made man, was applying direct heat. Clearly his struggle to land himself at the top of the social heap had worked, even if his dad's agenda hadn't changed. Was this a new Chase Cochran?

But then came the gaggle of slim girls with effortless, self-confident smiles—sticks, all of them, even in their winter-sports gear—and there went Chase's attention. I rolled my eyes at the jock's obliviously obvious tongue wagging.

"Side to side," I deadpanned, letting my gaze follow his. The girls turned their heads to smile at the attention they'd attracted as they walked by, and Chase was smitten.

"Oh, man. That's Kat from French . . ." He couldn't even

finish his sentence as he followed the toned backsides. Like iron to magnets, I observed.

"I'm sure Kat wouldn't appreciate you staring," I teased.

"No, it's just . . . She has a homework thing and I told her I'd do her. Do it for her," he quickly corrected, quite flustered. "With her. Whatever. Can we do the lesson another time?"

"Hell yeah. I'll call you." And he skied off to claim his prize.

I turned to face facts: There was still only one way to the bottom of this hill, and I'd learned nothing about how to get there.

My second trip down was no less clumsy than the first, but I was ready to call it quits. The lodge was immense, warm, and charming. It was almost enough to make me forget the bruises, jammed fingers, and throbbing knees I'd developed trying to come to a stop just outside the building's doors.

Almost.

I felt like one of the broken burglars at the end of *Home Alone* as I limped past benches of yammering skiers. I pulled my knit hat from my head and ran my fingers through my tangled, icy locks. I was presented with my reflection in one of the windows that looked out onto the slopes—ooof. Looked like I got lost somewhere between the washer and the dryer. I noticed pairs of eyes following me as I dragged my bedraggled ass toward the snack stand. I'm sure if I'd stopped to offer so much as a "hello" to a stranger, they would've just politely pretended not to see me.

If only they knew.

"Hey, Nica!" Oliver swung past me with a steaming cup of hot chocolate. "You look like you need to come crash by the fire."

"Long as it's more comfortable than the ground."

"Definitely. Here." He handed me his hot chocolate. "I'll get another. Sit. Before you fall over."

I took a welcome sip. The warm cocoa rushed over my tongue, and my cheeks flushed with warmth.

"Thanks," I said, appreciative of Oliver's genuine concern for my well-being.

"No problem. I'll join you in a sec."

The fire was built and roaring (or, more likely, someone just turned up the gas) by the time I got to the couches on the other side of the large room. No one else appeared as rough as I did, even though I'm sure they'd all tackled much more aggressive runs. I tried to temper my self-conscious thoughts as I drifted into the mix and found an empty spot on a couch. While I expected excited chatter and stories swapped from the slopes, it took me only two seconds to realize that this gathering by the fire wasn't here for idle chatter. Everyone here was focused on the words of one person: Topher.

The normally reserved kid had a wicked grin on his face as he pulled everyone closer just by lowering his voice.

"Oh, yeah," he said. "Total destruction. I can't believe you guys never heard about it. Nica, have you?" Everyone turned to scope my strung-out-looking visage as I froze in the headlights of Topher's question.

"Sorry. Have I what?" I felt a surge of panic at being put on the spot like that.

"Heard about the avalanche," he responded ominously. Unless "avalanche" was some sort of slang I was too much of a loser to know, I had to admit I had not.

I shook my head.

Topher's smile grew the way one's does when they know they're about to unleash a great story on an unsuspecting audience.

"It was 1846. The first settlement at Barrington had been completed by a collection of miners, trappers, and pioneers. Wasn't a huge city, just a hub for prospectors to get laid and families to kick up their heels safely for a night or two before continuing on the trail west. The government had even dropped real money to get a postal hub anchored in town, twenty years before the pony express would start helping to push letters and packages to California. Anyway, everyone knew it was an outpost in violent, difficult country, but no one had any idea that Whiteface was going to prove to be as deadly as it was."

I listened with rapt attention, as did everyone else, hooked by Topher's tale.

"No one knows if the avalanche was completely natural or if surveyors and prospectors set off some dynamite in the wrong place, but the mountain unleashed a wall of snow that took the town completely off guard. There was no time to run. The entire place was buried, like Pompeii under ice instead of ash. There're still rumors that the original buildings are actually underground, buried under a permanent layer of ice on the east side of town, closest to where Whiteface meets the valley."

Taking a look around at the faces of the other kids, I could see they were enthralled. Their wide-eyed stares were filled with visions of apocalyptic waves of white. I got a chill that subsided when a stuffy-nosed sophomore spoke up.

"Could it happen again?"

Topher solemnly shook his head. "There's no way of knowing. It could happen today or tomorrow or next week."

A new voice broke through—it was Oliver, returning with his hot chocolate and shaking his head.

"The Whiteface thing? It takes ice shelves centuries to build up like that. There's enough snow up there to bury us, but it isn't sitting on anything that'll come loose on such a massive scale. If it happens again, we'll all be long gone."

"But what if there's still a town here? What about those people?" Dana's cheerleading friend Annie asked with an expression of fear and trepidation, as if the lost people were ghosts who lurked on the mountain.

Oliver took a long breath. "I was speaking about humans more generally. Long gone."

Not everyone was amused by Oliver's slightly darker outlook on things, but I thought it was funny. Topher did too. His answer didn't seem to satisfy anybody else, and the crowd started to thin.

"I think we scared them," Oliver said.

Topher shrugged. "Whatever. Most of these guys like Noah more anyway." Topher looked at me. There was sadness in his eyes, and it betrayed his true feelings about the way the crowd had parted. I sensed he was lonely. Or maybe I was projecting.

"Screw 'em," I blurted out. "You had me on the edge of my seat."

An annoying chaperone interrupted. Lucy Mangione was an overbearing, angular algebra teacher who always wore red. "Getting dark, kids. Time to pack it in. Bus leaves in thirty."

I downed the rest of my hot chocolate and parted ways with the guys.

I don't think Jackson meant for me to hear his low, urgent tones as he leaned in to Dana's ear. In fact, he didn't even know I was there—"there" being the secluded hallway near the locker rooms. For my part, I hadn't meant to be spying, either. I was ready to get off this mountain as quick as I could.

I stopped at the snack machines and then I heard Dana's melodious laugh. I was used to hearing it ring out in the hallways at school, and I recognized it instantly—a distinct, bell-like jingle. I peeked around the corner from where I was struggling with my cash and saw Barrington's Most Popular hanging out with a group of fresh-faced girls near the slushy back entrance to the lodge. Chase's French muse, Kat, was among them. As I was considering moving closer to catch a hint of what they might be yammering on about, Jackson came down the hall. I froze. I didn't want him to catch me eavesdropping, but he was moving so fast that I ducked into an alcove. He breezed past me to put his arm around Dana. They chatted for a second before heading back toward me, where they slowed to a stop. Jackson rested his palm on the glowing vending machine. He bent close to Dana, his voice burdened with import.

"Can we talk?" he asked. Dana studied his face, trying to decipher his intentions.

"Sure. Everything all right?"

"Everything's fine, just . . . Come with me." It was the first time I wished I had total control over going invisible. I stayed in the alcove as he pulled her down the hall until they ended up on the back balcony of the lodge. I rushed to the edge of the balcony that faced the valley that Barrington nestled in and was high enough on the mountain to offer a pristine view over the town's twinkling lights. The stars hung bright overhead, like a reflection of our city in the sky. They were too wrapped up in their conversation to notice me. I guess I didn't have to go invisible to not get noticed.

"Secluded. Romantic. Jackson Winters, are you proposing?" Dana smiled, half joking.

Jackson laughed, but I didn't think it was funny. If he had a ring, I was one hundred percent ready to take a running leap right off the edge and into the void.

But it wasn't that. I could tell by the way his eyes wouldn't meet hers. It hit me that I read the situation wrong downstairs. This wasn't romantic. He'd taken her all the way up here in case she freaked out. Whatever this was, he'd been putting it off, I realized.

"When you were gone . . . well, you were gone for a long time, and . . . things, you know, things changed. No one knew where you were or if you were okay. I mean I know you've heard what I was like. I wasn't sure I how I felt then, and I'm not sure how I feel now."

My heart leaped into my throat. Was Jackson going to break up with her?

"About what?" Dana asked, expression darkening, slowly picking up on the same hint I already had.

"You know . . ." Jackson drifted off into a pause big enough to fill the nearby valley. "Us."

Oh my God! I was suddenly concerned I would shout out loud.

Dana stayed totally cool, her surface unrippled. She took a deep breath and squeezed Jackson's hand. Finally, her eyes found his and the unthinkable happened. As she gazed into his beautiful eyes, his face started to go blank. What started as a look of pained concern devolved into an emotionless mask.

And if that wasn't strange enough, she started to speak. Slowly. Deliberately. "Don't be silly. We're head over heels in love, Jackson. We always will be. There's no one else."

Jackson didn't blink. Didn't smile. Just took in her words and then leaned in for a kiss.

"Sorry. Don't know what I was thinking," he whispered. "You're perfect for me."

"I know," replied Dana, as her mouth parted to take his lips.

I wanted to wretch, but I knew the sound would give me away. Instead, I hurried off, leaving them behind. My mind raced, trying to process what I'd just witnessed.

It was impossible.

Jackson was a guy, sure, and their whims and wants changed quickly, but that was unreal. Dana had taken the conversation and not just shaped it, but fired the iron and literally bent it to her will. I guess it was possible she had Jackson wrapped so tightly around her manipulative little fingers that all she had to do was snap to get him to fall in line. The idea that she could so easily seduce him made me sick, but it didn't shake me to my core the way the alternative did. If Jackson wasn't on a wire-tight lovelorn leash, there was no easy explanation for the total one-eighty I'd just seen.

Was it possible that Dana had a power of her own?

12. ONE OF US

First seat on the left, directly behind the bus driver. I'd claimed the seat of intentional isolation, the seat that even your friends wouldn't ask to share with you. I'd even surrounded my impenetrable fortress with a moat: earbuds firmly secured and tunes already cranked. I didn't want to freeze out Oliver, but I didn't have a choice. If we shared a seat for even the half hour it would take to get back to the school parking lot, I knew I wouldn't be able to keep what I saw to myself. He wouldn't have any answers. As insane as it seemed, I couldn't stop the idea from turning over and over in my head. Was Dana one of us? Did she have a power? Was it even possible?

I knew the idea was crazy. Telepathy? Mind control? Wielding the Force at top Jedi levels? What I knew for a fact, though, was how Oliver would react if I told him. Even if I prefaced every word with an acknowledgment that I thought I might've gone off the deep end, it wouldn't be enough. He already knew I was jealous. I didn't like how

Dana had disrupted our band of outsiders. Seeing Jackson happy without me was painful. I wished I could prove to him that all these feelings and suspicions could be mutually exclusive. Wasn't there a slim possibility that while my judgment was clouded, it could also be right? Of course. But that didn't mean I was ready to mount this house-of-cards argument to my best friend.

It still hurt when Oliver climbed onto the bus and walked right by me. He was right in the middle of a story, charming Noah and a few kids from the back-of-the-bus crowd with a wild tale about Steve Jobs. It was like Topher's story about the avalanche—one of those stories people loved to tell because they knew it would enrapture an audience every time. It also told me that Oliver was trying. He liked these people and was reaching out in an effort to become friends.

Was Oliver moving on, too? Maybe he was a little bit tired of my teenage-girl pining, but the idea of being replaced as Oliver's best friend was even worse. I had to brush it off. I might've been a flavor of the month for Jackson, but friendships like the one I had with Oliver didn't work that way. But who was I to know? My Thai friend Lai and I were down to an e-mail maybe twice a month.

Peering over the back of my seat, I surveyed the other kids. Oliver wasn't the only one who seemed to have branched out socially. On the way up the mountain, the forty-some-odd kids had been segregated by social group.

Dana and Jackson had been the popular kids, mostly foot-ball players and cheerleaders with a few groupies to pad them out. Then there had been a handful of academic over-achievers, a few theater kids, and so on down the line, each carving out their own bus territory. Now, however, on the ride back, it looked like social anarchy. One would think they'd just survived the events of a Saw movie together, not spent an afternoon skiing.

It was so weird. Had these new friendships all been formed when I'd taken a bathroom break? There did seem to be one more outlier. Topher was only a couple seats back from me and across the aisle, sitting alone and vacantly star-ing out the window. That was a development I understood least of all. He and Noah had looked so happy together only hours earlier—what had changed? Was he that upset that no one stuck around after his story? I couldn't know for sure, but teenagers were notoriously fickle. It was exactly why I had to keep any and all suspicions about Dana close to the chest, at least until I had something a little more con-crete. If the evidence never came, I could just laugh it off as a crazy hunch that never came through. Staring off out of my own window, I cranked the volume on my phone and didn't look back again.

The next day I entered English excited to catch up with Oliver. I'd had enough time to put a little space between what I'd seen with Dana and Jackson at Ski Club and my high-riding emotions. It was also another day that had gone by without Oliver and me discussing Richard Cochran.

My disappointment was palpable when I found Oliver's chair—the one next to mine—empty. He was seated across the room instead, chatting it up with Noah and a couple other kids I recognized from the prior day's excursion. This was still going on? Oliver noticed me looking in his direction and waved me over, pointing to another vacant chair next to one of his new pals. I felt the pull to join him—maybe I'd like these other kids too—but it was waging a battle against my insecurity that was completely shocked Oliver would just abandon me like that. Before I could change my mind, the bell rang and Ms. Hansen sprang into action.

Ms. Hansen was a unique blend of classic California hippie breeziness and Rachel Maddow precision. Even her wardrobe blended the two, with her dark, thick-rimmed glasses offset by a diaphanous, dip-dyed scarf that almost swallowed her whole. A lot of kids liked her because she'd take any excuse to bring a snack. I liked her because she was smart. I guess the miniature Hershey's Special Dark didn't hurt either.

Her introduction to our new unit was interrupted by a shrill scratch on the loudspeakers. It was one of the office assistants calling down a list of a dozen or so students to the office. This was not terribly unusual in itself, but this was the third time it had happened that day. I didn't know all of the kids who had been named, but I knew enough of them to know they weren't all being called for more usual disciplinary reasons. In fact, the two previous lists had seemed particularly absent of the troublemakers who so frequently found themselves before the administration.

This one continued to follow suit. I winced, hoping my name wouldn't be included and sighing a breath of relief when it wasn't. Could it be Bar Tech up to something at the school again? My dad hadn't been asked to come to the school to perform blood tests, but he'd been obscuring his results as much as possible. If Bar Tech had grown tired with the inefficiency of their first attempt to track us down, had they doubled down their efforts on something more sinister? Of course, I was purely speculating, but you had to be careful when your top-secret superpower was on the line.

And I wasn't the only one who was curious. I heard a bit of chatter among my classmates, asking the same questions but with different possible answers. Was there a school prank no one had heard about yet? A bust on a large-scale exchange of Ritalin? An outbreak of lice? Those explanations sounded much more likely than a search for super-powered teenagers, but as one of those very kids hiding in plain sight in Bar Tech's company town, I knew better.

Ms. Hansen quieted our gossip, annoyed by the interruption to her meticulously planned class. What happened next wasn't exactly Ms. Hansen's fault per se, but I knew things were about to get ugly as soon as I heard one of high school's most dreaded pairings of words: "group project."

I instinctively turned to Oliver across the room. Thank God he was here. I couldn't imagine having to suffer through this with a stranger . . . until he dodged my eye contact and chose Noah instead. I had assumed working together would just be a formality, but I guess the time it took for me to make such a misguided assumption was more than enough for Oliver to change his mind. Great. I was so happy to know that a few hours at Ski Club had cemented them in a blood oath. I looked around the room, and everyone else seemed to have already fallen into partnerships as well. Suddenly, partnering with a stranger felt like a real possibility. I started to count my classmates. Was there an odd number? Nope, twenty-six even. I was pissed at Oliver for throwing me to wolves, but I'd still rather be his and Noah's third wheel than randomly paired up.

I locked gazes with the only other person in class without a partner. Chase Cochran's eyes lit up as I tried not to scowl. He crossed the room and casually dropped into what had formerly been Oliver's seat.

"Hey, partner," said Chase with a Cheshire-cat expression that almost suggested he was behind the whole thing.

I tried, but could muster only about half of a smile.

"Don't look so grim," he added. "You're going to hurt my feelings."

"Promise to work hard on this project?" I challenged him, throwing down the proverbial gauntlet.

"For you? Harder." Chase sobered up his smile and extended his pinky along with a stern expression.

"That doesn't include just writing your name at the top either," I added, in no mood to play cutesy with him. The temptation to see if he'd crossed his fingers behind his back was high.

"I promise," Chase vowed.

I smiled in spite of myself as we shook on it. Was this the Chase Cochran who'd pulled me up out of the snow and offered to give me a ski lesson? Or was it the one who'd gotten distracted and decided to chase other girls? I admitted, at least to myself, that he was a challenge in his unpredictability.

Dana caught me in the hall after class. Her usual solicitous self, she saddled up next to me like we'd actually spent time together on the field trip she'd forced me to go on. I took a deep breath, sensing my claws were already out and diamond sharp. To be fair, I reminded myself that I'd also avoided interacting with Dana on the trip at every possible turn.

"Nica, hey!" She fell into step next to me. I half expected her to try to link arms.

"Hey." She wasn't the least bit put off by my icy attitude.

She continued on with her usual small talk, which my ears were already buffering into a monotone droning. I snapped out of it when she pointed down the hall at Oliver and Noah.

She leaned in to my ear, keeping her voice out of earshot for anyone passing by.

"You think Ollie's into him? I think they'd be really cute together."

Ollie? I was ready to strangle her until my brain caught up and processed the rest of Dana's words. Into Noah? What?

The revelation hit me in a series of waves. Oliver never really talked about girls. I guess I'd just never given it much thought. Sure, I was more than willing to ruminate ad nauseam about Jackson, but some people were more private.

As soon as I saw Dana's face, I knew my entire internal process had just played out for her across mine. I recovered quickly, but it was obviously too late.

"Oh, no. I'm so sorry," she said with a look of mock concern. "I just assumed . . . I know you two are friends . . ."

Best friends, I corrected her internally. She continued to backpedal as I put more pieces together. I glanced back toward Oliver, but he and Noah were gone, already departed for class. How could he have shared something so personal with Dana before telling me?

I returned my focus to the girl in front of me. It was impossible to tell if she was secretly enjoying this. Dana pivoted, either finally taking pity on me or in an attempt to escape the awkwardness.

"I'm glad you had such a fun time at Ski Club yesterday.

I heard you might've had a little one-on-one time on the slopes with a certain blond football hottie . . ."

Her word choice launched a campaign of acid reflux. That said, though, I'd felt emotions at every stop on the spectrum for one Chase Cochran over the past few days. I couldn't admit it to Dana in a million years, but I enjoyed his seemingly relentless pursuit. It was usually charming just long enough for him to find a way to ruin it, often spectacularly.

"He did at least try." It was as much as I could allow myself to give her. I reminded myself, though, that it wasn't the first time Dana had not-too-subtly inquired about my romantic interest in Chase. If she could manipulate people, was she trying to manipulate me? Could it be possible that the sudden onslaught of flutters for Chase was a result of her somehow pushing me toward them?

"Would you say yes if he asked you out?" Dana was trying to be casual, but the hint of excitement in her voice made her preferred answer crystal clear.

"I don't know." I wasn't even sure myself, but making her happy was the last thing I wanted to do right now. "I should get to class."

"Yeah, me too," Dana agreed, but she was still glued to my side. "But I will say, I wouldn't be surprised to see the two of you a little more . . . friendly after another week or so."

A pop of a laugh erupted out of me at the idea. There

was not a chance in the world I'd ever go back to Ski Club. "Sorry . . ." My apology was a reflex. I wasn't actually sorry at all. "I'm glad I went"—another lie, I was really on a tear— "but I'm not sure Ski Club is for me."

"Oh, no!" It was like she'd just discovered her favorite cute animal was on the endangered-species list. "You have to come back." Her doe eyes were reaching anime levels.

I was actually surprised by how upset Dana looked. Had I misjudged her again?

"I know we didn't have a lot of time to hang out yesterday, but it will be different next time, Nica. One hundred percent more girl time. I promise."

Dana's sincerity hit me square in the stomach. I immediately felt bad for making fun of her, even if just to myself. Maybe Ski Club would be better if I gave it another shot. Oliver had obviously made the most of it. Maybe I just needed a little more practice.

I dug my heels in right there. Maybe I just needed a little more practice? Ski Club was miserable. I'd hated it. What was I thinking? I looked over at Dana, trying to keep the intense distrust off my face. Was she doing this to me?

"No," I said, as firmly as I could. "Thanks for the invite, but I don't think I'll be back."

Dana's face fell again. It was adorable and pouty, and I was beginning to see straight through it. I turned to head into fourth-period history class, but Jackson caught us right outside.

154

Leaning in to Jackson's shoulder like she needed the support to stand, Dana narced me out immediately. "Nica just told me she didn't have fun at Ski Club yesterday," she said, her mink lashes on overdrive. "I tried to convince her to give it another shot, but she's awfully stubborn. I'm so disappointed."

Dana gave me a little defeated wave and stumbled off like an ignored puppy. And Jackson looked like her overprotective owner. I didn't even want to deal with the guilt trip and tried to just ignore him and duck into class, but he blocked my way with his taller, broader frame. I took a few steps back, uncomfortable standing so close.

"What was that about?" His accusatory tone was both very clear and almost unprecedented.

"I don't know. Should I be apologizing that I agreed to go along on your stupid field trip and I didn't find my chi or inner peace or whatever everyone else apparently did?" I felt defensive and very much put on the spot.

"I knew it," he declared, bristling. "I knew you'd just agree to go and show up determined to have a miserable time."

"You do realize that sometimes people try things and don't actually like them?" I softened my tone, trying to diffuse the tension between us. "Maybe Dana shouldn't have presumed to know anything about me in the first place and, I don't know, maybe asked me before signing me up to go."

Our voices were rising with each block and jab. I could

feel the heat growing under my skin and eyes peering out our way from inside the classroom.

Jackson's fury wasn't having any trouble keeping pace. "Great, Nica. That's exactly what she needs. Another girl cutting her down with sarcastic, alienating bullshit."

"Right. Because Dana, queen of the school, is so emotionally fragile and desperate for friends," I snarled back. "And I just ruined her sweet and precious spirit by making her hear the word 'no' for once."

"Are you hearing yourself?" He just shook his head.

I knew I'd gone too far, but there was no way to take back what I'd said. I was angry with Dana, but the way Jackson looked at me was a million times worse. "Jackson . . ." I wanted to apologize, to backpedal, to admit my own envy and insecurities, but he'd heard enough already.

"I thought you, of all people, would be sympathetic to what she's going through. Dana's a great person. I've known her my whole life." He let the implication hang: I've known you for only a few months. "Dana is thoughtful, honest, and kind. You might not know her very well yet, but she wants to know you. She wants everyone to be friends, and if you can't even get over yourself long enough to just try . . . I don't think we can be friends either."

Jackson's ultimatum hung in the air as he ducked into class. He couldn't get away from me fast enough. Following him was the last thing I wanted to do, but the bell rang and forced my hand. I shuffled in, head down. I knew everyone was watching us, whispering. Oliver had abandoned me, apparently finding better friends in out-of-left-field Noah and Dana. And Jackson had dressed me down in front of everyone. Defending his perfect girlfriend's honor, no less. I wanted to go home.

I wasn't even certain that home would be far enough. I fantasized about heading to the airport and catching the next flight to LAX, then on to South America's biggest hub: São Paulo's Guarulhos International Airport. Then a smaller plane would carry me to Tierra del Fuego, the large island tip of Argentina. I'd have to spend a night or two, at least enough time to ride the Austral Fueguino, and then I'd board a ship in Ushuaia headed straight for Lydia. She'd be surprised to see me, sure, but I'd be in Antarctica—as far away from Barrington as I could get. How could she refuse me?

My due-south escape plan was interrupted by a now fourth group of names being called to the office. "Michelle Cabrini. Ted Bergevin. Nica Ashley." I didn't need a second push, gathering my things and heading straight out of the classroom.

The more distance I put between Jackson and myself, the more my marathoning heartbeat could slow to a jog. But, I realized as I approached the office, I was just replacing one problem with another.

I slipped into the office, reporting to the man running the

front desk. He told me to have a seat; Mr. Manning would be right with me. I did as requested, but realized as I picked up a magazine—I had no idea who Mr. Manning was.

I didn't have to wait long. A man in his thirties emerged from a back office, headed straight for me. He looked rather collegiate for an administrator, dressed in tailored flannel and dark denim. Only a well-manicured beard firmly separated him from the J.Crew-wearing student body.

"You must be Nica." He offered a hand to shake. "I'm Mr. Manning. The new guidance counselor."

He reminded me a lot my previous guidance counselor, Mrs. Henderson, who'd met with a suspiciously fatal car crash a few months earlier, when I'd first started looking for answers about my power and its connection to Bar Tech. Manning had a similar easiness and enthusiasm. But I had no interest in having any heart-to-hearts with him.

I tuned out a bit as he explained he was meeting one-on-one with all students to really get to know them as individuals. I hoped Manning's enthusiasm alone would carry me through the meeting, but he had to slow down and insist I actually contribute.

"I know it must be tough," he said, sufficiently empathetic. "Trying to join a social structure that's been in place for most of these kids since before kindergarten. But I'm an inviter, Nica. Do you know what that means?"

On a literal level, yes. You are the one who invites. But,

no, I have no idea what in the New Age hell you're talking about. Luckily, he answered for me.

"It means I invite you to view all this as a positive, productive challenge. I invite you to stand out. Don't feel like you have to blend in. Sometimes happiness can only come by embracing who you are and accepting where you stand. Fully. In front of everyone."

I didn't like the sound of that. He leaned forward to impress one last piece of advice, which chilled me to the bone:

"Follow Dana Fox's lead. That girl's got a good head on her shoulders."

The end of school couldn't come soon enough. I tore out of there as fast as I could. Head down, sunglasses on, hood up, earbuds in. It was the closest I got to disappearing without actually using my power. It was particularly cold that day, but even as the wind ate through several layers of down, I was just thrilled to be outside. Outside and alone.

Halfway through town, I passed Ebinger's and had a strong urge for chocolate. I desperately wanted to inhale their latest concoction, but not at the risk of running into Noah. Or Oliver. Peering in the window, I could see that the place was dead. An older couple occupied the only table in use, and Topher manned the counter, staring off again into a horizon of boredom. My stomach growled wantonly. I decided it was safe enough.

Topher didn't snap out of his way-off stare until I was directly in front of him, only half a dozen inches from nose to nose.

"Hi, Nica!" He booted to life. "Sorry. Sometimes when it gets really slow here, I just . . . go somewhere else."

"I know the feeling all too well," I replied, trying to swallow back all my sadness and fear.

"What can I get you?"

"I'll take one of whatever that smell is."

Topher nodded knowingly. "Today's special. Mayan hot chocolate with mini churros."

"Sold."

Topher continued to make small talk as he poured my drink. "Normally Noah and I work the same shift, which really helps to pass the time, but he changed his schedule so he could go to Ski Club."

"Again? Already?"

"I guess so. Might've just been some kids caravanning up." Topher shrugged it off, but it was clearly a sore spot.

I carried my treats to a corner table, keeping my distance from the bakery's other patrons. I dunked one of the mini churros right into the spicy hot cocoa. Drowning my sorrows had never been so delicious.

When the bell over the door chimed, I winced with anticipation. Misery had a way of finding me today, and if it walked inside right now, I was ready to take my spoils and run. I was strangely relieved when I saw that it was Chase. He noticed me and nodded a hello but headed to the counter. I felt a little miffed, but there was no way I was about to be desperate for his attention the minute he eased up his full-court press.

As he ordered, I couldn't help but wonder if he would just take his snack to go or if I was about to have some company. Before long I was squirming in my seat with nerves. What was going on? Had I been protesting a complete lack of interest in Chase a little too hard? I wondered if maybe this was Dana's influence or if maybe she was a convenient scapegoat. I hadn't gotten any closer to proof as to whether she was wielding any care-of-Bar-Tech psychic powers.

Chase walked over but didn't take the seat across from me. "Want some company? I don't want to interrupt if you're enjoying some 'me' time."

Maybe my defenses were down, but I was impressed with his restraint. In fact, I was kind of into it. "Sure. Go ahead."

When he sat down, I could see that he'd also ordered the special.

"Great minds." I raised my cup, throwing him a bone.

"Nah. I just told him I'd have what you were having," Chase admitted with a sly smile. "I've always wanted to say that. Besides, who could say no to adult Dunkaroos?"

I laughed. Not a conversational laugh or a put-on laugh or a "Hey, he's cute" laugh. Chase had just genuinely surprised me, and I could feel the stress of the day fading away.

He pushed his plate of churros into the middle of the table to share. "Don't worry; we can always get more."

For once, Chase was right. For the next hour or so, we talked and laughed and polished off a few too many mini churros. When he offered me a ride home, I accepted, happy to spend a little more time with him. As I navigated him to my house, listening to one of my favorite albums, which I'd stumbled upon in his recent playlists, I found myself in complete awe. Who would've guessed that Chase Cochran would be the best part of my terrible day? When we pulled to curb, there was something in the air. I could feel the inevitable; we were going to kiss. And I wanted to. It was the perfect seal to a completely unexpected afternoon, and I savored the ease. No sweaty palms, no butterflies. It was something new, I told myself as I climbed out of the SUV.

And maybe something good.

13. INVISIBLE DAY

I sat in a cold wicker chair on Oliver's quaint front porch, my foot vibrating like a nervous rabbit's hind leg. It was the only thing making a sound in the otherwise picture-perfect and totally quiet afternoon. Well, maybe not the only thing. From somewhere down the street, my ears caught the sounds of happy children pegging one another with snowballs. A fresh powder had fallen to Barrington's streets, and since the plows hadn't come through yet, the town had temporarily taken on the appearance of a perfect, sparkling snow globe.

I leaned forward in an attempt to apply pressure to my toes. I wanted silence. I wanted to appreciate the winter tableau for all its frigid serenity. After all, this was the carrot to Bar Tech's security stick, right? This display worthy of a Norman Rockwell painting is what every family in town was beaming at from their window as they congratulated themselves on choosing such a nice place to raise their kids and cruise into old age. I wanted to try to understand it, to let it bring a smile to my face, but all I could muster was a sigh. Was it really that easy to get people to accept the presence of a massive, invasive security force in their lives? Was peace and quiet so hard to find in the world? Was it really that revered? Even the families in Barrington with no connection to Bar Tech (especially those families) should know that they're living on the verge of *1984* in 2015.

Maybe the problem was that none of it seemed strange anymore. It was possible that adding a couple of patrol cars and stone-faced security men to the mix didn't even faze people anymore. What were they, other than the personification of the security and surveillance culture we read about on the Internet and see on TV? And what was that, other than a scandal that most people choose to ignore and live with? The problem wasn't that Barrington found itself out of step with the rest of the world. It was that the rest of the world was just catching up with Barrington.

Yet I still desperately wanted to feel the comfort that seemed to permeate the streets. It was no fun feeling like the last person on earth who had any sense or could see what was happening. Maybe the pulse could give me the power of ignorance next time, or at least a false sense of security.

I scanned the street for any sign of life, but with the exception of the occasional Bar Tech vehicle, it was quiet.

Dammit, Oliver. Where are you?

To be fair, he didn't know he was late. He had no way of knowing, because I hadn't told him I was going to be waiting on his porch when he came home. Things had been so weird lately that I didn't want him to try to avoid me, and the only way to force the issue was to drop in unannounced. I felt a little crazy, like a jealous wife waiting for her husband to come home from whatever dark bar or strange bed he'd spent the day in. Then again, "crazy" is a sliding scale, and the events of late were threating to slide right off the edge.

It seemed like every day this week brought with it some new complication, and while each new wrinkle was very exciting, every day brought me closer to "over it." Feelings for Chase, shade from Dana, and cracks slowly splintering my friendship with Oliver? Nope. No thanks. I was so ready to be done. I'm not a paranoid person by nature, but between my mystery contact and the reality-distortion field that Dana seemed able to summon at will, I wondered just how deep the rabbit hole went. At the moment, it felt bottomless.

The sun was beginning to set and my foot started tapping again. To calm my nerves and reawaken my legs, which were starting to numb in the winter air, I got up and started to pace. Oliver's mother would probably be home soon. I wanted to be gone when she arrived. Between the fact that she and I had never spoken after the accident, along with the conversation I was planning to have with Oliver, I was afraid that the mood might be more than a little sour. Considering how heated things had gotten in the car right before the crash, I was looking forward to reintroducing myself under much friendlier circumstances.

I didn't recognize the car that eventually pulled up. It was a small green thing, an oversized TicTac—a starter compact for a new driver. Was it possible Oliver had suddenly gotten a car? Or did this belong to someone else? I squinted to make out who was in the driver's seat. The bright winter sun prevented any definite ID, but it looked enough like Noah that I grumbled. Friend jealousy, I guess. I never thought romance would come between the two of us.

I hung at the far edge of the porch as Oliver stepped out and waved to the driver. I was trying to keep myself just out of sight. I didn't want to pounce melodramatically, but if Oliver stepped out of the car, I didn't want him to spot me and decide to get back in. I wasn't going to give him a chance to avoid me. His feet crunched over the fresh snow and I started—for just a second—to relish the fact that I was about to let him know exactly how I felt. Up the three small steps and to the lock. He pulled out his key, slipped it into the tumbler—

—and I walked straight into his peripheral vision.

"Why would you tell Dana?"

"Nica!" His eyes bugged out and the keys chimed against one another as they fell to the floor.

"Why didn't you tell me about Noah? You know I wouldn't care."

"Really?" He picked up the keys and then unlocked the door.

"Of course not, Oliver. You're my best friend. I love you for who you are, and I'd never question that."

"You know who I am? I'm Richard Cochran's son," Oliver declared, throwing me an unexpected curveball. "Where's the love for that?"

"That's different," I replied, suddenly embarrassed and feeling defensive.

"Is it? To me it's a secret that shapes my life, and when I shared it with you, look what happened. You told me to forget it. That it was dangerous. Weird. Difficult."

He stepped closer to me. I'd planned to come here and give him a piece of my mind, but I'd read the situation wrong. He was unleashing on me.

"I asked you for help," he said, "and you left me hanging. Know why I told Dana everything? Because Dana wouldn't do that. She has my back and accepts all of me. She wouldn't assume that she could tell me what to do based on how she feels about something."

Oliver landed blow after blow, and I just stood there and took it.

"She would never tell me to avoid knowing my dad because of who he is, either. You won't even help me get what I need to introduce myself to him." Oliver let that hang in the air. I kept my face from showing it, but inside I was dying. I had no way of knowing how much of his loyalty to Dana was the result of her manipulation, how much of it was out of anger and spite toward me, and how much of it—possibly—was genuine. In the end, it didn't really matter. What mattered was that I was no longer his only confidant, and that put our secret in danger. Despite how much his words hurt, I had to dig for one more thing.

"Did you tell her who your dad is? Did you use his name?" I gritted my teeth as I waited for the answer. The last thing I needed was Oliver being opened like a cheap can and spilling his secrets all over Barrington because he'd been tricked into believing Dana had his best interests at mind. His eyes flared and he didn't answer. I could tell he was thinking it was none of my business, but I knew that deep down Oliver understood the stakes. There's no way he would've said anything. Right?

"No," he responded. "Of course not."

His answer echoed like a shot. I tried to relax. Even though Oliver had perfected lying to me, I had to hold on to the hope that he was telling the truth now. He stepped into his house.

"Is that it, Nica? We done?"

"I'm sorry." I felt awful and didn't know what else to say. It didn't matter. The door slammed in my face.

• • •

That night my dad could tell that I was in a foul mood, but I refused to open up and discuss my failure as Oliver's friend. He pressed me to confide in him. He was worried about Bar Tech's extended radio silence. I wanted to care at that moment, but my mind kept returning to my own shortcomings. How had I suddenly become the bad guy in all this?

I couldn't stand to see Oliver hurting, and it completely ruined me that I was the cause of this particular pain. He had hidden the deepest, truest parts of himself from me and revealed them to someone I didn't think it was possible to trust. There was no way I was going to let that stand.

By the time I arrived at school the next morning, my mind was made up. If Oliver needed to prove a genetic link between himself and Cochran, I wouldn't make him stoop to lifting Chase's jockstrap so he could gingerly try to comb stray hairs off of them. I could get exactly what he needed by employing my hidden talent without anyone being the wiser.

What good was having the power to disappear if I didn't use it to help my nearest friend?

I made sure to stand off to the side of the chaotic first-floor lockers, where no one could accidentally bump into me. I lurked among people like a ghost until I spotted a harried Chase loping down the hallway, barreling through the crowd. Dressed in a black turtleneck sweater, worn gray cords, and hiking boots, he'd come from swimming laps, part of his coma-recovery therapy, and was running late. As he quickly finished drying his thick mane of blond hair with the gym towel around his neck, I stepped so close to him I could smell the distinctive scent of chlorine and woodsy cologne emanating from his glistening skin. For a moment I forgot myself and just stood there drinking in his fresh smell. Until I remembered why I was there. I spotted a couple of flyaway strands and yanked them out by the roots. He'd never miss them.

Chase winced and obviously felt it pinch. But he quickly ran his fingers through his hair, combing out the tangles, then bolted off to class.

I waited a couple of moments until everyone scattered and the corridor was empty. Then I opened my locker, dropped Chase's hair in a ziplock Baggie, and sealed it shut so that Oliver could get it tested for DNA.

With my mission accomplished, I set off to the top floor to find my next target—Dana—when I caught a glimpse of someone out of the corner of my eye. I jumped, and immediately realized the figure wasn't exactly in the hallway with me. He was outside it. On the roof. My heart stopped. It was a student—sitting parallel to the third-floor-hall window. Not doing much of anything. He reminded me of a monk or yogi: at peace, letting the sunlight ripple across his face as he took calm, relaxed breaths.

Then the bell went off, and the kid turned toward the window.

It was Topher.

He couldn't see me, as I was still invisible. But what really threw me was the fact that he disappeared as he rose to his feet. I was shocked. I stumbled back from the window and almost tumbled down the stairs but grabbed the railing in time.

First Dana, now Topher. Maybe I was going crazy. It was either that, I thought as I sprinted down the hall, or there were other kids with powers waiting to be discovered. And what the hell could Topher do? Could he go invisible like me? Didn't seem like it, since he would've had to climb through a window to get back inside. That or somehow drop safely to the ground. It must be something else. Could he conceivably teleport? Just pop in and out of reality and move from one place to another? That seemed like a possibility. In my brave new world, teleportation was reasonable— just another Thursday morning at Barrington High.

It took me a few moments to pull myself together and refocus on what I needed to do next. I'd sort out the whole Topher-mystery thing later. In the meantime I had to get back on track.

Finding Dana was easy. I stopped by the cafeteria. She breezed through the doors first and headed straight for the salad bar. After arranging cucumbers, tomatoes, lettuce, and olives with precision, Dana cruised to a long table at the

171

center of the lunchroom, where she perched like a royal as she waited for her sycophants to gather. I wanted to expose her—reveal her for being a manipulative, mind-controlling snake in the grass.

I recognized the first kid who sat down at her table, a drama geek named Scott Bozeman. He was wearing what looked to be a hand-me-down Pink Floyd T-shirt. His black horned-rimmed hipster glasses, chunky black boots, and green canvas jacket tied the ensemble together and screamed "outsider." Not exactly the kind of kid I would've thought to be in Dana's entourage, but they seemed to be close. Laughs and jokes flew back and forth as a timid girl joined them, a true, buttoned-up nerdette. I'd seen her hanging around the quad with the mathletes, but it didn't matter where I'd seen her before. It mattered that I was seeing her now, in a social group that didn't seem to be hers.

Stoners, jocks, musicians, straight-A students, and borderline dropouts all brought their food over and took a seat. Waves and smiles surrounded Dana like all these kids had known her since preschool. I suppose it was possible that some of them had, but I'd never seen this particular social arrangement during lunch before. To a passive observer, it would appear that Dana was doing the impossible and bringing students together in ways that no one had ever been able to do before. Hell, that's how it appeared to me. The question was how? And why? Social lines never blurred like this at Barrington, and I doubted her new friends were all there for the conversation. Dana was up to something. I was sure of it.

For the rest of the day, I kept a safe distance behind my nemesis. If she could manipulate people through force of will, I wanted to see it. If she had a plan, I wanted to uncover it. But the strangest thing happened: nothing.

I spent hours at her side and might as well have been following Justin Bieber through the halls of a middle school. I didn't see any signs of the behavior I saw her engage in with Jackson. Not one person's face fell slack. No one seemed to slip into a trance. They all just seemed to love Dana. She didn't demand anyone do her bidding or suggest to anyone that they so much as change their mind about where to sit. I thought for sure she'd at least try to coerce a teacher into changing her grade on a test or homework assignment; but no, she already had all As.

The last bell of the day rang, and I was ready to go home. I was exhausted and defeated. Staying invisible as long as I had didn't seem dangerous, but I could feel my whole body throbbing. On top of that, I was faced with the fact that I might've jumped to conclusions about Dana. Maybe I was wrong. Maybe what I witnessed between her and Jackson wasn't the result of a mutant manipulation. A cruel voice in the back of my mind kept flogging the possibility that the look that came over Jackson's face had come from another place: love. That was not something I was ready to admit.

I made my way to the front doors of the school and waited for everyone to leave for the day. I'd reappear in the thrum and walk out with everyone, maybe catch Oliver if I were lucky, hand off the hair, and head home to sleep for as long as I possibly could.

The gym doors to my left burst open and Dana came storming out. A perpetually angry, diminutive woman with bright red lipstick and a blond pixie cut—head cheerleading coach, Tori Brewer—followed. She pointed a clipboard straight at Dana's back like a weapon.

"Dana Fox, I won't have truants on my squad!"

Dana spun to face the woman, hands aflutter with dramatic gestures.

"You," Dana sneered, "don't get to make my schedule."

"Nor do you make mine," snapped the coach. "You missed three practices in the past week, and I warned you each time. I don't know what else is so important, but you'll have plenty of time to pursue it now. You're suspended until further notice."

"That isn't fair!"

A huge smile slapped itself across my invisible cheeks. Go, Coach Brewer!

"What isn't fair is the way you leave your squad hanging. It's selfish."

At this Dana squared her jaw and strode back toward her

coach. It was so aggressive; I thought I was going to witness a fistfight. Instead, Dana just looked the woman straight in the eye.

"If you don't let me lead the squad, they will look like fools during the first basketball game of the season. I don't think you want that. I think you want me to be up front. I think you want me to lead. I think you want me to make you look good."

Coach Brewer stared into Dana's eyes. I saw her face slacken—just like Jackson's. After a second of silence that felt like an hour, the coach smiled and put a soft hand on Dana's shoulder.

"You're right," Coach Brewer replied, suddenly contrite. "We're lucky to have you. See you at the game."

"Thanks, Coach. Glad we cleared up this misunderstanding." Dana turned, and her smile faded into a cold mask of self-satisfaction as she joined a group of chattering girls coming around the corner. They welcomed her with hugs and whatever the gossip of the moment was, while Brewer skulked back into the gym looking like she'd just made the best decision of her life.

Nononono! What happened to "suspended"? What happened to "off the squad"? Dumb questions, all of them. It was impossible to deny this time. Deep in my gut, I had to admit that there was a small, small chance that Jackson meant what he said when I spied on him and Dana on the balcony of the lodge. Brewer, though? Never. Not in a million years. This was a woman who openly referred to her squad tryouts as the "Trail of Tears." She didn't give a shit what people thought. She wouldn't change her mind for the president of the United States.

But she had for Dana Fox. All it had taken was a look.

That afternoon, I found myself back on Oliver's porch for the second time in twenty-four hours. He had no idea what I'd done, and I had no idea how he'd respond. I was pretty sure he'd be thrilled, but after our fight, emotions were tough to predict. I clenched the hairs in a Baggie in my fist, ready to make another deal. Thirty seconds after I pressed the bell, the door opened. Oliver looked me up and down like I was trying to sell him something. Maybe I was.

"You sick?" he asked, arms crossed defensively.

"No. I—"

"Didn't see you at school today," he reminded me. "Thought you were sick."

"I was busy. You gonna let me in?" Didn't look likely. I was ready to leave and call the whole thing off when he stepped aside.

Oliver's room was wall-to-wall video games, science posters, and vintage Star Wars action figures. He closed the door and I tossed the Baggie on his desk. He didn't pick it up, and I could tell he was running through the ways this could be a joke.

"I screwed up," I said. "I owe you this."

"An empty bag pays all debts," he said dismissively. "Is that a Thai thing?"

"Would you just look at it?"

He snatched it up and held it to the light to check the contents. His eyes brightened as he realized—

"Where'd you get them?" He was incredulous.

"From the source."

Oliver turned around and smiled at me for the first time in weeks. Then he hugged me.

I accepted his embrace and held tight. Relieved. The turbulence of the past few days had taken its toll. I didn't want to lose my friends. Especially not Oliver.

Which, unfortunately, meant there was one more towering, important can of worms I was going to have to open.

"I just want you to promise me something."

"Anything." Oliver shrugged.

"Stay away from Dana." I knew I was in trouble before he answered. He didn't exactly recoil, but he definitely scoffed.

"Should I even ask why?" Oliver looked skeptical.

Too late now. Might as well tell him everything. I dug in and lowered my voice.

"Something is up with her, okay? The way she talks to people. She can change them, change their mind and control them or something. I saw it at the lodge with Jackson and today with Coach Brewer."

"You spied on her?" Oliver looked horrified. "That's how

you're using your power now? To spy on our friends?"

"Yeah, but—no! She might not be a friend, Oliver. That's my point. She's manipulating people. You should see who's sitting with her at lunch. Kids that I don't think know each other's names are suddenly best friends because of her."

"That. Sounds. Evil. I'll bring gasoline. You should grab some torches," Oliver declared with a heavy dose of sarcasm.

"It's not funny." I was desperate for him to believe me.

"It's hilarious that you're so jealous. But there are plenty of other guys out there."

"I'm not . . ." I decided I wouldn't lie. "Honest truth? I'm seething with jealousy. But this is more than that."

"What is it?" Oliver demanded an explanation. Proof. Which I didn't have.

"I can't explain it . . . ," I admitted.

"'Cause it doesn't exist. Listen to yourself, Nica! You're building a conspiracy out of nothing because she reclaimed her old boyfriend."

Hearing those words felt like someone filled my stomach with rocks and threw it into the ocean. It took everything I had to not run screaming from Oliver's house. That was the exact same thing Jackson had said the day before when we butted heads in the hallway. *Don't panic. Can't trust him. Stay calm. Don't let him know.*

Prove it. That echoed above everything. If Dana had somehow gotten to Oliver, there had to be a way I could confirm it. My palms started to sweat. Then it hit me:

"I don't doubt it. I just don't want to take the chance that people find out about . . . you know . . . what happened at her house."

Oliver scrunched his nose up at me. "What are you talking about? Her party? I think she knows about her own party."

That was all I needed to hear. I checked every blink, every wrinkle in my friend's confused face to be sure. It was all too clear: Oliver didn't remember the pulse. Dana must've gotten to him. I left him standing with the Baggie in his hands.

My phone buzzed as I was making my way down his front walk. I didn't even want to look at it. I figured it would be some apology or tell off from Oliver, and all I wanted to do was forget it. Our friendship had been the only thing I cared about since I moved to Barrington, and I was afraid I was going to ruin it. It buzzed again, and I instinctively pulled it from my pocket. But it wasn't from Oliver. It was the mystery texter.

"We need to meet. NOW."

14. NOW YOU SEE HIM . . .

Impatient, but knowing I was currently the Odeon Cinema's only customer, I surreptitiously checked my phone. It was a triple-check at this point, but I was definitely at the right address. I had no choice other than to watch as the previews began to play. Would I have to find clues spliced into the film reels? That felt a little excessive. I considered checking under the seats, but I wanted to save that for a last-ditch effort. Instinct told me I'd just end up with a lot of hardened gum.

Errrrrr-EEEEEEK. The whine of old cushion was undeniable as someone sat down directly behind me. Either my afternoon was about to get a whole lot creepier or my unknown informant had arrived in the flesh. I started to turn, hoping to catch a subtle peek, but a deep, gruff voice stopped me cold.

"Don't turn around."

My mystery texter was just inches behind me. And he was unquestionably male. I shivered as I felt his hot breath against the side of my ear.

"I know you've set your sights on Dana Fox," whispered the deep, resonant voice. "You're right not to trust her."

Finally, a confirmation. "What do you know about Dana?"

"I know she's backed up her parents' story, that she was staying with relatives back east to take a break from Barrington. It's a lie," he stated without equivocation.

"So, she really was missing?" I remembered the posters plastered all over town, every last tack and staple solely the work of Jackson's two hands.

"No. She never left."

Whoa. How was that even possible? Barrington was a small town. Where could she even hide? But then the answer was so obvious.

"Bar Tech," I muttered.

"They recruited Dana," he affirmed. "Trained her. And when she was ready, Bar Tech just bided their time until it was the perfect moment for Dana to reappear."

So it was true. Dana's return was a comforting pacifier in the wake of our Bar Tech heist and Maya's escape, lulling the town back into the complacency of the Safest Town in America.

"She's got the entire school under her sway. But why? They trained her . . . for what? How do you know this?" It was obvious to me that he wasn't telling me the whole story.

"All I know is Blackthorne. That's the key." He was emphatic.

"What the hell is that?" My heart raced. It was so hard to not turn around. I finally had an ally, a partner, and it was so unfair that I had no idea who he was.

"You'll have to figure that out, and quickly," he ordered. "I've been watching Dana. She's only getting more powerful."

"How am I supposed to do that? You're the one with all the information." Mystery Texter was supposed to be my source.

"I wish I could give you more," he replied with an intimation of apology. "Don't trust anyone."

"Thanks for the heads-up," I snapped back sarcastically. I turned around to finally see who my Deep-Throat contact was. He was already gone. My eyes scanned the back aisle, catching a shadowy silhouette slipping out of the theater.

The movie had already started—a lame eighties action thriller starring Arnold Schwarzenegger. There was no way I could sit through that for the next two hours. With ten bucks down the drain and a lot more questions than answers, I had to get out of there.

Outside, the sun had just slipped below the horizon. Even the quaint streets of Barrington looked ominous over the haze of twilight. Was it the moody combo of a smoky purple sky and sodium streetlights, or was it the hefty reminder I'd just been given, that Big Brother was always watching? Of course Dana's underground takeover wasn't her own doing. She was the lackey, not the boss villain. My heart ached. I wished I could talk to Oliver. If he weren't so brainwashed.

With the temperature taking a steep drop at sunset and curfew nearing, the streets were empty. Except for one figure, just across the street. He was leaning against an all-too-familiar black pick-up. It was Jackson, the picture of cool, just standing there. Watching me. It was hard to tell at this distance, but it felt like a challenge.

In my mind's eye, I imagined myself running across the street, right up to him. I wanted to spill my guts and tell him everything. I wanted to tell him about Dana, what she'd done to me and Oliver and how she was manipulating him. He was in danger and he didn't even know it. I wanted to tell him about the deep voice in the theater. Most of all, I wanted him to wrap his arms around me and promise that we would figure it out. That we would solve the mystery of Blackthorne together. It was the only relationship I knew with him: keeping each other's secrets.

As much as I wanted to go over to him, I couldn't override my cold, hard logic. The voice in my head, not the lovesick teenage girl but the mystery man in the theater, beckoned low: Don't trust anyone. And as much as I wanted to give Jackson that exception, that he was *someone* not *anyone*, I couldn't. I tore my eyes away and started walking. I just wanted to go home.

Apparently, Jackson had other ideas. I didn't look over my shoulder, but he was the only other person around. I could hear his footsteps. Jogging across the street, coming up behind me, getting closer . . .

"Nica."

I ignored him.

"Nica!"

I turned on my heel to face him, arms crossed over my chest. Sure, the stance was a little obvious, but I didn't want to talk to him. Might as well be clear about.

"Heard you've been spending a lot of time with Chase Cochran," he said, accusatory, like an overeager prosecutor.

I shrugged. "Making new friends seems to be the new craze. Thought I'd give it a whirl. That all?" I turned to go, but Jackson followed.

"Most people don't refer to their hookups as friends."

"We're not hooking up," I snapped back dismissively. "He's my partner in English."

"Oh, I see. I'm doing my Shakespeare project with Noah. Hasn't involved any making out at Ebinger's yet. Maybe I've just got something to look forward to." His tone was hostile, not like a guy drowning in love for the head cheerleader. It was undeniable. Jackson was jealous.

Was this Jackson's true self peeking out from behind the veil Dana had cast over him? It was wishful thinking, sure, but what else could it be? And maybe it made me a horrible person, but I was happy to see him, even if he was furious with me. It was real. And he cared a whole lot.

"You know what? We did kiss," I confessed, enjoying that the green-eyed jealousy monster was on the other foot for once. "It has nothing to do with you."

"He's an asshole, Nica," Jackson proclaimed. "He just goes after girls, like Maya, until they give him what he wants, and then he's gone. Out of their lives. Done."

I stared up into his eyes as I lit the fuse on my next rocket. "I already know how that feels."

It took everything I had to hold the stare—a steely gaze that I would not be the first to break. *You*, I screamed at him inside. *You had me and then you were gone.* The seconds were aeons, but he looked away.

I had won.

All too quickly, it was painful to have him back. Just this glimpse of the real boy I loved, passionate and alive again. But I knew this moment of clarity would be brief. He was just an escaped prisoner, soon to be reclaimed by the warden herself.

"I have to go." I was too tired now. Resigned. "I just don't have the time." As soon I turned my back on him for a second time, I knew he wouldn't follow. The tears were like fire against my frosted skin, each one fueling the long walk home.

Twenty minutes later, I found myself at the end of my own driveway. The one, singular desire I had was to go inside and let my dad take over with his favorite school-night routine. We'd talk about my day and then his, or at least what he considered safe to my limited security clearance. Then he'd feed me. From the window, I could see that he was hard at work on Mediterranean kabobs and homemade hummus, one of my favorites.

It just made me feel that much more guilty, because I had already made up my mind about what I needed to do. I became invisible, sneaking in through the garage and silently padding my way upstairs. I knew that if I didn't do it now, I might chicken out. But my emotions were high, and if I was going to break my dad's trust—go against the one request he had made absolute—I had to do it right now.

I slipped into his office, closing the door—my hand wrapped in my sleeve—right behind me. Spying on the good guys. It was a weird sensation. I knew the right way to do it. Plead my case to my dad, telling him everything I knew and all of my suspicions, and then see what he'd offer to share. But what I feared was most likely true: that my dad would choose to protect me above all else and whatever he might share would be too little, too late. If my dad knew anything about Blackthorne, I needed to know now. The deep voice at the theater had impressed upon me that time was of the essence, and that meant slicing through red tape. Even if that red tape was my dad, secret agent for the Department of Defense.

I pivoted toward Marcus's vault of a filing cabinet. I didn't know where he kept the key, but I had a hunch that I could get a preview of its secrets with just my bare hands.

I leaned over the cabinet and pressed flesh to metal. Immediately, my invisibility transferred to the steel exterior. Jackpot. It was still locked, but I could see the clearly marked tabs of every precisely arranged hanging folder. The first few were incomprehensible to me—words, numbers, places I held no associations to—but about halfway back I had to hold my breath. They were names of my classmates. And judging from those included in their company—Jackson Winters, Oliver Monsalves, Maya Bartoli—they were students who had passed my father's blood test with flying colors. Or failed miserably, depending on which way you looked at it. There must have been almost two dozen. It had been here all along—a neat catalog of every superpowered student at Barrington High.

Another name stood out as I poured over them—Topher Hansen. But he seemed like an odd man out. I knew I was circling something with the remaining kids, some commonality. It all came together when I realized the name that was missing: Dana Fox. Excluding Topher and Maya, every kid in my dad's cabinet was a card-carrying member of Ski Club. This was it. This was the proof I'd been looking for.

The X-ray preview of the filing cabinet's treasures was suddenly insufficient. I needed to get inside, to comb through every last file for any mention of Blackthorne. But where was the key? I searched the room high and low to see if it was tucked away in any possible nook or cranny, but I came up empty-handed. Resigned, I pulled two bobby pins out of my messy coif. It was a long shot, but I'd have to try it the old-fashioned way.

I wondered if Googling "how to pick a lock" put you on the government's radar, or if I needed to upgrade to bomb research before I'd make somebody's list. It was something I'd seen a million times in movies and on TV, but I had no clue how to actually do it. The lock gave way after only a few seconds of jiggling. It was a miracle, but considering the week I was having, it was more like the universe was just starting to make good on its debt. With the cabinet open, I was overwhelmed by the amount of content inside. It would take me hours to even speed read every confidential document from the NSA and Department of Defense, and my dad was already probably wondering when I would get home. He had just been slicing the vegetables when I got home, which gave me about another five minutes or so before he'd loaded the skewers.

Keeping my ears attuned for any sounds on the stairs, I started to scan the contents of every folder for one word, the only word. But page after page, document after document, there was nothing. About halfway through the first drawer, a shrill ring shattered my concentration. The landline was hooked up on my dad's desk, and he often fielded his calls in here. He never admitted it, but I assumed it was because it was the furthest from my earshot. I had to get out of here—

fast. Sliding the folders back to a close and giving them a once-over, I quickly closed the doors and slipped into the hallway just as Marcus reached the top of the stairs, taking them two by two.

I caught my breath, still invisible but propped against the wall, as he answered.

"Hello? Oh, Richard! Thank you for returning my call."

The smart thing to do was to take this opportunity to run downstairs and declare my "arrival," assuring my dad wouldn't find out about my invisible mission into his expressly forbidden private files. But Richard Cochran was on the line and he didn't know I was right outside the door. I had gone this far—eavesdropping was just the cherry on top.

After a series of not-so-pleasant pleasantries, my dad's one-sided conversation sounded a lot like a brush-off. My dad said he'd been trying to get Cochran on the phone for days. It made me feel terrible. Marcus's job, not at the hospital but working undercover for the Department of Defense and by association the NSA, had been made exponentially more difficult by my arrival in Barrington and subsequent top-secret mutant status. My dad had spent years penetrating Cochran's inner circle, but now he had an even bigger priority: me. My dad's determination to keep me safe was in direct conflict with his number-one mission from Cochran: finding my gifted peers and me.

"I understand that things are changing at Bar Tech, but

now isn't the time to be making rash decisions. I . . . No. No, sir."

I could hear the resignation in my father's voice. He was letting Cochran take this battle. I just hoped he had a long game.

"Yes. Good-bye."

Crap. I took off down the stairs as the phone clicked against the receiver. Weaving through the living room and kitchen, I slipped back into the garage to grab my backpack and coat, which I'd hidden for safekeeping. As I walked back inside, I shouted, "Hey, Dad!"

He gave me a hug as soon as I'd unloaded my bag and winter gear. I'd have never known he'd just gotten off a contentious phone call if I hadn't been there to overhear it. The man had a hell of a poker face. Trying out a lie of my own, I told him how excited I was about dinner, but in my mind I was still riffling through the files upstairs. Why those kids? Was it a coincidence they were all in Ski Club? Dana was recruiting them, but for what reason? And was that why she was so adamant that we become friends? Did Dana know about my power? Had Oliver or Jackson shared my secret? I wasn't ready to ponder the consequences of that bomb. I was stuck with not enough of the big picture.

The next day at school began with an intense sensation of déjà vu. It was the second day in row I'd arrived with a mission of greater importance than my own education. Despite my bigger goal (the ever-present "What is Blackthorne?"), I had made headway only in the Dana Fox mystery. The phantom at the theater had told me she was a trained Bar Tech recruit and I had betrayed my father's trust to discover that Dana was now recruiting superpowered kids of her own. While the how was clear—Dana had used her mesmerizing mind to relieve me of both of my friends—today I was determined to delve into the why.

I took a swing with the first Ski Club member I saw. *Grady Walters, you're up.* I caught up to him in the hallway, attempting my most charming smile. We didn't really know each other, but he was one of those sort of semipopular, sort-of-academic, second-string athletes who never quite excelled at any one thing.

"Grady! Hey!" He looked nervous. I reined it in. "I'm writing a guest article for the school blog about the resurgence of Ski Club. I was hoping you could answer a few questions for me."

Less nervous. "Sure."

I loved the nice kids. Unfortunately, that was about as far as I got. As I walked him to the music wing, I asked as many questions as I could think of that might give me just a glimpse of what was really going on, but was only met with sound bites of sunny skies and picket fences.

"Dana's great." Don't I know it.

"Ski Club has brought together a whole new friend group across different cliques." How sweet.

"I really feel like I've found myself."

Come on. This self-help-lingo bullshit was really starting to get on my nerves. But it would continue for the rest of the day. Every member I tracked down and cornered was thrilled to discuss their new favorite extracurricular activity. It was Jackson's and Oliver's identical responses on a much larger scale. They were an army of Stepford wives, parroting back exactly what Dana wanted the outside world to hear. I was almost impressed with how much control Dana had wielded over so many people in such little time. Maybe the girl deserved valedictorian as well. At the very least, she could probably talk herself into it.

I'd managed to avoid the queen bee herself for most of the day, but we shared last period World Cultures, and there was no way around it. Dana cemented that when she took the open seat right next to me. I wanted to play it cool. The longer Dana viewed me as a nuisance, not a threat, the better off I'd be.

Dana led with her usual sunshine and small talk. "Ready for the test? I've been hearing all day that it's brutal."

"Oh yeah?" I wasn't about to brag, but I'd been riding a pretty easy A in the course all year. Granted, I'd been to four more continents than Mr. Kile, but we had a silent understanding where I wouldn't correct him on his pronunciation if he didn't refer to me as "Barrington's own world traveler."

"I studied a little last night. I'll be fine," I said. Maybe it was a little braggy.

"I hope so. I heard you've had a renewed interested in Ski Club, but we can only take members on if they can keep their grades up." Dana's smile hadn't waned an ounce, but the hint of chill that entered her voice had me on high alert. A renewed interest in Ski Club? What was she talking about? I hadn't told anyone I wanted to go back to that emotional garbage dump.

Dana continued. "Junior year is just really important, with college applications right around the corner. Hate to see your GPA start to slip." The longer she went on, the more confused I felt. The bell announced the beginning of eighth period, and Mr. Kile dove right in, handing out the exam.

As I penciled in my name and the date at the top of the stapled pages, I couldn't stop thinking about what Dana had said. Her words about Ski Club and the unnecessary droning about my grades just repeated in my head. I tried to push past it, doing my best to concentrate on the multiple-choice questions in front of me. But with each question I answered, the next became more and more difficult. It wasn't the content itself. I knew the unit material inside and out. It was the actual words on the page. It was like being so tired that you can't stop your vision from splitting into two. By the time I reached the end of a question, I'd already forgotten how it had started.

When I glanced around the room, I could see that everyone around me was already on to the essay section. I checked the clock and almost fell out of my seat. We'd just started, but somehow there were only five minutes left. Then I saw it out of the corner of my eye. A languid grin turned up the side of Dana's mouth. She looked at me when she stood up to hand in her test and I knew. I knew that smile was just for me, and I couldn't think straight because of her.

Renewed interested in Ski Club. Hate to see your GPA start to slip. It had been a threat, a threat she'd immediately followed through on. Not because I wanted to go back to Whiteface, but because I had been talking to her minions. Of course they'd reported back and now Dana was marking her territory. She was flaunting her power and leaving me floundering. At least that was what my daily growing paranoia told me. I could hear the whispers already. Nica's losing it. Losing her friends, her grades, just completely losing her shit. It didn't matter if Dana had forced me to bomb the test or if it was just the stress getting to me. There would never be any proof. I scribbled in random answers for the remaining multiple-choice questions and handed the rest of the exam in blank.

I already had my bag slung over my shoulder and bolted from my chair the second the last bell sounded. I had to get away from Dana, and I couldn't stand to look Mr. Kile in the eye. Storming through the halls, I wanted to vanish and never come back. It had been bad enough to watching Dana manipulate Jackson and push Oliver away from me. But having her inside my head? It was too much. I couldn't be one of her puppets, but I was starting to realize just how high of a mountain I'd need to climb.

It took something truly strange to stop me dead in my tracks. By chance, I'd caught the most unlikely pairing out of the corner of my peripheral vision. At a table in the back of the library, Oliver and Chase were sitting and studying. Together. When I was sure they hadn't seen me, I slipped inside. Gliding into the empty stacks, I triple-checked my surroundings and then went invisible. It felt so easy now. Had Oliver asked for a sit-down? Was he going to tell Chase they were brothers? Or was this one of Dana's moves? Chase was one of the only people I had left to turn to. It would make sense for her to pull him out from under me. And who better to administer the poison than a jilted best friend? There was only one way to find out. Up on my tiptoes, I headed straight for them.

As I got closer, I could see they were surrounded with books and papers. My worry grew deeper. What if Chase wasn't Dana's latest target but rather her link to Bar Tech? Chase was Cochran's son; only months ago he'd been eager to turn over Maya, his own girlfriend. Here he was now in all of his baby-executive glory—practically a damn student ambassador!

This time, however, my internal tirade was paranoia. Closer yet, I was able to see the text on the strewn-about papers. It was chemistry homework.

"So, helium, neon, argon, krypton, xenon are all . . . ?" Oliver asked.

"Noble gases," Chase responded. I could tell he was a little excited to know the answer.

"And what makes them special?"

"They all have eight electrons."

"Which means . . . ?" Oliver looked at Chase, expectant.

"They're stable?" Chase thought about it another moment. "Inert."

I felt like a jerk. Oliver was Chase's tutor.

"Well, okay. I think that does it for today." As Oliver called their session to an end, the visage of teacher and devoted student fell to reveal two teens not quite comfortable with each other.

"Uh, thanks. My dad said he'd have a check for you at the end of the week. I'll bring it to school on Friday."

"I don't mind picking it up at your house, if that's easier. It's on my way." It was obvious to me how eager Oliver was to go to the Cochrans', but I doubted Chase could see it too.

"I thought you lived closer to downtown," said Chase. Either way, Oliver was caught.

"I do. I'm just over there . . . a lot. You know, friends."

They sat awkwardly for another second. "Hey," started Oliver. "Can I ask you something kind of weird?"

Chase was clearly thrown off guard by the request. "Uh, sure?"

"You're an only child, right?"

No, no, no. Don't go there, Oliver.

"Yeah, dude."

"Me too. I was just wondering . . . do you ever wonder what it would feel like to have a brother or a sister or something?"

Oh, Christ, Oliver. That is not smooth. He was lucky that Chase wasn't the sharpest observer of human behavior and the implication went right over his head. He just laughed.

"It could happen. My dad's always threatening to marry someone younger. Probably kind of weird, but I'd get used to it."

"Yeah, probably," Oliver said with a hint of sadness.

I winced through another thirty seconds of awkward silence until Oliver finally got up and left. As soon as he was out of sight, I doubled back into the stacks to go visible again. Safely reappeared but still out of sight, I fluffed my hair a little and smeared on some quick lip gloss. I didn't want to stop to think about what it meant, but I knew I cared about how I looked in front of Chase.

"Nica! Hey!" He was packing up but looked happy to see me. I leaned over his study materials.

"Chemistry, huh?"

"Yeah . . ." He shifted his weight, a little reluctant to talk about it. "My dad hired me a tutor. I thought I'd be able to blow him off after a couple sessions, but your pal Oliver is persistent."

I wanted to know more, if only to hear if Oliver had made it all the way to Cochran Senior yet. "Why the sudden interest in academics?" Heaven help me if he repeated any of Dana's "junior year" jargon.

"I wanted to impress you." Chase could only hold it deadpan for a few seconds. "My dad insisted that I get my grades up. Said they need to be strong enough that I can get into any private school without too much elbow grease."

"Are you moving?" I asked, genuinely surprised. Bar Tech was headquartered in Barrington. Why would its CEO be going anywhere?

"Honestly, I don't know. My dad can be an impulsive guy. He says we always have to be ready, because he never knows where Bar Tech is going to take him next. Probably gives the same speech to his employees." He said it like a joke, but there was more pain under the comment than humor. He pushed it off with a rakish grin. "Glad to know you'd miss me, though."

The temptation was strong to flirt back and indulge for just five minutes, but my brain and hormones were battling it out. My brain won out. I was too busy shuffling the puzzle pieces to maintain a witty repartee. Where could Bar Tech even move to?

"Of course I would." It was true, the best that I could give him. "I have to get home. A lot of homework." A lame excuse, but the only one I could toss over my shoulder as I waved good-bye. I wasn't sure if my father was ready to talk, but I was running out of options.

On the way home, I assessed my situation. Dana was clearly growing more powerful, or at least starting to seriously target me. It's possible she was just great at mind games, but I suspected it was much more than that. Blanking on the entire test was like forgetting how to tie my shoes. Even accounting for nerves and stress, it was unlikely I'd loop them together and trip that hard. In the midst of my analyzing, I passed Ebinger's. I walked straight by it at first, but my mind took a hard left turn. I had to bring up what I saw at school with Topher—had to—if only to balance out the friends I was losing and the secrets that were slipping into the shadows. I returned to Ebinger's door.

There was Topher, daydreaming as always. The bell announced me and snapped him out of it, but it was a little too late. This time he couldn't cover up the fact that he'd been caught.

"Oh, uh, hey, Nica. What can I get you?"

"Got a minute?" I asked, cutting right to the chase. He gestured to the other kid on staff that he needed a break and started to come around to the front of the counter. I shook my head. "Out back."

We ducked through the kitchen and through a ratty screen door into an alleyway. If there were ever an appropriate place to talk secrets, this was it.

"I want to talk about the pulse."

Topher's face twisted into a scowl. I kept talking before I lost him.

"I saw you. On the roof. I know what you can do."

"You have no idea what you're talking about." His face flashed fear.

"I do! Look . . ." For maximum effect, and to demonstrate my control, I let my invisibility ripple down my entire body. It was foolish, showing off so cavalierly, but I had to stun him or I risked never getting him to talk. Topher's jaw dropped. "Please don't lie to me," I begged. "We need to have each other's backs."

"I won't lie: You sound crazy." He backed away from me.

"Topher! Come on!"

"I don't know what the hell is wrong with you, or what fucking prank you're playing, but I don't want to be a part of it."

"You're already part of it. You have to accept that."

"Get outta here, Nica," he ordered, face reddening.

"I saw you vanish right off the roof."

He opened the back door and tried to make a quick exit, but I grabbed his arm and pulled him back out.

"Please." I stared right at him, my desperation never more apparent than at that moment.

"Leave, Nica. Be careful. They're watching you."

Slam. And he was gone.

They're watching me? Who the hell was he talking about?

I turned to see a shape at the end of the alleyway. Jackson.

"Hey!" I shouted. It was part accusation, part epithet. Of course, the slinking coward turned and ran. But I wasn't about to let him get away.

15. TRUST NO ONE

This was Dana's fault. I knew it with all my heart and soul. As I marched across the pavement to confront Jackson about it, I became a self-righteous missile. They wanted to play dirty, huh? They wanted to break up relationships and shatter trust. For what, Dana's ego? So she could comfortably rule the school like the dictator of her own small country?

So much for wanting everyone to be friends.

I caught up to him as quickly as I could.

"Jackson!" I shouted. I was determined for this to end here and now. I sprinted to the end of the alleyway, dodging the trash cans and boxes that sloped down from the solid brick walls. I burst from the end of the alley and swiveled right, the same direction I'd seen Jackson head, but he was already gone. How? Could he fly now? Had Dana picked him up in an invisible car?

Okay, probably not that one. But I wasn't ready to rule anything out.

I saw his truck sitting across the street. The windows

were tinted enough that we couldn't make eye contact, but I could spot him behind the wheel, his broad shoulders leaning forward as he cranked the engine. The car roared with the horsepower trapped beneath its hood, and for once—maybe the first time—the sound didn't excite me. Now all I heard was a taunt: "You'll never catch me."

If I had Oliver's speed, things would've been different. I would've crossed the street in less than a second and stood in front of the car. I'd have made him choose between running me over or getting away like he clearly wanted. I'd have made him tell me what was happening.

My heart pounded at the thought, but it was just a fantasy. I was no Oliver. Jackson sped the wrong way down a one-way street and blew through a stop sign. He broke at least three traffic laws before he disappeared around a corner, but conveniently, no one was around to even take down his license plate number.

I trudged home. At least my dad would understand.

"Nica, don't lie to me!" My dad was shouting before I was even through the door.

It was tough to get me to cry. It wasn't even a matter of provoking the emotions that would normally result in tears; it was mostly that the energy expended crying was never worth it so I always held it back. I didn't find it to be a release. It gave me a headache and left me drained. This was different, though. The tears came down my face slowly at first, but began to rush as the depth of the shit I was in became more and more clear with every extra kick in my dad's volume. I'd been broadsided by a mistake—a disaster of an oversight. In my haste to get to the truth, I had shattered something between my father and me: trust. And all it took was a bobby pin.

I had no idea what was wrong. I certainly wasn't expecting Marcus to be full of quiet, angry fury. I'd planned on spilling my guts, but only because I wanted to, not because he demanded it. The evening I'd been imagining unfolded gently, starting with him asking me what was wrong. I'd try to figure out where to start, and he'd tell me it was okay, to start at the beginning. Tell him everything. As the events of the past few days spilled out, he'd pull me close and tell me everything would be okay. We'd get to the bottom of it. Together.

But he seemed so angry that rational talk wasn't likely.

He shook his head in disappointment. "You went behind my back."

"What are you talking about?" I asked, truly mystified at first. The words had barely dropped from my mouth when I realized exactly what he was talking about. He knew. Somehow he'd figured out that I'd gone through his files.

"There was one thing—one thing—that I didn't want you knowing, Nica. I told you about me, and Cochran, and my work for the government because those were things that

I decided were okay for you to know. They were important and they were necessary."

Okay, think fast, girl. Maybe he's bluffing. Maybe he just suspects you went through his files and he wants you to confess. Don't give that to him. Play dumb.

"Dad, I have no idea—"

"Who taught you how to lie?" he asked, more sad than angry. "It wasn't me. It wasn't your mother."

I wanted to answer him and shout back: Fear. Life. Bar Tech. But sarcasm didn't seem the right route at the moment.

"You've got such a good poker face, Nica. That's what's really scary. I believed you all the time. I wanted to. But I can't anymore." They were harsh words to hear from your dad.

In my mind, I worked through my escapades from the night before. There's no way he saw me. That much I was certain of. I'd been so careful, so quiet. I saw each moment clearly as it played back for me—turning the cabinet invisible, checking the names on the folders, and picking the lock. It had gone so well. I paused my playback as I remembered slipping the folders back and leaving the room. Oh God.

I'd never checked to make sure the drawer locked when I closed it.

"Your bobby pin broke the lock. I found this jammed in the tumblers." He dropped the small, black, spherical tip onto his desk, like a physical period to his accusation.

And there I stood, unsure of how to respond. My friends were abandoning me, I'd lied to my dad, snuck behind his back, broken his trust, and I felt so alone. Sadness piled on top of frustration piled on top of anger. I couldn't hold them back and I couldn't control them. I didn't feel like there was anything I could control anymore. Everything around me seemed to be falling apart.

"I had to." I spit it out from clenched teeth, the only thing keeping the floodgates from splitting wide open.

"Had to?" He looked at me, shaking his head in disbelief.

It wasn't enough to acknowledge how broken things were. He was making me pick through the shards and hold each one up so I could explain why.

"It's the only way I can protect myself," I declared, feeling more vulnerable and lost than ever before.

"I can protect you," he replied, his anger and disappointment slowly softening. "All I want to do is protect you, but I can only do that if there are things you don't know. The minute you know is the minute you're a target, Nica. And now I can't trust you, either." His words were true. Maybe he couldn't trust me. But they connected to something inside me like a baseball to the crack of a bat.

I suddenly found myself on the offensive. "You can't trust me?" I cried, tears erupting. "You're the one hiding things. I snuck behind your back because there was no other way for me to get the information I needed. You don't think I can handle this situation, so you keep me in the dark. "

"Scarier things are lurking in the light," he responded lovingly.

"I didn't break into your files for fun, Dad. All I know is that you're a covert operative for the Defense Department. Are you NSA? Intelligence? Does anyone else know what's going on here?"

"There are leaks everywhere, Nica. Even in the NSA. The fewer people who know about me, the better for my cover. And the better for you."

It wasn't the full disclosure I was hoping for from my father, but it was a start. "Just as long as someone's watching out for you."

"Of course there is. Now tell me what's going on at school."

I took a deep breath. For all my high-minded rhetoric about how I tried to be honest and truthful with him, there was a lot I had to explain that he didn't know. Small things, little secrets that didn't mean much individually but added up to paint a large, dangerous picture. I wouldn't classify any of it as lying. In that light, I almost understood why my dad would hide things from me—pieces of the truth that didn't seem like information I should concern myself with. I can't say I wanted our relationship to continue that way, so I decided to lay everything on the table. Especially my suspicions about Dana.

"Ever since the pulse went off the night of Dana's party, our powers have stuck around," I finally admitted.

My dad pursed his lips and cocked his head. "Everyone's?"

I nodded. "Jackson conducts electricity. Oliver runs. Fast. Like, lightning fast." I knew I was betraying their secrets, but I also knew I had to trust my dad. I wanted to protect them.

"What do they have to do with Dana?" he pressed, anxious to know more.

"I think she has the power to control people's thoughts. That's why I had to see your files."

"Controlling people how?" My dad's mind was working overtime to process all this.

"The power of persuasion," I answered, the details sketchy. "Her group of friends has been expanding, drawing in kids from every clique and corner. None of them have anything in common except for the fact that they are all a part of Ski Club, which Dana organizes."

"She's recruiting them," he said.

"Her own personal army," I said, feeling the tension between us had finally dissipated. Connecting the dots of a mystery can do that—bring people together. As it had brought Oliver, Jackson, and me together not that long before. I decided to let loose the biggest secret of all. "You ever heard of 'Blackthorne'?"

My dad did a double take. "Where did you hear that name?" He looked scared—as scared as I'd ever seen.

"Someone's been texting me."

"Who?" he demanded, getting right in my face.

"I don't know who yet, but he's on the inside. My own personal Deep Throat. The only clue he's given me so far is 'Blackthorne.'"

"It's connected to Bar Tech," Dad confessed, barely able to fill in the blanks. "I've heard the name kicked around. The details are way, way above my security clearance. You think Dana's involved?"

"Maybe." I shrugged uncertainly. "It would make sense. She disappears, mysteriously returns, and then starts hanging out with superpowered kids—one of whom is her old boyfriend."

"Why haven't you joined them?" my father asked quizzically. His impassive expression indicated he sensed that I was still holding something back.

"I almost did." Dare I give him the real answer? The whole saga of Jackson and Oliver with all the gory details? I considered it for a second but realized I could sum it up—honestly—in a way that was much easier to understand. "I don't trust her," I stated plainly.

My dad nodded, accepting my explanation for the moment. "If you get close to her, do you think you might have a better shot at figuring out what's going on?"

"Yeah," I agreed, "but I also have a better shot at becoming a brainwashed soldier for her. What about Cochran? Any way you could get more on Blackthorne through him?"

Dad shook his head. "Cochran is playing things closer to his chest than ever. He's got his inner circle, and he's freezing me out."

This rang true with the conversation I'd overheard on the phone last night.

"I don't know if it means anything," I interjected, "but Chase mentioned something weird about how his family might move soon. Could be nothing, but it struck me as odd. Especially if something big is happening. Why would they leave in the middle of it?" My question hung in the air.

My dad responded. "Maybe we should take Cochran up on that old dinner invitation."

It was almost too easy. I'd nearly forgotten about our standing invitation to dinner at the Cochrans'. It had been extended by Chase's father months ago, back when I'd first arrived. At the time, I'd done everything I could to avoid going, but given the wall we'd hit, I realized it was time to accept.

Chase, of course, was thrilled to hear I'd be coming over and pressed his dad to say yes. After all, he'd been doing everything possible to get me to go out with him.

"A chaperoned date," he joked as he followed me through the hallway after lunch one day. "How romantic."

"Beggars can't be choosers," I snapped back, enjoying having the upper hand for once. At least it felt like I had it.

As we stood outside the Cochrans' main gate, waiting to be buzzed in with our flowers and wine, I tried to figure out how to frame this. Our trust was tenuous, and I didn't want my father to think I was hiding anything from him. Still, the situation with Chase was complicated. I couldn't say that, though—at least until I sorted out my own feelings about Jackson. Chase was so obviously wrong for me that I didn't even know how to begin explaining myself—other than I was utterly confused.

We rode silently through the off-putting gate up to the sleek modern house, where Richard Cochran was waiting to meet us with a handshake already extended.

"Marcus! Nica! I can't believe it's taken this long!" Cochran declared, giving me an unwelcome embrace. It was just a friendly greeting, but I already didn't trust the words coming out of his mouth. He was dressed way too nicely, to the point that it felt like a subtle power move.

Chase, clad in a tight T-shirt and skinny designer jeans, affectionately took my arm while Cochran shook my dad's hand.

"Come in," Cochran insisted as he hustled us into his grand foyer and beyond.

An array of fancy appetizers was out on the steel and glass coffee table. There was hummus, green and black olives, and a spread of exotic cheeses. Chase quickly cornered my dad over the Spanish goat cheese. As if my palms weren't sweaty enough from their man-to-man, I was also left alone, face-to-face, with Richard Cochran.

"So, Nica, how's school?" he asked innocently, like any other father might inquire. I tried to play it cool and pretend that the question wasn't loaded with a million ways I could tip him off to things he didn't know about my friends or me.

"Good. Chase and I have a project together—" My sentence ground to a halt as Oliver suddenly walked into the room.

Cochran couldn't have been happier to see him. "Oliver! I thought you'd left already."

Oliver just smiled, enjoying the look of shock on my face.

"No," he said. "Chase and I had just finished studying when the bell rang."

"Then stay for dinner!" Cochran said with a bright smile.

"Thanks, but I really can't." Oliver's refusal sounded pretty weak.

"Nonsense," Cochran retorted. "You're staying."

Cochran's insistence was so forceful and definitive that I had to wonder whether this accidental run-in hadn't all been neatly orchestrated.

What kind of game was Cochran playing? Whatever it was, Oliver was in. He agreed to eat with us. This night was already off the rails and careening for disaster. Maybe I never should've come. It was too late to change my mind though. The Cochrans' private chef whisked us into the baronial dining room. It was time to eat and time to dig for info.

The food was amazing: grilled Colorado leg of lamb, roasted-beet salad with arugula and pistachios, and risotto with pea tendrils. Truly, for as much as I distrusted most of the people around me, I couldn't say that the meal was anything less than a symphony in my mouth. My dad even looked the other way when I sampled some of the Napa pinot noir wine. I needed it to get through the stilted conversation, the small talk, and the tension of sitting at a table with my ex–best friend, my wannabe boyfriend, and my worst enemy. It could've been the alcohol's gauzy lens, but Cochran didn't really seem so bad when he wasn't strutting around as a money-grubbing, DNA-altering, corporate monster. He sounded just like any other dad as he boasted about Chase's achievements, how his grades were up this year, and how his future was bright.

Oliver chimed in a handful of times to compare the ways in which he was excelling too, and each time, Cochran beamed. Chase didn't seem as thrilled. There was an undercurrent of competition, and I had to wonder how aggressively Oliver was trying to ingratiate himself into this family. Was Oliver just trying to be part of the conversation? Or had he already told Cochran the truth? There was no way he'd already said something, right? When that particular bomb went off, it could take the entire family with it.

Besides a rundown of Chase's grades and accomplishments (I had no idea he'd almost received Student of the Month twice) that seemed to impress even my own father, there was very little useful information to be gained from dinner. I blamed myself. I'd worked every angle I could think of, short of standing on my chair and shouting that I knew someone in this room could tell me more about Blackthorne. I was hoping that maybe Dad and Cochran would load up on brandy over dessert and something might spill out, but otherwise I was ready to get going.

A caramel *budino* was presented for dessert, and I used the opportunity to take a breather. Excusing myself, I headed down Cochran's labyrinthine halls in search of a bathroom.

"To the right." I jumped at the sound of Oliver's voice and spun around to find him following me.

"And you just happened to be tutoring here tonight?"

"No. I planned this," he admitted quite baldly. "I wanted to be here as soon as Chase told me you were coming."

"Why?"

"I wanted you to realize Cochran's not the monster you think he is," declared Oliver.

This still felt so incredibly wrong, but by getting Chase's hair I'd given my implicit blessing to the whole thing.

"How long has Cochran known?" I asked.

"Since I started tutoring Chase a week ago. Once I told Cochran, he wanted to make sure he had a way to help support me."

"What about Chase?"

"You can tell him, I guess."

"I'm not getting in the middle of this." I shook my head, not wanting any part of this family drama.

"He'll figure it out eventually."

I was stunned by Oliver's uncharacteristic coldness. He was acting as if no one else would have feelings about any of this, as if he were the only person was mattered. In fact, he was acting—more than a little bit—like Dana. I felt queasy at the thought. Could she be involved in this as well? I knew she'd driven a wedge between Oliver and me, but could she have pushed him into Cochran's orbit? Could she be influencing Oliver right now?

"He doesn't know about . . . your power, does he?" I asked with trepidation.

Oliver couldn't lie to me. He didn't even try to hold back his grin.

My voice went quiet. My heart started to palpitate. I wanted to scream. "Why would you tell him?"

I expected a snarky, heartless answer, but instead Oliver seemed hurt. "He's my father, Nica."

"You're going to get us all rounded up and used as guinea pigs!" I warned, thrusting a nasty finger in his face. "This is

215

the man who's been responsible for what's happening. He's been using us as guinea pigs. God knows what else he has planned." I didn't feel safe anymore, not around my friend and definitely not in Cochran's house.

"You don't know what you're talking about," Oliver blurted back. "There's so much more."

My face registered confusion, and I was primed to ask another question when Chase interrupted.

"There you are! Dessert's almost gone."

"Actually, I've got to go," I said, leaving Oliver behind. Chase was rightly confused, but I hit him with a kiss on the cheek and it shut him up.

"Nica's leaving," he announced as I pulled him into the dining room with me.

"Sorry," I muttered. "I have a paper due tomorrow."

My dad read the fury in my eyes and knew to play along. Our good-byes were fast and polite. I felt bad leaving Chase hanging, but I pulled him aside and assured him this had nothing to do with him. I told him I'd see him at school.

The next time I saw him, my world would be in pieces.

School rolled around, and I dragged myself from class to class, sticking to the fringes where I was eking out my increasingly isolated existence. My goal was nothing more than to get through the day without getting my heart broken or spirit crushed by some new turn of events. I was closing in on freedom when I rounded a corner right into Dana Fox. She smirked, and I got the sense she'd been waiting for me.

"You shouldn't be so mean to Oliver." Dana's tone was so insistent and demanding that it sounded like a veiled threat or warning.

I tried to brush past her, but she stayed in my way. I tried to avoid her eyes. I didn't want a repeat of my history-test disaster. "I don't know what you're talking about."

"He said he saw you at Chase's last night and that you weren't very nice to him." Nothing escaped Dana. Clearly she knew all.

"I'm glad you're so concerned," I shot back, continuing on my way.

"If it's because of who his dad is . . ." She deliberately left it dangling, like a wayward participle.

I stopped in my tracks. "He told you." So much for not having my spirit crushed. It was like Oliver was determined for our secrets to get out—or at least to spread to the people who wanted to exploit us the most.

"Oliver's my best friend, Nica," Dana proclaimed. "We tell each other everything." It was said with a certain amount of unmitigated glee.

"That's adorable. Make sure to tell him Nica says 'Hi,' and 'How could you?'"

"Not everyone has a good relationship with their father," Dana remarked. "It's a very special thing, what you have. Let Oliver make his own decisions."

"Oh, that won't be a problem." I wasn't going to stand in Oliver's way any longer.

"And work on your empathy, Nica. You'll need it." Dana turned and shuffled off to her class, leaving me with an uneasy feeling that I hadn't heard the last of this.

I returned home to a front door hanging wide open. For a split second, I feared the worst: Bar Tech had come and taken my father. My characteristically quick walk turned to a trot and nearly a sprint as my mind processed the possibilities. When I hit the front step, I breathed a sigh of relief. My dad stepped out with two duffel bags. No one had taken him. No one had hurt him. He was safe after all.

"Dad!" It was a relief to see him. Dana could be a bitch, but there was the slightest sliver of truth to what she said. I didn't always appreciate my relationship with my father as much as I could.

He didn't even look at me. I should've known something was wrong the second I opened my mouth. Was he angry with me again? I followed him out to the driveway, where he was loading the bags into the back of his car.

"What are you doing with two duffel bags?"

"Sorry. Do I know you?" My dad asked with a perplexed expression.

The sound I made in reply was a mix between a laugh, a snort, and some granular *hoccck* in the back of my throat. The only appropriate response. In the span of a second, I went from assuming he was kidding to realizing he wasn't to checking myself. This was my house, right? And this man—I recognized him—he was my father, correct? I fell into a feedback loop and couldn't answer.

"Dad. It's me. Nica. Your daughter."

"I don't have a daughter." His eyes got wide as he eased his way to the driver's door, backing away from me like I had rabies.

Nothing—nothing—had prepared me for that moment. What could? Turning invisible for the first time wasn't even a comparison to the shock wave that hit me when he said that.

"Listen," he said, continuing to back away. "You look confused. Is there someone you want me to call, or . . . ?"

This was really happening. My own father had forgotten who I was. How was that possible? Had he hit his head? Not that I could see. Early Alzheimer's? I doubted it could happen so suddenly. It had to be Dana's fault. My rage boiled over into a gasp and a choked scream. She'd convinced him, controlled him, manipulated him into thinking I didn't exist. And where was he going? Where was she sending him? Would he ever come back?

I probably should've just gone invisible there and then. Let my amnesiac pseudo-dad figure out what happened later. Instead, I charged him, still insisting. I hadn't meant for it to seem crazy. I was literally throwing myself at him.

"Dad, please. You've got to remember me."

But he didn't remember. His brain had been wiped clean of me—the good and the bad. I was so sorry for breaking into his files, for breaking his trust, for breaking his heart. I hadn't meant to lie, I didn't want powers, and I didn't want things to end like this.

He just saw a whirling, weeping maniac and jumped in his car, cranking the engine. He rolled the window down. "Get the hell off my property or I'll call security."

I was stunned into silence. I didn't need that grief, so I backed away, apologizing. "But where are you going? What am I supposed to do?"

He stared at me, looking confused until the *waaaaahnk* of a Range Rover's horn in the distance broke it. The instant he turned to look at the car, I vanished. When he looked back, I was gone.

He didn't know it, but I was still standing in the doorway watching him as he sped off toward the unknown. Invisible to my own father.

· · ·

The rest of that night was a total blur. I didn't have anywhere else to go, so I thought staying in the house would be fine. Who knew where my dad was going? I was in a daze, alternating between tears and standing at the threshold of the front door, daring myself to slip into the night and go after Dana. My thoughts became dark and twisted. More than once I stared at the kitchen knives, jutting from their wooden block, and told myself to just take one. Bring it to Dana's. She'd never even know I was there. . . .

She didn't know who she was messing with.

As much as I wanted revenge, I also knew that I wasn't a monster. I reached out to Jackson and Oliver. Neither answered my calls or texts. Were they just avoiding me? I couldn't be certain. I tried reaching out to my mother, too, knowing that she was well out of Dana's grasp, but was met with an automated message informing me that extreme weather conditions had disrupted communications at the base. I had no one left to talk to. Dana had, essentially, iced me out of my own existence. In a cruel twist of fate, I'd truly become the invisible girl.

Night turned into day, grief turned into sleep, and I woke up to the bright morning sun and someone pounding on my front door. The incessant *thumpthumpthump* felt like it was smashing directly into my brain as I got up and stumbled down the stairs. I fumbled with the lock and paused. What if it was Bar Tech Security? I almost didn't care. Whoever it was, it was at least another human being, some kind of company. I figured I'd take my chances and opened the door.

My visitor was a girl about my age, but the sun hit her from behind and silhouetted her face. I couldn't see who it was until she stepped forward to give me a hug.

"Hey, girl. Miss me?"

It was Maya. She was back.

16. BREAKING IN

I poured a stream of hot, black coffee into a purple ceramic mug and handed it to Maya. She clutched it, happy for the warmth and the pick-me-up. I poured a second cup for myself, hoping that the caffeine would help me refocus. In the ten minutes since Maya had arrived, I'd begun to feel better. Less alone, at least. Her presence was comforting, familiar. In a way I felt like I was back at the beginning, just arriving in Barrington and being pulled from my loneliness by Maya's kind hands.

At first I hadn't even known what to say. When I'd answered the door, my moorings were loose. I had nothing to hold on to, and I felt the darkness closing in. The hug that she offered as soon as she stepped forward was so genuine and full of love that a spark lit deep within me. I didn't know how long it would stay aflame or if it would spread and catch and bring me back, but in that moment it was enough.

"Come in," I said, barely getting the words out. Maya

crossed the threshold and entered the house. I closed the door behind her and locked it. Neither of us knew what to say next.

"You look exhausted," she said, concern etched across her face.

Maya looked remarkably rested, at ease, and more beautiful than I'd remembered. She was a far cry from the terrified girl who'd left town in the middle of the night so long ago.

"I can't believe you're back." We stuttered over each other's words, each trying to be the first to explain, but got nowhere. She laughed. Then I laughed. Just a chuckle, but that little flame in my soul grew. I'd never been so happy to see anyone in my life.

I settled in kitty-corner to Maya at my kitchen table, ready to hear her story. "Okay," I said. "You first."

She sipped her coffee. "The first few weeks I stayed with my sister in Chicago. But people around the university began to talk and ask too many questions. So I thought it was best to keep on the move."

"You've been traveling all this time?"

"Mostly in the east," she admitted. "Trying to stay off the grid." She'd also taken the opportunity to strengthen her abilities during her self-imposed sabbatical.

"How," I asked, eager to hear if her methods were like mine, "did you even get your powers to stay around without the pulse to activate and reactivate them?"

"Exercise," she declared. "Not physical, but mental. By the time I hit the road, I already felt my telekinesis fading, but I was determined to hold on to it. I spent a lot of time practicing."

"I'm impressed," I said truthfully.

"Anger's a great motivator, Nica. All I could think about was how pissed I was at Bar Tech and Cochran and Chase. At having to leave Barrington—even if it was just for my own safety. And then rage at feeling my powers draining away. I'm one pissed-off chick."

"Glad you got in touch with your inner demon," I joked. This seemed to be the fuel Maya needed, the raw materials that she could burn to keep her strong. "Do you ever worry that it's dangerous?" I asked. "Using your emotions as a catalyst?"

She shook her head, defiant. "It's a release. Almost therapeutic."

I nodded, able to relate to that very feeling. How many times had my jealousy or anxiety resulted in a flutter of invisibility that I had to hope no one was witness to? The practice had helped me concentrate to get to the place where I could control it myself.

"You picked a helluva time to come back to all this shit," I joked.

"It was weird, but it was almost like I felt your anguish two thousand miles away. Drawing me back."

I spilled my guts out to Maya about every crazy thing

that had happened since she was gone, capping it off with Dana's miraculous return and the terrifying way Dana not only turned Jackson and Oliver against me but my own father as well. Luckily, no one knew Maya was back. This seemed to be my trump card, to be played very cautiously.

Maya wasn't surprised by what I recounted to her. What was most important was that she and I work together. Her intense emotions had pulled her back home without thinking about how dangerous it could be. The first thing she noticed was Bar Tech's pervasive presence near her house. Security wasn't heavy, per se, but there were enough agents afoot to raise a red flag.

"Will you go check it out?" Maya pleaded. "Without anybody knowing that you were there." She raised her perfectly arched right eyebrow.

"I will"—I leaned over and grabbed Maya's wrist—"if you help me with my dad."

Maya finished her coffee and started to spin the cup in a slow circle. "How?"

"I don't know exactly," I admitted, "but you're the only one I can trust. Dana doesn't know you're back, so I know you aren't under her control."

"How do I know you're not?" Maya shot back. "You're cooped up in this house. Your dad supposedly just walked away and left you alone. . . ."

I could see her growing nervous. We were both in a precarious position.

"Sorry," she said. "Maybe that was harsh. I don't doubt Dana's up to something, but I'm not just going to drift around Barrington waiting to get caught up in whatever it is. If we could fight back, that might be different."

"I'm not sure exactly how I've been able to dodge Dana's power and influence other than by my own sheer force of will," I explained. "From the moment she returned, I've suspected she wasn't telling the truth about where she'd been and what happened to her. Perhaps my doubt and mistrust protected me just enough from falling under her sway. I can't prove anything to you right now, but if you can trust me—for just, like, twenty-four hours—maybe I can."

"I don't know. . . ."

"Stay here and give me the day to find proof. If I can't, I won't hold it against you if you decide to just go under the radar again. But you and I might be the only ones who can stop Dana."

In my gut I knew that the other benefit of keeping Maya around was for her sheer power. Invisibility was amazing, but it wasn't a weapon. I was stealthy—and sure, I knew how to throw a punch—but I couldn't go up against a real enemy the way she could when she was unleashed.

Maya looked at me and nodded. "It's time we take those bitches down."

I didn't bother going to school that day. I couldn't be sure it was safe for me to walk the halls of Barrington High anymore. If Dana could get my dad to walk away, what else was she capable of? I didn't see the situation escalating to violence, but I didn't want to put myself in a situation where it was unavoidable. I had plenty of absences I could burn through before they would start to affect my future potential, and weighed against the possibility of Dana destroying my future, I'd choose absences time and time again.

Maya didn't stick around to talk. She didn't tell me where she was off to, but after settling in, she said she'd be back later. I assumed she was snooping around town. I could only hope that she meant it when she said she'd stay away from her parents' house. Her emotions were as fragile as they were volatile, and I was afraid she might do something regrettable if Bar Tech Security spotted her.

But at the moment—5:19 p.m., to be precise—that was all out of my hands. I was back in my father's office. I'd been here most of the day, going through every document and shred of paper in his files. Blackthorne came up nowhere. I couldn't find anything about any projects—private, public, or otherwise—with that name. I even did a computer search using my high school's account for a LexisNexis database.

If the mystery were an assignment, my teachers would be proud of how thorough my research was, but I'd still flunk without evidence or a conclusion. How hard I tried was not going to win me any points in this situation.

I tried to connect students' social network pages to e-mail addresses and then tried common passwords on the offhand chance anyone was dumb enough to use "password123" in the year 2014. No one was. The strangest piece of all was just that Dana had no online footprint. Her name came up in relation to her disappearance, but she had no Twitter, no Facebook, no Instagram, no Snapchat and no e-mail account that I could find. She was playing it smart. She knew that if someone like myself tried to link anyone to her, they'd follow the threads back to a gaping void. In Dana's world, all roads led to nothing.

I put my feet up on the desk and leaned back in my dad's office chair. It squeaked ever so slightly as I swiveled back and forth, my eyes searching for an answer. I didn't want to disappoint Maya, and I didn't want to disappoint the mystery texter. My back was completely to a wall. It was time to come up with something, and fast. What was I missing? What path had I not yet traveled? There had to be a clue I'd missed. With a hearty shove, I sent the chair spinning in a circle. Think, Nica. The small divots and imperfections in the ceiling blended to a blur, and when I closed my eyes, I saw a flash of pink.

I'd overlooked something. I snapped forward with a start. My brain knew it. I'd seen something and missed its significance. Pink. I stood up, my senses at the ready. I had to find it. I scoured over the desk and reopened the broken, unlocked cabinet. Didn't see anything remotely pink. I spun back around to the computer, the monitor . . . nothing. I got up and walked around to the other side of the desk, the side I would've faced walking into the room. There it was.

A pink pad of sticky notes.

I grabbed it and expected to find something written on the top piece of paper, but it was blank. Then I looked again: No, it wasn't. That's why I'd overlooked it the first time. Whatever my dad had written down, he'd peeled off and taken with him—but I could read the imprint of what he'd written on the chunk of pad he'd left behind. It was faint, but the top line clearly was one word that started off "BLAC" before the press of his pen became too light to make out. This same word appeared to end with "NE." My heart started to race. He'd discovered and written down something about Blackthorne? The next line down read . . .

Dammit. It was so hard to tell. Definitely a number. Looked like "37.510" followed by "98.333." What the hell did that mean? I fell back into the chair. Another wall. Maybe even completely unrelated. What if the word wasn't "Blackthorne"? What if it was but the numbers were from something else?

This was useless. I needed something more direct. It was Friday night. While I sat here struggling to put the most basic pieces together, there was an overnight trip for Ski Club Dana and all her friends would be gathered up on Whiteface, probably plotting against the entire town as they raced down the mountain and drank hot chocolate. As soon as I had that thought, I knew exactly what I had to do.

I had to go straight to the source. If this all revolved around the members of Ski Club, I'd have to go back.

This, I thought, arms wrapped around my body as I slouched my way up a slushy, icy service road, had somehow sounded much more heroic in my head. When I'd first been struck with my grand plan, I thought I'd just drive to Ski Club, go invisible, and see what I could see. In the space of a minute, I realized that wasn't going to work. First of all—no car. Hadn't helped my social life; wasn't helping now. On top of that, anyone I'd be comfortable enough to borrow a car from, like Oliver or Jackson, was no longer in my corner. What was I going to do, steal Oliver's mom's? I honestly considered it, but it was too much trouble. I couldn't very well bike to Whiteface, and—at almost six in the evening—the school's buses had long since taken the kids to their destination and were probably still up there, waiting to bring them back in the morning.

Probably.

I couldn't remember. Did they wait, or did they head back to the school and send a different driver to pick us up? School wasn't too far to walk, and it wouldn't hurt to find out. I decided that was my best play. I knew I couldn't wear layers, since only the stuff that touched my skin would stay invisible, so I threw on some sleek Under Armour that offered the best chance of keeping me warm and headed off into the dark, cold night. The only other thing I brought was a small GoPro camera I'd picked up overseas, so that I could record whatever I saw. One way or another, I was coming back from this trip with proof.

Out the office door I went and off to find Bus 18. Sitting on the cold cement floor for an hour and waiting for one of the drivers to open the doors to the bus was the worst. By the time I followed him on board, I was freezing and ready to call this whole adventure off. Luckily, he was a big fan of a heated bus and cranked it up well into the seventies. Not so luckily, he also turned out to be a reggae fan who really liked singing along.

I sat in the very back, doing my best to ignore the deluge of sharp upstrokes and lilting backbeats as I warmed up. What would I find up on Whiteface? Some horrible experiment? A plan to go to war with Barrington, using mutant teenagers as weapons? Or just a girl who was so lonely and desperate to be popular that she was willing to force her totally unaware peers into surrounding her with warmth, praise, and friendship?

I got so lost in thought that I didn't notice the bus had shot right past the turn it needed to take to start up the mountain. I didn't notice anything was off until the incline increased severely and the road got jarringly bumpy. I didn't remember this from my last trip up here. By now it was too dark to get a good look at where we were. I felt the same fear and loss of control that I'd experienced in planes jetting through rough air. All I wanted to do was get off, but that wasn't an option. I wasn't in a position to yell for the driver to stop. I just had to hang on and wait it out. The jolting road gave way to smoother terrain before long, though this new pavement was just as poorly lit. My neurons fired with new, unspeakable possibilities.

What if the driver knew what I was up to? He couldn't. What if this was a trap? Where was he taking me? It didn't make any sense. He couldn't know. There was no way. But the reality was that we were not on the road to Whiteface. We were headed somewhere else, much higher up the mountain. Finally, after what seemed like an eternity of driving into a craggy void, the bus slowed down and came to a stop. I tried to get any view out the window that would give me a sense of where we were. There had to be a house, a barn, something with at least a light on. There wasn't. I was in the middle of goddamn nowhere on a mountain in the middle of a freezing January night. And the driver was standing up, turning around. My blood froze. He cracked his neck to the side and looked like he was going to open his mouth to say something—but I was the only one there to say anything to. I braced to be caught.

"'Noooo woman, no cry. No woman, no cry . . .'," he crooned to no one in particular. I was so relieved I wanted to hug him. He wasn't a villain taking me deep into the woods to be eliminated; he was just a dude who liked to sing to himself. And his voice wasn't half bad. It still didn't explain where the hell we were, or why we were there. He didn't park on a desolate mountain pass to work on his Bob Marley. Then a radio chattered from the dash:

"One-eight, one-eight. Come in, one-eight."

The driver picked up a handset by the wheel and held it to his face. "Ah, this is one-eight. Go for one-eight."

"Cochran's predicting an eight-thirty release from the lodge. Copy?" He rolled his eyes and shook his head but adjusted his attitude before he rolled off a reply.

"Well, I ain't goin' nowhere else, so let 'em take their time."

The lodge? But we weren't anywhere near the—

Then it hit me. I could see it clearly in my mind's eye: the building I'd spotted from the lift. The one that Chase told me had been shut down. Bar Tech was still using it—or at least Dana was. Suddenly "Ski Club isn't just about skiing," was taking on a whole new meaning. I had to get off this bus. There were two options: yank the door handle and run out the front, or open the emergency door and escape from the back. Neither option was all that smooth, and both were likely to convince the driver that the bus was haunted by a furious poltergeist, but I had no choice.

I chose the one that seemed most cathartic and kicked open the emergency door. The alarm wailed, and the driver let out a gasp so sharp I feared for the health of his heart. There was no turning back now. I leaped into the darkness and circled the bus, looking for a way to the "lodge." There had to be something, even if it was perilous and dark. The vehicle's halogen headlamps illuminated a gravel path about ten feet from where we were parked that extended into the woods. It dropped off into black after just a few feet, but it was wide and straight enough that I could make out the edges with a little bit of squinting and some help from the moon. I was on my way.

Fifteen minutes later and I was still walking, shivering in my guts, with no building in sight. Had I been hasty? No, this path had to take me to wherever that voice had broadcast from. It was the only thing that—

CRUNCH! I stepped off the path and into six inches of snow. I yanked my foot back, but ice-cold jets of pain were shooting up my leg already.

"Shit!"

The path couldn't just dead-end in the woods. As I hopped on my less-freezing cold leg and tried to swat the remaining chunks of ice and snow that clung to the other, I saw light. I looked up. The path hadn't dead-ended; it just veered sharply to the right—and straight to the back of the concrete bunker. The "lodge." The very same one I'd expected to see. My body tingled from excitement now instead of just the cold. Every step closer was like ripping a layer off a mystery package, and I was desperate to know what was inside. Only one thing stopped me from charging right to the door:

Guards. Of course. Oh, but I was patient. I was a monk. I was ready to stand out in the cold on one leg until sunrise if it would reveal to me what was going on in this lodge, what was going on with Dana, and what was going on with Bar Tech's master plan. What might've been a few minutes felt like a second while the guard had a smoke. When he put it out under his boot, I knew I was going to have just the smallest of windows to follow him into the facility and only if he opened the door nice and wide.

He did.

I kept quiet and matched his pace as he clomped inside on heavy, black treads. Knocking them against the wall to get the snow from deep in the nooks and crannies only helped disguise the sound of my wet feet squeaking gently against the linoleum floor. I ditched the shadow game and held tight to a corner, taking in my surroundings. This place was nice. High ceilings, cool, relaxing blues and purples on the walls. It didn't even look like a lab, but more like a mix between a doctor's office and a spa. As my heart stopped pounding, I heard soft, coffeehouse music drifting quietly from speakers above my head. I blinked to make sure I wasn't hallucinating. I don't know what I was expecting, but this was downright surreal. I held close to the wall, trying to map the place in my mind as I moved deeper inside. I could hear what sounded like muffled shouting in the distance and followed it. Guards passed by, oblivious to my presence as I came to rest outside the doors of what looked like a high school gym. The sounds of a pitched battle—grunts, groans, shouts—echoed from within. What the hell was going on in there? Gladiatorial combat? I patiently waited for the doors to open so I could slip inside. It wasn't long before two female medical technicians in white answered my prayers, throwing the door open the entire way and hurrying out.

"The scope and reach of our patents allows biological products . . . ," the younger woman with a pixie haircut said as she whisked by me with trays of blood samples.

"As long as the genes are isolated from their naturally occurring states," the older and obviously more senior of the two women added, carrying a stack of medical tests and readouts.

Without a second thought, I slipped inside, and the

door clanged shut behind me. I was so eager to get into the restricted area that I wasn't really paying attention to what they were discussing.

Nothing could've prepared me for what I saw.

There were two teenagers with individual powers being put through a battery of tests. Although I didn't know their names, I recognized them by sight as kids from school. The petite girl with a perky ponytail was wired with electrodes. She was bending and melting steel rods of varying thickness with her bare hands. The tall guy with the blue-dyed emo haircut, also wired, was freezing objects with the slightest touch. A platoon of a dozen intense scientists and medical personnel with clipboards and iPads observed and noted every detail. They had drawn vials of blood, which were being analyzed and processed in centrifuges along with high-tech PET scans and EKG and EEG readouts.

Chief among the scientists was my biology teacher—Mr. Bluni.

I reeled. I'd never imagined anything like this in my worst nightmares. I was aiding and abetting Mr. Bluni with his genetic research paper. Which wasn't just any research paper or project. It was for Bar Tech.

Suddenly that brief conversation I'd overheard on my way in took on a whole other meaning. Those women were talking about biological patents. My brain scanned through the many genetic studies and articles I'd read for Bluni. I recalled reading about how adrenaline and insulin and other various genes had been patented. Bluni had been interested in how genetic traits were inherited and passed along from generation to generation. Then I thought about all those blood samples they'd had my father draw from the kids at school. Maybe Bar Tech didn't want to sell those of us with powers as weapons. Maybe they wanted to isolate the specific genes that gave us our ability and patent them. If Bar Tech could extract these genes, they could do that. They would own us. Our unique biology. And then they could transfer those genes to others. In a matter of time, Bar Tech would be able to grow its own army—or sell the technology for billions of dollars.

As I struggled to keep my breathing steady and my invisibility up, one nagging thought pounded to the core of my very being:

Could I have just found Blackthorne?

17. STRANGER IN THE NIGHT

I wasn't the only one watching. High above the fray, I could just make out Richard Cochran surveying the horde from his position in a pristine glass office. This, of course, wasn't surprising in the least, but the person right at his side hit me like an old-school fist to the kidneys. It was Oliver. It was so painful to see my best friend becoming complicit in the work of the very person looking to control us—or worse. I couldn't know now how much of his determination to join Cochran was his own or created by Dana's influence, but either way the paternal draw was undeniably strong.

At the same time, my own father's departure had left me with a still-gaping heart. What was Dana hoping that would accomplish—force me to join their group? I was beginning to doubt my own ability to not follow directly in Oliver's path. Not ready to submit to defeat quite yet, I decided if I could find my way to Cochran's war room, maybe I could piece together another part of the puzzle.

The facility was a labyrinth unkind to those who did not

know its geography inside and out. I found myself moving farther and farther from my destination, but as my mother always said, sometimes the scenic route pays off. In this case, she was right, but in a bitterly unexpected kind of way.

I had noticed that Jackson wasn't a part of the display in the large training hangar, but I hadn't stopped to consider why. Now, with him right in front of me, I knew. The secluded hallway I'd found myself in featured a large Plexiglas window that peered into a slightly smaller training space. Jackson was alone. It reminded me of the movie moment when a formidable villain would show off his or her prowess, letting the hero know the only possible outcome was a crushing defeat. However, in this scenario, Jackson had no idea he even had an audience to show off to.

I watched as he powered through a series of exercises and was floored by how much his powers had advanced since the last time I'd seen them on display. There was a gigantic board rigged with hundreds of small lights that he was able to control by calling up different patterns, like lighting up every other bulb or creating patterns—an assortment of shapes and stripes. Then I watched as Jackson powered up an electric grid—the same kind that was usually surrounded by chain-link fence and HIGH VOLTAGE—STAY OUT—and calmly placed his hands directly on top of it. Jackson closed his eyes; he was as calm and collected as I was terrified and panicking. As the grid grew to a whir, Jackson's skin began to tint an icy blue like what I had witnessed the night of Dana's homecoming party. But instead of losing consciousness or control, Jackson continued to absorb the raw power—and then wielded it as his own.

Hands off the grid, Jackson was able to create an electric field that encircled his body. It was a perfect sphere, like Glinda the Good Witch's bubble, but with a lot more X Games and blue-raspberry Gatorade thrown in. Using his supercharged body as a battery, the sphere grew larger and more tempestuous, twisters of electricity swirling on the surface like a Jupiter storm. He pushed the field toward a variety of test objects— wood, paper, plastic—most of which burned in immediate combustion upon contact with the shimmering blue.

Jackson's eyes were so dark with focus and raw power that a stormy gray had completely polluted their clear waters. Logically, I knew it was Jackson, but I didn't recognize him. I knew then I had to drag myself away. Watching this pod version of one of my closest friends was too disturbing for me to continue. With only adrenaline and an overwhelming rush of emotions to propel me, I finally found a stairwell that led up to the second floor.

The upstairs of the building was more of an observation deck than a second floor. There were windows in all directions, a 360 view of the entire floor below. Just rotating around on my heels, I could see the group training together. Jackson and others who were practicing more unpredictable powers were in more private areas. I was lucky to find that Cochran and Oliver were still here, now with a third man joining the conversation. It was my mild-mannered biology teacher, Mr. Bluni.

The men were midconversation, but I did my best to play catch-up. He might be on Bar Tech's payroll, but Bluni commanded authority. At the moment he was updating Cochran on the progress of his genetic research. He was confident that once they isolated the specific gene the patent could be expedited by Bar Tech's contacts in Washington.

Cochran didn't seem impressed. "We're still missing the runaway, right? Maya Bartoli?"

"Unfortunately, yes. Security is confident they'll be able to bring her in. She'd been staying with family in Illinois, and then disappeared. There are only so many places she can hide," replied Bluni. "We'll find her." That didn't seem to warm Cochran over.

Cochran turned to Oliver. "Why don't you head downstairs and join the others? Mr. Bluni and I have a few more technical details to cover."

Oliver looked disappointed to be excluded from the grown-ups table, but he quickly agreed and did as he was told. It was weird watching him walk by, completely oblivious to my presence. I heard his voice echo back in my mind, asking how I could spy on my own friends. I didn't have a good answer, but it was becoming easier and easier.

With Oliver gone, Cochran and Bluni got back to business. Cochran heaved a big sigh of skepticism. "My biggest concern here remains instability. Yes, their powers have been developing at an impressive rate. And with proper training those abilities are able to be honed, but—"

"Not just honed. Improved. Expanded," Bluni said, jumping in, but this just irritated Cochran further. He wasn't buying what the biology teacher was selling.

"It doesn't change the fact that they're adolescents. I know scientific interest is high in our research—"

Bluni jumped in again. "High would be a massive understatement. The minute we successfully implant genes in embryos, we'll have a five-year waiting list at 200 percent of our initially proposed rates."

"That's a long way off to see results," Cochran groused, none too pleased.

"Scientific progress demands patience," said Mr. Bluni.

"Then it's a good thing I'm still in a position to decide how my own money is going to be spent. Bar Tech needs to start monetizing its significant investment now."

It was a command, not a request. I scurried out of the way as Cochran's fervor whisked him out of the room and then followed him out.

I stood around shivering in the snow for nearly an hour, waiting for someone—anyone—to drive back down the mountain so I could get the hell out of there. As my luck would have it, Cochran was the first to leave. An eager young Bar Tech Security officer, hoping to make a good impression on his boss, brought Cochran's Range Rover around. He cranked the heat up at full blast, making it nice and toasty inside for Cochran's drive back to Barrington. While Cochran was busy conferring with one of the other scientists, I darted along the opposite side of the car and slipped in undetected. I hunkered down on the floor of the backseat, praying that Cochran wouldn't hear me breathing. Fortunately, he listened to the Denver classical radio station. They were playing Beethoven's *Eroica Symphony*, drowning out any and all other random sounds, inside and outside the vehicle.

During the ride, I considered taking Cochran hostage and demanding to know what he'd done to my father. But as I had no weapon to threaten him with, it seemed unlikely that abducting him would work. I knew I had to enlist Maya if I had any hope of combating Cochran and Bar Tech and getting my father back safely.

Cochran made it home quickly and without any violence on my part. I waited until he was well inside his house and all the lights were out before I slipped out of the car and scaled over his property wall to freedom.

By the time I hoofed it home, I was ready for a long, hot bath. But I was so exhausted and spent that I couldn't do much more than shed my clothes and crawl into bed.

· · ·

The next morning, Maya and I watched the video clips I'd taken at Whiteface on my laptop. It might've looked like cheap, found movie footage, but it was just as disturbing playing on a small screen as it had been in person. Maya dug her fingers into her hair when Cochran mentioned her name, and I couldn't be sure, but I thought I saw a few items on the table twitch. She brought her finger down on the computer's space bar, freezing the video.

"I can't take another minute of it," she confessed.

I silently agreed. It was terrifying and nauseating, and I was sitting with one of the only people in the world who would understand exactly what I was going through. I hoped it was horrible enough to make her stay, not horrible enough to convince her that she was crazy to ever have come back to Barrington. I guess those two weren't mutually exclusive.

"I wish I'd come back sooner," Maya declared. "What are we going to do?"

Before I knew what was happening, I was crushing both of our rib cages with a hug of monstrous proportions. Maya let out a cough, a mix of surprise and from the sheer force of the blow. I released her from the hug, suddenly a little sheepish. Maya didn't miss a beat.

A look of intensity came over her face. "We need a plan," she announced.

I nodded in agreement, but all I had been trying to do was build a plan. It would've been much easier if every step I'd taken was a failure or a trick or swept out from beneath my feet. Not to mention, I didn't trust anyone. What would my mystery texter say about Maya?

"It's just hard to wrap my brain around," she admitted.

"We have a new enemy now," I quickly reminded her. "Dana."

Maya shook her head. "I think it just feels that way. She might have a more personal grudge against you, but Dana's just another cog in the system. We need to think outside of that."

I felt like I was watching Maya become an adult in real time, and I wondered if she saw the same thing in me. She got up off the kitchen stool and started to pace. After a few darts back and forth, something seemed to shake lose.

"You've been trying to piece it together, figure out what's going on . . . ," she continued, "but now we know."

"At least we know some of the details," I countered.

"That means it's time for a shake-up in our strategy," Maya replied. "We need to go on the offensive."

She said it with a force that made me immediately want to rally behind her, but what did it mean? There were only two of us. Even if we had enthusiasm and positive thinking on our side, they weren't an army of superpowered teenagers. I pushed her to continue. "What are you thinking?"

"I'm not sure," she muttered. The pacing continued to turn the wheels in Maya's head.

"We need to get outside the Barrington bubble," I said. "Break the story. Even if it's just a part of it."

I saw the flash of the lightbulb in her eyes. "We'll be whistleblowers."

My mind roared ahead, catching up to Maya's as we both landed on the same idea.

"My mom." I voiced it aloud. "She's a journalist. She can help us tell the outside world what's really going on in Barrington. And she'll be an effective bargaining chip to help get my dad back."

Maya smiled.

I knew my dad would be opposed, as well as maybe even the entire government, but it wasn't like I could call up the Department of Defense or the NSA and ask them for an alternate plan. Who would I call anyway? My dad never told me who else he might be working with in Barrington—if anyone. My dad would also probably be in huge trouble for revealing his true purpose to his sixteen-year-old daughter, but one problem at a time. Why, yes, Ms. Receptionist, my dad is an undercover agent for the DoD who recently had his memory wiped by a teenager who can control minds. I was hoping I could speak to his superiors, to find a way of handling this without exposing their top-secret mission. There was no way I'd make it past the front desk.

Maya was already handing me her burner cell. "Call her."

I pulled her number (they were extra long to call the South Pole) off the fridge and started to dial.

"Even if she leaves today, it'll be a couple days before she can actually get here," I said.

There was a delay until the line started to ring. One ring, two . . . I crossed my fingers that I wouldn't be on the receiving end of the same automated message from my last attempt, but as soon as the recording clicked on, I knew exactly what it was going to say.

"Shit." I shook my head, discouraged, and angrily hung up the phone. Of course Lydia had to be at the farthest outpost on Earth when I actually truly needed her. It was unfair to blame my mother, but I knew this was one I really couldn't pin on Dana Fox.

Maya heaved a weighty sigh. "We'll keep trying."

"I'll e-mail her, too. It could be a while, though."

"In the meantime, we need a backup plan." Maya was working another nugget of an idea.

"Lay it on me." I poured myself a second cup of coffee. Dad wasn't here to stop me, so I might as well find the slightest of silver linings. It was going to be a double cream and sugar, too. "Are you sure we're the only ones?" Maya asked. "The only kids affected by the pulse who haven't been enlisted in Dana's Ski Club?"

I imagined the folders upstairs in my dad's office. I'd

seen them together in the halls, together on the slopes, and together in Bar Tech's very special version of 24 Hour Fitness. I could think of one other outlier, but he'd already said no right to my face.

"There is one other person," I proclaimed. "I saw him vanish off the school roof."

"Who is it?"

I sighed. "I already tried to get him to help, but he just stonewalled me. There's a difference between not joining Ski Club and signing up for the rebellion."

"Let me try," insisted Maya.

"I don't think—"

"Nica, I can be very convincing. I talked you into being my friend, didn't I?" She was right about that. If not for Maya's determination, we never would have said two words to each other.

"Topher Hansen. He works at—"

"Ebinger's. I remember him. Uh, Nica . . ." She hesitated. "I really hate to say this, but . . . you're going to be late to school."

We laughed together at the absurdity. "I'm really glad you're back," I told her, genuinely happy that she'd decided to stick around.

"Me too." Maya returned the smile.

Four hours later, I'd made it to lunch without a hiccup. Dangerous as it was to show my face, I was staying quiet, polite, and below the radar. I'd successfully avoided Dana and Jackson and the other kids. Lunch, however, was a place a little trickier to not stand out these days. My first instinct was just the table farthest from Ski Club, but unfortunately, that one was already overpopulated with the Drama Club. So I settled on easy targets that still were a considerable distance from Dana's cronies: freshmen.

The table was only about half full when I sat down at the leaner end. They all looked up, surprised, but didn't say a word. A few shuffled their chairs in the opposite direction, putting a little extra distance between them and myself. I tried not to smile. At least I knew they'd leave me alone.

"Where have you been hiding?"

I looked up. Oliver sat down in the seat across from me with his lunch.

"I haven't been hiding anywhere," I replied coolly, keeping up my guard. "Why aren't you eating with your brother and Dana?"

"Because I miss you, Nica," he answered with a smile as he took a bite of his vegetarian pizza. "I just wish we could be friends again."

"I didn't know we weren't," I said. I sensed Oliver had a reason for seeking me out beyond friendship. "What do you really want, Oliver?"

"You're wrong about Dana," he insisted. "She's got our best interests at heart. If you'd only listen to her . . . give her a chance to explain about things, you'd understand."

I looked around the quad, suddenly feeling vulnerable. Was this some sort of an ambush? Oliver would try to break down my resolve and then Dana would come in for the kill. She wanted to turn me, and now she was using Oliver as an emotional weapon to lure me. I put my fork down on my half-eaten Cobb salad and got up.

"The only thing I understand is that she's using you to get to me. Tell Dana to do her own dirty work." I turned and walked away, fighting back the sob that nearly overtook me. I needed backup. And soon.

I ditched the remains of my lunch and dug out my phone. I scrolled through my texts for any communications from Maya, or better yet, my mom. Nothing. I tried calling my father's cell phone. I hoped that his being away from Dana had freed him from her influence. But I was stunned to hear that his number was disconnected—no longer in service. I then tried to text him. The message that bounced back said it was undeliverable. I tried again. There must be a mistake. But it really looked like my father's account had been closed. There was one person left who I hoped would help me.

In fact, besides Chase, the most recent text exchange of record was still between the mystery texter and me. I was pretty sure I had unraveled the identity of Blackthorne. I quickly typed out a text. "I've got something for you." Vague enough. My thumb hesitated over the send button for just a few seconds before I committed to it. Hopefully, it was enticing enough that he'd respond.

When I stepped out of class the following period, Dana was waiting for me. "You think you're so clever, that no one knows your secret or what you've been up to."

"What did I do? Take your seat at lunch?" My voice was so thick with sarcasm, a pool was forming at our feet.

"I see right through you, Nica. The little girl who wasn't there. Except I know you were. Sneaking around Whiteface. Spying."

How could Dana possibly know I was there? Was she just playing a hunch? I decided not to give anything away.

"That's quite an imagination you have." It wasn't the most creative of brush-offs, but it would do. I started to walk away from her, heading down the hallway, but Dana's long legs kept pace easily.

"You're the one imagining things," she said with a cold, threatening tone as she stalked toward me. "Inventing conspiracies. Psychiatrists call that paranoid delusion. I hear electroshock therapy can be very successful over time. Then again, some patients never recover. And with your father missing, who knows what will happen to you?"

"You have no proof of any of this," I responded, looking her right in the eye. Dana knew I had a power—otherwise she wouldn't have tried to recruit me to Ski Club so intensely— but there's no way she could guess that I had the ability to become invisible. There's nothing that could've given away my presence.

"Luckily, infrared cameras pick up all sorts of things," she declared. "We have about thirty of them installed at the lodge."

Except those. I knew damn well that my heat signature would show up on one, even if I was invisible to the naked eye. Dana whirled in front of me and caught my eyes with hers. I tried to tear them away, but I couldn't. She had me. Just for a second. Just long enough.

"You may think you're immune to me," she said, practically whispering. "You'll break. Everyone does."

I felt my mind begin to spin, truth and lies combining into a colorful swirl that I couldn't make heads or tails of. What had happened last night? Had I wandered out into the woods alone, confused, and upset? Had I hallucinated that building and all those kids? Was it all a response to fact that my dad had left me?

No. It was her. She was fucking with my head. I tried to shake her claws loose from my brain.

"I know what you can do, and it's not going to work on me," I vowed, taking a strong step forward and backing her toward a row of lockers. "I know you took my dad from me. I know you think you can break me. You can't."

Dana looked around for a lifeline, one of her friendly minions to step in and whisk her away, but we were alone. I think I even saw a brief flash of fear.

"I just want to be your friend," she responded humbly.

"Keep telling yourself that." I wasn't buying her bullshit anymore.

"I think you need help, Nica. Serious mental help."

You do, a voice in my head agreed. With every ounce of mental strength I could muster, I hung on to what I knew to be true, even though Dana was trying to toss me off like an angry bull. I was so mad and confused that I could barely see straight, and I had to back away before Dana broke into my brain completely.

When I left her, it took only a second for her to compose herself. I saw a creepy grin cross her face as I slunk farther away into the school.

I headed home and crashed, downing Advil to fight off a headache. I couldn't stop staring at my phone. I'd survived the rest of the school day. My optimism was telling me that I'd scared Dana off, but I suspected she was just licking her wounds, preparing to come back bigger and badder, a perpetually poked hornet nest. I was willing my phone to come to life, but I had been waiting for hours and had little faith left. All I was asking for was one little buzz, just one little vibration to let me know my source had gotten my message.

I'd set Maya up on the fold-out bed in the living room. I had thought about offering her my dad's room—it was empty, after all—but it was just too weird. I couldn't stop hoping that he'd come through the door at any moment, throw his arms around me, and apologize profusely. There was no way anyone could ever make him forget his own flesh and blood, his only child. But I was still waiting. The longer I could keep the fantasy alive, the longer I could keep the reality from tearing out my heart.

Adding to the mountain of emotional upheaval, this radio silence from my mystery texter had thrown an even bigger wrench in the works. How long would I have to wait to hear back? What if I didn't hear? What was the appropriate amount of time before I had to assume that my only other ally was missing in action? On the flip side, if my covert meetings in Barrington public places were truly over, I felt like I had to tell Maya everything the Mystery Texter had shared. If something happened to me, she would be the only one left. Trusting no one wasn't working.

I knew I wouldn't be able to sleep without at least one more attempt. I snatched up my phone and opened my messages, pulling up our conversation. Still nothing. I didn't know what to say. Not sharing specifics over the phone had been rule number one when we'd sent Maya out of Barrington. It felt even riskier to break that now. I settled on "Are you okay?" I hoped it communicated urgency without giving anything away. I rolled onto my back, my eyes boring into the ceiling, waiting for a response. My vision went soft as my body finally began to succumb to the complete exhaustion. In just a few deep breaths, I was out like the dead.

Not dead enough to not bolt upright at the sound of someone in my room hours later. My sleepy eyes tried to focus on the blurry form—not Maya's—but the voice tipped me off the second it rolled off his tongue.

"Shhhhhh. Keep the lights off."

I was terrified. The gruff-voiced stranger from the theater was in my bedroom. I could make out only his silhouette, the same long winter coat he'd worn at the theater.

"You shouldn't have texted me. It's not safe. I text you. I set the drops and the meetings." It was a whispered lecture, but his tone was absolute. "You better have something good."

I was still trying to catch up to how he was in my house. I knew I'd never been able to sneak past our very own Bar Tech home security system. How on earth had he? I doubted asking would get me anywhere, though. *I have my ways*, he'd say, impatiently.

"I have Blackthorne," I said, proud of my work. I told him everything I'd seen on the mountain, how Mr. Bluni and Cochran were going to patent the gene so that they could grow their own army of supersoldiers with Dana as their fearless leader.

"Did you hear the name referenced? Did someone actually use the word 'Blackthorne'?"

I could hear the disappointment, but my mind reeled. How could Blackthorne be anything else?

"No," I reluctantly admitted, "but the program, what they're doing . . . It's a huge secret right under the town's nose. What else could Blackthorne be?"

He went silent, and I stared into his shadow, trying to make out his identity, but he was too much in the shadows. It sent an honest-to-God shiver down my spine. I pulled the blankets tighter up around me.

"You're getting closer, but that can't be it. Whatever Blackthorne is, it's secret even inside Bar Tech. We're still missing something, something bigger."

"That's it? 'Something bigger'?" My voice rose as I mocked his cryptic styling. "I need more to go on and I'm tired of this charade. Tell me who you are!"

But he was gone, a swift exit out the window, without another word.

18. FASTEN YOUR SEAT BELT

I woke up the next morning to the smell of freshly brewed coffee and what I'd now memorized as the signature spicy vanilla scent of Ebinger's Bakery. I didn't quite bound down the stairs with the energy of a kid on Christmas morning, but there was a distinct spring of excitement in my normally lethargic stumble.

While I was expecting muffins or croissants or maybe even a crumb cake waiting for me, I was surprised to see Topher in addition to the most beautiful breakfast spread. He and Maya had already helped themselves, spreading Ebinger's house-made hazelnut spread onto this morning's brioche. A slight chill came over the mood as I added myself to the mix, and I got the distinct feeling that I was interrupting something. Several baked goods later, I knew why. Maya had snuck out to the bakery early, intent on bringing Topher into the fold. She'd gotten a lot further with him than I had—he was here, at least—but he was still full of reservations.

"I'm not an idiot," he began. "I knew from the minute

Dana Fox not only acknowledged that I existed but insisted we become friends that something was going on. Girls like her don't just suddenly talk to guys like me."

"She signed you up for Ski Club too?" I tried to relate.

"Not exactly. After I said no, she worked her charm on Noah. He signed me up and seemed so excited about it. I just went with the flow."

Lure 'em in with your boy du jour. I was starting to see the repetition in Dana's playbook.

"When I didn't go back, she seemed to cool off for a bit. At least until you got in the middle of it," he said, that "you" rolling off his tongue to pierce me.

I, per usual, had no idea how I'd made things worse. "What are you talking about?"

"Noah. He left me because of you."

He could tell I wasn't putting any of the pieces together.

"Well . . . sort of. Dana found out we were friendly and warned us that you weren't the kind of person I wanted to be hanging out with. After she heard about the night you came to the bakery, Noah broke up with me. I don't know how she does it, but she has all of them just wrapped around her finger."

I felt terrible that I had been the cause of Topher and Noah's breakup, but I was honestly more curious as to how Topher seemed to be completely immune to Dana's influence.

"I'm sorry about Noah," Maya said sympathetically. "But you're right—he's not the only person Dana's taken away. And we know how she's doing it."

Topher leaned forward, looking at both of us, intrigued.

I jumped back in. "Dana has an ability, too, just like I do. And Maya. And you." He grimaced. He didn't seem quite ready to admit to it, but he wasn't shouting protests either. "She can control people's thoughts. I know it sounds crazy, but—"

"I believe you." Topher pursed his lips. "In fact, I think I've seen her do it. And for some reason, my skepticism, and maybe my power, makes me immune to it. I think that's why she gave up on me."

"I don't get it," I said, mystified. "How would being able to teleport stop Dana's power from working on you?"

"I can't teleport," Topher said. "I can astral project. It's why I'm always staring off at school and at the bakery. It's because I'm literally somewhere else."

I had heard of astral projection before. Chalk up another one for Lydia and her New Agey friends, but Maya looked confused.

"It's like being in two places at once," Topher explained. "I can leave my physical body behind and travel in a second to anywhere I want to go. I look like and sound like I'm really there, but it's more like . . . like a hologram. I can snap back to my corporeal body at any time. I've even spent the whole day at school that way, as a sort of challenge to myself. Which sounds like how you caught me."

I smiled. It sounded a lot like how I'd been experimenting with my power. With Jackson and Oliver being distant for so long, I had forgotten how nice it was to have other people I could relate to, in the full "I'm-a-superpowered-teenager" way.

Topher continued. "It's also how I knew Dana was full of shit. My projected self is completely unfazed by her power. I've watched her straight-up lie to people and get away with it."

"So, you've seen how powerful she is," I said, thrilled that I had found another ally. "How she's changed everything so quickly. You have to help us."

Topher didn't respond and didn't look so convinced. Maya saw his hesitation and moved in for the close.

"Dana's smart. She's used to getting her way," Maya reiterated, locking eyes with Topher. "We don't have a lot of time, but I think if we fight back—not just close our eyes and hope she'll go away, but actually fight back—we can take her on. Use the element of surprise. Get our friends back. I don't know about you, Topher, but right now I think fighting would feel really good."

Maya's speech had me sold, but I wasn't the one she needed to sway. We both looked to Topher.

"You really think we can beat her?" he asked, still wavering between leaving my house or staying.

"Yes." Maya's reply was fast, assured, and decisive.

I wasn't nearly so sure, but I also knew when to keep my mouth zipped shut.

"So, what's the plan?" As soon as Topher asked the question, I realized we might lose him as quickly as we'd gained him. I was hoping Maya would chime in with another deep pull, but the silence was ominous. Then inspiration struck and I jumped in.

"Well, for starters," I said, interrupting the silence, "you can help me get in touch with my mom."

"This low-budget operation doesn't even have phones?" Topher joked, but it was clear he didn't hold a lot of confidence.

"Nica's mom is a journalist," Maya proclaimed. "We think she can help protect us by publicly exposing Bar Tech."

"Unfortunately, I haven't been able to get ahold of her for almost a week. She's in Antarctica. That's where you come in." But Topher was already shaking his head in doubt.

"I think Antarctica might be a little out of my reach," he confided, unsure about the plan I proposed.

"Are you sure?" Maya was pressing Topher hard. "The only way you can get your power to develop is by pushing it to the limit."

I didn't want to bully Topher into anything. I was trying to be different from Dana, not just like her. I remembered, though, that Maya had once been Dana's very own Mini Me. I decided to try another strategy.

"Can you tell us more about how your power works?" I asked Topher, truly interested in his ability. "What have you learned using it?" I had made a habit now of carrying gloves in my back pocket. I was sure Topher had similar nuances that only his power could provide.

"Well, for starters," Topher began, "ever since it started about six months ago, after the pulse, I haven't gone farther than my aunt's house in Los Angeles. I spent last summer there, so I know the place really well. That makes my projection easier. I have to imagine in my mind—like, a real 3-D place—before I can project myself there. It helps to create an anchor of sorts. But usually it's just around town. Sometimes maybe Denver."

"Have you ever projected anyone else along with you?" I asked.

"No one knew I could do it at all until about five minutes ago," Topher confessed. "It's not like I've been advertising for passengers."

"So Noah doesn't know?"

Topher shook his head in confirmation. "No one does."

"That's probably for the best," Maya chimed in, injecting a note of caution. "The less that Dana can get out of him, the better."

I continued on ahead. "Could we try? Just somewhere in town, somewhere you know really well, and go from there?" It was a first step—a tiny, baby step on the way to Antarctica—but we had to start somewhere. Topher had placed his trust in us, and now I wanted to earn it.

"So you're really serious about this Antarctica thing?" Topher's expression was a cross between amusement and incredulity.

"Yes," I answered. "If it's possible."

"It's possible in theory, I guess," Topher accepted, still highly skeptical. "The farther away I project from my own body, the more I can feel it. There's a physical sensation to it, like a tether with just a little bit of elastic to it. The farther I go, the more it stretches and the harder it is. I've projected from my house to school all day, but when I went to California? It was a workout. Twenty, thirty minutes max."

"It sounds like a muscle. I bet you can strengthen it with more practice."

I shot Maya a look. I didn't like how pushy she was being.

"I've done some research," admitted Topher, now on the defensive. "Even some of the best, most highly trained spiritualists have fallen into deadly comas when they've pushed their powers too far."

"You have to wonder, though," I replied. "Their form of astral projection might be a little more . . . psychological than yours. It's possible that those guys in comas might've just done too much peyote."

Topher laughed.

I continued. "How about a test run? Try to bring me

along on your projection, just somewhere close in Barrington. A place you're already comfortable going."

He sighed and chewed his lip as he pondered my request. "Okay," he finally relented. "Let's try it."

"Tonight?" I was eager to mobilize.

"I can't. I'm closing the bakery and then curfew. Tomorrow morning?"

I looked at Maya and we nodded in unison. Then I smiled: "Tomorrow morning."

After an uneventful day at school, I hurried right home to see how Maya was doing. She was getting a bit of cabin fever being stuck in the house all day, but boy did she put that bottled-up energy to work. The floor was clean enough to eat off of, and she'd perused my dad's cookbook collection in preparation for dinner.

I was excited to see my dad's old-fashioned pasta maker out on the counter. I had found it once in a deep pantry dig, but Dad was reluctant to use it. I wasn't sure if that was because it had been a wedding gift or because of his deep aversion to refined carbohydrates.

A deep red sauce was brewing on the stove. "Smells awesome," I said, inhaling the fragrant aroma of tomatoes, basil, and garlic. "You're hired."

"Thanks," Maya responded, quite proud. "It's a traditional Italian dish I learned on *Top Chef*. *Festa dei guerrieri*, the warriors' feast. Seemed appropriate."

"I've never heard of it, but I'll happily eat it when it's ready." Maya grinned as she stirred the sauce. I could read between the lines. She'd spent the whole day trying to distract herself but couldn't stop thinking about being so close to her family and her old life.

"Try not to worry, okay?" I tried to reassure Maya, but it wasn't the same thing as being together. I knew that because I was missing my dad something fierce. I didn't want to think about the awful things Bar Tech or Cochran might be doing to him.

"Yeah, I know. Thanks." She turned her attentions back to cooking dinner, but I knew I hadn't completely assuaged her sadness.

My phone buzzed in my pocket, and I dug it out. My first thought was that it might be Lydia, back online on the other side of the Antarctic storm. I switched gears as soon as I saw the sender. It was Chase. I felt an immediate pang of guilt and angled the phone away from Maya. I still hadn't found a way to bring up that I was kind of, sort of—to be fair we hadn't put a name on it, either—flirting with her ex. I didn't want to betray the holy covenant of female friendship, but at the same time, my tenuous relationship status seemed like such small potatoes next to the bigger problems we were dealing with. Maya was too concerned with Bar Tech and Dana and getting our lives back to be pining over boys. At the same time, I had to admit I was dying to open the text.

The phone buzzed again. Make that texts.

Are you okay? Not the subtle flirtation I had been hoping for.

You're 40 minutes late. Text me back when you get this.

Late for what? I racked my brain, but I couldn't remember making plans for a date with Chase. Then I remembered and immediately felt like a total jerk. It wasn't a date.

It was our stupid Shakespeare project. I had completely forgotten about our English assignment, and right along with it, our plans to collaborate. I quickly sent a response.

Sorry—totally lost track of time. Will be right there! I knew I had to keep some semblance of my life intact. And I didn't believe Chase was trying to ambush me either. In fact, the more I thought about it, the more I thought going to his house might be a good idea. Maybe I could even find out something about my father's whereabouts. Maybe Chase knew something he wasn't even aware of. Something he overheard his father talking about.

Unfortunately, that left me to deal with Maya and the dinner she had made for both of us. I decided it was time to come clean and tell Maya the truth. I took a full-body breath.

"Maya, I'm so sorry to bail on you, but I totally forgot I promised to work on this group project for English class tonight. I should only be gone for a couple hours. Totally understand if you want to eat before I get back." Okay, maybe just part of the truth.

"Oh." Her disappointment prevailed only for a few seconds. "No worries. I'll be here when you get back." She said it with a resigned laugh, but it still made me feel awful. I was already pulling on my winter layers, ready to get out ASAP.

I tried to rationalize leaving Maya behind to go hang out with Chase. We weren't hanging out, I corrected myself. We were doing schoolwork. A required assignment. Shakespeare, at that. I'd barely had a chance to read *Twelfth Night*, but it certainly reminded me that you don't always end up with the person you expect to. Maybe I had been Olivia, desperately (and foolishly) chasing after Cesario only to have Sebastian rightly fall into my lap. So much had changed since Oliver had bailed on me and I'd been forced to partner with Chase. The door was open to Cochran Manor when I arrived. I shouted a tentative and echoing "Chase" into the void. No response. The grand entry foyer was dark. I danced back and forth on the front porch for a bit, but it was just too cold. I let myself in, calling out Chase's name and slowly making my way inside.

"Chase?" Again no response. I began to get a little worried. Why were all the lights out? Had I made a mistake coming here alone? I dug out my phone, pulling up the flashlight app, when I heard a voice.

"Marco!" It was a shout from a distance, but I was almost positive it was Chase's voice.

"Marco!" Definitely Chase. I could hear the mischief in

his voice. Was this a game? If so, I was in no mood to play.

"Polo?" I replied, trying to pinpoint the direction of his voice.

"Marco!"

I moved through the dark house, focusing only on the sound of his voice. At least until my foot made a distinct crunch on the floor. When I looked down, I could see a trail of snow on the floor. Not the real thing, of course, but the glittery, fake stuff used to decorate fancy department stores for Christmas.

"You're getting warmer . . . ," Chase said playfully.

I could hear him from the next room over. I followed the trail of snowflake breadcrumbs down a short hallway. When they made a sharp left into the great room an audible gasp escaped me before I could stop. The already beautiful room had been turned into a winter wonderland. Hundreds of hand-cut paper snowflakes clung to the windows and hung from the ceiling in cool shades of blue, silver, and white. They were softly illuminated by an equally impressive number of LED Christmas lights in the shape of stars. Chase stood in the middle of it, a mysterious wrapped package in his arms.

He smiled, proud of his handiwork. "The whole candles-and-flowers thing felt a little played out."

"How many dance committee girls did you have to charm to steal all these decorations?"

270

"Ye of little faith. I did every last one myself." He set the wrapped present down, holding up his hands for examination. "I even have the paper cuts to prove it."

I moved in for a closer look, but I quickly realized that was a sly trap as well. His arms encircled my waist, and I could feel our hearts volleying off each other's chests as he kissed me.

When we came up for air, Chase's face was expectant. "Are you holding out for your present, or will you just say yes already?"

"What am I saying yes to?" He was definitely wearing down my resistance.

"You, Miss Ashley, just agreed to be my date to the Winter Formal. No backing out now." He grabbed the present again and handed it to me. He almost seemed more excited about the gift than the charmingly Pinterest romantic gesture he'd created in his own home.

As I unwrapped the box, I realized I couldn't even remember if I ever knew about the dance at all. It seemed so insignificant and normal in the towering shadow of what was really going on in Barrington and my life. I was nervous to see what Chase had bought for me, not sure if I was ready for an overly generous gift as well. Expensive to me might've been pocket change to Chase, but it didn't mean I'd be any less worried about breaking it.

That just made the present all the more perfect when I

saw it. I knew immediately it hadn't cost him a dime, just lots of hours of hard work. Gently nestled in pastel tissue paper was our completed Shakespeare project.

"I promised not to make you do it all yourself. This just seemed like the next obvious step."

I flipped through the neatly bound folder. I was just skimming, but it looked like he'd done a really good job. Cute and with a secret literary strength? How did I end up in this situation?

"I totally understand if you want to give it a more thorough read before we hand it in. I worked pretty hard on it, though, so try to be gentle."

"It's wonderful. Thank you," I said, a bit suspicious about his magnanimous effort to win me over. I smiled at him. Something was off. Chase wasn't smiling back. "What's wrong?"

He hesitated before answering. "I've just had a rocky few days," he confessed.

"Do you want to tell me about it?" I braced myself for something awful. Had Dana swayed him with her lies? Or had his father?

"I found out I have a brother."

Oh, man. I chided myself, relieved. Not that he knew but that his angst and turmoil wasn't about me.

Chase continued, and it was like opening the floodgates. "I only found out two days ago. Though I've had suspicions about Oliver's sudden and intruding presence for a while."

"Oh my God." I tried my best to sound like this was news to me.

"It's Oliver." He looked to me for a reaction.

"What?" And the Oscar goes to . . .

"You know the worst part? Oliver and my father have so much in common. Suddenly, all of my tutoring sessions have turned into awkward family bonding time. Oliver has so many questions about scientific developments at Bar Tech, and my dad is excited to have a son to share them with. He doesn't seem to notice that I'm completely lost in the conversation." Chase's pain ran deep. "Plus, he told me to keep Oliver a secret, and I barely see my dad anymore, so I can't even talk about it with him."

It reminded me that I missed talking to my dad . . . and my mother. I felt abandoned, like I'd been suddenly orphaned. I couldn't help but feel incredible sympathy for Chase.

Chase probably hadn't expected his romantic girl trap to end in a cuddle session in front of the Cochrans' stunning limestone fireplace. Or maybe he had. I certainly hadn't.

As curfew started to close in, Chase offered to take me home. It was a quiet drive, our hands clasped and resting against his thigh as his four-wheel drive delivered me home safe and sound. I might not have had any parents to report home to, but I like to think they would've given the date a stamp of approval.

The following morning Topher arrived at my house bright and early for our attempt into the great unknown: an astral projection built for two. It was a little awkward, as I was looking for him to lead, but I had to keep reminding myself that he had never done this either. I hoped this just meant we'd end up better friends on the other side.

"Should we sit together?" I asked, trying to keep my ideas as broad as possible.

"Oh. Sure."

I sat next to him on the black leather sofa in the living room.

"Where to?" Topher asked, like he was a polite taxi driver instead of a teenager about to attempt to project our collective consciousness through space.

"Don't you want to decide?" I offered him the option. After all, it was his ability I'd be riding shotgun on.

"I've basically mentally mapped all of Barrington at this point."

I gave it a moment's pause. Was there a trip that, if successful, we could also use to our advantage? Back up to Whiteface was certainly an idea, but the mission seemed risky enough on its own without adding Bar Tech's secret lab to the mix. Then I was struck by another option.

"We could check in on Maya's family." It was something I probably should've made time for sooner, but at least if it worked now and we needed a quick escape, we could be out of there in an actual split second.

"Sure." Topher shrugged and then offered his hand, and we interlaced fingers. "I'm just guessing, but it seems logical that we should touch. I think I should try to walk you through what I do and then, hopefully, when I project, you'll be there too."

I couldn't help but think of my mother. This kind of teenage experimentation would be right up her alley. In fact, it was only a few steps removed from all those transcendental yoga retreats she'd done through the years.

"Close your eyes," Topher continued. "I start by imagining my destination with as much detail as I can. So, for Maya's house . . . Sorry. This is so weird, explaining my thought process and trying to use my power at the same time."

I could hear him take a deep breath and refocus.

"Try to imagine the street and all the houses," suggested Topher. "It's usually pretty quiet there, maybe a car or two. Maya's house is in the middle of the block. It's windy today, too, the kind that whips right through your clothes."

I did my best to paint Topher's picture in my mind. I had passed by Maya's house a few times and was able to conjure up the two-story white brick colonial with steel-gray shutters.

"Now what do we do?" I asked, anxious to be transported across town.

"Open your eyes," ordered Topher.

275

And just like that, there we were, standing across the street from Maya's house, but instead of the vaguely impressionistic image I had held in my mind, it was real and vibrant, my eyes filling in all of the details I hadn't known to add myself. I was simultaneously awestruck and little nauseous.

Topher tugged me along to take a few steps. "Yeah, it's weird the first few trips. Got to get your sea legs."

That was an understatement. I felt like I was standing on a platform suspended above a turbulent sea. Everything rocked back and forth. I couldn't get my bearings at first. My stomach was flip-flopping, and I was hit with a massive wave of vertigo.

"I think I'm going to be sick," I muttered, barely able to get the words out.

"Just pick a point on the horizon," Topher instructed, "and keep your eyes locked on it. That will help."

I took several deep breaths and did as Dr. Topher ordered. I stared at the end of the street where it intersected Main Street on the outskirts of town. After about thirty seconds I felt my nausea slowly subsiding. Another thirty seconds later and I knew I was more in control, more comfortable navigating this strange and amazing out-of-body experience.

I then headed toward the front stairs with Topher. Each step felt like its own mini adventure. Maya's house was just across the street, but to me it seemed like an impossible distance to cover.

"So, how does it work?" I asked, trying to keep my mind focused and redirected to the task at hand. "We look solid—like real people. I'm not falling through the floor."

"That's all still in R and D," Topher replied, letting his inner geek shine. "I like to call it 'physics lite.' As humans, so much of our behavior is determined by our ability to predict outcomes. As far as I can tell, my astral body behaves like my real body would, but only because that's what my brain expects to happen. When I consciously push those boundaries . . ." He paused to demonstrate.

Topher put his hand on the stair railing and started to push. After a second, the resistance gave way, his hand passing straight through the metal bar.

"I can break the rules. I've only just started messing around with it, but in theory, I should be able to walk through walls. Run incredibly fast. Maybe even fly. I just have to wrap my mind around each thing first. But really, I'm not a scientist. It's equally possible I've just watched *The Matrix* too many times."

"Well, I don't feel the need to challenge physics anytime soon. It's weird enough just being here," I admitted, feeling more comfortable and starting to get into the swing of things.

Topher and I circled around the house, keeping our distance while we peeked in the windows. No sign of Bar Tech Security anywhere. Nothing seemed amiss. Maya's mother was in the kitchen, sipping coffee and talking on the phone. I heard the garage door opening up. I saw Maya's father pulling out in his Jeep Cherokee, presumably off to work. All in all, a normal morning.

"You ready to go back?" I asked Topher. My stomach definitely felt better, but a distinct fatigue had taken its place, like I'd run a marathon or something.

Topher nodded. We crept behind the trees and made sure no one was watching as we vanished into thin air.

Before I knew it, I was back on my couch, safe and sound, sitting next to Topher. The sensation I experienced felt similar to the first few seconds out of a vivid dream, where your body doesn't immediately respond to your brain's requests. As soon as it would listen, my hand covered my mouth. I'd spoken too soon about that nausea.

Topher, on the other hand, was excited and energized.

"Next stop Antarctica," I said with a hopeful smile. Unfortunately, his cold feet reemerged.

"I know you want to talk to your mom, but Antarctica is really far away. I don't even know what it looks like. Some fuzzy vision of snow and ice could just as easily land us in Siberia."

I knew the risks were great, but I felt as though I was out of other options. Then I remembered: the photos that Mom had sent with her Christmas gifts. I ran upstairs to retrieve them.

A few minutes later, Topher had spread them out on the coffee table like a collage. He was still hesitant. "It's a start, I guess. But there's no context, no reference point. I don't know if it's enough."

My brainstorm was drying up rapidly.

"Did your mom send you any videos? That might have a better sense of space." Topher was clearly groping for something—anything that might help him help me.

I shook my head . . . almost ready to throw in the towel. But then I remembered the base did have their own website. I grabbed my laptop off the table and punched the research base into Google.

Sadly, their website wasn't nearly as state-of-the-art as their facilities. Then I had another thought: the street-view function of Google. It had helped me get around in numerous foreign cities, especially those where people were happy to given directions but I was completely incapable of understanding their language. It seemed like a stretch, as Antarctica didn't exactly have streets per se, but . . .

There it was—not the entire landmass, but the interiors and exteriors of some of the most important scientific outposts that had been built there—including my mom's temporary home.

"This help?" I asked Topher, showing him what I'd found. It was an Internet miracle. The photos had the slightly strange distortion of a 360-degree view that had been pieced together by individual photos, but it was much more detailed than the image of the parking structure that I'd conjured up.

Topher continued to click around the map, matching a few images up to the ones my mom had sent along. "I think we can work with this."

I was so excited that I almost missed it. As Topher moved along Google view, I saw an accompanying series of numbers. A pair of numbers with lengthy decimals; they were longitude and latitude coordinates.

Just like the ones I'd found on my dad's desk.

Topher's cell phone interrupted us. It was Perry, the owner of Ebinger's Bakery in a panic. One of the other workers had horrible food poisoning, and he was shorthanded that morning. Could Topher please fill in for a couple hours, just until his boss finished with his deliveries? He'd pay Topher double.

"Sorry about this, Nica," Topher apologized as he threw on his parka and ski cap and hurried out the door.

Topher promised that Operation South Pole was a go, and we planned to make our move during the Winter Formal. Yes, it would take us away from the dance, but it also seemed like the most opportune time to go. There was no way Dana Fox would miss her own Queen Frostine coronation, and we'd be safe from her for just long enough.

As soon as Topher was out the door, I sprinted to my

dad's office to reclaim the scrap of pink paper. Sink or swim, I supposed. With a shaky pinky, I pressed down the enter key. My knees wobbled, and I fell back into the office chair as the coordinates loaded in front of me—dead in the center of a place called Blackthorne, Virginia.

19. GIRLS' NIGHT OUT

My fingers clacked over the keys, opening tab after tab in my browser, as I searched for anything I could find about Blackthorne. I spent hours trying to figure out what was the connection between this town and Bar Tech? There didn't seem to be much of a there there. It was mostly farmland. The nearest town center was almost fifteen miles away. No gas station, no post office, and no high school—just miles of produce waiting to be plucked from the ground.

As with most American farms, the crops had been reduced from a variety of vegetables to the standard corn and soybean combo, but other than that, it might as well still be the early 1900s in Blackthorne. So had my dad been wrong? Or was I? These coordinates didn't seem to lead to a place that would interest Bar Tech in the slightest. I closed the browser window and decided to sleep on it.

But first I gave Maya a complete report about her parents. She was relieved to hear that, but the isolation from her old life was really wearing her down. She was . . . well . . . I hoped she was going to be okay. Circumstances had certainly thrown her from her course, but she was tough and smart—maybe more so than any of us. After all, no one else had been able to hold on to her power through sheer force of will. Whatever came her way, she seemed like she was going to be able to make the most of it.

I slipped under my covers not long after ten. I'd hardly closed my eyes when my phone buzzed. I rolled over and opened an eye to see if it was another creepy message from the mystery texter. Instead, the text was from Chase.

Bball game w/me tomorrow?

Not sure kinda busy :/ was the reply I eventually settled on. *Too busy for your bf?* he fired back. I smirked. That was a loaded reply, considering I'd never thrown around the "bf" term. *Maybe. #topsecret.* Thought that might give him enough to think about that I'd have time to fall asleep. *Bzz-bzz.* Nope. Lightning Fingers replied in seconds. *U can have top. Doesn't have 2 be secret* ;) I blushed. That was forward. And hot. I was so flustered, I couldn't decide on a reply that wouldn't escalate—and even though that was tempting, I wasn't ready to wake up next to Chase. I decided to leave it there. I put my phone on silent and rolled over in search of sleep. That last text kept flashing in my mind, along with a whole host of exquisitely dirty thoughts. Jackson would never say anything like that. He was too much of a gentleman—"was" being the key word. But rather than mourning the loss anymore, I was ready for a change of pace. I tossed and turned, trying to shake it, but my eyes fluttered back open.

Sleep wasn't coming anytime soon.

When it did, it came hard, and I floated through oblivion for the next eight hours straight. When I came to the next morning, I felt good. It's amazing what rest can do for the heart and soul. For a second I even forgot what a disaster my life was. Even better, I drifted downstairs to find that Maya had already made coffee and gotten started on pancakes. Steaming mugs were set out for both of us, and she was cleaning up her trail of utensils and dishes as she went. I was beginning to feel like a guest in my own house.

"How many people you planning on feeding?" I asked, nodding to the three bowls of batter waiting to hit the skillet.

"Went a liiittle overboard on the mix," Maya admitted with a smile, "but I figure we might as well go hard. Gonna have a long day, so best to get off on the right foot."

Weakness grabbed my ankles and tugged. I suddenly didn't know if I could face another night of living like a combatant. Hadn't I lost enough already? And with my mother decidedly off the grid and my father disappeared to who knew where, I felt totally rootless. It had been so long since I'd felt free. Going with Chase to the game tonight would let me feel it again—even only if for a few hours.

"You think we could maybe postpone until later with that?"

Maya wasn't stupid. She picked up on the sound of me planning something that I wasn't saying. "Something come up?"

"First basketball game of the season is tonight, and Dana's heading up the cheerleading squad."

I saw Maya flinch. The news pained her. "What else is new?" Not too long ago she would've been at the game, cheering her heart out. Not anymore. So much had changed.

"Think about it. Cheerleading might be the only thing that'll get her to drop her guard long enough for me to snoop around, maybe talk to people who aren't under her influence." The more I thought about this, the more I realized it was a good plan. "It won't be for long," I promised. "It's too good of an opportunity to pass up."

"Do what you got to do," Maya replied, her frustration apparent as she beat the pancake batter into submission. "Time is wasting, Nica."

She finished making the pancakes but didn't say another word.

The second-quarter buzzer sounded, and the gym was primed to explode. Fans, signs, parents, and students were packed into the stands, tighter than a traffic jam. The Barrington High band tore through brassy arrangements of old standards and modern anthems. My ears caught some Katy Perry in the mix, and I was impressed that it sounded as good as it did. Even more impressive was the smooth transition into a rowdy version of "You Shook Me All Night Long."

We were up thirty-two to twenty-six, not the kind of lead that called for nails to be put in anyone's coffin, but enough that spirits were high. I'm not a huge sports fan—it all seems pointless to me, and my presence at the game was definitely due to Chase—but I have to admit that even I was swept up in the celebration. Perched high in the stands, I cheered the sounding of the air horn like an ancient Roman gladiator fan, frothing at the mouth, screaming for victory. This was war. Sort of. At least somebody was winning something, I thought, as our team's red-and-blue-jerseyed players huddled in a circle below. I watched them chant, cheer, and throw their hands in, all to keep themselves pumped through the short interval before the next round of pitched play.

I hadn't expected to see Jackson at the game, but there he was, seated several rows below us, closer toward the floor. Although Dana and her cheerleading posse were on the sidelines, cheering on the team, Jackson kept turning around and staring at Chase and me. Fortunately, there was nothing scandalous to really see other than the fact that Chase and I were sitting together. No blatant acts of affection on either of our parts, which was fine by me. I tried to act cool, calm, and collected—not my most natural state. But I felt like I was doing a pretty good imitation of not caring that Jackson was there.

Then Chase took my hand and pulled me closer. He

hadn't made a move all night, but something seemed to come over him. I squirmed a bit but then gave in to the moment. He looked into my eyes and said one word: "Snacks?"

"How romantic," I quipped, and playfully scooted away. "You want me to get you nachos? That why you brought me?"

"Popcorn."

"I thought we were going to dinner after this," I snapped back, hoping he'd be loose enough to spill some more details about what his father and Oliver were up to.

"I consider popcorn an appetizer," Chase announced humorously.

"You and I have very different definitions for food."

"Opposites attract," he said with a smirk.

Dana might've been the one I was worried about controlling people's minds, but Chase's smile was a close second. That thing was a weapon. He wielded it expertly.

"Fine, but you're paying," I proclaimed.

As I tramped down the steep bleachers with Chase's ten-dollar bill folded in my hand, I kept an eye out for Dana. The last thing I wanted was to come face-to-face with her. I wasn't exactly undercover, but if I was careful, I could get out of there without causing a scene. It was strange. Everything seemed normal. If one were to show this scene to a random assortment of strangers, not one would point out that the people here seemed to be under the spell of a power-mad teenager. It was enough to make me wonder if maybe, just maybe . . . Stop it. That was Dana's suggestion, still kicking around in the back of my head. I knew it was planted there, but I had no idea it had reached its roots so deep. Was there any way of permanently weeding it out?

The smell of hot, fatty snack foods seemed to do the trick for now, and I followed my nose out the gym doors, through a small crowd, to the snack table. The selection was a rainbow assortment of candy and chips, pretzels, hot dogs, and dozens of other pleasure-delivery devices that ostensibly had some nutritional value. I ordered Chase's popcorn, some gummy bears for myself, and two sodas. I turned to head back and walked right into Oliver.

"Hey, Nica," he said casually, as if we were still the best of friends.

I was so surprised, I almost dropped the treats I was carrying. How long had he been behind me? Was he watching me? Following me? Or was this a complete coincidence?

"Hey." I didn't make eye contact. I couldn't, after seeing him in Cochran's office at the lodge. I tried to get past him, but he mirrored my steps. He'd caught me and wouldn't let me go.

"I understand you're pretty upset," he confessed.

No shit, Sherlock.

"I'm glad Dana's keeping you updated," I retorted, assuming this was going to take a sharp turn into "cryptic warning" territory, another shot across the bow to remind me to back off. Instead, Oliver seemed sad.

"I want to apologize for how I came across at lunch the other day," he said contritely with a hangdog expression. "It wasn't like me."

I checked his eyes to see if he was under Dana's spell or not. It's not like they'd be glowing red or anything, but I'd started to get a sense for that look, the one that indicated Dana had taken hold. I couldn't quite identify it, but it was so subtle to begin with that I couldn't be sure. . . . I continued to play my cards close to the vest and say as little as possible.

"Little late," I muttered, my hurt feelings from being rejected still very raw.

"I also heard you visited Ski Club."

"We're not gonna talk about this here."

Oliver stepped closer to me, the way Dana sometimes did. His attitude turned on a dime. For a second I saw a flash of the old Oliver.

"You got it all wrong, Nica. Cochran's not a bad guy. The more I've gotten to know him, the more sure of that I am. Bar Tech does a lot of good to people all around the world. The genetics program is really about helping save lives."

I tried to process what Oliver was telling me, but it was a warped and corrupted version of reality as I knew it. This was crazy. 100 percent nuts.

"Did Cochran also tell you that he wants to patent the gene that gives us our power?" My tone etched with a major dose of cynicism. "He wants to own us, Oliver. To profit off of us. And to sell the technology."

"That's not true," he declared. "He believes our genetics will offer medicine exciting new ways to help soldiers who've been injured in combat. To help those who have terminal diseases. Bar Tech's devoted to medical research and progress. He'll watch over us and make sure we're protected."

"He certainly has a funny way of showing it," I snapped back. As I finally strong-armed my way past him and back toward the gym, I honestly wasn't sure I could ever believe him again.

An hour later, after being beat down for nearly the entire game, the Lakeville High Trojans reached deep and pulled out a win that dropped the jaws of everyone in the gym. It seemed impossible, but our team had gotten cocky and Lakeville took advantage, sinking a series of three-pointers, taking advantage of some loose elbows, and leaving every last ounce of blood, sweat, and tears that they could on the court. The tables turned so quickly that our team didn't even have a chance to course correct, and Barrington's fans left with their heads in their hands. I was disappointed, sure, but I couldn't overlook the symbolism of the situation: A team about to be crushed pulled out a win by playing smarter, faster, and never giving up. I clung to this, my very own inspirational sports metaphor to help keep the night from becoming crushingly shitty.

As Chase escorted me across the school's parking lot to his car, he was supremely bummed, and my encounter with Oliver had thrown me for a total loop. What should've been a walk filled with gentle touches and small kisses was silent and sullen. If it hadn't been, I don't know if I ever would've noticed Maya standing in the shadows between the cars. My feet ground to a halt. I thought about telling Chase and trying to hide, but it was too late: Maya was already staring right at us. Me. I was caught.

"Don't mind me," Maya quipped. "I wouldn't want to interrupt date night."

Chase's head snapped to the source of the voice, and I knew he recognized it. It looked like . . . Well, as far as he knew, he was seeing a ghost.

"Maya? Oh my God . . ." Chase was truly shaken to see Maya standing right in front of him.

"Miss me, Chase?" Maya slunk toward us between the rows of cars, top lit with sodium shadows and light.

I took my eyes off of her long enough to notice that the windows in the cars closest to her were starting to vibrate.

Chase stood there for a moment, totally speechless.

"Maya's been staying with me." I came clean right then

and there, about as much as I could, at least. "It isn't safe for her in Barrington, and I didn't want word to get out." I shot a glance to Maya. This was where things could get truly dicey. Maya and high emotions did not play well together, as evidenced by the pulsating metal and glass on all sides of her. Her powers were at the whim of her building fury. I was praying Chase didn't notice.

"Where did you go? What, I mean, where—where have you been?" he stammered.

Please don't be stupid. Don't tell him why you really left.

Maya, much to her credit, played it totally cool. "My family was falling apart, okay? I know you weren't really paying attention to our relationship by the time I had to get outta here, so forgive me for not making it crystal clear."

Wasn't much Chase could say to that, and while he tried to formulate his next words, Maya stared me down. "I'm here for Nica."

I gave Chase a quick peck on the cheek. "Go home. I'll catch up with you later."

"No, I want to . . ." Chase looked so confused that he couldn't even finish his thought.

"Chase, there are a lot of things you're good at, but this is not one of those things. Let me handle it, okay? Go."

To his credit, he did. Got right in his car and left. I hoped I'd made the right decision. Maya waited for him to pull away before she continued.

292

"Snooping on Dana, huh? You didn't have to lie to me, Nica. We're in this together."

I felt awful at having deceived her, but I had been keeping tabs on Dana, too. "I know, but Chase and you have history together. . . . I wasn't sure you could handle it. Not that there's really much to tell. Nevertheless, I didn't want to dump one more huge change in your lap."

"If I could handle him, I think I can handle this. I get it. Things have been rough and you drifted together. I just hope you have better luck with him than I did."

I was relieved. It seemed like Maya was going to avoid a major meltdown. I decided to fill her in on the last detail, too. "It's not at all serious, but we're going to the Winter Formal together this weekend, too. Just so you know."

"Oh, good," she said quite matter-of-factly. "I'll see you there."

"What? You can't come!" That came off harsher than I'd meant it to. "I mean, no one knows you're here."

"They will," she declared.

"What do you mean?" I started to get a very uneasy feeling.

"I'm sick of floating around this town in the dark at night. I want to have my life back. And that means going through her." Maya's eyes narrowed at a target over my shoulder.

I turned around and saw Dana, still dolled up in her cheerleading uniform, heading to her car. I spun back to Maya.

"No, no, no. Bad idea. Terrible idea," I whispered, pulling her into the shadows behind some trees. "Our one advantage right now is that Dana doesn't know you're back. You can't blow that."

"I have to, Nica. I don't have any other choice." She shoved my hand off her arm and took to her target like a missile. "Dana! Dana Fox!"

Dana froze in her tracks as Maya emerged from the shadows. Even though all our plans were about to crumble around us, I took what little glee I could in watching Dana's eyes almost bug out of her head. She'd been totally in control until this moment, aware of each move anyone in her circle made—hell, aware of each move I made—but she hadn't seen Maya coming until she stepped into the full glow of the streetlights.

"Maya. Oh my God, hey!" Dana came in for a big reunion hug.

Maya didn't move. She closed her eyes, and without even breaking a sweat, flung an unsuspecting Dana to the ground with barely a look.

"Don't even," said Maya. "I want to get a couple things straight." Emboldened by the warning shot, I had Maya's back and followed her toward her dazed prey.

"You," snarled a very pissed off Dana as she spotted me advancing toward her.

"I know. I'm everywhere these days, huh?" I snapped

back with a shrug as Dana recovered, brushing pebbles and pavement from her palms.

"You put her up to this?" she accused, referring to Maya's sudden reappearance in Barrington.

"Not at all," Maya responded. "I've been wanting to do that for quite a while."

"You know she's screwing your ex," Dana pronounced, revealing her nasty true nature with surprising venom. Her cool and collected mask of sweetness was finally giving way to something real and ugly.

"First of all: Nica's not," Maya replied confidently. "Second: We just tabled that discussion, and I think it'll work out fine."

"Whatever. You freaks deserve each other," Dana barked back with utter contempt.

She started to push herself up to her feet, but the steel-eyed Maya took two steps toward Dana and forced her back to the ground without even a touch. Dana struggled to get up again, fighting against whatever force Maya was exerting, to no avail. Reality seemed to shiver as Maya applied a second wave of psychic pressure that bore down on Dana's chest like a boulder. Dana gasped and tried to catch her breath. The fear and terrified realization in her face that Maya was a formidable opponent almost made me feel pity for Dana. Almost. I enjoyed watching Dana cowed and overwhelmed with such apparent ease. Yet, despite the power I felt, I was also hit with an unexpected sadness. In that moment, the tables had been turned. Maya and I were the bullies.

"Here's the deal: Nica told me everything," Maya announced, clearly enjoying being in control of the situation. "I know what you're up to, and I want it to stop. I want you to leave Nica alone. I want you to let her have her friends back, and I want you to bring her dad back—whatever that takes. And I want you to know your place. I'm never going back to being number two around here. Ever."

I watched as Maya's jaw clenched, and a moment later Dana was lifted into the air and dropped roughly to her feet. "Understand?"

Dana remained silent. She wouldn't give us the pleasure of repeating it. She folded her arms defiantly and just glared back at Maya and me.

"Say it," demanded Maya, "or we're going to have a problem."

I felt proud of Maya, who had so evidently embraced her abilities and come into her own during the months of her exile.

"The problem is that you're here," Dana snarked back, unbowed by Maya's display of impressive power. "I don't even have to give you bitches the chance, but I will: Get out of Barrington. Both of you. Or I won't be responsible for what happens."

I knew that Dana's threat was clear and unequivocal. She'd go to war with us in a heartbeat.

Maya's nostrils flared. That was not the answer she was looking for. I braced myself as Maya started to press harder, crushing the breath from Dana's lungs like a human tube of toothpaste.

"Maya," I cautioned, "let it go."

The cheerleader began to turn shades of purple and blue as she tried to suck air into her useless lungs.

"Stop!" I yelled, worried that she would actually kill Dana right there in the school parking lot.

Maya wouldn't stop, or perhaps couldn't. She was losing control, and the furious look in her angry eyes said she wanted to kill Dana. I froze, trying to figure out what to do to defuse the situation. I couldn't let this go any further, but Maya was much more powerful than I was. If I tried to physically intervene, would she turn her rage on me?

I took my chances and grabbed Maya by the shoulders. "Stop it!"

Finally, something shook loose. I saw the shift in Maya's eyes as she snapped back to reality, huffing like she'd just run a marathon.

Dana sucked in air, her chest heaving up and down as she quickly came back from the brink of unconsciousness. Released from Maya's hold, Dana scrambled backward and then launched to her feet and ran for her car.

"Let's go," Maya ordered as she threw her hood up to

hide her face from the rest of the crowd still emptying out of the gym and retreated back into the darkness.

As I followed Maya away from the school and her dangerous public display of powers, I felt something horrible brewing all around us. I should've known this was the beginning of the end, but I was so overwhelmed by the fact that our cover was blown that I couldn't focus on what had just happened. I could only think about what would happen next.

There was no way I could go to the Winter Formal. For that matter, there's no way I could let Chase go to the Winter Formal either. If Dana and Maya ever found themselves together in the same room again, there was no telling what could happen.

All of that was on the tip of my tongue that Friday night when my doorbell rang. I was sitting on my bed in sweats and a T-shirt, waiting for that chiming *bing-bong*, dreading it, and hoping that maybe the dance would just get canceled. After all, Dana knew the stakes; Maya seemed out for blood. Dana could easily have gotten the event shut down if she were concerned enough, but she wasn't. Once the moment in the parking lot passed and she'd filled her lungs with air again, she must've convinced herself that Maya was just making an idle threat. She was so wrong.

At the same time, I knew there was no easy way to explain all of this to Chase, which is how I'd let things get this far. I stayed out of school after the parking-lot incident and kept dodging his insistent calls and texts that we discuss Maya's reappearance. I kept hoping some random turn of events would remove the wall at my back and allow me to make a smooth escape: *Sorry, Chase. Can't go to the dance. My dad needs me to pick him up from somewhere in Florida. Sorry, Chase. Can't go to the dance. The world's about to end.* I mean, anything at this point would be better than answering that bell. But nothing had come up. The situation was this: Chase was at my door, ready to take me to the dance, and I was going to have to let him down because of a war that only I, his ex, and Dana knew was brewing.

I took slow steps down the stairs as the bell rang again, rehearsing what I could say to him and coming up empty over and over again. It was like I was watching someone else as I stepped to the door and opened it. Chase's muscular fame stood in the doorway, beaming at me. Strong, handsome, and smooth in his designer dinner jacket, he looked every inch the suitor I knew he would. I didn't swoon, but I allowed myself to stare. I couldn't help but fantasize about him scooping me up and whisking me away, but before I could get much further, his face fell.

"Where's your dress? I thought you'd be ready."

"I can't," I said apologetically.

"You can't get dressed? I can help you with that." He smirked.

"No," I replied, shaking my head and trying not to laugh at his one-track mind. "I can't go to the dance with you, Chase."

A curtain of silence fell between us.

"Can . . . Can I come in?" I silently stepped aside as he continued. "If this is about Maya . . ."

"There's a lot going on in my life right now," I confessed, "and you are by far the best part of it." I took his hand in mine. "Let's be honest though: We are not part of the same . . . social . . . anything . . . at Barrington. You've seen what's happened over the past couple weeks; you aren't blind."

"So what? Dana doesn't like you. I don't like her either."

"It's worse than that. Trust me. You've worked hard to get where you are and have the friends that you do. And I don't want to ruin that by dragging you down."

He looked like a genuinely hurt puppy.

"Maybe I ended up where I am so that I could meet you."

Ahhh, don't make this so hard!

"Chase . . ."

"Nica . . . ," he mimicked.

Part of me just wanted him to leave. Another part wanted to leave with him.

"None of that matters. I really like you."

"It's not that simple."

"It is! I promise! Look, maybe it's dumb, but Mr. Manning

has this thing he told me about being in high school. He said that everyone wants to fit in, but really it's more important to stand out. I want to stand out, and I want you to stand out with me. Honestly."

My head was in a full-on wrestling match, pitting what I wanted against what was right. In the moment, I made a bad choice. I agreed to go to the dance.

And life would never be the same.

20. A TRIP TO ANTARCTICA

It's true: Barrington was basically a corporate-owned police state operating in the guise of a wealthy, idyllic small town. But damn, did their high school know how to throw a party.

I hadn't given much thought to my expectations—a low-lit gym, some streamers, a punch bowl surrounded by the same cookies they offered at lunch—but this was something else. Barrington High was a choreographed dance number away from every American-high-school-movie formal I had watched abroad on bad bootleg DVDs and always assumed were a complete and utter fabrication. The biggest surprise of all? I was actually having fun in spite of my life being in a complete free fall. I felt a little like I was partying aboard the *Titanic* as it was sinking into the frigid North Atlantic waters.

The music was pounding in my chest and Chase was matching me song for song. It was a far cry from Dana's Homecoming bash, where I'd deliberately kept to the margins and tried not to call too much attention to myself. But that night something had taken over me. I was having too much fun to worry about the blisters I knew were growing in my unpracticed heels and the shade Jackson was throwing from his perch against the wall. If my life was going to go down the tubes, I was going to at least have a bit of fun before the end. After the insanity of the past few months, all I wanted to do was smile, amped up on dance-pop fuel and raging teenage hormones until I was ready to drop.

I raged on in blissful ignorance, looking like a grinning idiot spinning under the lights with my arms in the air for another thirty seconds or so before Topher tapped me on the shoulder. I could tell immediately that he wasn't having such a good time.

"We should get going!" He had to shout over the music, and I could still barely hear him.

"Going where?" Chase interrupted.

"Topher just needs an extra set of hands," I announced. "Be back before you know it."

And off I went, leaving Chase alone on the dance floor, completely baffled about what just happened.

Topher led me out of the densely packed throng of partiers, and unfortunately, right past Oliver. He didn't notice me though, as he was completely focused on his dancing partner: Noah. Both Topher and I winced as we saw it, and I took the lead, pulling my friend straight past. Topher looked heartbroken, but we had bigger fish to fry.

In keeping with exactly how it would play out in one of

those high school movies, the high-octane dance jam faded out into a slow song. The floor cleared out and refilled with couples. Hand in hand, Dana and Jackson made their way to the center. I wasn't expecting the accompanying gut wrench, but I felt it loud and clear. From a distance they were perfect. She was a shimmering angel in his arms, all that lustrous hair tumbling down her back in old-Hollywood waves. Jackson looked every bit the hero to her heroine, dapper and filling out his suit in a way that few high school boys can. But I just didn't buy it anymore. Suddenly their "perfect couple" was like a reality-television construct I could see straight through. Maybe I was projecting, but so much of my intense jealousy had already fallen to the wayside. I could tell that Jackson wasn't happy; he resembled a Ken doll posed into position with a stuck-on plastic smile. I turned away to follow Topher and felt a distinct change in my longing. Instead of wanting Jackson, I was just sad for him.

Topher and I snuck out of the dance and climbed the stairs to the second floor, moving deep into the English department and about as far away from the gym as we could get. He lifted a gigantic set of keys from his pocket.

"Lifted them off the janitor," he admitted with a sense of glee. "My biggest crime to date."

I followed him inside with a grin. "Stick with me, kid. I'm a terrible influence."

We'd chosen the remote department lounge in advance,

both for its lack of windows and its comfortable couch.

We settled into position, Topher's laptop set up with the view of Antarctica open in front of us. We'd blazed through a quick mental refresher and everything was set. Everything, I noticed, except for locking the door. I bounded across the room to lock us in from the inside—only to have it fly open almost right into my face.

I was expecting all of Ski Club, so Chase's handsome face was a surprise. At least until I read it as decidedly unhappy.

"An extra set of hands, huh?" He stared daggers at Topher.

"It's not what you think. I promise," Topher declared, not getting up.

I pushed Chase out into the hall. "Go back downstairs. It's a long story and I can tell you later, but the sooner you leave, the sooner I can come back."

"You're kidding, right? I'm just supposed to be cool with you upstairs alone with this guy? Nica . . ." Chase was staring me down but he looked so worried. It was sweet enough to soften my edge.

"How about a compromise? You stay out here and watch the door."

He didn't love it, but he didn't throw it back in my face either.

"Do you trust me?" I asked.

He nodded, if slowly.

"Okay. Then I'll see you in about twenty minutes."

"Twenty minutes?"

I closed and quickly locked the door behind me, making sure Chase couldn't just barge in while Topher and I were in the middle of things.

"Is he going to be a problem?" Topher looked just as worried as Chase did.

"I don't think so. Let's do this."

"Now or never," he echoed as I settled back onto the couch.

We each took another minute to stare into the computer and look over my mom's coordinating snapshots. Topher wrapped his fingers around mine when he was ready.

I felt the bone-chilling cold the moment I opened my eyes . . . and immediately shut them again. It took a while for my brain to really process it. I knew I wasn't physically cold. My body was more than eight thousand miles away in centrally heated suburban Colorado, but the strain of that distance was like the coldest slap of wind chill I'd ever felt against my face.

I squinted to see what I could make out. It was stupendously bright—brighter than any natural light I'd ever experienced. Antarctica's summer sun glared down with all of the intensity of the Sahara but none of the heat. Unfortunately, all it did was light up the thick snowstorm, simultaneously coming down from the sky and whipping across the frozen tundra horizontally. Perhaps worst of all was the deafening roar. I couldn't really feel the wind, but I could hear it loud and clear. I felt like I'd been dropped into the middle of a punk-rock show.

"Topher?" I couldn't even hear the sound of my own voice. I tugged on his hand in mine, worried. "Topher!"

As soon as he looked back at me, I knew the clock was ticking. "Let's go," he said. "We're not going to have a lot of time."

But as soon as he said it, we both realized, *Let's go where?* It was just shades of white in every direction. Snow blindness. The reflection of sun off snow was so intense that "direction" became meaningless. I pointed in one direction. Topher nodded, and he and I stumbled ahead. With every step I prayed and hoped that I might find my mother at the end of the world.

With every haggard step, all I found myself thinking about was *The Little Mermaid*. Not the Disney film with the catchy tunes and fairy-tale romance, but the childhood-scarring Hans Christian Andersen version, where she disintegrates into sea foam at the end. When original-recipe Ariel was given human legs, every step felt like daggers. The picture book had left me in tears for days, but this was even worse. Now I was living it.

After a few fruitless minutes wandering in endless whiteness, I started to second-guess the whole mission. The very reason I hadn't been able to reach Lydia by phone was the inclement weather. How could I have thought I'd be able to beat that directly immersed in the elements?

I could see that Topher was ready to accept defeat. "I think we should go back. I haven't felt this sick since my first time. Nica?"

I couldn't even answer him. I was feeling it, too. Worse than the brief excursion Topher and I had taken in Barrington a few days earlier. I felt light-headed, dizzy, and extremely desperate. Almost claustrophobic in that expanse of whiteness, which felt confining and scary. This was my plan A. I didn't have a plan B to fall back on.

"Nica? This was a bad idea!" Topher shouted. "We can't see anything."

I agreed and was nearly ready to throw in the towel when I saw something. It was a faint splash of color on the ground, poking through the frozen white landscape. I crouched down to get a better look, hoping that it wasn't just a subzero mirage. The yellow was coated in ice and dirt and snow, but it was real. I smiled when I realized exactly what it was.

"Topher!" I pointed, and he squatted down for a second opinion. "It's a guide rope."

Topher nodded his confirmation. "They put them out here in case people get trapped in a storm. If we follow it, we might be able to get to the base."

The clock was ticking away. I knew Topher was ready

to turn back, but I was prepared to beg. "Please. Just a few more minutes."

Without a word, he nodded and took off after the narrow trail of yellow. The pain I felt in every muscle and joint—most likely the sensation of stretching our astral tethers to their very metaphysical limits—was just as intense, but now hope was driving each and every step.

I was only about five feet away when a building came into view. Even through the veil of bright white, I recognized the McMurdo Base Station immediately. I had made it. There was still one more obstacle. The door.

"We're going to have to go right through it," said Topher, pointing at it.

I nodded and recalled how his astral hand had slipped through the staircase railing just the other day. We rested both hands against the door.

"Just remind yourself we're not really here," Topher reiterated. "We have no mass. The rules of physics do not apply."

I was amazed to see his hand and arm push mine straight through the door. He was actually talking himself into it. Topher then reached back for my hand and pulled me through with him.

Once inside the station, it hit me that I still had no idea how to find my mom. We knew from the satellite images that all of the buildings were simply designed for the utmost longevity in Antarctica's extreme conditions. Luckily, in my case, simple also meant gridded. It was only two hallways before I found Lydia's name on a door plaque.

My mother just about died of a heart attack on the spot when she opened the door. "Nica? How did you . . . ? Who . . . ?" She couldn't finish her thoughts, and as she slumped against the doorframe, Topher and I moved inside and shut the door.

"Mom, look at me," I commanded, trying to get her past the initial shock of seeing me appear out of nowhere. She turned with a hand to her head, like she was afraid her brain might slide out if she didn't hold it in.

"I can't explain this to you now, but you need to look at me and understand this is real. This isn't a dream. This isn't a hallucination. This is an emergency."

"H-how . . ." Lydia couldn't put two words together, she was so overcome.

"I'm in danger. Dad is in danger. Barrington's not the place everyone thinks it is. Bar Tech owns it, and they are experimenting on kids. They've been doing it for a long time. The world needs to know what's going on here." I might have been only two cinnamon-roll side buns away from R2-D2's projected Princess Leia, but I had never seen my mother react so seriously.

"I need you home, Mom. More than ever." I knew this was all a shock to her system, but I had to make her understand the enormity of what was happening back home.

Lydia's eyes finally began to focus. She nodded, processing everything I had just said. In a matter of seconds I watched a fierce, protective lioness emerge from behind my mother's damp eyelashes. Ever the journalist, I knew she had a million questions she wanted answers to, but time was of the essence.

"I can't explain right now," I continued, "but it has to do with Bar Tech. Just come home. Now."

"I'll be there as soon as I can. I love you, Nica."

That was all I needed to hear to give me strength. The trip was over, and seconds later we were back in the teachers' lounge. This time I wasn't so lucky with the nausea. Topher recovered a little faster, though my stomach's reaction was no help to his.

"What now?" Topher asked.

I was still a little spacey. I couldn't believe I'd finally made it to all seven continents, even if that last one required a large asterisk.

"We get Maya. Lie as low as possible for the next couple days until my mom gets here. Hope Dana leaves us alone if we do."

When we stepped back out into the hallway, I was surprised to see it completely empty. Where was Chase? I supposed it was possible he'd taken a quick bathroom break, but it sent a shiver of apprehension down my spine.

"Let's go." Topher was already locking up the room.

I followed the throbbing bass back downstairs to the gym. The dance was just as energetic as I'd left it. I hoped that also meant no one had noticed Topher and I were gone for almost thirty minutes, but I knew better than to be too cocky about it. Dana Fox had a way of knowing exactly what I wanted to keep from her.

I started scanning the room for Chase. I visibly jerked when an arm slipped around my waist. There he was, finding me before I could find him.

"Where did you go? I thought you were worried about me," I teased him, at least until I could see that he was not in the teasing mood. I changed my line of questioning: "What's wrong?"

"Maya's here. I don't know what happened exactly, but she seemed really upset. It gave me this really weird sense of déjà vu. . . ."

I immediately knew what he meant even if he didn't. I had almost forgotten about Chase's memory loss following his coma a few months earlier. He might not have remembered exactly the chaos that happened when Maya got upset, but his subconscious seemed to. I had to get to her right away.

"Where is she?"

He shook his head, unsure. "She tore out of here a couple minutes ago."

I tried the door to the nearest girls' bathroom, but it

was locked when I tried to open it. My instincts were right. "Maya? It's me. Open the door."

There was a long pause before a *click* and the door cracked open just a sliver. I slipped inside, shutting it behind me. I knew she was in trouble as soon as I saw the state of the bathroom. It looked like someone had thrown a full-on tantrum, but Maya was beautiful and unharmed, huddled in the middle of the floor. She was weeping and the room was in shambles. Every mirror cracked or shattered, the fluorescent lights overhead flickering and barely hanging on to the ceiling, every paper towel dispenser emptied with the towels themselves tossed about like a tornado had hit them. It was all the more frightening because I knew she hadn't done it with her hands.

I approached her like a wounded, cornered animal, crouching, hands outstretched, eyes low. "Maya, are you okay? Can you tell me what happened?"

Maya's voice was cracked and throaty. "I never should've come back to Barrington. I thought maybe I'd scared Dana the other night, but she just went straight for the jugular."

My mind was racing. I'd barely been gone half an hour. The dance seemed undisturbed. What had happened that left my friend so broken? "What did Dana do?" I asked as gently as I could.

"I tried to talk to my old friends. Annie, Maddie, Jaden, and Emily from cheerleading squad. They called me an imposter. They said Maya Bartoli was dead. Then they demanded that I leave."

My insides curdled, and it reminded me of the living nightmare of my father's blank stare, of his threat to call the police on his own flesh and blood.

"Maya, I'm so sorry. After my dad and what happened at the game the other night . . . I never should've let you come to the dance."

It was in that moment that I saw a spark in her eyes. A switch was thrown, turning Maya from sad victim to bold aggressor. She peeled herself up off the floor and turned her rage on me. "No. You never should've let me stay."

The room was suddenly alive again. The glass rattled off the mirror frames, crumbling into the sinks. The light above us was rocking back and forth, almost tearing itself wire by wire out of the ceiling tiles, finally shattering into a million shards of glass.

"Maya—" I tried to interrupt, but there was no stopping her.

"Poor Nica," Maya exclaimed, her eyes getting wide with anger. "Sad and alone with no one to turn to. You needed me. You needed help. Do you remember what happened when that was me? When I was alone and I needed help? You sent me away! You and your friends stayed here together—safe—and I had to go off on my own. I had to grow and suffer because no one here could handle it."

I was afraid. I was afraid of my own friend. I didn't know if she'd hurt me on purpose, but I didn't think she'd stop the bathroom from eating me alive.

"I'm done being a good soldier, Nica!" Maya shouted, advancing toward me. "I'm not going to fall in line with your plan and try to pull everything into a neat solution. This is war. There will be casualties. Dana's going to pay."

Maya stormed out of the bathroom, and it was like a bomb exploded. I dropped to the floor and covered my face as glass flew and metal warped and the light finally made good on its promise, crashing to the floor inches from my huddling form. I couldn't stop shaking, but I had to stop her.

Unsteady, but on two feet, I opened the door and stumbled back out into the hall, scratched and bleeding. Maya was already out of sight, but I knew exactly where she was headed.

When I reached the gym, I didn't understand what was going on. The music had dropped to a schmaltzy ballad, but no one was dancing. Instead, it was almost deathly quiet except for the soprano melody and strings. All eyes were on the far wall, lit up with some sort of slide show.

I pushed through the crowd, simultaneously trying to get a better look at what was happening and attempting to find Topher and Maya. I had to stop her before she reached Dana. As the pictures came into view, I didn't recognize them at first: cute kindergarten class photos, a girls' soccer team, elementary-school art projects that only a parent could love. I didn't pick out the recurring figure until she entered her awkward middle-school photos. I was putting it together like a slow-motion car crash—all of the photos were of Maya.

As they eased into high school, I could only watch in horror. She was sparklingly photogenic in each captured moment: from being the only pretty girl in the Science Olympiad, to her stint as captain of the cheerleading squad, to photos of her year on homecoming court, and all the way through to her with Chase at a dance in the weeks before she disappeared. I felt the bile rise as I read the banner fading in above the photos: IN MEMORIAM. Soft sobs began to fill the room as friends and strangers mourned their loss.

It was so much worse than I'd even thought. Dana hadn't brainwashed the entire school—not to mention the entire town—into forgetting Maya Bartoli. She'd brainwashed them into thinking Maya was dead.

It was hard to spot Maya in the crowd, but I finally set my eyes on her. She was crying along with the rest of them. What did they even see when they saw her? How had Dana distorted the truth? Did the real, living, and breathing Maya just bring up a blank? I knew it didn't really matter, though. The emotional damage was real. And it was catastrophic.

As I looked around at the tears and the quietly shaking shoulders of my fellow classmates, it was clear that they all genuinely believed they were suffering the passing of a friend, one who was actually standing among them, a ghost at her own funeral. No one here was free enough of Dana's distortion field to understand the truth. I wanted to scream. *What the hell are you people doing? Do you understand the pain you're causing?* But they didn't. They thought that the Maya among them was a basket case.

I turned to Maya with "don't" on my lips, but it was too late. The tears that stained her face dribbled from eyes that had rolled fully back into her head. She wasn't blinking, and I could see that there was nothing left but the whites of her eyes, crisscrossed with the bright red lightning bolts that were her strained and shattering blood vessels. In that instant, I felt a powerful, inescapable truth in my gut.

We were all going to die.

21. SHAKE, RATTLE, AND ROLL

I'd never considered what it would be like to perish in a building collapse. Being wiped from the face of the earth by a car crash, or a plane crash, or the violent protestations of an angry mob as they turned against their government had all been real possibilities in my travels with Lydia. I'm sure we'd stayed in places that sat on jittery tectonic plates or were known to have been in the path of deadly storms, but I'd never witnessed anything of the sort and never lay awake in bed at night fearing that the ceiling might collapse onto me. It struck me now that I hoped it would be quick.

A mess of multicolored electronic noises broke the photos into crazy patterns and lines. They snapped right back the first time, but then—*bzzrkkkt, bzzrkkkt*—the projector fritzed twice more and the smiling faces of Maya and pals didn't come back. The bulb exploded with a brilliant white snap. One-hundred-some-odd kids and chaperones flinched at the same time, covering their eyes and yelping in surprise.

"Everyone okay?" shouted a voice from across the room.

The replies all came back positive. The glass and sparks were contained within the machine, so no one had been hit with debris, and no one needed medical attention.

Except for Maya. Unnoticed in the aftermath of the sudden shock, she was still standing next to me in the back of the room near the soda machines, looking for all the world like she was having some sort of terrifying standing seizure. She wasn't convulsing or foaming at the mouth, but I knew she wasn't in control. Her fingers twitched like they were playing a complex concerto or counting to one million in a way that couldn't be easily comprehended. Her feet were beginning to lift off the ground. She rose barely an inch at first, then began to warp the air around her as she rose, causing it to shimmer like heat off of sunbaked pavement. The waves rippled up her body and crashed over her head, silent and gentle. I tried to follow the ripple outward from its conception point, but it quickly vanished.

This first wave of energy pulsated through the room so low and slow that it didn't even register as a physical phenomenon. It didn't create a wind or a shock. It wormed its way into people's ears and guts, spinning their senses and dropping them to their knees. One girl to my left fell to the floor and vomited. The chaperones were still recovering from the exploding projector and found themselves caught off guard by the new turn of events. Panic seized their faces. Was that an earthquake? What the hell was going on?

The last time Maya's powers had threatened the school, they'd been new, untested, almost useless in her clumsy hands, but that was before she'd trained herself. Before she could rip tree stumps from the ground and toss Dana around like a rag doll with nothing more than her mind and an endless supply of anger. It was impossible to know where those reservoirs were held or how they were formed, but whatever they were, they were real and very, very dangerous.

The second wave of energy came as a powerful thunderclap. It shattered every bulb in the ceiling and wrenched the projector down from its mount. Decorations ripped from the walls, and the snack bar in the corner was demolished. The sound served as whip crack that started a stampede of terrified teens. As they ran for the back, they came to a dead stop at the surreal sight of Maya, hovering two feet off the ground, head back like she was going to ascend to heaven.

Her fingers still twitched so hard they looked like they might wrap around themselves and break. My eyes caught Oliver's through the crowd—they were wide with fear. Though he knew about Maya's power, he'd never seen it manifest like this. Neither had Jackson or Dana herself, from the looks of things. They were equally wide-eyed and stunned. A third wave began to build at Maya's feet. More than just a ripple, it seemed to be bending and mirroring the reality around her. As it grew, swelling like a piece of blown glass that I knew was going to burst, I searched for my voice.

"R-run! RUN!" I shouted, realizing it was the only thing I could do at that moment to save people from the destruction that was sure to follow.

That snapped everyone out of it. The sudden crush of panicked bodies slamming into mine sent me spinning to the floor. My hands shot to my face and throat to fend off the feet that threatened to crush my windpipe. A hand burst through the crowd and yanked me up. It was Chase, and I clung to him as he threw his body between the crowd streaming for the exits and me.

"We got to get outta h—"

The third wave came and stole his words. It wasn't like the other two, loud and frightening. No, this one was almost silent. An explosion free of flames but furious in its destructive force. The molecules of the air itself were blasted apart from one another, torn asunder by Maya's terrible power. The room was leveled in the blink of an eye. Kids tumbled over tables, and tables tumbled through walls. Bricks collapsed into sand. The soda machines erupted into geysers of neon and sugar water. Every door and window in the room burst into pieces and sailed into the parking lot. Chase was yanked away from me so fast he looked like he shared Oliver's power. I was sent soaring at the same time and slammed into the remnants of a wall as the ceiling came tumbling down.

Then there was nothing: vague shapes in the dark,

popping colors that danced across the backs of my eyelids, but no thoughts, no sounds. I couldn't have stayed out for very long, since Maya was still standing in the same spot when I came to. She was covered in dust like a cheap stage ghost, shivering and crying. I wanted to leap to my feet to console her, but my body was unresponsive. My first horrified thought was that I'd been paralyzed, but the reality was that I was trapped under a pile of debris. It was too heavy to move, and I had to take to wriggling out from under it. I pulled my legs free and wobbled to my feet.

I noticed all the bodies. Some people must've made it outside, but those who hadn't had been tossed by the blast. I couldn't be sure if they were alive or dead. Hell, I could barely be sure of my own status in the land of the living. "Chase?"

No reply outside of a few groans coming from others who were rising to their own stunned feet. Sirens wailed in the distance, and the sound carried in through the ceiling, which was now open to the sky. I limped toward Maya, hands outstretched to comfort her, maybe even help her off the newly minted battlefield. Instead, her head whipped up and she shrieked, sending me back through the air with a flick of her wrist. I crashed down into a broken cafeteria table as Maya started to run, flinging away anything in her path with little more than a look and a wave of her hand. When she reached the back wall, she ripped the rest of that down the same way and stalked off into the night.

A dusty, bleeding hand fell onto my shoulder. "Hey, you okay?" Topher asked.

I turned and pulled him into a hug. I wasn't okay. I was terrified, ready to crawl into my bed and never come out— but I wasn't about to let him know that.

"We've got to get help," I said, as if that wasn't already clear.

"First we've got to get outta here," he proclaimed as he grabbed my hand and led me into the blown-out hallway. It was borderline apocalyptic, covered in garbage and debris that had been displaced in the wake of Maya's psychic freak-out. Topher held a finger to his lips as we slipped past the mouth of another hallway. He pointed out a group of kids huddled around someone on the ground, and in my rush to make sure that everyone was okay, I made a huge mistake. I ignored Topher's shushing and opened my mouth.

"Is somebody hurt?" One head turned toward me, then another. My stomach sank. All of Dana's minions. Then Jackson turned around, hoisting Dana to her feet with one muscular arm.

Shit.

"Stop her!" Dana shouted.

Topher and I bolted. He tore down the hallway behind me, pulled even, and in seconds, blew right by. It hit me that my three-inch heels, though plenty sensible for a dance, might as well be cinder blocks in this situation. I kicked the dressy spikes to the side and stepped on the gas, barefoot. It felt good. I caught right back up to Topher and shouted for him to hook right, up the rapidly approaching stairs.

FWAH-BOOM! A searing, liquid fireball hocked from down the hall exploded in the space we'd occupied seconds earlier. It melted lockers and tore the water fountain from the wall, sending a geyser of water flying free from the exposed pipe. Through the soaking spray, I saw Dana leading her army down the hall, right on our heels.

As we took the stairs two and three at a time, Topher tried to pin down our next step. "Where are we going?"

"To the Bridge!" We cleared the last steps, hit the landing, and there it was: An eighty-foot-long hallway enclosed by floor-to-ceiling sheets of plate glass, the Bridge connected the original high school that we were in to an expansion built a few years before I arrived. It was as futuristic and stupidly expensive-looking as the rest of the architecture in town that Bar Tech had a hand in and definitely wasn't a smart place to hide or fight, but it did have a set of steel fire doors at each end. As at any high school concerned with security and safety, they were installed there in case of emergency. Should there be a fire, or God forbid, a shooter in the halls, the doors could be remotely or locally closed, locked, and set to contain the problem. We passed through the first set, spun around, and slammed them shut with a metal-on-metal clang.

In that same instant, a blindingly bright halogen light roared to life on the other side of the giant glass panels. Topher and I turned away, but the light moved with us, keeping us from getting a good look at where it was coming from. I didn't need my sight to recognize the sound—the familiar grit and holler of a hovering helicopter. The glass barely dulled the noise, and Topher had to scream to be heard.

"Holy shit!" Topher exclaimed, looking terrified. "Are they from Bar Tech?"

"Unless you arranged transportation for us," I barked back, "I'd say yeah!"

As if to confirm our suspicions, a disembodied voice crackled over the bird's loudspeaker: "The situation has been contained. Please exit the building. Again, the situation has been contained."

They were either lying or had no idea what was going on. Either way, I wasn't about to turn myself over. Topher and I kept running. About halfway down the Bridge, the fire doors I'd closed behind us began to slam back and forth in their frames. Someone on the other side was giving them a beating. Instead of holding firm, one exploded from its hinges and flipped past us, scarring the floor in a flurry of sparks. I turned to see a Bar Tech Security guard the size of a mutant linebacker—like he'd injected himself with all the steroids in the state—hulking in the empty frame with a smoking bazooka. He charged with a guttural howl, Dana and the rest of her militia right behind him. A deranged-looking group of students flung the remaining fire door in our direction and missed by inches. Instead of taking my head, it smashed through one of the glass panels and careened into the parking lot below.

The helicopter repositioned itself, arcing high over the Bridge and coming level with us on the other side. As its floodlight blinded us for a second time, a voice cried out:

"Nica! Look out!" That sounded like Oliver, I thought. *Look out for what?*

A silver glint answered at the very edge of my peripheral vision. I turned away from the searing light to look out the opposite window. What I saw took my breath away. It was a bus. One of our shiny, high-tech, Bar Tech–supplied wonders of public transportation, except this one was suspended in the sky, twirling on the end of a wild, invisible string. And coming straight for me.

I spotted Maya in the parking lot below, wild-eyed, arms still extended from the effort of directing the vehicular projectile my way. The battered fire door was embedded into the roof of a car a few inches to the side of her. She must have thought the door was aimed at her. And now she was reacting like any wild animal would—by going on the offense. Unfortunately, I was standing directly between her and vengeance.

As the last seconds of my life ticked by, the bus grew closer and filled my entire field of vision, like the mouth of a giant coming to swallow me whole. It no longer sparkled in the light, it was consumed by shadow, a monolithic structure about to lay waste to what seemed like the entire world.

I didn't see what hit my chest, but the force of the contact ripped me off my feet and lifted me off the ground. I soared backward as the bus hit the glass at highway speeds, nearly rupturing my eardrums with its sound and fury. It tore through the steel like paper and pulverized anything less tensile. It stayed partially intact as it bisected the Bridge but met with the helicopter in midair when it erupted out the other side. The resulting explosion lit up the night and rained flaming chunks of debris down on what was left of the Bridge.

I landed on my back, and the air cracked out of my lungs. In the split second before he rolled off and vanished, I saw Oliver checking my face to make sure I was conscious and alive. He was gone before I could catch my breath. Had that really just happened?

I rolled to my stomach and took in the situation. The Bridge was no longer a complete hallway—it was a left side and a right side with a chasm at its center. Both remaining ends groaned under the newly misappropriated weight, threatening to collapse and crush us all under their free-falling weight. The half I lay in was bent maybe thirty degrees down, enough that I could feel the slope, but not so much that there was nowhere for me to go but to tumble out the bottom to the earth below. Dana and her cohorts, now trapped on the other side of the gap from me, were in danger of meeting the same fate. In fact, for the first time in weeks, their numbers worked against them. I was just one small girl; the demolished building could support me just fine. The dozen or so kids trying to get to their feet in the crippled section opposite me? Not so much.

"Nica!" I turned around and looked up the incline to spot Topher clinging to one of the fire doors we'd been sprinting for when the bus made its appearance. "Up here! We almost made it!" It wasn't far, just twenty feet or so. I could make it. I knew I could.

The chaos had me so distracted that I didn't notice the water until I tried to stand up. Broken pipes and erupting sprinklers released rushing rivers of water down the linoleum surface, making any sort of foothold impossible. The only way to get to the top was going to be on my stomach. I stayed low and hung on, turning my head to the side to keep from gulping down the gallons of filthy water flowing into my face. With all the strength I had left, I put one hand in front of the other and pulled myself against the tide. Each time I slipped and fell back, Topher screamed down at me to keep going. More than halfway there, I heard a series of cracks beneath me, and the hallway dropped a few feet. The jolt threw me, and I tumbled back, catching the edge of the broken floor as I went over the edge.

"Shit!" I looked backed up to Topher, but there was nothing he could do without putting himself in danger. I was dangling on my own with no way up and a long way down. Invisibility wasn't going to make the fall any less deadly, and the torrential waterfall splashing over the edge was only hastening my demise. I could recognize bad news when I saw it. "Topher, run!"

"Not until you're safe!" he shouted back. The gesture was brave, but putting himself in any more danger was pointless.

"If your power can show people the truth about Dana, you need to find Jackson. You need to find Oliver, and you need to open their eyes!" Topher looked terrified, but I knew my words were hitting home. "Go! Get outta here!"

As if to show him things would be okay, I reached into the deepest recesses of my strength and pulled myself inch by agonizing inch up over the edge and flat onto the floor. He didn't move—he just looked past me, over my head. *What the hell are you waiting for?* I rolled onto my back to follow his gaze and saw Dana running toward the gap, angry crowd at her back. She practically roared as she hit the gap and leaped into the air, leading her minions into battle. They each followed suit, jettisoning over the chasm with a powerful shove from the petite girl I saw being tested up on the mountain that night.

"GO!" I screamed to Topher in the second before they all landed on our side of the Bridge. He threw the door wide and disappeared to the other side. I could only hope I was a desirable-enough target that no one would even notice he'd vanished. Dana hit first, and the impact drew a bone-jarring rattle from the structure. As the rest of the mutants landed, I closed my eyes and waited for the whole thing to give way. Each one seemed to crash into the floor harder than the last, and as I looked into their dark eyes, I knew they weren't planning on showing any mercy.

Jackson fell last, slowing his descent on a large blue ball of lightning. I kept thinking this must be a mistake . . . a bad dream. He strode over to Dana's side, and they each grabbed one of my arms, yanking me to my feet without a word. This wasn't a nightmare. This was my life. Were they going to toss me off the edge?

"It didn't have to be this way," announced Dana, sounding victorious. "What are you even fighting for?"

"Bar Tech will never own me," I declared, defiant. Then I shut my eyes and prepared for the worst when I heard Topher yell—from behind me. Everyone turned to see him standing on the side of the Bridge that Dana's A-Team had just fled. He was projecting himself to distract them.

"Hey, assholes!" Topher taunted, waving his arms with abandon. "You only got one of us!"

With the precision of a general, Dana gestured and half

of the students swarmed back to where they came from. Of course, Topher would be long gone by the time they got there. I closed my eyes to take advantage of the moment, planning to turn myself invisible and punch my way out if I had to—but when I opened my eyes again, I was still solid. I tried again. Nothing. What the hell? Was this because of the astral projection? Had we gone too far? Had I lost my own power? Dana turned back to me just in time to catch the surprise on my face.

"Oh, relax. There are some people who are going to be very happy to see you." Her fist landed in my face and the lights went out.

22. RECKONING

There were dozens of TV monitors. It looked like the inside of NASA's launch station or a live television booth or an evil genius's lair. Bar Tech Security really was ubiquitous. They were everywhere. Every monitor was a different camera, a different angle on our quaint mountain town. And there were so many. Every street corner and business and traffic light framed in closed-circuit black and white. Except tonight's views were not Barrington's bread and butter, the deceitful facade of gleaming modern amenities and fake folksy charm. Instead, Barrington was in ruins.

The high school had been just the beginning. Maya was a natural disaster, tearing Barrington apart street by street. She had set her sights on Dana, but a true storm had no goals, no enemies. She had one mode: annihilate. As soon as Maya had returned to town and shown me how her powers had developed, I had fantasized about her wreaking havoc on Bar Tech, destroying the secret facility on Whiteface, taking Cochran down. But this was not what I'd hoped for.

I couldn't root for her, destroying homes and hurting people without a hint of restraint or remorse. Maybe even the idea that she'd ever been in control was just as foolish and shortsighted as the town's blind eye to Bar Tech's omnipotence. An hour ago, she had been a seventeen-year-old with unprecedented power. But now? Maya wasn't a person anymore. She was a force.

Still, I couldn't help but wish for just an ounce of Maya's strength. Contained in a glass office, my view of operation headquarters was so unobstructed I could almost hear its mocking laughter. Four walls, even just of high-quality glass, were enough to contain her. Of course, I could turn invisible, but that wouldn't do me any good. I reminded myself, though, that even my superficial power was in question. I hadn't been able to use it when we were trying to escape the school, when I really needed it. And it didn't seem to be improving, no matter how much I tried. I had two options. Watch the televisions or will my power back to functionality. They felt equally fruitless.

The waiting didn't seem so bad when I was suddenly faced with the alternative: interrogation. I watched as Richard Cochran and Mr. Bluni approached. They may have shown their differences when I'd watched them fight at the lab, but they were now unified in their position against me. I tried to imagine how this would go, but all I could picture was the two of them jockeying for bad cop. Bluni sat first.

"Nica," he started, with a heavy sigh that I guessed was trying to communicate his "aw, shucks" disappointment in me. "I gave you the opportunity of a lifetime. To become part of something historic that will transform humanity for the better. This could've been so much easier if you had just decided to cooperate. Instead, you decided to hold in all that jealousy and angst and insecurity. It didn't matter how hard Dana tried to befriend you. You were just stubborn. And look at where it's gotten us. I hate to say it, but . . ." He tossed a long look to the monitors over his shoulder. "This is all your fault."

I laughed. I could normally talk myself into a whole lot of guilt; I could find a way to make my latest problem entirely my fault, but if this Psych 101 tactic was how Bluni planned to break me, he was shit out of luck.

"Right, of course," I snapped back. "Because I irradiated pregnant women to see what would happen to their kids." I didn't care that I was locked up in the center of enemy territory. If all I had left was my dignity, I wasn't going to let them put this on me.

"Lashing out at those trying to help is a perfectly normal response. We had just hoped you were better than that. That you'd see the big picture." Bluni continued on his high horse. "That's why we're here now, Nica. To offer you one last shot to work for scientific advancement. Medical progress. To join your friends and pave the way for the future."

God, where was he getting this? It was like Bluni had found a direct line to Newspeak.

"I'm actually quite certain that helping you and my friends and community are mutually exclusive," I declared. I could at least take some triumph in the cracks of Bluni's cheery facade.

Cochran pushed ahead, cutting through the niceties. "We need to control this. Maya is going to keep hurting people, including herself, until we can stop her. She's your friend, right? All I'm asking for is your help."

Richard Cochran's game was certainly better than Bluni's. I'd give him that, but it didn't mean I was an idiot. There was nothing I could do to help them stop Maya, at least not inside this glass cage. I wasn't sure what they were really digging for—maybe just to see exactly what I knew, or perhaps what we had planned, or maybe they even knew they had a whistleblower on their side, the yet-to-be-revealed mystery texter. I crossed my fingers he was still out there. I knew I had to toe the line.

"I'm sorry. I can't help you," I replied. "You were right. I'm just a kid." Maybe they'd try to force it out of me, but I had plenty of fight left. Until I was jacked up on Sodium Pentothal, my lips were sealed.

"Fine," Cochran said, a flash of anger showing. The tone of an impatient parent had slipped into his voice. "We can do it without you. It's all over now, anyway. Our patents are on the fast track for approval."

The man Oliver and Chase called father turned on his heel and marched away without a second's hesitation. Bluni lingered behind. I couldn't tell if I'd angered him more or if Cochran had. I was still unsure as to why the two were at odds.

"You think you're doing the right thing, but you're not protecting anyone," asserted Bluni. "Not even yourself. There is no Barrington without Bar Tech. More than half the town works for the company."

I ignored Bluni's threat and just stared off over his shoulder. It wasn't quite a showdown, but I considered myself the winner when he finally slunk off.

Alone again, I had all the time in the world to ponder the meaning of their visit. It was possible that they just wanted to know what I knew, but that didn't seem to warrant the presence of Bar Tech's two heaviest hitters. The bigger question was what they were dancing around with all of the vague "end is nigh" omens. Cochran had said he was shutting it down for good. But shutting what down?

I remembered what Oliver had told me about Cochran, about how he'd been forced to financially invest in developing Barrington's superpowered offspring as the alternative was a much more sinister ending. I'd written it off as bullshit, easy Bar Tech propaganda that was being delivered by demented daddy dearest and smoothed over by Dana's powers. Had I been wrong to discount it?

Obviously, it had been told with as much positive spin for Cochran as possible, making him look like a sympathetic leader stuck between a rock and a hard place. But removed from that context, it did seem totally possible that Cochran hadn't been interested in the program from the beginning. It was certainly high risk and was even now, more than fifteen years later, waiting on rewards. Chase had said that his father was a businessman first, eliminating the original atmospheric research that had filled Whiteface's now-refurbished facilities. I hadn't even considered how much those renovations must've cost. Not to mention the millions or even billions Bar Tech invested in scientific research. I knew there was more to it.

That would have to wait because I heard more approaching footsteps. It seemed unlikely that Cochran or Bluni would be back for more. I braced myself. It could be Dana. If I couldn't escape her, would her powers be able to wear me down? It was the first time I'd considered a truly dark ending to my current situation. At least I knew I wouldn't surrender to Dana without a hell of a fight.

When he appeared around the corner, I gasped. I was surprised, for sure, but I didn't know whether to be elated or terrified. It was Chase. "Nica!" It was a hushed call as soon as we made eye contact. He tossed a weary look over his shoulder as he hustled up to me. "Are you okay?" He pressed a palm flat against the glass, and I immediately felt like I was in my own Lifetime movie.

I hadn't responded yet, but he kept talking. I was trying to get a read on him. I hated that I was even thinking it, but Chase as my white knight was too good to be true. We had gotten separated at the very beginning of Maya's stage-five meltdown. It was enough time to go running to his father and for Cochran to break the news to him gently. *Sorry, son, but your girlfriend is playing for the other team. Time to man up and close ranks.* Maybe it was a little militaristic for the J.Crew Cochran men, but I got the idea. Family first.

"Can you hear me in there?" Chase tapped his fist against the glass a few times, recapturing my attention.

"Yes." I nodded. "Sorry. Being held captive by your dad is a little overwhelming." I didn't like hitting Chase with a litmus test, but I didn't know what else to do. It wasn't even personal. Oliver and Jackson had been taken from me as well. I just needed to ascertain Chase's loyalties as quickly as I could.

I still felt like a jerk. Chase looked like I'd slapped him. "I don't know what to say to that. He's my dad; I can't change that. But I'm here. I can get you out."

"How?" I asked, immediately suspicious, but Chase was already digging the necessary tool out of his pocket. A white rectangle the size of a credit card emblazoned with a Bar Tech holographic image.

"I swiped it from my dad's office," Chase said as he slipped it inside the door's digital lock.

Here I was, receiving a miraculous rescue, but it only made me question it more. He had stolen it from his dad's office? Obviously, it was his father's company, but Bar Tech was no mom-and-pop business. Just because Chase was Cochran's son didn't mean he had the run of the place.

As the light flashed green and the door swung free with a small beep, I considered a second, possibly worse option. What if it wasn't Cochran Senior who had pushed Chase to my aid, but Dana? As soon as I thought it, I immediately recognized it as the slyer, smarter move. Instead of Chase's father having to reveal his true colors (what kind of good parent locks up teenagers?) and asking him to narc out his girlfriend, Dana was the perfect solution. Dana could've talked him into a betrayal he'd see with only undying certainty. No torn loyalties or moral choices; only a blind surrender to the lure of Dana's snake eyes.

His hug, squeezing the air out of both of lungs, certainly felt genuine. Chase took my hand, pulling me ahead, but my heels instinctively dug in. He turned back to look at me, incredulous.

"Come on! We have to go now." I could see it play across his face as he finally figured it out. "Jesus Christ. You don't trust me?"

I wanted to apologize and just run off into the unknown winding corridors with him, gunning for safety and trusting he'd pull me free of his own father's maze. But I had already lost too much. I didn't know if I was more afraid that Chase had betrayed me, or the surprise of one more person being ripped from my heart.

"I want to," I answered hesitantly. "It's just . . . well, it's a little convenient, isn't it?" It felt like I was punching us both in the gut. "You finding me minutes after your dad has trapped me here? An eager shoulder to cry on?"

I slowly backed out of the glass cell. If my hunch was right, I wanted at least a running chance before getting shoved back inside.

"I don't know what to say to that," Chase replied, hands held up as if to say "I'm no threat" and "I come in peace." "I trusted you when you asked me to. When you wanted to lock yourself in a room with Topher. I just stood by, no explanation. Hell, I guarded the door for you!" He clenched his jaw and gritted his teeth, trying to calm the anger worming its way to the surface.

"I tried to get you to stay away from me," I retorted. "I told you it might not be safe for you."

"And you know what that means by normal-people standards? That means 'I have trust issues.' That means 'I'm not sure how I feel about you.' That means 'Jackson Winters jerked me around and I'm still mooning after him.' Not 'Kids at our high school have superpowers and I'm one of them.'"

Did Chase know that? Or was he just assuming I was one

of them? It didn't matter anymore. Not a single resident had missed Maya's display under Barrington's extra-bright streetlights.

"If you want to go it alone, fine. Take it." He held the Bar Tech keycard out to me, an offer. "I'm sure I'll get a lecture, but no one will lock me up."

I'd never seen Chase look so worn down and defeated. I reached for the card . . . but took his hand instead.

"You promise you can get me out of here?" I asked, scanning his face one last time.

"I promise," Chase vowed.

I held his gaze. I couldn't be 100 percent sure of his loyalty, but I wasn't ready to be quite that cynical yet. "Here goes nothing," I announced as I used all my concentration to vanish before Chase's stunned eyes. His mouth hung open as he watched his own hand and arm, which were holding mine, start to disappear. In a matter of seconds he was gone.

"Whatever you do, don't let go of my hand," I ordered.

Chase tugged, and this time I followed. I was light on my feet, jogging alongside Chase through overly lit hallways and down metal staircases.

Security guards were combing the halls, checking doors, never realizing that they weren't alone. As Chase and I silently passed room after room of labs and computers and storage, something occurred to me. I knew right away it was exactly the kind of thought I should shy away from, but it refused to be denied. Why was I running away when every answer I'd ever wanted was in this very building?

My heels dug in once more, squeaking to a halt as my rubber soles gripped linoleum. I almost wrenched Chase's arm out of its socket.

"What is it?" Chase whispered, suddenly alarmed by my resistance.

I materialized and so did he. I pointed at the keycard he was holding in his left hand. "That's your dad's keycard?"

"Yes. Nica, come on. We've got to move." Chase was losing patience with me. At least one of us still had their head on straight. We could hear footsteps and voices from somewhere down the hallway.

I continued on. "Which means it will open any door in this entire building."

Chase didn't like where this was going. At all. "Yes . . ."

I had already made up my mind.

"I can't go yet. There are answers here, and I might never get an opportunity like this again." I knew that I risked losing my chance to escape, but I'd already decided on this, and damn was I committed.

"You realize this is absolutely insane, right?" Chase proclaimed, nervously scanning up and down the corridor for signs of Bar Tech Security.

"Yes," I acknowledged. "Completely and utterly."

"But that's how you roll, right?" Chase sighed, shrugged.

I nodded. He waved his arms like an overly enthusiastic college tour guide. "Where to?"

"Where would you get yelled at the most for sneaking into?"

Chase was sobering quickly. "The executive floor."

Three minutes and a special elevator later, I was in the belly of the beast. The executive floor could be accessed by only a handful of Cochran's most-trusted employees. It also had the coolest collection of mint-condition arcade cabinets I had ever seen.

"Always keeping me on my toes, Bar Tech," I muttered as I scurried past them with Chase.

"I'm not surprised. My dad has almost as many at home."

"You mean . . . you've never been up here before?" I asked, incredulous. I was confused, as Chase seemed like he knew exactly where he was going.

"Nope."

"Then how do you know . . . ?"

Chase pointed dead ahead to the double doors at the end of the hall. "Easy. That's the biggest office." He moved for the doors.

"Wait," I said, stopping in my tracks as I tried to assess the situation. "What if he's in there?"

Chase shrugged. Then he knocked. I winced, ready to run, but there was no response. We used the keycard and the doors swung open.

The office was spectacularly beautiful, impeccably decorated and designed. It was all browns, blacks, and creams. Spare Asian minimalism mixed with high-tech wizardry. Everything from the recessed lighting to the wall of concealed video monitors was controlled via a remote. It looked more like one of those insanely expensive luxury hotels than a business office.

Pushing all tangents aside, I headed straight for Cochran's computer. It was comprised of several slim monitors on his sleek, midcentury desk. With a secure office in an entirely secure floor providing more than ample security, Cochran's desktop was still password protected.

I realized that I had no chance in hell of hacking into Richard Cochran's personal computer. Still, I did have access to my own secret weapon. I turned to Chase, hoping that his status as the Cochran prodigal son had reaped some rewards along the way. "Any idea what your dad's password might be?"

I could see in his eyes that this was his do-or-die moment. Would he really betray his beloved father for some cause he wasn't even a part of? Or would he come to his senses and finally stop me and protect his family's empire?

"Takamori1877," he announced. "His passion is Japanese history—specifically Samurai Japan. Saigo Takamori was one of the great samurai warriors from the nineteenth century. Some say he was the last true samurai."

"Funny. That was my guess," I quipped as I typed the password on the keyboard and then headed right to the drop-down search function.

My first search was for Blackthorne. There was a lot of what I already knew, but stark confirmation directly from the devil's playbook. Bar Tech had bought up almost all of the public land. The files also revealed that Cochran had made several recent trips to Virginia, meeting with local politicians, contractors, engineers, and researchers from the state's best tech school. The project was certainly gearing up, seemingly under most of the company's noses. Only one woman, whom Chase identified as Richard's loyal assistant of more than fifteen years, was cc'ed on any of the correspondence. The spending was coming out of a special fund Bar Tech had formed for corporate charitable donations. As no one seemed to care too much about Bar Tech's philanthropic efforts, it was the perfect place for Cochran to hide his secret spending.

Next I tried my own name and my father's. As I'd suspected, Cochran had been isolating my father for weeks before Dana brain-wiped him clean and he was sent out of town.

"Looks like your dad knows more about me than maybe I do," I announced to Chase. Not only did he have details of my ability and its functions, likely thanks to Oliver and Jackson via Dana's superpowered wiles, but my habits, friends, absences from school, and medical records. The rabbit hole was tempting, but I knew I couldn't get stuck on the smaller details.

"What about Whiteface?" Chase asked, peering over my shoulder, eager to find out every secret his father kept.

"Jackpot," I replied with a smile.

This time there was not just what I already knew—the secret facility, Dana's role, gene patents, Bluni as the program's lead researcher—but what I definitely did not. Details on Cochran's computer showed that the training facility was not the only atmospheric research lab that had been gutted and refurbished. While the main lab, Bluni's headquarters, was the crown jewel, the remaining five labs were among Cochran's collection of dirty little secrets. Each former lab had been outfitted with the most rigorous lock system and accompanying keypad, but the real kicker was in their new content. Cochran had outfitted each unit with a truckload of C-4 explosives. I didn't know much about explosives, but for some reason Richard Cochran had been squirreling away enough to blast Whiteface into two. Unfortunately, it didn't say why.

When I heard the door's lock click open, it was like I had summoned him to answer the question himself. With nowhere to go, I yanked Chase down directly under the desk. I tried to go stealth again so we could have a chance to sneak out or at least hide somewhere a little less obvious.

My fingers shimmered but quickly returned to fully opaque. Chase shot me an urgent "hurry up" look. As hard as I tried to relax, focus my energy, and disappear, my body wasn't cooperating. Which made me only more desperate and panicky. But it wasn't happening.

Luckily, Cochran wasn't headed for his desk chair. He was too busy shouting back and forth with Bluni. "This Maya Bartoli shitstorm? This is all on you, Bluni. You were so caught up in your research lab you never realized how dangerous an enemy she could be to us."

"This isn't my fault, Richard," Bluni barked back. "This incident at the school has nothing to do with the science. It's an isolated aberration."

"Isolated? She's rampaged half the town. She's the exact worse-case scenario that every researcher warned the board about before you told them every lie they wanted to hear and convinced them that these traits were safe to harvest and implant in others. I don't know if it's better or worse when your fearless leader drinks the Kool-Aid too."

"Bartoli wasn't one of my kids," he answered defiantly.

"You're right; she's not. But Nica Ashley is. And you let her run wild." Cochran waved his hands around the room, presenting his office in its full glory. "The keys to the castle? My job? I know what the board promised you upon delivery of genetic patents. I might be getting pushed out, but I still have my people here."

Holy shit. I couldn't believe what I was hearing. Richard Cochran was no longer pulling the strings at Bar Tech?

"Fine. Great, in fact. The timing couldn't be better, because I am so tired of bailing out this ship you insist on sinking," said Cochran. He picked his laptop up off the desk, along with the single framed photo on the desk: Cochran and an eighth-grade Chase. "Enjoy it while you can." He departed with a smirk, leaving everything else behind him as he stormed out of the office.

Though Bluni didn't know he had company, Chase and I were reeling in Cochran's wake. My brain was scrambling to catch up: Cochran's reluctance to make the superpowered kids a real project at Bar Tech. Dana's recruitment tear through Ski Club and their training facility on Whiteface. Blackthorne, Virginia, Cochran's most top-secret projects. And his most recent acquisition: enough C-4 explosives to warm the heart of a Bond villain. I could feel that final piece clicking into place. It filled me with equal parts satisfaction and terror. It was time to get crazy.

Though Chase tried to stop me with every available limb, I climbed out from the under the desk. Bluni didn't even notice me until I spoke.

"I know what he's planning," I said boldly.

Bluni dove for the desk's panic button. The alarm had barely sounded before two security guards barreled into the room.

"Leave her alone!" Chase shouted, rising to my defense, but it was chivalrous in gesture alone. He was quickly in the same zip-tie cuffs I'd been wrangled with.

He and I were being dragged away, so I shouted out as much as I could. "Cochran's not abandoning Bar Tech. He's going to rebuild it. He has another site in Virginia that he's hidden from the company. It's called Blackthorne."

This seemed to at least get Bluni's attention. But why was I sharing? Why did I want to help Bluni, a man equally as vile as Cochran himself? Because I had figured out Cochran's endgame.

"He has all of Whiteface rigged to explode. He's going to bury Bar Tech, the town, and everyone with it."

Bluni didn't flinch, but I could see his hand beginning to tremble. He looked away, instead turning to the guards. I could see his time as Bar Tech's grand master already ticking away. "You know where to put them. And get me a location on Cochran. ASAP."

23. ESCAPE

Chase's hand was warm, and I squeezed it like a charm, the only source of heat and light in the otherwise frigid cell. It was so cold and dark, that "cell," wasn't even accurate. Compared with the rest of the building's architectural merit and postmodern grandeur, this felt like the dirty basement that Bar Tech had forgotten to finish. Its own Soviet gulag. The thought gave me chills. How many unfortunate people had been locked away in this place? While the realization that Chase and I weren't the first to rot in this hole was upsetting, even worse was the fact that we were on deck to be the last. I couldn't fix the past, but I was very focused on the future—the one that involved catastrophic destruction and the burial of Barrington. Every distant rumble and clank put me on edge, each one sounding for all the world like the beginning of the end. I sat silently, fists clenched, waiting for the reaper to arrive in the form of Cochran's avalanche, roaring down the mountainside to pulverize us. "Your dad's an asshole," I blurted out. Not the nicest thing to say but a bit of an understatement in my opinion. Not uncalled for, but I knew it probably wasn't the right time to say so. When was, though? I didn't want to start a fight, but I had to let Chase know how I felt. He squeezed my hand back.

"It's just not like him. It's not the guy I know."

"No one here is who you think they are," I said sadly, thinking about Jackson and his abrupt transformation. "We've all kept secrets from each other. I'm not proud of it, but we did."

"If I could just talk to him . . . ," said Chase, trying to wrap his head around the recent avalanche of disturbing revelations about his father.

"It's too late for that, Chase. We have to get out of here and we have to try to stop him. Talking will just get us killed."

Chase scooted across the floor to the slot in the thick door. "What are we gonna do?" he asked, as if I had some magic solution to our current predicament. "Can you shrink us and slip through here?"

I remembered that I hadn't actually discussed the specific details of what I was and wasn't capable of with Chase. In lighter circumstances, I probably would've laughed. But Chase was getting audibly frustrated—I hoped more at the situation than my attitude. A third voice interrupted.

"I have a better idea."

The voice came from behind me. I turned around to see Topher standing behind us with Oliver at his side.

"About time," I said matter-of-factly, and then ran toward them for a hug. In my excitement, I'd forgotten that they were simply projections, and my efforts sent me breezing right through their spirit forms and nearly crashing into the wall. "Right," I said, noticing Chase's spooked look, triggered by our friends' sudden, ethereal appearance. "Uh, so, Topher can—well—long story, but it's him. Just separated from his body. Astrally projecting. This is what I was doing at the dance. I had to get to my mom."

"But isn't she . . . ?" Chase shot me a bewildered look.

"Yeah, down in the South Pole. And Topher and Oliver are in town at Ebinger's."

"Oh. Duh." Chase looked more confused than ever.

I turned and looked at Oliver. "You saved me at the school."

He blushed and looked at his feet, embarrassed by the attention.

"What happened with Dana?" I asked.

"There are places in my brain she didn't get to," he replied. "It took seeing you in danger like that, but it was so clear. You were about to get hurt. I had to do something."

His explanation sent one thought blazing across my brain: What about Jackson? If Oliver was moved to action, why wasn't he? Did he not care about me? Or not care enough?

"It took me a while to find him," remarked Topher. "But

I didn't give up. I kept thinking about what you said—that I was the only one who could open his eyes."

"And he did," Oliver chimed in with a warm smile. "I'm so sorry for the way this all happened. I can't believe what a dick I was."

"You were, but it wasn't your fault," I said, just relieved to hear Oliver sounding like himself again.

"I could've fought harder," Oliver retorted guiltily. "I should've been stronger."

"And I should've been a better friend," I shot back, feeling my own pangs of guilt. "All Dana did was shove a wedge into a crack I created."

Chase jumped from behind as his brain kicked back into gear after being blown wide open. "Hate to break up the good vibes," he interrupted, "but you want to tell them what's going on?"

I started to pace as I relayed to my friends the information we'd discovered and the actions Bluni had taken; how we'd ended up in here, with no idea of where Cochran was or what he was up to.

Oliver was the first to jump in with a semblance of a plan. "Topher, how far away is the bakery from here?"

"Ten, maybe twelve miles," answered Topher.

"That's where we went for . . . the projection," Oliver explained to me. "Once I'm back in my body, I can cover that distance and be back here in like two minutes. It might be a fight to get in, but if Topher can find where the keys are, I might be able to break you out."

"You aren't a fighter," I reminded Oliver, stating the obvious.

"No, but I am angry," he countered, holding out his hands and curling them into balls. "This is a fist, right?"

I grinned. "That'd be it."

"Then I think I'm all set," affirmed Oliver. "And I promise I'll only fight if I have to. If I'm quick enough, no one will even notice I'm here."

I glanced over at Chase and Topher. "Work for you guys?" They both shrugged their approval. No objections.

"Okay then," Oliver said, nodding at Topher. "See you all in a few." Oliver and Topher blinked out of sight. And just like that they were gone.

"You really think this will work?" Chase pressed, doubt written all over his face.

"No idea," I replied honestly.

"Has Oliver ever thrown a punch outside of a video game?" Chase asked, trying to muster up a bit of humor in an otherwise grim situation.

"It's the only option we have," I reminded him. "If Oliver says he can handle it, my fingers are crossed and my hopes are high. Have a little faith."

After a few quiet minutes with no sign of Oliver's arrival, I began to worry that my own faith was misplaced. Chase knew better than to point out that it had been much longer than my speed demon friend had predicted, but the silence just made me antsy. I looked through the small window in the door and noticed the hallway our cell was in had a wall of security monitors on the other side. No one was posted to watch them—was all of Bar Tech Security still downtown, cleaning up Maya's mess?—so I was free to observe the dozens of different angles feeding in from all around the facility. I scanned past labs and meeting rooms, bathrooms and hallways, but didn't see any indication that Oliver had arrived.

Come on, man. Where are you?

My eyes drifted to a segment of monitors focused on the perimeter of the building. Dozens of attentive guards were still on patrol. So much for my hope that Maya had been a large enough distraction to make this any easier on Oliver. One screen displayed a lonely back corner of the structure, a single guard leaning against the wall by a door. I looked past it—

—and right back as something blasted out of the nearby tree line and clocked the guard in the temple. The force nearly knocked him off his feet, and in an instant, Oliver appeared on-screen. He tried the door, but it was locked.

He stooped and searched the guard for a keycard. Seconds later, he was in.

I nudged Chase. He looked at me questioningly.

"He's here!" He joined me at my side and peered through the slot. I pointed out a second monitor, where I'd picked up Oliver's journey into the facility, then a third, then a fourth. He was tough to follow, popping from hallway to hallway, but he was making his way to us when he stopped and whipped around, like something spooked him. There was nothing there, but he seemed to look relieved and started talking to someone. Topher! After a few seconds, Oliver grinned and sped off the way he'd come. I lost him, but Chase picked him up three screens over and four down. He peered through a thick window, checkered with rein-forcement wire, that looked in on a large office. That must be where the keys are kept.

"No way he's getting in there," mumbled Chase, coming to the same conclusion. Oliver looked around and blasted down the hallway, where he lifted a sizable trash can off the ground. A second later, the wastebasket burst through the glass like a rock through paper. An alarm began to sound as Oliver hopped in through the busted glass. Chase was shocked. "How'd he do that?"

"Speed," I realized aloud. "Inertia. Once an object starts moving at a certain speed, it'll keep going that speed, even if he stops. Like in a car accident." I shuddered at the memory of the wreck I'd experienced in Oliver's mother's backseat.

"So however fast he can run . . . ," Chase added, mulling over the ramifications of inertia.

". . . that's how fast he can throw anything he can hold," I chimed back, completing the science lesson.

Bzzzzzt! The door lock disengaged and Oliver popped it open. He ran in for a hug, which I returned at full strength. He turned to Chase, arms wide—

—and paused. Chase was not diving in to reciprocate the embrace. The brothers looked each other up and down, wary. There was no spite, but no warmth either. Chase extended a closed fist. Oliver gave him a pound. They both offered a small nod of understanding. This would do for now.

"Now can we get the hell outta here?" I asked as I eagerly strode out of the detention cell.

If we could've run as fast as Oliver, the escape would've been so much smoother. From caged to free in ten seconds flat. That wasn't happening. Our legs were still stuck in first, while Oliver zipped down each new hall like a race car with a brick on the gas pedal. After making sure each was clear, he'd gesture for us to follow and we'd catch up as fast as we could. This worked for the first few floors we ascended through the mazelike complex, but we were quickly met with resistance. The alarm triggered by Oliver's trashcan-through-the-window trick was still wailing, and the sound was drawing guards—not just from outside, but from within the recesses of Bar Tech as well. We could hear them pounding down the same stairs we were galloping up, and Oliver signaled for us to turn around. Speed wasn't necessarily in our favor anymore. Hiding would have to do.

We dove under the stairwell as gruff shouts and thick boots clattered by. I squeezed Chase's hand and wished I could vanish. More than anything, I wished that I could make Chase vanish with me, too. None of this was his doing, but here he was, being hunted just like one of us. When the last guard passed through the door, we hustled back up the stairs. We were going to have to rely on the world's fastest teenager to get us out in one piece.

"There they are!" The shout came from behind us, from a burly guy with a beard that wrapped his face like a werewolf's.

Oliver looked for something to throw. Nothing. The hall was white and bare. The security guard held up an automatic weapon—whether it was loaded with bullets or a beanbag, we had no way of knowing—and barked at us to freeze. Chase and I obeyed. We were caught, and our hands went up. Oliver made a familiar fist. He didn't think he could take this guy, did he?

Fwoom! Oliver fired himself down the hall like a human rocket. My eyes couldn't even trace him until he was less than a foot from our captor, where he emerged from his speedy blur with his fist aimed for that bearded chin. Knuckles met jaw with a crack, and the guard dropped to the floor as Oliver rolled past him and sprang back to his feet. He brushed himself off and jogged back over to us.

Chase enveloped him in a massive bear hug. Oliver's voice was a muffled struggle as he gasped for air until his brother let him go. "We cool?"

"We're cool," Chase announced with an approving nod.

It was only a short sprint to the exit, and we found ourselves outside, alone in the dark, with most of the Bar Tech Security force still confusedly scurrying through the building behind us. Oliver ground us to a halt.

"Wait here."

"For what?" I shouted, ready to run until my body collapsed, just to be away from this place. Oliver pointed at a pair of headlights growing larger in the distance.

"Our chariot awaits."

In a few seconds, a large white Ebinger's Bakery van with Topher behind the wheel screeched to a stop in front of us. Oliver rolled the sliding door back and ushered Chase and me inside. We froze at the sound of a dozen guns being cocked and aimed at our backs. A single pair of hands began to clap.

"And Cochran says you're all like Maya," a familiar voice proclaimed. "You're much more in control and far less dangerous."

I turned to see Mr. Bluni leading a phalanx of guards closer and closer to our position. Even though his words were big, I could tell he was a little uneasy, approaching us like we were kicked pit bulls, ready to attack.

"Grab them!" Bluni ordered the guards.

Oliver and I didn't even need to speak—he knew to run. Just like I'd told Topher when I was barely hanging on to the remnants of the Bridge, it was better for one of us to remain free than none of us.

A few of the guards spun and peppered the road with shots, but Oliver was too fast to be hit. He'd already cleared the road, vanished into the woods, and was probably halfway to Denver. Topher was yanked from the driver's seat and tossed into the back of the van with Chase and me. Bluni hopped in with three guards. Two more took the front.

"Where are you taking us?" I demanded to know as my wrists were bound once again with a zip tie.

"To offer a trade," Bluni replied after a moment of consideration. As soon as Chase and Topher's wrists were tied to match mine, Bluni pounded on the wall between the drivers and us. "Move!"

The van lurched out of the lot and peeled around the back of the Bar Tech offices. I tried to keep Bluni talking as the vehicle left the smooth pavement of the lot and hit a much bumpier patch of road. The rocky ride reminded me of the bus ride to the lodge, only that hadn't taken us anywhere near Bar Tech. We were going somewhere else entirely.

"Whatever you want," I said, "we can't help you."

Bluni scoffed. "Maybe you can't, but your boyfriend here can." He focused his eyes on Chase.

"Just say it, man," Chase responded. "I'll do it."

I shot Chase a look. He didn't have to give in that easily.

"She was right about your dad," Bluni declared. "He took a company helicopter, and we tracked him on his way to the top of Whiteface. Probably getting there as we speak. I assume that's where he's going to set off his charges and destroy my work."

Your work, I sneered in my head. Bluni was talking about our entire town. Our home. Many lives. To him it was all just an experiment, one wrapped up in his ego and lust for power.

"But I'm gonna offer Cochran a trade. He gives up," Bluni stated as he whipped a pistol from behind his back and leveled it at Chase's head. "And I won't kill you in front of him. All you have to do is convince him to let you live."

Fear gripped Chase's face. He could tell Bluni wasn't bluffing with idle threats.

Chase turned to look at me.

Bluni shook his head. "She can't help. This is on you."

I looked to Topher to see how he was handling the turn of events and noticed his eyes were focused on a point far, far away. At first I thought his almost catatonic state was brought on by stress, but then I remembered the times I'd caught him "daydreaming" at work. He wasn't trying to retreat into his head. He was projecting. But where to? What was he looking for? Maybe he was trying to find help. I couldn't ask him, so I decided to try to stall and give him the time he needed to complete his mission.

Before I could say a word, I saw Topher's eyes suddenly spark back to life. "He's here!" Topher's words were urgent and joyous.

I had no idea what he meant and neither did Bluni, but he wasn't taking any chances. "Who's here?" he demanded.

Topher refused to answer. His eyes were wild, his skin slicked with the slightest sweat. It was clear he knew something that we didn't, like he'd just returned from some sort of religious journey. Maybe he had.

Bluni cocked his gun and pointed it at Topher's chest. "Who. Is. Here?"

Suddenly, the sliding door rumbled wide open as if to present an answer. The guard closest to it turned, surprised, and was yanked off balance by an unseen force. He hit the floor at a strange angle and had time only to shout once before tumbling out the door and into the night.

Bluni pivoted and fired two shots at whatever had taken

the guard, but there was nothing there to catch his lead. The dark, snowy woods raced by, the wind reached in and slapped at our faces, but neither man nor beast presented itself as the culprit. Bluni inched toward the door, gun thrust out ahead of him. He steadied himself with one hand as the van continued to sprint over the rough-and-tumble road, unaware that a man had just been lost.

I was so close to leaning forward and shoving Bluni with all my might, sending him to join his unlucky employee on the side of the secluded road, but the other guards were too close. If I pushed Bluni, they might decide I was the next to go, or worse, just put a bullet in me. I gritted my teeth and let him explore. I settled back next to Chase and Topher, who was staring off again, back on whatever adventure he—
BANG! BANG! BANG!

Bluni leaped back, firing wildly. "Someone on the roof!" he shouted, and his men leaped into action. On a matched-three count, they threw open the back doors, ready to blow away whatever they saw. But again: nothing. The man on the right gestured to the man on the left to move forward with him. They took their time, step after step, Bluni at their back. I saw another opportunity to move in for the tackle, but I couldn't take the chance that one of them would turn and fire as we charged. Chase edged forward, but I nudged him back and shook my head. He and I would wait until we knew what was going on.

Even with the side and back doors open, it was eerily quiet in the van as the trio peered around each door and checked on top of the roof.

"Nothing, sir," reported the guard on the left.

I didn't believe it was nothing. Either Bluni was losing his mind more every minute, or somebody was toying with us. My instincts told me the other shoe was about to drop, but I couldn't ever have predicted it would come down swinging and screaming through the open panel in the side of the van.

In the form of Topher. Who, amazingly, was still sitting right next to me.

The guards and Bluni didn't realize the second Topher was just an illusion. All they knew was that they couldn't shoot at him. If they missed, the bullets would tear through the thin metal partition separating us from the front and possibly kill the driver. One of the guards took a swing and lost his balance as his hand passed right through the projection's face. Momentum carried him off his feet and into the wall. If he hadn't cleared out of the way, I don't know if I ever would've seen the completely unnatural gust of whirling, swirling snow tumbling along the road behind the van. It looked like the Tasmanian devil was right behind us, which could mean only one thing.

No way. It was Oliver, hot on our heels. He must've

been the one to open the door and yank the guard out, and now he was catching back up to us to finish the chaos that Topher started. There weren't many steps left for Bluni and his men to take before they'd find themselves falling out of their ride, and Topher's "angry ghost" act was proving effective at shrinking that distance to a razor's edge.

The remaining guard caught me looking over his shoulder, at Oliver right behind him, and spun around. Without breaking his incredible stride, Oliver grabbed the man's weapon and twisted it, directing a burst of fire harmlessly to the ground. The guard tightened his grip on the gun, and Oliver came to a complete stop—for just long enough to rip the shooter out of the van. Before he'd even bounced off the road, Oliver took off for us again.

With just Bluni and one Bar Tech goon left, it seemed like we actually had a shot at making it out of this. With a cry, I leaped to my feet, lowered my shoulder, and charged at an unprepared Bluni. I caught him in his gut, doubling him over and sending him out the back. He dropped his gun and grabbed the wildly flapping back door, clinging to it by his fingertips.

At the same time, Oliver sped up and jumped onto the second door, slamming it shut into the face of the remaining guard. The guard flew back toward Chase, who head-butted him in the chest and sent him tumbling out the side door. Even with his wrists bound, Chase was able to slam the side door shut, leaving us three on one to finish Bluni. He'd already crawled his way back inside. Disarmed, but no less dangerous, he tackled Chase into the rigid metal wall. *WHANG!* The back of Chase's head ricocheted off and left him dazed. I connected with Bluni from behind. He whipped around and shoved me back, dangerously close to the rear door that still hung wide open. Oliver was no longer right behind us. He was nowhere to be seen.

"Oliver! Hurry!" I shouted as I heard loud footsteps clang over our heads. He was on the roof! Then I heard the screech of brakes. He must've leaped in front of the van! While the driver's decision to avoid hitting the mystery runner who appeared out of nowhere was a good one for Oliver, it was a poor one for the rest of us on this icy back road.

I grabbed Chase and held him tightly as the entire vehicle flipped. The force shook Bluni loose and tossed him like a rag doll. He bounced out the flapping back doors and straight up into the night sky. At this point I had no sense of what was up or down, so it was probably an illusion, but the last I ever saw of my science teacher was him disappearing into the stars.

Over and over and over and over we rolled, like clothes trapped in a dryer. By the time we came to a stop at the bottom of a shallow ravine, I wasn't sure I'd ever be able to walk again. Chase groaned as he hoisted himself upright.

"Guys? Guyyyys?" Oliver's voice echoed through the woods, drawing nearer every time he called for us.

"Anything broken?" I half coughed, reaching over to Chase.

"Don't think so," he remarked, quickly checking his body for any major injuries. "You?"

I flashed a thumbs-up. "On top of the world."

Above us, the sliding door opened as far as the twisted metal would allow, and Oliver peeked in.

"You guys ready? We've got to get to Whiteface."

24. ASSAULT

One more step. One more step. One more step. This was my mantra, and had been for the last half hour as Oliver, Chase, Topher, and I trudged through swirling sheets of snow that got denser the closer we got to the peak of Whiteface. We'd been walking for what felt like hours but was probably only twenty minutes; trying to follow the road the van had been speeding down before it crashed.

The farther I trekked, the less visible the road became. Each new blast of icy wind threatened to freeze my bones inside my skin, and I felt as lost and blind as I had on my trip to Antarctica with Topher. Just like on that journey, I was filled with tension and terror, drowning in the knowledge that I was treading the line between life and death and daring it to snap beneath my feet. When Topher and I had projected to find my mom, the urge to turn back and go home had almost won out—the difference this time was that failure would leave us with no home to go back to.

"They really went for realism with this Winter Formal, huh?" Oliver cracked.

His joke might've gone over better if any of us were dressed for the weather, but I wasn't prepared for this and neither was anyone else. I was still in the thin, tattered remnants of my dress from the dance. We had only the two coats we'd swiped from the dead guards in the front seat of the wrecked van to keep us warm. My feet were stuffed into the oversized boots of the driver, which did just enough to keep snow and ice from soaking through and threatening my toes with frostbite. My hands were a totally different story, and I wiggled my fingers nonstop to avoid giving them a chance to freeze solid.

At the front of the line, Chase held up a hand, drawing us to a halt. "Shhhh!"

We strained to hear anything over the howling wind, but there it was. A hum. Chase pivoted toward it and started hustling even harder through the snow.

"That's a helicopter," he said, convinced.

To my ears, it could've been a distant generator, but I took Chase's word for it and followed as fast as I could. Oliver sped past us and looped back seconds later with a report.

"There's something there! A building or something!"

I dug deep and grabbed Topher's hand. He'd been silent since we crawled out of the wreck and had stayed that way the entire time.

"C'mon. Almost there." I could tell the bitterly cold air

was getting to him. It took him a second to find me, even though I was right next to him.

"Then . . . can we rest?"

I knew some of the symptoms of hypothermia were sluggish thoughts, movements, and speech, and I began to worry. If we didn't get inside very soon, I had the feeling Topher was going to be in trouble. The hum of the helicopter Chase predicted grew louder and began to take on the familiar shudder of rotating blades. All signs pointed to us being on the right track. A few minutes later, the intensity of the snow dropped off. The fluffy sheets didn't slow, but something was breaking it up enough for me to make out where I was.

That something revealed itself to be a complex of low concrete bunkers jutting out of the mountain around us in the shape of a horseshoe, us standing at the mouth. They were perfectly camouflaged by the snowbanks that sloped up to their flat roofs, nearly invisible in the storm. Perched on the helipad in the center of the arrangement was a Bar Tech helicopter, blades roaring and sucking in a vortex of snow. Besides a helmeted and headphoned pilot, I couldn't make out who was seated inside. If there were any guards on board—or if Cochran hadn't yet run inside—we were going to have trouble. I decided we'd take our chances.

"Spread out!" I shouted so that the guys could hear me. "Cochran isn't triggering any explosives from out here. There's got to be a way in!"

Chase and Oliver stayed low, trying to avoid detection by the pilot as best they could. I threw one of Topher's arms over my shoulder and helped drag him through the snow to the closest bunker. We were greeted by a thick metal door, which was surrounded by even thicker concrete. Not a good sign. A keypad sloped off the surface to the right, but I had no idea how to even begin guessing numbers that might result in success. And the cold was beginning to get to my brain as well, slowing my thought processes to a crawl.

A bolt of electricity ripped through the air and detonated against the building a few feet to my left. Instinctually, I tried to go invisible, but my body still refused to cooperate. I shoved Topher to the ground as three more bolts slammed into the building in quick succession. Leaping to my feet, I faced down the person I already knew was responsible for the attack: Jackson.

He was storming toward us from a few dozen yards away, brilliant bolts of blue circling his hands so fast that his arms appeared to terminate in ball lightning. I raised my hands up and out to the sides. It felt silly to be surrendering to the guy I'd been in love with just a few months ago, but I didn't have any other choice. Under Dana's control, I had to assume that Jackson was ready to do anything she demanded—including killing me. A misstep could mean being fried alive by his hands.

"Jackson," I started gently, carefully, "you don't know what's going on."

"He doesn't need to." The sickening lilt of Dana's voice, followed by her lithe form, crept out from behind a large transformer half buried in snow. She thrust her hand to the right, and Jackson did the same. With a flick of her wrist, she fired a bolt of blue from his hand. "It's better that way."

Oh my God. It seemed impossible until she repeated the action with her other hand. I dodged the resulting blast and realized I was witnessing the result of Dana's powers pushed to the max. Forget brainwashing people; forget forcing them to believe lies—she'd fully infiltrated Jackson's brain and was using him as a marionette of devastation. I ran for shelter around the side of the nearest bunker, stopping to lift Topher and drag him with me. There was no avoiding the fact that the only way I was going to get into these buildings was by going through Dana and Jackson—but how? And why were they even up here—protecting Cochran?

"Cochran's trying to destroy Barrington, Dana!" I shouted over the roar of the helicopter engine. "Is that what you want?"

"He helped me realize there's a big, big world out there waiting for us, Nica. You of all people should know that. Biology is destiny. And our biology is worth a fortune. You think being head cheerleader is all I aspire to? We can write our own ticket. Control our own destiny." Her voice was cold and cruel. Unwavering.

"You know Cochran thinks you're a liability!" I shouted back, hoping to get through to the part of her that still had an ounce of compassion left.

A volley of bolts fired from Jackson's hand, which Dana directed up and over the bunker providing my shelter. I couldn't risk darting back into the open, so I sat tight, clutching a shivering Topher, and hoping that none of the projectiles would find their mark. This time around they didn't. I couldn't be sure I'd be so lucky on the next.

"A liability"—she laughed—"is what Bluni was."

Did she know he was dead? I couldn't tell.

"He let his coup go to his head and started making mistakes," Dana elaborated. "I approached Cochran and suggested we do something about it."

"He's going to destroy the entire town! All of your friends! Your family!" I peeked around the corner to see Dana barely shrug.

"What loyalty do you feel to them, Nica? They're weak. Boring. Worthless. Most people are, really. You, me, Jackson, Oliver, and Topher . . . We're different. We're special. We're the next phase in evolution. Survival of the fittest."

"They don't deserve to die," I countered, desperate to stall for time.

"Maybe not, but life chose winners. Us. Let the losers go."

WHAM! A blur struck Dana's abdomen and sent her crashing to the ground. I caught a glimpse of Oliver, fast as a jet, coming around for a second pass before she'd even picked herself up. He connected low, yanking her legs out from underneath her.

"Get him!" she screamed.

Oliver leaped from side to side as Jackson leveled a series of crackling balls of lightning his way. It was impossible to connect with a target moving at his speed, and Oliver drew their fire with a near smile on his face. Each time Jackson missed, a new crater was formed in the snow frozen to the buildings behind Oliver. Frustrated, Dana forced Jackson to fire wildly—her mistake, our advantage. None of the shots found their mark, but one went wide enough to connect head-on with a door. Keypad locks be damned. These buildings weren't designed to withstand the onslaught of electricity raining down on them. The door flew off its hinges and clattered into the bunker.

"Go, Nica! Get inside!" screamed Oliver.

I didn't hesitate. Dana threw Jackson's arms wide and used one hand to fire at Oliver, the other to fire at me. Clouds of snow blew up from the ground as each shot missed. The path was clear, but I'd never make the distance if I had to drag Topher behind me. I held up, weighing the thought of leaving my friend behind to freeze in the snow against leaving—

potentially—all of Barrington to the same fate. Before I had to make the impossible call, Chase vaulted down the roof of the bunker and dropped into the snow next to me.

"Your ex is pretty pissed," he snarked. "I hope it's not because I took you to the dance."

I didn't have the heart to tell Chase how deeply I found myself mourning what had happened to Jackson. In the same moment I'd realized that Dana was using Jackson as a puppet, I'd realized I could never truly get over him. He was too kind to deserve what was happening to him, too trusting, too sensitive. If he and I ever had another chance—if we somehow both survived today—I swore I would tell him how I felt. I would try to get him back.

"It's not funny," I snapped at Chase more cruelly than I meant to.

"Sorry," Chase muttered, struck with the realization that as much as I'd grown to like him, I'd never feel the same way about him as I felt about Jackson.

"Grab him," I ordered, pointing at Topher. "Oliver's got Dana distracted, and I think we can get inside."

Chase grunted as he wrapped his arms around Topher and lifted the leaner kid onto his back. "It's not a superpower, but . . ."

"It'll do," I finished with a small, appreciative smile. "Ready? Three. Two. One!"

Chase and I tore out from behind the building. I was relieved to see Dana and Jackson's backs turned, still trying to put down Oliver. It was going to be an impossible task, but I had to hope that was exactly what would keep Dana busy. She absolutely hated anything that wasn't going her way and wouldn't stop until she had total control. Halfway to the entrance, we passed the helicopter and I lost the sound of Chase's footsteps behind me to the thunderous drone of the machine. I couldn't risk looking back. I had to stay focused on that door. Thirty feet. Twenty feet. Ten feet.

I threw myself inside and around the corner to avoid any fire that might be lobbed in my wake, but the only thing that followed was Chase. Cheeks red and short of breath, he lowered Topher gently to the metal floor before leaning against the wall and sucking short gasps into his lungs. I'd felt the burn too—the oxygen was just a little bit thinner up here, and it made everything more difficult. My lungs ached and my muscles burned, but we were so close now. I picked up where Chase had left off and helped Topher to his feet, pulling him away from the door and deeper into the facility, where it was warmer.

The guts of this building were not as polished as the interior of the base that had served as the training facility for Dana's army. This was all industrial pipes and concrete, catwalks and dim lights, which probably could've served as a model for a level in one of Oliver's favorite video games.

I followed the heat, figuring that the more used and useful portions of the construct would be home to whatever Cochran was trying to access. Topher came back from the edge as he and I hobbled on. Chase caught up as we advanced slowly through the drab corridors, lit only by giant warm bulbs.

I checked each shadowy corner for rooms or offices that the president of Bar Tech could be stowed away in, working on bringing his horrific plan to life. I'd lost track of all the times I'd turned left and right down the cloned subterranean corridors and was ready to slump to the ground when the hallway dead-ended in a massive circular room. It was carved from the metamorphic rock of Whiteface, fitted with a grated floor and ceilings that stretched so high that they vanished into darkness.

Cochran stood on the far side, working in front of a lit console. The soft *clickety-clack* of keys wasn't enough to mask the clang of our feet on the grate, and Cochran threw a "one second" signal over his shoulder. "Almost there, Dana."

Chase cleared his throat. I wished I could've seen Cochran's face in that moment—caught red-handed by his own son. Even the body language of his back seemed crushed. His broad shoulders drooped as he turned around, knowing exactly whom he was going to see.

"Dad," Chase said, entreating his father to listen. "Please don't do this."

Cochran shook his head. "It's already done."

Chase ran across the room to the console, Topher and me right behind him. A countdown on an old desktop computer gave us five minutes.

"What is this, Dad? How do we turn it off?" Chase started to freak.

"This is where we used to launch our satellites from," Cochran announced proudly. "I retrofitted a few things for my needs."

I took in the room with new eyes: This is where it had all started more than seventeen years earlier. I tried to imagine the massive satellite and rocket sitting over this platform, scientists racing around, performing last-minute checks. Never knowing the disaster that was about to strike and wipe out the entire lab, exposing our pregnant mothers to electromagnetic radiation, which mutated their unborn children's genes.

"It's better this way," Cochran said, trying to put an arm around his son and lead him away.

Chase shoved him off. "Don't touch me! Turn it off!"

"I can't, Chase. It's over. Come with me." Cochran turned to the rest of us. "All of you. You've proven yourself as valuable assets." He was so calm, but it was clear he knew the levels he had sunk to. Just because he wasn't a gleefully cackling villain didn't mean he wasn't a villain all the same. He started to back away as he spoke, and I doubted he meant what he was promising. If we went with him, who's to say that he wouldn't turn on us in an instant? Chase, Topher, and I stayed firmly planted where we were.

"Chase!" Cochran snapped angrily. "These two can stay if they want, but you don't have a choice. Let's go!"

Chase shook his head, defiant. "You're wrong. I do have a choice. I choose my friends." Chase stood firm, proud. A man at last. That was the last thing he'd ever say to his father.

With barely a tear in his suddenly steely eyes, Cochran turned to abandon us—

—only to be sideswiped by a familiar blur that tossed him to the cold metal ground. Oliver! He was a step ahead of the searing-hot electricity that arced through the air. Without slowing down, he traced the curve of the room, directing as much of Jackson's fire as he could to the cylindrical rock wall all around us. Not a bad idea, until the bolts started to crack off large pieces of rock, sending boulders hurtling down on top of us.

"Look out!" I screamed, leaping for safety. Out of the corner of my eye I saw Chase jump free and Topher roll out of the way. That distraction was all it took for me to miss the mammoth chunk of falling rock slam into and through the metal in front of me. I met nothing but air on the way down. A second earlier and I would've been crushed. A second later and my hands might not have found the edge of the grate. Though I could feel my fingers crack and twist, they stopped just short of breaking, and I was able to hold myself up. My shoulders and chin rested on the bent, drooping metal, while everything below my waist dropped off into empty space. I scanned the room and noticed Cochran was gone.

"Oliver! Follow Cochran—you need to stop him!" I cried, but I couldn't see my friends through the sparks and dust that had been kicked up by the cave-in.

What I could see was Dana, limping through a cloud of crushed rock with a deranged grin on her face. "Dana. Help." I knew it was useless, but I could feel myself slipping. I desperately needed her to give me a hand or I was going to fall. Without a word, she drew close and stared down at me. "Please . . ."

All she did was lift her foot and bring it down. Hard. Grinding my fingers. The pain shot through my arm, and I pulled my hand away, which left me dangling from one hand. I closed my eyes as she lifted her foot again, ready to bring it down on the only thing left between the end and me. I tried to picture my dad and his bright, reassuring smile that always made me feel as if I could do anything I set my mind to.

A bolt slammed into the back of Dana's head, sending her out over my head and spiraling into darkness. I didn't hear her land.

A moment later Jackson's hand reached down to me. I didn't know if I could trust him, but I had no choice. He pulled me up and then in close to his chest. I clung to him tightly. It had been so long since he'd held me in his arms.

"Forgive me," he murmured.

"I . . . I . . . What . . . How . . . ?" I felt dizzy and confused.

"She never had me, Nica. I just let her think she did. It was the only way I could find out what she was up to. How else could I have found out about Blackthorne for you?"

I shook my head and looked at him, wondering if I'd heard him right. "You?" I cried, pulling away and looking him directly in the eyes. "You were the—"

He cut me off with a severe nod. "I'll tell you everything. I promise. After we stop Cochran."

I searched his eyes to see if his was lying to me. All this time, he'd just been pretending? I couldn't believe it, but I also had to admit that it made a certain amount of sense.

"I don't know if we can stop him," I said, unsure if I had any fight left in me.

"Then we can at least make him pay." He grabbed my good hand and led me out of the facility as more rocks began to fall to the floor, destroying what was left of the room behind us.

By the time Jackson and I wove our way back through the concrete halls and reemerged outside near the helipad, Cochran's escape copter was already lifting into the air.

It moved slowly, swinging wildly from side to side as it struggled to take off in the high winds and nearly blinding drifts of heavy snow. He was clearly comfortable leaving his two sons, Chase and Oliver, now united in a newfound disgust and abhorrence for their father, behind to freeze to death on the mountaintop.

Oliver saw Jackson first, but I held my hand up as soon I saw the fear in his eyes. "It's okay. He's back."

But Jackson didn't seem happy. His eyes flashed the same color blue as his hands, and I could tell that anger had consumed him. He aimed his hands as the helicopter lifted higher and higher, ready to fire a blast that would bring the whole thing down in flames.

"NO!" screamed Chase, leaping in front of him.

I couldn't understand Chase's desire to protect his monstrous father, but then, I wasn't the one in that position. Would I do the same for my father if the shoe were on the other foot? The two rivals locked eyes, each daring the other to stand down. Neither one so much as flinched until Jackson lowered his hands and the helicopter vanished into the darkening sky.

Jackson, Chase, Oliver, and I barely had a chance to breathe before the first explosion. When it detonated, it sounded like a pleasant rumble—a distant firework celebrating an obscure holiday. I knew the awful sound signaled death and destruction, but I tried to hold on to hope—however tenuous a fantasy—that everything would be okay. My friends reeled back. Jackson grabbed my hand and tugged, frantic.

"Run, Nica!"

My feet stayed firmly planted in the thin layer of snow and ice. I shook my head.

"It's over," I muttered.

"No, it's not!" Jackson yelled back. "We can get out of here!"

"And go where? Stand under the avalanche?"

My memory of Cochran's secret documents reminded me that my friends and I were just out of harm's way: above and a quarter of the way around the mountain from the path of the avalanche. We were so far away that it took a full thirty seconds for the reverberations to weave their way through the solid rock and ripple beneath our feet. A second, third, and fourth explosion sounded. One after the other, they echoed the whole way down the mountain.

Everyone relaxed—barely—as they realized I was right. From our vantage point, it was impossible to get a look at the fire and ice that surely erupted into the air, but I could picture the small concrete bunkers bursting outward in orange and yellow flames. Not only was all the evidence of Bar Tech's training camps being erased, but the ground beneath them was being shattered. A solid line of broken stone and unstable ice would reach from the first explosion to the last, breaking a sheet of earth and snow cleanly off the surface of Whiteface and sending it hurtling at our small town below.

The sound of crashing snow was unmistakable and all encompassing. I imagined the rescue workers in the streets starting to turn around. I imagined kids awake in their beds wondering what the roar in the distance was—the roar that was growing louder every second. I imagined parents looking up at Whiteface in horror, wondering how much time they had. Long enough to say good-bye?

Standing up here, helpless, was almost worse. It wasn't a death sentence, but part of me longed to be among the doomed so that the guilt wouldn't haunt me for the rest of my life. This was my fault. The war that had sparked between Dana and me had metastasized into something that touched each of my friends and now many more people I didn't even know. Sure, the five of us up here would survive, but what would it matter if our families didn't? Not to mention we'd be trapped up here with no way of getting down, short of walking. There I was, full circle back to "death sentence" again. But there was no way to stop a wall of snow.

Or was there?

"Maya," I gasped. "Where's Maya?" The boys looked at me like I was crazy. "Topher, we have to find her!"

"She could be anywhere in Barrington by now, Nica," Jackson interjected. "Or dead."

I wasn't accepting this for an answer. No. I knew where she was. I called up Bar Tech's bank of screens in my mind, the ones from which I watched her unleash chaos just an hour or so ago. I hadn't been paying attention to the details, but I tried to focus. What street was she on? In which direction was she walking? What could I see and what could it tell me? I had to hope my recall was accurate and I wasn't just seeing what I wanted to see. Oliver could run down there and check, but we didn't have time. There was what—a few minutes before Barrington left the map?

An hour ago she was walking north up Laurel. Where was she going?

"Guys, if you take Laurel north from the school," I asked, "where does it go?"

"Uh, um . . ." Chase tried to land an answer. "Nowhere, really. Dead-ends in a cul-de-sac near the base of the mountain. Just woods."

I knew it! There was nothing left for her here. She'd finally leaped straight off the deep end, and there was nothing for her to do anymore but run. Luckily, it seemed like she was running in the right direction to do one last thing before disappearing for good.

"Last time she left, she told me that she'd spent time in the woods, that she'd centered herself there. She needed to calm down and regain control of her powers. I bet you anything she's doing that again, and it's right where we need her to be." I strode to Topher's side. "Take me there."

"She just laid waste to almost half the town!" Topher barked back, shooting me an "Are you insane?" look.

"Topher, please," I begged. "I need to talk to her. We all do. She needs to know she's our only hope."

Chase, Jackson, and Oliver looked at one another. I hoped they realized I was serious. "She can stop that avalanche if you can get us there!" Topher shook his head. "Now or never, Topher!"

"Now or never," he muttered, grabbing my hand. I took Chase's, Chase took Oliver's, Oliver took Jackson's, and we all closed our eyes. Topher exhaled heavily, trying to find peace at the center of this disaster. His breath slowed. He focused at some unseen point and rolled his head in a circle, loosening his neck—and there we were. Five of us, together, in the woods at the edge of town. Sure enough, the rumble of the avalanche was as I'd imagined it. Distant but intense. No doubt something awful was headed straight for us. I strained to see our target in the dark.

"Maya!" I shouted.

The boys chimed in, calling Maya's name in a mad hope that somehow she would hear us in time. As I tried to get her attention, Topher controlled our location, projecting us from one place to the next, disappearing from one segment of the woods and reappearing in the next. We moved deeper and deeper, closer to the avalanche until I turned around—and there she was. Totally alone.

Maya was bruised and bleeding, a vacant look still haunting her face, though her eyes seemed brighter than ever; silver stars set in her skull, waiting to explode. She didn't seem particularly surprised to see us; instead, she was content. Relaxed. Maybe resigned to what was about to happen.

"Nica . . . ," she said quietly, pointing over my head in the direction of the encroaching disaster. "Can you see it? It's coming."

"Maya, listen," I said, as the others drew close around us, silent and terrified—trapped between an unforgiving wall of snow and a girl with godlike powers. Her wide, trembling eyes floated over me like I was speaking a foreign language. "Forget everything that happened back there." I indicated Barrington before looking her dead in the eyes. "Right now this is all that matters. I know you're angry, but you're the only one who can stop this."

"No one can stop it," she muttered, sounding lost in a dream. "This is what happens to a town that makes monsters."

"That's not true, Maya." I locked eyes with her. "Cochran was responsible, and Cochran already got away. These are innocent people being punished. You can take all your anger and all your sadness and all your rage and turn your back and let this happen, or you can stop it."

As I talked, I could see the familiar ripples flitting through the air around her, ducking and weaving in and out of reality. I needed them to grow. I needed those deadly indicators of her power to swell to the size of a mountain.

"I need you to think about who you want to be—like Dana and sell us all out for Bar Tech? Or are you Maya Bartoli, the girl who fights to the end?" This seemed to click; my words brought her back from the edge. It was as if she'd snapped out of a deep trance and saw us standing there for the first time. Shock turned to concern, and concern turned to resolve. She didn't have any questions about what she needed to do.

"You guys need to get out of here," proclaimed Maya.

I shook my head and took a step toward her instead of away. So did Topher and Chase and Oliver and Jackson.

"No. This is our fight, too," I replied, reaching for her hand.

She was shocked when her fingers passed right through mine. But we all tucked in as close as possible, forming a protective circle of friends around Maya as she stared down the avalanche and began to unleash her psychic energy in waves.

Just like at the dance, it started with a rumble, long and low, then a crack, then an explosion that shook the snow from the trees. Each of these shocks passed right through us as we stood in awe at the center of the storm.

Maya gritted her teeth and pulsed over and over, each one larger than the last, until she fell to her knees, howling like a demon was trying to rip itself from her body. As she convulsed, the snow began to melt away, and the mud it left behind began to boil. We all took a horrified step back as a circle of heat and immense power spread from her in a concentric circle, tossing boulders and tearing up trees by their roots. She seemed to the enveloped by the earth itself as her power tore the forest apart.

In that second, I realized I'd taken my eye off the avalanche. I'd been so focused on Maya that I'd forgotten to look up. When I did, there was no time, no time, no time. I screamed as the fury of untold tons of rock, snow, and ice plowed into us, enveloping my fractured world in darkness.

25. BARRINGTON REDUX

I inhaled deeply, the fresh pine and frozen air enveloping my senses. Light filtered down in glowing pockets among the centuries-old evergreens. Snow and a baked forest floor crackled beneath my feet with each leisurely step. The woods were alive with birdcalls and racing squirrels, the hustle and bustle of fauna's daily life, but I was taking it slowly. A true stroll without purpose or destination, besides meditation and decompression.

My mother had been waking me up for five a.m. yoga since she'd arrived three days earlier, along with an entourage of Internet journalists and cable news reporters whom she'd alerted about Bar Tech and Richard Cochran in the wake of my "visit" to Antarctica. Lydia had pulled every string she could with *National Geographic* to get airlifted out of McMurdo Station and on the first flight north to Denver. I was so happy to have her there that I'd indulged her habit with a smile.

"I had everyone at McMurdo doing it," she'd bragged.

"They were grumpy at first, but they all agreed: Sun salutations at dawn is the only way to start your day."

I didn't have the heart to tell her that I'd rather be underneath my flannel sheets and down comforters. I did, however, appreciate some company in my afternoon commune with all things Mother Earth. Tall and stoic as ever, Jackson followed along, about half a step behind me. If I was honest with myself, his presence, along with the endless pine grove, was what I'd missed the most. I could just make him out in my peripheral vision, but I could feel our connection with every step. When the pulse had first hit and he and I had discovered our powers, the woods had become our safe haven from Bar Tech's relentless eyes. I hadn't thought about it in so long because the delicious memory had turned so painful, but it was where we'd shared our first kiss. Well, our first real kiss. There had been the tentative one in his Mustang, ruined by Dana's ghost and my insecurities. But the one that had led to more? That had happened here, the same cold air filling our lungs as our blood had turned to fire.

Even now I could feel the warmth radiating off of his body. It was slight—dampened and contained by layers of polar fleece and Gore-Tex and waffled cotton—but his return to my side had heightened my senses for every ounce of familiarity and pleasure I'd been deprived of since Dana's reappearance. I bristled even at the thought of her, once again a ghost for Jackson and now a harrowing specter of mine as well.

Ever an emotional lightning rod for me, Dana was a reminder of all of the psychological rubble that still needed to be cleared in the wake of the past month's events. I knew how right it felt to have Jackson back at my side, but neither of us had even begun to unpack the meaning of it. And then there was Chase.

I hated to admit it, but I think Chase had been the first to read the writing on the walls. He had kept his distance in the days after the avalanche, texting to let me know he was okay, but nothing more. Oliver had been splitting his time between the two of us, so most of what I knew was through my recently restored best friend. Chase was struggling with his father's secrets and betrayal. Luckily, he had a brand-new brother to shoulder some of that weight. I knew first-hand that the sudden loss of a parent was a gut punch, but I had also seen the look in his eyes when Jackson had exposed himself on the mountain as a double agent working, not for, but against Bar Tech. Jackson's heroic moment had been a restorative one for me.

For Chase, however, it might as well have been the nail in the coffin of our relationship. I hated knowing I'd hurt him. Chase had pushed for it, fought for me, shown he wasn't the invulnerable jackass that he wore right along with his letterman jacket. After I'd lost my friends and my dad, he had been my only lifeline. At the same time, though, I think he and I had both known that my heart had never fully strayed from Jackson. Even after we'd been captured by Bar Tech Security and banished to their darkest dungeon, Chase had called me out on my lingering feelings.

That surprise was still working me over. Not only had Jackson strung Dana along since she'd been unable to satisfy him with a credible explanation for her reappearance, but he had also been my very own mystery texter. It made me rethink every encounter Jackson and I had over the past month, not to mention my interactions with the shadowy informant.

Jackson had known exactly how to attract my attention and exactly how to earn my trust. Breathing against my neck in the dark theater. Sneaking into my bedroom in the middle of the night. I'd even finally been able to connect the dots as to how my informant had gotten past our house's formidable Bar Tech Security system. It may have been a real stumper for a house burglar, but not for the guy who had harnessed the power of electricity.

All along, I'd thought Jackson had chosen Dana, but really he had chosen me. Jackson once told me to trust him. I'd thought I had been discarded, abandoned, but in fact Jackson had been my guardian in the shadow. He'd helped me every step of the way, staying close when I thought I had lost him, watching over me when I thought I was invisible, confident above all that I would be the one to help him take down Dana and Bar Tech when the time came. Jackson believed in me. It was proof of everything I had ever wanted to hear from him, and he had communicated it all without a word.

But did he trust me? That was the bad taste that lingered as my mind tore every last detail to shreds and pieced the tiny pixels back together. I couldn't stop asking the question. Why had it been so important that I remain in the dark? I was reluctant to break the easy silence, a rarity in my life, but I had the guy right here.

One last calming breath. *In through your nose, out through your mouth*, I could hear Lydia correcting me. God, I'd missed her so much.

"Why did you keep it a secret?" I asked, my voice initially abrasive to my own ears. It hung in the air, the final mystery in my days of reflection and retrospection. There was no accusation in my voice. I just needed to know. "Why didn't you just tell me?"

I wanted to look at him, and slowed my pace, falling into stride. It was too much to stop, but I glanced over as he mulled his answer.

"I can see how it might be hard for you to understand," Jackson started. He wasn't defensive, but I could tell he wanted to explain. "I just had no idea what was going to happen. I hoped that Dana wouldn't get to you, but I couldn't know if she would. I also didn't know if I'd be able to go on resisting her. It felt safest to compartmentalize everything, keeping my secret and feeding you what information I could. It was the hardest thing I've ever had to do."

Thinking about the situation from his point of view didn't erase how he had made me feel. I had felt so alone, so lost, so separate from everyone that mattered to me, and so hurt. But those were all facts, out to bleed honestly in the open. Jackson had suffered, just as alone as I had been, but had required an all-important mask, a lie of how happy he was just to keep up appearances.

"I'm sorry," I apologized. It wasn't my fault, but at least I finally had someone who knew how I had felt. "Part of me just can't believe it's over."

"I'm not so sure that it is," Jackson replied, always the pessimist. He was probably right. "This is who we are now. Who knows what's going to happen, but what's important is that we continue to live our lives. I'm not going to wait around for Bar Tech's—or whoever's—next move." He stopped in his tracks, swinging around to face me.

His blue-green eyes were a shock to my system. I had missed their unwavering stare and the way they still made my whole body unsteady. He took my hands, and my quivering knees silently thanked him.

"You know what? I was wrong," he continued. "It wasn't keeping secrets straight that was so hard. It was pretending not to care about you, pretending like you weren't the person that I thought about every morning when I woke up and every night when I couldn't sleep."

I pulled him against me, and he kissed me like we'd never left the woods, like Dana had never come back to Barrington. But somehow it was better, more passionate. Maybe because Jackson and I had weathered so much pain and survived.

The reunion lasted until I couldn't feel my toes and fingers. I'd had enough cold for multiple lifetimes. The woods would always be our place, but I had to go home eventually.

Thankfully, home had been restored as well. In ways I could never have imagined. In those first dark days after my father's disappearance, his house had become a husk, a bed to sleep in, without him. Fortunately, Maya had saved me just when I needed saving the most, when I was at my lowest and needed a friend. I never imagined that the frenetic, somewhat overbearing cheerleader who'd introduced me around my first day at Barrington High School would come through and have my back when I thought I had no one else. Maya had held out her hand and I'd taken it.

All of which made me take a long, hard look at myself. Why was I always underestimating my friends and my nearest and dearest? Trust in others was not something that came easy for me. It terrified me to know how much I needed Oliver and Maya and Topher and Jackson. Where would I be without them?

And how would I have made it this far without my parents? They were constantly surprising me.

When I walked inside and found Lydia and Marcus together in the same room—an elusive simultaneous appearance—it filled me with so much joy that I could hardly believe it. They were making dinner together, maybe the one part of their relationship that had always been an easy collaboration. I guess they'd done a pretty good job with me, too.

My dad wasn't sure exactly what had happened after he'd left the house in a hurry that day, but his foggy memory had cleared not long after Dana's defeat at Whiteface. He'd barely made it through town that day when two Bar Tech Security cars had stopped him and taken him into custody. They must have drugged my father, because the next thing he knew, he'd woken up two days later in one of Bar Tech's secure black-ops facilities somewhere in the mountains of Western Pennsylvania. He was kept prisoner in the bunker-like compound until all hell broke loose back in Barrington. Luckily, a sympathetic guard, with two children of his own to protect, realized that the shit was about to hit the fan when Cochran disappeared, and he released my father.

Dad checked into a random motel somewhere outside Pittsburgh under a false name and then booked a flight back to Barrington.

Lydia, however, had beaten him to the punch when she'd

arrived in Barrington with the media brigade, eager to dig up the details of Cochran's shady dealings. It was decidedly not a sitcom-family homecoming, but the three of us had hugged like it was.

Dad had been bowled over by the details of what had gone on in Barrington in his absence. He remembered Dana coming to the door under the guise of selling raffle tickets for the Booster Club. He and I had both been surprised to find an actual receipt in the kitchen junk drawer. Dana Fox: a vision of school spirit until the very end.

"You okay with me going back to being the parent around here?" Dad asked the next morning while making a mile-high stack of blueberry pancakes for my breakfast, like he used to do when I was a little kid.

"Relieved, in fact, to hand over the reins. Besides, you keep the place a lot cleaner than I do," I replied, so happy to be sitting across the kitchen table from him again. I watched him smile with pleasure as I smothered my pancakes with fresh Vermont maple syrup and devoured them in huge bites. "Not to mention make the best blueberry pancakes ever."

His eyes were moist as he tried to fight back his emotions. "I'm sorry I wasn't there when you needed me. I'm sorry I forgot you. That I nearly lost you."

I hugged him, so relieved to have him remember he was my father. "Does this mean you'll let me take my road test?"

Okay, maybe it wasn't the best time, but I was a town hero. At least secretly. How could he say no?

"Can you parallel park yet?"

"I'm . . . working on it."

"Go ahead and schedule it. We'll practice next week. By the way, that's the reason I failed my driving test the first time. My parallel parking sucked."

"You failed something? That's a first."

And just like that, my father and I were laughing again.

Next week. Just the very concept gave me pause. What else would next week bring? What was Barrington going to be like free of its Bar Tech Security and the curfew? It wasn't like Bar Tech was gone forever. Richard Cochran was out there somewhere, licking his wounds but planning, reformulating. Control of Bar Tech had been taken over by the Department of Defense until they could conduct a thorough investigation of every department and all their research. No doubt the company would rise again, if under a new face and a new name. Reinvention is the backbone of American business after all. The official story as reported, of course, told it a little differently.

The version that was reported by the media explained that Bar Tech's headquarters were being moved as a result of the nearly catastrophic avalanche. Blame for any misconduct was placed squarely on Richard Cochran's shoulders. The technology being developed by Bar Tech was far too valuable to be housed in a town that was so vulnerable to natural disasters. If the avalanche had powered all of the way to Bar Tech's headquarters, billions could've been lost. And why hadn't it? The story was light on those details

I'd had a recurring nightmare as a child about drowning in a tsunami. Frozen in fear, I'd watched the wall of water tower over me, taller than the Empire State Building or Mount Kilimanjaro or any of the very tall things I'd seen in my short time on earth . . . and then break, rushing down at impossible speeds and burying me in stories upon stories of deep blue water. I'd swim up, kicking as hard as I could, but the light at the surface would be fathoms too far to make it without refilling my lungs. But then I would wake up, gasping first for air and then shrieking for my mother as soon the fear had quelled enough to force words from my mouth. The wall of snow barreling down White-face had been my nightmare come to wintery life, but the differences were stark.

For one, it was thunderous. And it grew louder and louder, almost deafening as it tumbled down the face of earth and rock. But for the first time in my nightmare, I wasn't alone. My friends were with me, staring down the white monster together. Our words were drowned out and unlike the wave, where the water hovered over me at its peak for what felt like forever, the snow came far too fast. When the snow hit, barreling through us like the end of the world, there was no swimming. The snow was real and unkind, and it swallowed Maya whole just like her power swallowed it. Two creations of equally matched mass and force pitted against each other, ending both in a violent flash.

Our astral bodies had been knocked back to Whiteface a split second after impact. It had taken a few moments, disoriented by my sudden return, for the tears to come. Maya had saved my life—our lives. She'd saved the whole town, but she was buried under an endless depth of snow. Fear had turned to grief as I realized that the white wave hadn't been my tsunami at all. It had been Maya's nightmare, and she wouldn't be waking up.

I still couldn't believe she was gone. So little time had passed between watching her get her heart torn out at her own memorial service and her self-sacrifice to save all of Barrington. Maya, too, had been a force of nature, unable to harness her great power, able only to point it in a direction. Regardless, I was racked with guilt. I'd asked her to stay. I'd asked her to help. What if I'd been able to stop Cochran before he'd set off the detonations? Would Maya be with us now?

That "us" was growing in size, too. Not only had Lydia joined my dad and me, but our house had felt a bit like an orphanage for my friends these past few days. I hadn't told them much about my dad's job, his real job for the Department of Defense, but they did know that he had been working the inside of Bar Tech and knew about all of our powers. Lydia, obviously, had learned when Topher and I had projected to Antarctica, but she was catching up very quickly. It was a huge change for Jackson, Topher, and Oliver. Loving, caring adults they could talk to.

As part of the attempt to help all of us get back on our feet and settled back into our everyday lives, everyone had been invited over for dinner. Jackson arrived first, while my parents were cooking and laughing in the kitchen, and even though it had been only an hour or so since our walk had ended, I was incredibly glad to have him back at my side. Topher and Oliver arrived about fifteen minutes later, and I was surprised to see Chase in tow. I was a deer in the head-lights, my fingers still intertwined with Jackson's, but none of us said a word. Regardless, I pulled my hand free of Jackson's. There was no need to rub it in Chase's face.

While the guys were arguing with my father about college football team rankings, which I had less than zero interest in, I wandered outside to get a breath of fresh air. I stared up at the glittering night sky. I certainly wasn't one to get philosophical all about life, but sticking around in Barrington for more than a few months seemed kind of awesome to me. Who knew what the future would bring for any of us? I certainly had no clue. About the only thing I knew was that I wanted my future to be in Barrington—at least until I graduated high school.

Still, I had to wonder . . . Were there other kids out in the world beyond Barrington with powers? Had the pulses affected others in ways we might not know for years to come? Or were we the only ones with enhanced abilities? And would we pass on those powers to our children? Or would those genes die out in some kind of genetic drift? I chuckled to myself. I'd actually learned something from Bluni's research.

"See those three stars, all in a row?"

I turned around to see Oliver. "That's Orion's Belt," he said, pointing to the constellation. "The three major stars across are called Alnitak, Alnilam, and Mintaka. The other two—Betelgeuse and Rigel—make up his shoulder and his foot. And up there, in that arrow shape?" He pointed near Orion. "Those are the seven sisters. They're named after Atlas's daughters, who were said to be the objects of Orion's affections."

"You may be able to leap tall buildings in a single bound, but you're still kind of a really big nerd," I said with a glib smile.

"Tell me something I don't know."

"Don't ever change," I quipped.

"Dinner's ready," my mother called out as she opened the sliding-glass door to the kitchen. The fragrant aroma of curry, basil, coriander, and other Thai spices wafted out, beckoning us back.

Oliver and I set the table while my parents lined the food up buffet-style. When we were all seated, it felt like we were gathered for a special occasion, a birthday or Thanksgiving or at least the kind of dinner where someone would make a toast.

But it was just a Thursday-night dinner. That was special enough.

Oliver had already started stuffing his face, but he paused mid-chew when I stood up, water glass in hand. A sweeping gesture. Everyone looked surprised. It was very unlike me, which I was reminded of as soon my mouth went cotton-dry.

"Um, I just wanted to say something," I began. "We've all been through a lot this year, and I guess I wanted to say thank you. Thank you for taking care of me, watching over me, listening to my problems, and"—I smiled slyly at Oliver—"calling me on my shit."

Oliver shrugged and grinned back. "Anytime."

"I'm just really glad you're all here." Maya weighed in the back of my mind again as soon as I'd said it. As I sat back down, I silently wished that she were here, too. I figured everyone else was having the same thought; there was no reason to say it out loud.

Dinner was nice, even if I found myself occasionally wincing at its cloying Hallmark Channel charm. I rested my hand on Jackson's thigh, under the table and outside of anyone's sight. Out of the corner of my eye, I caught his surprised smile before he could temper it. It was just nice to touch him—to know he wanted to be there with me. And so what if I got a little thrill that he and I were the only ones to know?

An interruption came with the loud ringing of a cell phone. For a moment no one recognized it as their own, looking around only to see who would silence the rude disturbance. Then my dad stood up from the table. He looked a little nervous as I watched him, putting the pieces together. I hadn't recognized it as his ringtone—it had been a jazzy version of the *Top Gun* theme, and incredibly embarrassing, as long as I'd known him—but I watched him move across the dining room and kitchen to a cell phone nonetheless.

At first I was a little sad that he had finally given in to to my desperate pleas to join the twenty-first century, but added his confusion and delay together with the look of concern and realized his devotion to 1980s Tom Cruise had not wavered: The ringing was, in fact, a second cell phone— his Batphone, a direct and private line to the Department of Defense. And now they were calling.

He answered, ducking out of the room in a gesture of politeness but what I knew was really a move for privacy. I couldn't help getting up to follow him. I walked out of the kitchen and turned left like I was headed for the bathroom, but doubled back toward the stairs. From the faint sound of my dad's voice, I could tell he'd padded upstairs to his office.

Instinct told me to follow, but we'd been over this so many times. We trusted each other, and everything was out in the open now, at least among our immediate family.

I forced myself to sit down at the base of the stairs. I could wait a few minutes for him to tell me himself. Maybe it was nothing—or maybe it was an update about Bar Tech or even a new assignment. Or perhaps they'd located Cochran, found something to charge him with. That was probably a long shot, but who said it had to be bad news?

At least I wasn't alone.